"Thrilling up to the last page, titillating from one sexually charged scene to the next, and captivating from beginning to end, the last of the Royal Four series displays Bradley's ability to tell an involved, sexy story. If you haven't yet read a Bradley novel, let yourself be seduced by the mistress of the genre!"

—*Romantic Times BOOKreviews*

"Have you discovered the bawdy charms of Celeste Bradley? Laced with intrigue and adventure, she has quickly become a staff and reader favorite and with each book we just fall further in love with her characters. This is the final book in the superb Royal Four quartet, with her most dangerous deception yet!"     —*Rendezvous*

### THE ROGUE

"Once you've read a Liar's Club book, you crave the next in the series. Bradley knows how to hook a reader with wit, sensuality (this one has one of the hottest hands-off love scenes in years!) and a strong plot along with the madness and mayhem of a Regency-set novel."     —*Romantic Times BOOKreviews*

"Bradley continues her luscious Liar's Club series with another tale of danger and desire, and as always her clever prose is imbued with wicked wit."     —*Booklist*

"Celeste Bradley's The Liar's Club series scarcely needs an introduction, so popular it's become with readers since its inception . . . Altogether intriguing, exciting, and entertaining, this book is a sterling addition to the Liar's Club series."     —*Road to Romance*

### TO WED A SCANDALOUS SPY

"Warm, witty, and wonderfully sexy."
—Teresa Medeiros, *New York Times* bestselling author

*More . . .*

W9-ASO-822

"Funny, adventurous, passionate, and especially poignant, this is a great beginning to a new series . . . Bradley mixes suspense and a sexy love story to perfection." —*Romantic Times BOOKreviews*

"A wonderful start to a very looked-forward-to new series . . . once again showcases Celeste Bradley's talent of creating sensual and intriguing plots filled with memorable and endearing characters . . . A non-stop read." —*Romance Reader at Heart*

"Danger, deceit, and desire battle with witty banter and soaring passion for prominence in this highly engrossing tale . . . Bradley also provides surprises galore, both funny and suspenseful, and skillfully ties them all in neatly with the romance so as to make this story more than averagely memorable." —*Road to Romance*

"A fantastic read . . . Bradley successfully combines mystery, intrigue, romance, and intense sensuality into this captivating book." —*Romance Junkies*

### THE CHARMER

"Amusing, entertaining romance." —*Booklist*

"Bradley infuses this adventure with so much sexual tension and humor that you'll be enthralled. You'll laugh from the first page to the last . . . The wonderful characters, witty dialogue, and clever plot will have you wishing you were a Liar too." —*Romantic Times BOOKreviews*

### THE SPY

"Only a clever wordsmith can make this complex, suspenseful tale work so perfectly. Bradley pulls us into the wonderful world of the Liar's Club and gives us a nonstop read brimming with puzzle after puzzle." —*Romantic Times BOOKreviews*

"With its wonderfully witty writing, superbly matched protagonists, and intrigue-steeped plot, the third of Bradley's Liar's Club historicals is every bit as much fun as *The Pretender* and *The Impostor*." —*Booklist*

"A must for readers of the Liar's Club series and a good bet for those who haven't yet started . . . I unhesitatingly recommend." —*All About Romance*

"Ms. Bradley has an effortless style to her prose."
—*The Romance Reader*

"A Top Pick . . . the best of [the Liar's Club] so far. Bless Celeste Bradley . . . She just seems to get better at it as she goes along."
—*Romance Reader at Heart*

## THE IMPOSTOR

"Bradley carefully layers deception upon deception, keeping the intrigue level high and the tone bright . . . Readers will race through this delightful comedy of errors and eagerly anticipate the next installment."
—*Publishers Weekly*

"With delicious characters and a delectable plot, Bradley delivers another enticing read brimming with the mayhem and madness that come with falling in love when you least expect it. The devilishly funny double identities, witty dialogue and clever twists will captivate."
—*Romantic Times BOOKreviews* (Top Pick)

"Don't miss this second book of the Liar's Club series. With humor, passion and mystery, it's absolutely delightful in every way! I can't wait for the next one."
—*Old Book Barn and Gazette*

## THE PRETENDER

"Totally entertaining."
—*New York Times* bestselling author Julia Quinn

"An engaging, lusty tale, full of adventure and loaded with charm."
—Gaelen Foley, *USA Today* bestselling author of *Lord of Ice*

"Bradley certainly knows how to combine engaging characters with excitement, sensuality, and a strong plot."
—*Booklist* (starred)

"Bursting with adventure and sizzling passion to satisfy the most daring reader."
—*Romantic Times BOOKreviews*

"A charming heroine and a dashing spy hero make *The Pretender* a riveting read . . . [E]ntertained me thoroughly from beginning to end."
—Sabrina Jeffries, *USA Today* bestselling author of *After the Abduction*

# Look for these other books by
# Celeste Bradley

## THE LIAR'S CLUB

*The Pretender*
*The Impostor*
*The Spy*
*The Charmer*
*The Rogue*

## THE ROYAL FOUR

*To Wed a Scandalous Spy*
*Surrender to a Wicked Spy*
*One Night with a Spy*
*Seducing the Spy*

**Available from St. Martin's Paperbacks**

# Desperately Seeking a Duke

## Celeste Bradley

St. Martin's Paperbacks

DESPERATELY SEEKING A DUKE

Copyright © 2008 by Celeste Bradley
Excerpt from *The Duke Next Door* © copyright 2008 by Celeste Bradley.

ISBN: 0-312-93968-X
EAN: 978-0-312-93968-7

Printed in the United States of America

St. Martin's Paperbacks edition / March 2008

St. Martin's Paperbacks are published by St. Martin's Press, 175 Fifth Avenue, New York, NY 10010.

10 9 8 7 6 5 4 3 2 1

*This book is dedicated to my father, Fred Epps, who loved to read and loved to laugh. He never knew his little girl would grow up to be a writer, but I think he would have been tickled pink.*

*I'd like to gratefully acknowledge the support and assistance of dear friends and family. Without you all I would not be able to face the empty pages. Thank you, Bill Bradley, Darbi Gill, Robyn Holiday, Kim Jacobs, Cheryl Lewallen, Jennifer Smith, Cindy Tharp, Alexis Tharp, Cheryl Zach (aka Nicole Byrd), and, always and forever, Mia and the Banana. I'm also pretty damn fond of my editor, Monique Patterson, and my agent, Irene Goodman, who keep the hard stuff going while I have all the fun.*

# Prologue

I, Sir Hamish Pickering, being of sound mind but ailing body, do make my last will and testament.

I've climbed as high as a man can, despite having twice the brains, wisdom, and fortitude of the layabout aristocracy. Yet, a woman can wed as high as her looks will let her, up to a duchess if she may.

There, my own daughters have failed me miserably. Morag and Finella, I spent money on you so that you could marry higher but you weren't up to snuff. You expected the world to be handed to you. If any female of this family wants another farthing of my money she'd best set herself to earn it.

Therefore, I declare that the entirety of my fortune be kept back from my useless daughters and be held in trust for the granddaughter or great-granddaughter who weds a duke of England or weds a man who then becomes a duke through inheritance, at which time the trust will be released to her and only her.

If she has any sisters or female cousins who fail, they may each have a lifetime income of fifteen pounds a year. If she has any brothers or male cousins, though the family does tend to run to daughters, more's the pity, they will receive five pounds apiece, for that's all I had in my pocket when I came to London. Any Scotsman worth his haggis can turn five pounds into five hundred in a few years' time.

A set amount will be given each girl as she makes her debut in Society, for gowns and whatnot.

Should three generations of Pickering girls fail, I wash me hands of the lot of you. The entire fifteen thousand pounds will go to pay the fines and hardships of those who defy the excise man to export that fine Scots whisky which has been my only solace in this family of dolts. If your poor sainted mother could only see you now.

Signed,
Sir Hamish Pickering
Witnesses,
B. R. Stickley, A. M. Wolfe
Solicitor's firm of Stickley & Wolfe

# *Chapter One*

*England, 1815*

It likely signified nothing especially portentous, but when Miss Phoebe Millbury, proper vicar's daughter, met the man of her dreams the first part of him she fell in love with was his arse.

Up until that moment, the lush ballroom full of brightly clad dancers was like a dream—but not a good one. Phoebe moved through the strange landscape of her first Society ball seemingly without touching foot to the ground, as insubstantial as a ghost and just as unnoticed. What was she doing in this glittering world of the *haute ton*?

*Go to London and land yourself a duke*, the vicar had told her. *Fulfill your mother's dying wish.*

As if it were that easy.

*And don't let it happen again*. Oh, the vicar hadn't said that bit out loud, but the message had been perfectly clear. She must maintain propriety at all times, be demure and sensible and modest, as she had been for many years now, and never, ever slip down that unfortunate path again.

Which left her little in the way of means to win the attention of the aforementioned duke. Her gowns were all right for a country girl making the rounds of the village sick and infirm, or even for a dance at the local assembly rooms—not that she'd ever dared dance under the vicar's watchful eye—but they were hardly up to the rich London fashions worn by nearly every other lady in the room.

Nor was she a slender beauty like her cousin Deirdre, or even her widowed Aunt Tessa. She'd never had cause to mind her looks before now, she reminded herself, and she was far more fortunate than some. She slid a glance to one side of the ballroom to spy her other cousin, plain Miss Sophie Blake, as she took a seat in the row of chairs unofficially reserved for girls who would never dance.

*Land yourself a duke.* That would be a dream come true—which was ironic since it was largely the vicar's doing that Phoebe no longer dreamed such unlikely dreams.

Oh, she'd been a believer once upon a time. Once upon a time she'd been fifteen and a true romantic—a dreamer of the highest order.

One handsome dancing master later, she'd been cured forever. Since she apparently had no ability to discern dream from reality—nor even right from wrong!—the only way to be truly safe was to follow the rules very carefully. One could count on the rules, in a way that one could not count on what people said.

Or the way that one felt.

Phoebe sighed. It didn't seem to bother Sophie to sit out the music, but Phoebe would rather like to eventually dance with someone. He didn't have to be handsome, or even titled, as long as he had bathed semi-recently and didn't step on her feet . . .

That's when she spotted the hard, masculine buttocks that punctured her dreariness like a pin to a bubble.

The rest of him wasn't bad, either. Looking at the broad shoulders and dark waving hair of the man dancing with his back—and his heavenly posterior—toward her, Phoebe licked her lips and reminded herself that she was not that sort of woman any longer. She was never going to sin again.

*Oh yes, please.*

No. Never again.

*Pretty please with a chocolate drop on top?*

It was without a doubt the finest arse she had ever seen, clad in snug black breeches, with the tails of his evening coat falling just so over the well-developed . . .

The gentleman shifted his weight from one side to the other and Phoebe's eyes nearly crossed.

*Delicious.*

She let her gaze travel all the way down and then slowly back up, inch by inch. He was beautifully made, as if someone had taken every woman's ideal of broad shoulders and long muscular legs and ordered just the right man to fill the bill.

He turned his head.

His snowy cravat emphasized a truly admirable jawline, which in turn set off the high cheekbones and forehead that Adonis would not have been ashamed to sport. Dark hair curled over his forehead and collar, a bit too long and a bit too wild, as if even in his fine clothes he was not quite completely tamed.

*I like him not quite tamed . . .*

He finally turned bodily in the dance. His smile flashed white. His crisp bow at the end of the steps revealed to Phoebe that his belly was as flat as her cousin Sophie's bosom and that his chest was broad and deep.

Furthermore, his trousers fit even more beautifully in the front.

A rush of heat flooded Phoebe's veins. She glanced warily about her, for she would not want her cousins or her chaperone to catch her being so bold. She'd only been in London for a week and so far she'd managed to fool them all, even during her nerve-racking presentation at court.

No. Deirdre, the elegant and fashionable cousin, was surrounded by her usual coterie of admirers and didn't seem to have any attention to spare. Sophie, the unfortunately tall and awkward cousin, was across the ballroom, doing her best to hide in the crowd and was much too involved in the impossible process to so much as glance Phoebe's way.

Aunt Tessa, who was not much interested in chaperoning any of them, not even her own stepdaughter Deirdre, was busy exchanging gossip and barbed commentary with her equally fashionable clique of ennui-afflicted Society wives. Phoebe was safe.

Then the man before her laughed, a deep chuckle that rumbled through her body, causing a shiver in parts best left unmentioned and setting off alarms of all sorts within her. She knew what *that* feeling signified!

Oh, heavens. Not so safe, after all.

She was interested in a man—interested in *that way*—for the first time since she'd become infatuated with her dancing master, nearly ten years ago.

And that hadn't ended well at all.


SO FAR DURING the evening, Lord Raphael Marbrook, titled by courtesy if not by legitimate birthright, had managed to slip through the crowd at the ball without incident. He'd skillfully avoided some cuckolded husbands, thrice ducked encounters with card-playing lords intent on winning back what they'd lost in the past, and even managed to dance right past his predatory former—married—lover without her becoming aware that he was anywhere nearby.

Another hour and he could make his excuses. Even his half brother Calder could say naught about him evading family duty on that score. It was only the threat of being forced to attend the even more boring parade of virgins at the assembly rooms of Almack's that compelled Rafe to be here at all.

"If I have to waste time going wife-hunting, you have to

go with me," Calder had vowed, his tone promising dire consequences indeed. This would be Calder's second wife, for he'd lost his first wife, Melinda, only a few years into their marriage.

This was particularly unfair since there was no possibility of Rafe himself finding a *first* wife among such upright and respectable members of Society. Still, the Marquis of Brookhaven's considerable black and brooding wrath was best avoided, if possible.

Not that Rafe was afraid of his brother—they were of a size and age and neither had ever come out the clear winner in any of many boyish brawls—but he had a particular agenda to put before Calder regarding some improvements on the Brookhaven estate and it wouldn't do to unnecessarily provoke him beforehand. Only Calder could approve the changes, for Rafe had no power over their father's legacy. He was not the real son.

Of course, the irony was that Calder didn't give a damn about Brookhaven. Oh, he did his duty. No one starved and the production remained stable, but Brookhaven could be so much more!

Brookhaven didn't stir Calder the way it did Rafe. The only things that stirred Calder's icy blood were his factories. He remained fascinated by the machinery and the efficiency, while the ancient grandeur of Brookhaven was lost on his logical mind. He dismissed the magnificent hall as "that drafty pile of stone" and the loyal cottagers, the pumping heart of Brookhaven itself, as "those backward rustics."

Being the acknowledged bastard of a marquis had its ups and downs. On one hand, having been raised at Brookhaven along with his half brother, he'd had all the advantages of privilege and education that Calder, the true heir, had enjoyed. On the other, he'd spent those years knowing that while Calder had the promise of a title and real power, all he himself would ever have was an allowance and a courtesy "Lord" before his name and the scandalous reputation he'd worked so hard for—but now repented.

After all, generous allowances were spent as easily as any other sort of money and he'd devoted years to enjoying his to the limit. Women, cards, spirits—all without any of the tedious responsibilities that came with legitimacy. Everyone expected the Bastard of Brookhaven to come to a bad end and Rafe had spent most of his youth proving them right to the best of his ability.

Yet, there was no point now in regretting his youthful indiscretions. Apologies would get him nowhere with Calder. Only time and effort could ever prove to his brother that he was ready for more solemn duty.

And the duty he wanted was Brookhaven.

Now, as he paused to speak to one of his more respectable acquaintances, Rafe absently twitched his shoulders. For the last several moments he'd had the eerie, neck-tingling sensation that he was being watched.


PHOEBE'S SINGLE GOVERNESS, who'd only lasted a few weeks, had once told Phoebe that if she hadn't had bad luck, she'd have had no luck at all.

Her luck was in full force tonight, for just as she'd decided that that was indeed the manly and muscled arse with which she wanted to spend the rest of her life, everything went perfectly, horribly wrong.

He lifted his chin as his genial brown eyes scanned the room—and then his gaze was genial no longer, but was now intensely locked on hers.

Something struck Phoebe in the vicinity of her heart—and a bit lower—a powerful and startling attraction that far surpassed mere interest in his anatomy. The impact quite stole the breath from her lungs.

*Lightning.*

Then she realized the worst of it. She'd been caught looking.

*Oh, bugger.* Without thought, Phoebe ran for it. Right into a servant carrying a full tray of champagne flutes. The high-impact collision propelled the poor man, his tray, and all its contents directly into the spinning mass of dancers behind him.

Immediate uproar ensued. Horrified ladies screeched, angry lords cursed, amused musicians hid their smiles. And then everyone began to angrily look about for the culprit.

It was her most horrible nightmare come to vivid life. Phoebe braced herself for the worst.

Rafe couldn't believe it. The poor servant hadn't stood a chance against the shapely missile aimed his way. Glass and champagne sprayed far and wide, leaving a perfect half-circle of madness with the girl at the obvious apex.

Oh, damn.

He strode into the fray and, grasping the girl by the hand, danced her into the pattern as if the two of them were mere passers-by, continuing with their spirited country reel.

She gasped at his firm handling. "Sir, what are you doing?"

He gazed nonchalantly ahead, moving them in and out of the dance. "Oh, did you want to stay to see how things pan out?"

She glanced over her shoulder and then, paling at the chaos, resolutely looked away. "Well, but—we haven't been properly introduced!"

"I won't tell if you won't." They reached the end of the pattern, now far across the ballroom from the spill. A waltz began. He grinned down at her, for she was dancing in earnest now, moving *him* along as quickly as possible. "Are we late for something?"

She sent him a piteous glance. "My aunt Tessa!"

Rafe looked over his shoulder to see an extremely elegant lady with an extremely plagued-off expression upon her face, casting about the ballroom with snapping eyes. Oh, dread. Not the infamous Lady Tessa. "Care for some air?" he offered casually.

Phoebe nearly melted in gratitude. He was a god and a hero. "Don't mind if I do," she said with all the nonchalance of a woman who had just escaped the firing squad.

He danced her to the terrace door, whisking two full glasses from a footman's tray with the fingers of one hand as they passed. The man only bowed with a wry grin on his face. *Points for style,* his expression said.

Points for flat-out male perfection, Phoebe's heart said.

She put out one hand to hit the latch and they danced outside with nary a pause in their waltz. Three stone steps led down to the terrace from the door. He wrapped one arm firmly about her waist and whirled her right off her feet, dancing her down the steps without spilling a drop of champagne.

It was a bold, dashing move. Phoebe laughed aloud, startled out of her worry about the chaos behind them.

He smiled down at her as he set her back on her feet. "That's better. What has that awful mess back there to do with us? We were dancing."

She caught her breath and stepped back slightly, still feeling the solidity of his broad chest against hers. "I get the feeling that you dance your way out of trouble often, Mr.—"

He bowed deeply, still balancing the glasses in one hand. "Marbrook, at your service, milady."

Phoebe laughed again and curtsied. "My thanks, sir knight. I am no lady, however. My name is Phoebe Millbury, of Thornton."

He straightened with a grin. "Might I offer you a glass, Phoebe Millbury of Thornton?"

She eyed the glass dubiously. "Proper young ladies do not drink champagne."

"Proper young ladies don't douse the ballroom in it, either."

She shuddered. "Don't remind me." She took the glass. "I suppose I'm already in enough trouble this evening." She sipped it. "Oh, that's rather nice!" She took another, larger sip.

"Whoa, there." He took the glass from her. "You might want to wait a moment, since you've never had it before."

It fizzled delightfully going down and warmed her stomach. Suddenly the incident in the ballroom seemed less deadly and more amusing. She giggled. "Did you see their faces?"

He shook his head. "Two sips and she's gone." He tossed the rest of her glass over the railing. "You, Miss Millbury, are what we gentlemen would call a 'lightweight.'"

She curtsied. "My thanks for your timely rescue, Mr. Marbrook. It was very nice to meet you, but I ought not to be out here alone with you."

"You're not going back in there, are you? Lady Tessa looked thoroughly frightening."

She hesitated. "You know my aunt?"

He grimaced. "Everyone knows Lady Tessa. I only wonder what Lady Rochester might have done to be blackmailed into inviting Lady Tessa this evening."

She gazed at him with one brow raised. "I ought to defend my aunt. She has taken a great deal of trouble to launch me in Society."

He smiled, the corners of his mouth crinkling. "Launch? Like a rocket, to rain destruction on innocent ballrooms everywhere?"

She shook her head, a rueful grin slipping through her arch pose. "No, I fear I did that all by myself."

"I am partly to blame. I startled you—though not half as much as your . . . examination startled me."

She went very still, her gaze frozen on his face. "I'm sure I don't know what you mean," she said testily.

"Yes, you do. It is only fair that I have my turn."

Her brows crinkled slightly. "You're an odd man, Mr. Marbrook."

He smiled. "Hold still."

She did so obediently, but he could sense her fingers twining nervously behind her back. She wasn't as cool as she'd like to pretend.

She was a pretty girl . . . but not an exceptionally beautiful one. Her fair hair shimmered in the moonlight, the many different colors combining to defy categorization. Was she blond or brunette? It was a mess, part falling down, part twisted up high to show off her neck and rounded shoulders. It was mutinous hair, as if her inner rebellion could not be truly contained.

In the ballroom, he'd been struck by the blue of her wide, vulnerable eyes—like a hazy summer's day—but in the moonlight they washed almost clear to sparkle like diamonds as she gazed up at him.

He tipped a finger to her chin, absorbing the delicacy of her features one by one. Her lips were sweet and curved rather than his usual preference for full and sensual and her chin tended toward pointed. She was stubborn, he'd wager.

She reminded Rafe of a porcelain doll—if porcelain dolls came outfitted with stunning bosoms. If they had, he might have been inclined to play with them a bit more in his curious boyhood.

"Well, do I pass inspection, sir?"

Don't kiss the pretty girl. The pretty girl likely has friends in high places and a papa with a pistol.

Do *not* kiss the pretty girl.

Unless perchance he could convince the pretty girl to kiss *him* . . .

He decided to chance it. He leaned close, putting his lips close to her ear. "You know, I'm told I'm quite good at making rockets explode."

"Oomph." A small fist made forceful contact with his waistcoat.

She tossed her head. "You're not *that* handsome."

He stepped back, grinning and rubbing at his stomach, his estimation of her moral fiber strengthened. Right, then. No jaded, innuendo-laden Society banter for this lady. "I suppose I deserved that."

She was shaking her hand from the sting of the blow. "Indeed. That was beneath you. I have a very heroic view of you. Do not spoil it."

Heroic? There was no reason for the spread of warmth in his belly. The opinion of a silly debutante mattered not at all.

Although she did look fine in the moonlight, bosom high and shoulders back, the light of battle in her eye. And that shot to the stomach—that had been no playful slap. She'd meant every bit of it. Apparently, country girls from Thornton struck hard.

He bowed deeply. "My apologies, Miss Millbury. I was much too bold." When her defensive stance eased, he gave her his most charming smile. "Where is this Thornton, that it breeds such warrior damsels? It sounds a harsh place— Thorn Town."

She smiled back, as if she could not resist. She would not be the first.

"On the contrary. It is said that it was named when a long-ago king rode by with his entourage of knights one winter's day and called the valley 'a worthless briar patch.' As a jest, he gave it to his least valued knight on the spot."

"Ouch."

She smiled. "Ah, but that is not the entire story. When the poor knight returned to his valley in the spring, he was stunned by the beauty and scent of the landscape, perfumed by many thousands of roses left to grow wild by some chance of wind and storm. Since he did not wish his capricious king to take it back, he named his manor Thornhold and the village he built for his cottagers Thorn Town. The king and his court never deigned to visit, and so never knew that he had given his lowest knight one of the most beautiful portions of England."

She was quite transformed as she spoke. Her voice took on a dreamy quality and her eyes grew soft. Rafe found himself utterly captivated.

"A fanciful tale." He kept his voice low, so as not to break the spell.

She continued to gaze somewhere far away. "Indeed. I used to imagine that I was the lady of Thornhold, won by the clever knight from the king's favorite, and brought to the manor in the dark of a midsummer night. When I awoke, I looked from my marriage bedchamber out to a sea of roses and swore to my love that I would keep the secret forever."

He chuckled. "Put a lot of thought into that, did you?"

She pursed her lips slightly, but he thought he detected a twist of humor there.

"Well, there is a variation where the king's favorite comes to steal me back and I am taken away from Thornhold in the dead of winter and the roses never bloom again."

He laughed, delighted by the fancy. "And if you do not return to Thornhold now, will there be no more rosewater for the baths of Thornton?"

She laughed and a pleasant sensation warmed the pit of Rafe's stomach. On impulse, he wrapped his hands about her waist and swept her up to stand upon the bench.

She gasped and teetered. "Mr. Marbrook!"

Once she steadied, he released her and made a flourishing bow. "O, Lady of the Roses, I am but a humble knight, scorned by my king. But I have a valley of exquisite beauty beknownst only to me. I shall bestow this valley, which fades next to your own beauteous glow, if you will only grant me your love!"

She gazed at him, wide-eyed, until he thought he must have mistaken her nature and shocked her too deeply with his actions. Then a smile teased her lips before she donned a haughty mien. "Who are you, lowly sir, to offer nothing but a tangled bramble patch and expect a wife?"

"It is not a bramble patch, lady fair, but the garden of Eden itself."

She lifted her chin disdainfully. "And in this valley of roses, would you expect me to be your lady or your chattel? Would I be allowed a mind of my own, sir knight?" Her gaze became distant. He had the feeling she was somewhere else entirely for a moment. "Would I be chastised for being myself?" she said softly. "Must I keep hidden behind a mask of others' making?"

Her words resonated against something old and raw within him. *Hidden behind a mask of others' making.* Yes, he knew what that was like.

"No," he whispered. "There, my lady is a queen in her own right. There, my lady can do no wrong." He pretended to pull something from inside his coat and presented it with a bow. "I offer you a single rose from my valley—for one of my roses is worth a hundred of any other in everlasting splendor."

A dreamy expression replaced the haughty one as if Miss Phoebe Millbury entirely forgot the role she played.

"Everlasting splendor," she repeated softly. She reached to take the flower, and in the moment when their fingertips touched, Rafe could have almost sworn that something did actually bloom between them.

Nonsense. He blinked, then stepped back, intentionally shattering the moment with a short laugh.

His abrupt motion caused Phoebe's balance to shift. The sole of her soft dancing slipper skidded on the dew-dampened bench and she began to topple into his arms.

# Chapter Two

The dark-eyed knight—er, gentleman—caught her easily, taking her breath away with the ready swiftness of his strong arms. One instant she was on her way to an embarrassing sprawl on the stones of the terrace, the next she had two large hands wrapped about her waist and her entire weight taken on a broad chest. Only one foot remained on the bench, on tiptoe at that, yet he smiled up at her astonished face as easily as if he carried a pillow—although she knew very well she was *not* stuffed with feathers!

Then it struck her—that spreading warmth, that humming of her nerves . . . that wonderful, dreamy, dangerous feeling that she'd thought she'd banished from her senses forever.

*Again. I want to sin again . . . and again . . . and again . . .*

She pushed her hands on his broad shoulders to lift her bosom away from his chest. *I will not be a creature of animal passions. I will be a . . .*

His shoulders were rigid with muscle, hard and flexing beneath her palms. He would be a miracle of manliness without his shirt—like one of the workers of the fields when they thought no women were about . . .

*Stop it!* Obviously a firm grip was needed, for she was . . .

She was sliding slowly down his long, hard body, inch by inch. Her softer flesh melted and molded to his as he gradually lowered her to stand on her own. It was a lovely trip down, and over far too soon, although some part of her was aware that he'd intentionally drawn the entire process out to a vastly improper length.

He was being very bad. She was being much, much worse, for she was not only allowing it, she was enjoying it. He was big and handsome and he liked her—Phoebe, simply Phoebe.

Not the demure, perfectly behaved daughter of Mr. Millbury, the vicar. Not the scandal-waiting-to-happen girl who had spent the last ten years waiting for her secret to erupt and ruin her future forever. Not Aunt Tessa's well-dressed creation at her first London ball.

Simply Phoebe.

"Marbrook." She sighed his name, just like a heroine in one of those tawdry novels she wasn't supposed to read.

Rafe's mouth went a bit dry but he wasn't complaining.

He stole a long, admiring glance down her décolletage, then found his gaze actually drawn back to her face. She truly did look like a milk-fed country girl who wouldn't turn up her nose at a good pudding or a good laugh.

On the other hand, she was finely dressed and moreover, she was at Rochester's ball, which meant she was neither common nor friendless.

It was past time to return Miss Phoebe to her chaperone. Yet, for some reason, he did nothing but remain where he was, standing a bit too close, with his hands about her waist, a bit too high, staring down at her as she stared back up at him.

Her blue gaze was like a cool clean pool, the sort that could wash away any sin.

"Are you a rake?" Her voice was husky in the quiet, yet the words rang loudly in his ears.

*Rake.*

He smiled slightly, despite the sudden and shamed

pounding of his heart. *A rake indeed.* Worse, actually. *I am a bastard.*

Suddenly he had the overpowering urge to become precisely what she thought him—an honorable man with only the best of intentions.

But not yet. Right now he didn't want this moment with Miss Millbury from Thornton to end. He tucked her closer into him, until his thighs pressed alongside hers and her breasts moved against his chest as she breathed.

Phoebe allowed it. After all, it wasn't much closer than two might stand while dancing. She did not take offense.

*When will you take offense? When he ravages you in the garden?*

She hushed that thought, for it held the taint of the vicar's voice. Besides, the opportunity of being ravaged in the garden by this man might be too interesting to pass up.

"Although that is probably the champagne talking," she said out loud. "I am beginning to see why young ladies are not supposed to drink spirits. It does strange things to one's guard."

As in slaying it, beheading it, and burying it in the aforementioned garden. But no matter.

He crinkled his brow, not losing his smile. "I wish I was in on that conversation, but I fear I have no idea what you and the champagne are talking about."

"The garden," Phoebe informed him, opening her eyes to gaze up at him again. Goodness, wouldn't she love to have this man stretched out in the flowers for her exploration? She sighed deeply. He did not hide his interest in her neckline, but it was only a rather politely admiring glance. His gaze came directly back to meet hers again.

"I see. Is it a fine garden or a poor one?"

Her eyes grew heavy-lidded as she let her gaze travel over his lips close to hers. "A very fine one. The finest."

"Does it suit you, this garden you speak of?" His voice

deepened, betraying a hint of . . . vulnerability? "Do you like it?"

Her heart melted. "I like it above all others." She longed to embrace him—nay, to sink into him like water spilled in desert sand. "I wish . . ." She bit her lip. "I wish it were mine."

His gaze went to her lips and stayed there. "Do you truly want this garden to be yours?"

*Oh, yes, please.* Her heart was both racing and at peace. It was an odd thing, to have found what one was looking for so desperately, when one didn't even know one was looking.

Gazing up at him, at his fine clothing and dark hair and delicious mouth and the shadow of masculine cheek and jaw . . . The wrapping was quite perfect—including that posterior view, which still lingered in her mind's eye—but it was something more that tugged at her as if he had her soul on a string.

His eyes. It was if she was looking into still water, only the self she saw was the half of her she'd been missing all the days of her life.

Magic. Old magic, like in those stories her cousin Sophie was always reading. "I believe I am bewitched," she said huskily.

His eyes knew. "Are you?" he said.

She could not look away. It was as if he recognized her as well, as if he could see directly into her and always had.

The astonishing thought that followed was that she had the distinct impression that he liked what he saw. Which was impossible.

Wasn't it?

Yet, the longer he held her gaze trapped in his—the longer the silence grew and blanketed them, isolating them in a moment out of time—the more she began to believe in the impossible.

In his eyes, she saw herself as beautiful and more. She felt understood, as if her very nature were bared to his observation and he saw no wickedness, no inherent flaw, no dark and decadent seed of sensuality—or at least if he did, he didn't mind it one little bit.

His expression was one of acute fascination. It was as if she were the first woman he'd ever seen—which was nonsense. Only . . . it didn't feel like nonsense. He seemed as surprised by her as she was by him.

Wouldn't it be lovely if it—if he—were real?

Rafe couldn't tear his eyes away from her, which made no sense. She was a mess, really, in that fine but unflattering dress, with her hair clumped into that unwieldy bun . . .

It would be long, perhaps to her buttocks. It would curl around his fingertips when he stroked his hands through it and dragged it forward to drape over her bare breasts . . .

Need hit him so hard he could scarcely draw a breath. Not lust—well, not simply lust, at any rate. It was *need*, much like the need for air, or water. He needed her, in all her sweet boldness, in all her clear-sighted wholesomeness, in order to go on.

But this was nonsense. There was no such thing as "the one." There was no shortage of ladies eager to be his lover. Women surrounded him, glittering, stylish creatures with polish so perfect and hard that it seemed as though they had crystallized.

She was nothing like that, this country girl with the vulnerable eyes and the resolute chin. She was so unpolished that his fingers twitched with the urge to discover every rounded texture she possessed.

Before he knew what he was about, before he could stop the impulse—the *need*—his head tilted down to kiss her.

It wasn't a real kiss—more of a breath of a touch, mouth to mouth, a sweet, nearly chaste brush of softness to firmness. It wasn't really a kiss—except in that it was a kiss that turned Phoebe's entire world sideways forever.

His big hand came up to cup the back of her head and the not-kiss lingered. They stood, pressed together, their only movement the rising and falling of their chests, the pounding of their hearts.

He groaned aloud, then froze, as if hearing himself in surprise. He pulled back from her, his breath coming fast. "God!"

Phoebe was a bit breathless herself. She wrapped her arms about herself, feeling cold without him close. "The vicar would say that God had nothing to do with that . . . although I have always wondered if that were really true. I mean, if God created us and if we—"

He was looking at her oddly. "The vicar?"

Oh. Perhaps it was a bit early to bring up the vicar. Then again, it was a bit early to be kissed on the terrace, so there. "The vicar is my father. Mr. Millbury, vicar of Thornhold in Devonshire."

"Ah." He wrapped his arms about her and pulled her close against the chill, dropping his chin on the top of her head with a deep exhalation. "Of course. Your father is the vicar. How . . . fitting."

Rafe was very surprised at himself. He'd always been a bad seed, but manhandling the vicar's daughter in the dark? That was low, even for him.

Not to mention the danger that at any moment, this country vicar would emerge from the ballroom and demand a betrothal at the business end of his blunderbuss.

Betrothal. Wed.

Something rather interesting rolled through Rafe.

Wed to pretty Miss Phoebe Millbury, unfashionable little nobody fresh from the wilds of Devonshire. Now, why did that thought hold him caught in its warm, generous, pliant embrace for so long?

He very nearly opened his mouth to propose on the spot.

At the last instant, he caught himself. He could hear Calder now, carrying on about the ills of impulsiveness. Rafe leashed the strange possessive urgency that this girl mysteriously incited within him and firmly tied it down. The Season had scarcely begun. There was plenty of time to get to know Miss Millbury better.

Besides, the idea appealed. The thought of spending the summer in her company, courting her, surprising her with small gifts—just enough to delight her without turning her head, mind you—driving her through Hyde Park in his phaeton . . .

He would do this properly. He would play the gentleman for her. There was plenty of time.

A new calm descended, smoothing the jagged edges of his earlier frustration with Calder's highhandedness. An unhurried courtship of Phoebe Millbury would be just the cure for his current restless dissatisfaction.

And then, when his investments paid out and his ship came in, he would approach her very respectable father with gold in his pocket and his hat in his hand. Perhaps with Calder's backing, that would be enough to convince such a man that his daughter should wed a bastard.

Then, just in time for their seasonal return to Brookhaven he would wed her with all appropriate fanfare. Then he would wrap her up and stick her in his pocket to be his talisman against the stifling pressure of being forever in the shadow of the perfect scion, the Marquis of Brookhaven, Calder Marbrook.

He smiled easily at his delightful Miss Phoebe Millbury. She smiled back, shyly at first, then with a growing confidence. Oh, yes . . .

She was the one.

# *Chapter Three*

It was simple enough for Phoebe to make her way unnoticed back to the spot where she'd first seen Marbrook. She arrived without attracting attention, and why would she? After all, she was one of many unexceptional girls garbed in white muslin with matching wistful expressions. Hopefully her own mien would be seen as bashful and overheated, not aroused and excited.

What had she just done?

She reddened further, thinking of his rather telling silence once she'd mentioned the vicar—and the way he'd respectfully guided her back into the ballroom, so different from his teasing manner before—

"There you are!"

*Tessa.* Phoebe took a fortifying breath and turned to face her chaperone with an innocent expression on her face. "Yes, aunt?"

Lady Tessa was the niece of the current Duke of Edencourt and had been a great beauty in her day—which was not so long ago, come to think of it, since Tessa was but one-and-thirty years—but her stunning looks hadn't been enough to compensate for her famously vicious personality.

Polished and perfect and unkind whenever it suited her. Phoebe supposed that Tessa had gotten by on her beauty for so long, the woman simply couldn't understand the concept of getting by on good character and kindness.

Tessa made it a point never to frown or purse her lips. The muscles of her face never moved if she could help it. It preserved her beauty, just as she claimed, but it gave her an eerie quality, as if she had been turned to stone by Medusa. Lovely but cold as alabaster.

She'd finally married not-so-well and had burned through her not-so-wealthy husband's money in record time. Her much older husband, who had once been wed to Phoebe's mother's sister, had promptly paid her back by dying as quietly and unceremoniously as he'd lived, leaving her with pretty trappings, empty accounts, and his only child, his daughter Deirdre, to raise.

This made Tessa, by some contortionist calculation, something like an aunt to Phoebe and, as such, she was a suitable chaperone for her launch into Society. At least, that was how Phoebe's father, the vicar, had explained it. Phoebe thought the entire matter was a bit of a stretch and that the vicar would have been better off simply admitting that he wasn't interested in the job and that he meant to gleefully fob her off on the caustic and sometimes offensive Tessa.

"You stupid girl!"

Very well, make that "often offensive." Phoebe remembered to blink innocently. "But Auntie, what did I do?"

"I saw you dancing! Who were you dancing with?"

Quickly, Phoebe ran down the mental list of men she'd been properly introduced to. "Was it Sir Alton?"

"No, he had dark hair and he wasn't a stooping old heron like that idiot Alton. I didn't see his face—but I don't think I introduced you to—"

"You introduced me to Mr. Edgeward." Who was tall but not too tall, dark and fairly young. She hadn't danced with him—but then again, she wasn't claiming any such thing, was she? It was very important not to lie. Lying was a sin. She had enough of those under her belt so far this evening.

*Oh, my.* What a rather intriguing image that conjured . . .

Tessa deflated. "Oh. Edgeward. Well, don't waste your time with that slow-witted farmer. You girls are here to attract dukes, not ditchdiggers."

"Aunt, Mr. Edgeward has more acres than most lords and he's a very intelligent man—he is simply on the quiet side." Nor did he have any interest in Tessa's sort of sly gossip, which meant—in Tessa's vernacular—he had nothing useful to say.

Tessa let out an impatient noise. "Where is your cousin Sophie? If that girl has hidden in the library again—"

"I'm here."

Both Phoebe and Tessa whirled in surprise to see the speaker, standing no more than a yard away.

Unlike the other maidens on the marriage mart, Miss Sophie Blake was rather hard to miss, for she was fully as tall as any man in the room—with the possible exception of Mr. Edgeward—and as narrow and straight as a pencil. She had arrived only yesterday to join their party of competing debutantes, journeying alone from her home in the north, with one small trunk of clothing and one large trunk of books.

Her unfortunate height might have been more easily overlooked had she possessed a handsome figure, or a lovely face, but Sophie had inherited all the worst of the Pickering trademarks. Her blue eyes were nearly as pale as milk and her hair was the ruddy sort of blond that made one think of runny marmalade. Her features were as bony as her figure and her nose . . . well, one truly needed a much bolder personality to carry off such an imposing ancestral feature.

Combine that with a complete lack of interest in fashion

or style, a tendency toward clumsiness, and a sharp mind that made most men feel a bit stupid, and one had the complete recipe for a wallflower of the first order.

Sophie had been given the same small allotment of funds that the rest of them had, but Tessa had claimed it all for rent of their house and preordering the gowns.

Sophie hadn't cared. "I came here for the experience of travel, and to see the history and grandeur of London. I have no intention of wasting my time looking for a husband."

Now she stood before them in a ill-fitted ruffled concoction hastily purchased by Tessa. Her wispy hair was escaping its combs, her spectacles were slightly askew, and she had a smudge of dust on her chin.

"You asked after me, Tessa?"

Sophie might be retiring and a bit on the shy side, but she had a way of gazing evenly at people whom she found mentally deficient in some way—which compared to her was nearly everyone—that always seemed to cause Tessa's hackles to rise.

As they did now.

Phoebe looked away as Tessa made clear her opinions on Sophie's carriage, manner, and appearance, trying not to hear the hissed insults while at the same time remaining at the scene so Sophie might not be left a complete victim to Tessa's ire.

After all, Sophie had distracted Tessa from Phoebe's inexplicable disappearance from the ballroom, which was appreciated.

*Coward.*

*Oh, yes.*

But there was no deflecting Tessa when she was in full fury. "And as for you, Phoebe Millbury—"

*Oh, dread,* as Mr. Marbrook had so eloquently put it.

"—I don't think your father would approve of this tendency to wander! Must I write to tell him how you've taken to slipping away with strange men—"

Phoebe gasped. "But that's not—" Careful. Don't lie. "I was most properly introduced to Mr. Edgeward. And I only stepped out for a bit of air." Which was all true. Mostly.

Tessa narrowed her eyes and leaned closer. "Phoebe, your father warned me to take great care with you. You do not want to cause an *incident*, do you?"

Phoebe went cold. *The Incident.* That's what the vicar always called it, when he could bring himself to mention it at all. The vicar wouldn't tell *Tessa,* would he? No, surely her father wouldn't reveal Phoebe's humiliating secret to Society's most vicious gossip—even if she was almost-nearly related to them?

Phoebe closed her eyes against the possibility. God, if all these people knew! They might know, even now, right this minute! She opened her eyes to gaze around her in a panic.

Those women over there, with their heads together—were they talking about her?

She could almost hear them. "There's that Millbury girl . . . the one that ran off with her dancing master when she was only fifteen . . . he ruined her and abandoned her, can you imagine that? Just left her there, half-naked in the inn room, for her father to find the next morning!"

They would turn and gaze at her in a moment, all their scorn alive in their eyes . . .

*I'm sorry,* she wanted to cry out. *I didn't mean to be bad. I was only left a bit too alone for a bit too long. I went a bit too far—*

No. No, she was imagining it again, just as she had so many times in the past ten years.

No one had ever learned what she had done so long ago. The vicar had concealed every detail and Terrence

LaPomme, musician and seducer of gullible young girls, had never been heard from again.

She'd been the model vicar's daughter ever since, never giving her father the least reason to worry about her behavior—

*Alone on the terrace with Mr. Marbrook, sliding down his hard muscular body, his large hands tight on her waist, his lips almost touching hers . . .*

—until tonight!

Hurriedly, she covered her shock, hiding the wave of alarm that swept over her. Tessa knew nothing, and Phoebe intended to keep matters just so.

But Tessa had abruptly pasted a sweetly welcoming smile on her face to greet the couple now approaching them. "Deirdre, my pet! Dancing has put the loveliest bloom in your cheeks! Is it not becoming, Your Grace?"

Phoebe managed to curtsy before Tessa's elbow made contact with her ribs, but Sophie was a bit late off the mark. "Oomph!"

Straightening, Phoebe saw her other cousin, Deirdre, sweeping elegantly toward them on the arm of the only actual duke in the room.

If Sophie had inherited the least attractive Pickering tendencies, then Deirdre had made off with all the good ones. She was just tall enough to be elegant and just slender enough to be stylish while still packing all those things men desire in a woman. Her hair was the color of sunlight and her eyes were a deep sparkling blue that made Phoebe, who had previously liked her own sky-blue eyes, feel as though hers had faded somehow. Even the Pickering nose, nonexistent on Phoebe and overly prominent on Sophie, on Deirdre took on an aquiline elegance that made Phoebe feel just a bit underbred.

Of course, Deirdre, having been raised by the ruthlessly social-climbing Tessa, made the most of her good fortune.

Every gown she owned was lovelier than the last, and all fit her excellent figure to perfection. Deirdre was here to win.

So far she had the highest score. None of them had actually danced with an unmarried duke until now.

There was the fact that the duke on Deirdre's arm was over seventy years of age and was currently about to pass out from his brief turn on the dance floor, but one would never know it from the blazing look of triumph in Deirdre's eyes.

"There'll be no living with her now," Sophie muttered to herself. Phoebe had to agree. In the past week she'd learned that Deirdre was spoiled, selfish, and vain—and now it seemed she would be made all the more unbearable by this evening's coup.

Seeing Tessa and Deirdre side by side, Phoebe was struck by the pure resemblance that had nothing to do with facial features or hair or eye color. Every supercilious line of Tessa's posture and attitude was perfectly reflected in Deirdre.

This alternately annoyed and stirred pity in Phoebe. It surely could not have been easy to be a child in Lady Tessa's house, yet Deirdre could be such an entirely selfish being that Phoebe sometimes had trouble holding onto her compassion.

She vaguely remembered Deirdre as a child, for they'd played together on occasion when they were very young, until Deirdre's mother had died and her father remarried Lady Tessa. Then the family gatherings at Thornhold had ended.

Sophie's family had never visited, for Sophie's mother was bedridden from a riding accident years ago.

Although their mothers were all sisters, it seemed that Phoebe, Deirdre, and Sophie had nothing at all in common . . . except the desire to win the Pickering trust.

That was why they were here, in London, sharing this

house to stretch their stipends and vying for the few dukes currently available on the marriage mart.

"I'm glad it is you I share a room with," Phoebe murmured to Sophie.

Sophie blinked and turned to look at her in surprise. "You are?" A swift smile flashed across her bony face, then it was gone. "Thank you."

Phoebe gazed at her cousin in astonishment. For just a fraction of a second Sophie had looked . . . *pretty*? No, that wasn't possible, was it? It was a trick of light and shadow and her first taste of champagne. Phoebe peered closer.

"What is it?" Sophie dabbed at her chin. "Didn't I get the smudge off?"

No, Sophie was as she had been before—unfortunately plain.

And she, Phoebe, was unfortunately wicked.

Never again. No men. No trembling knees. No secret touches. Not until her wedding night, with her hopefully not-too-disgusting husband, who hopefully wouldn't be very observant about a silly little matter like her mislaid virginity.

Tonight's episode had been a mere moment out of time, an uncharacteristic break spurred by a moment of panic. He'd saved her from an unfortunate scene and she'd been polite about it.

Nothing more.

*Wouldn't it be wonderful if Marbrook were really a duke in disguise?*

Wonderful, but not likely.

# Chapter Four

Back in the ballroom after smoothly inserting a blushing Phoebe back into the dancing throng, Rafe spotted his brother, Calder, holding up a column on the other side of the room.

People sometimes asked Rafe if looking at Calder was like looking into a mirror. It always reminded Rafe of that astonishing moment when he was eight years of age, when the imposing man who'd taken him from beside his mother's deathbed brought him to the grandest house he'd ever seen and showed him to a finely furnished nursery.

"Calder," the man had called out. A boy just Rafe's size had emerged from a corner filled with books and had bowed to the man. "Yes, Father?

Looking at that boy . . . yes, that had been like looking into a mirror. His eyes, his nose, even his curling dark hair— the other boy had taken them all!

That seemed to be the very thought crossing the other boy's mind as well. Long-lashed brown eyes had darkened and narrowed, focusing on the large, friendly hand resting on Rafe's shoulder.

"Calder, this is your new brother, Raphael. He is my other son."

*Other son.*

Resentful fire flashed in the other boy's eyes, ending

Rafe's newly born hopes of having the brother he'd always longed for.

"*I* am your son," Calder had stated firmly, furiously, proudly. "*He* is nothing but your bastard."

Perhaps it wasn't right to hold the words of a hurt and shocked eight-year-old boy against the man he'd become, but Rafe still heard them, still saw them in Calder's gaze, still felt the blow to the grieving, lonely heart of a lost boy in a stranger's house.

Calder had been the first person in Rafe's life to call him a bastard, but he was by no means the last. Now it was no longer news, of course. He'd known this world and its people for a very long time. He was nearly one of them, warily welcomed—as long as he remembered his true status.

Rafe would never forget his first sight of Brookhaven. Rolling up that long drive with his head and arms hanging out of the carriage window, he'd seen that golden evening sunglow upon the white stones of the great house and thought perhaps he was seeing the gates of heaven itself.

The marquis had smiled at his abrupt infatuation and later had taken him through the gallery. Hand in hand with the stranger now called Father, Rafe had gazed at the portraits of Marbrook men long gone and seen his own eyes painted on the canvases.

It was as if he'd been lost, even happy as he was with his loving, teasing mama. She was a memory, a wisp, a feeling of warmth and happiness that would never return. What there was to take her place was Brookhaven. The very earth beneath his feet—and on his hands, for he never tired of playing in it—vibrated in harmony with his own heartbeat. The land, the trees, the fields, the stone walls twining over the hills like ancient, illegible writing . . . those were his skin, his bones, his flesh, the creases of his own palms.

Father had watched that love grow, at first satisfied, then proud, then at long last—too late—worried.

Little boys don't understand inheritance law, don't think in terms of legitimacy or illegitimacy. He'd learned that his brother would someday have Brookhaven. He'd assumed he would share it, as he shared the nursery and the governess, the toys and the books.

Calder must have known, but he'd said not a word to Rafe on the subject. Kindness or subtle vengeance? There was no way to know. Their relationship grew quickly in the hothouse conditions of that nursery, for who else was there to play with? Their brawls became fewer, though never disappearing completely. Their accord, while sometimes uneasy, strengthened them both. It was something, to never be alone, to always look across the room or the desk or the dinner table and see the one person who knew you best—whether they liked you that day or not.

Until that day . . .

"I'm sorry, my boy, but you must see how it is. Calder is my heir." Large, sympathetic hands on his shoulders.

He'd shrugged them off. "Then make him share it. Build a wall down the center of Brookhaven. I want the side with the house."

A smile, sad and proud at the same time. Rafe had known then.

"Even if I didn't have Calder, you could not have it, Rafe. The title, the lands, all is entailed to my legitimate heir. If not to Calder, then it goes to another branch of the family entirely. I have a distant cousin in Kent. He is a farmer, a country squire. Imagine his face when he received that knock on his door!"

The jest fell flat, for Rafe hadn't the breath to laugh even out of politeness. He'd believed—he'd put *faith* in this man, in his brother, in Brookhaven itself. He'd thrown himself into his studies, trying to catch up to Calder, trying to be as good a son, willing himself to become worthy of this new life. He'd come home . . .

To a home that would never truly be his.

At the moment, the true heir, the Marquis of Brookhaven, looked as though he were trying to hide behind a potted palm—as if a mere tree could afford much cover for a great lout like Calder. He appeared to be gazing with interest across the room at this year's crop of maidens fair.

Rafe snorted to himself. Knowing Calder, he supposed his brother planned to coolly shop someone from the lineup of twittering virgins, check her bloodlines and her teeth, and have her properly bridled by the end of the first month of the Season.

Then the systematic breeding would begin, something that Rafe truly didn't want to picture. Calder in bed would probably be as boring and predictable as the ticking of a clock—at least, that was what Calder's previous wife had claimed once in a passion of furious disappointment.

Rafe had steered clear of Melinda's restless search for distraction but her words had only confirmed what Rafe had long suspected about his brother. All work and no play made Jack a very dull lover.

Smiling, Rafe crossed the room to join him. Rafe normally avoided his taciturn brother if at all possible, especially in social situations, but tonight not even Calder's dour visage could taint his buoyant spirits.

Rafe grinned at Calder when he reached him, and even cheerfully clapped him on the back. "I can see you're having your usual delightful time."

Calder slid him a sour glance. "Can you not see the jig I'm dancing?"

Rafe leaned a shoulder against the pillar and regarded the teeming ballroom with new affection and appreciation. "Ah, simply look at all the pretty girls here tonight. Surely you can find someone who meets with your approval?"

"Unlike some, I'm not in the market for a face or a figure. I'm looking for a wife with—with something else to offer."

"Blue blood to further refine the Marbrook breeding book?" Rafe grinned. "There's a packet of thoroughbreds here, although I admit you won't want to hold out for looks as well."

Calder lifted one shoulder, evidently too bored to shrug with both. "There isn't a woman here worth looking twice at, either way."

Rafe turned to gaze at his brother. Should he broach the topic of his impending engagement now? No. It would only garner him another lecture on impulsiveness. Still, it wouldn't hurt to hint in that direction.

"I spotted a lovely girl tonight. I think you know the family. Her father is Mr. Colin Millbury, a vicar. Her great-grandfather was Sir Hamish Pickering. You remember hearing stories about him, I'm sure. Crotchety old Scot who bought himself a knighthood?"

"Ah, yes." Calder lifted a brow in halfhearted approval. "At least she's not one of those shipping heiresses. I can't abide shipping heiresses. Entirely too full of themselves."

"No, she's not at all overreaching. Her aunt is Lady Tessa, wed to Cantor. You knew Cantor quite well, didn't you?"

Calder gave him an appraising look. "I did at that." Then his interest sharpened. "Pickering, eh? There was quite a fortune there, if I remember correctly, although it didn't seem to last. What ever happened to it?"

Trust Calder to check the price tag. "I imagine it was piddled away like most fortunes."

Calder slid a glance his way. "Hmm. Well, I suppose you'd know all about that."

Rafe exhaled slowly. "You're improving. It took almost four minutes for you to mention that this time."

Calder's lips barely twitched. "I strive to please."

Rafe folded his arms and gazed at the marble floor. "Once again—I did not piddle my portion away. I invested it. Investments take time to come to fruition. Ships take time to come in. You should know that, of all people."

Calder shrugged and looked away, his interest lost. "I have no desire to argue tonight. I came to find a wife."

*A wife.*

Rafe gazed across the room where Phoebe stood with her family. She was no longer smiling, but the expression of grave reflection on her face suited her nearly as well. She might be whimsical but she was not silly. He felt the pull all the way across the room, as though she were tied to him—and he to her.

A day ago that thought would have sent him running. Now, it only seemed to bring a sort of peace.

For the first time Calder seemed to notice his distraction and raised his own gaze to the other side of the room. "Which one is she?"

Rafe repressed his possessive smile and pointed Phoebe out to his brother. "There, by the musicians. Standing next to the blonde." God, she looked radiant even at this distance. What was she thinking of, to make her cheeks so rosy?

The same thing he was, no doubt.

Calder gazed thoughtfully across the room. "The . . . er, motherly one?"

Rafe tried very hard not to roll his eyes. Calder could be such a stick sometimes. Why not simply say, "the lady with the stunning bosom"? Then again, Rafe didn't care to have his brother notice his future fiancée's figure at all. "Right. That one."

"The blonde is prettier." Calder pursed his lips slightly. "But she looks like a good sort, I suppose. Cheerful. Decent connections as well. Old Pickering was in trade, but two generations later no one gives a damn as long as the family's reputation is good."

For Calder, such commendation was as good as applause.

Rafe relaxed. There would be no battle over his engagement to Phoebe, as long as he took his time and did things right and proper.

Then again, if Calder could see the value in her, others would as well. Perhaps he should secure her sooner.

Sooner sounded good to him. The sooner he had Phoebe to himself, in his house, in his arms, in his bed—

Yes, most definitely sooner.

# Chapter Five

The next day Phoebe awoke to find Aunt Tessa shaking her with a rather violent hand.

"For pity's sake, wake up, Phoebe! It's all of nine o'clock. Goodness, you sleep like the dead!"

That should pose no problem for Tessa, for her shrill voice could surely rouse any lifeless churchyard.

Aunt Tessa's face took on the oddest expression, making Phoebe hope she hadn't said that out loud.

"Put on your wrapper and come to my sitting room, at once," Tessa said tersely.

Oh, drat. She must be in some sort of disgrace. Somehow Tessa had learned about that encounter with Mr. Marbrook last night. Yet who could have told? Phoebe resolved to give nothing away, hoping that Tessa knew somewhat less than the whole truth.

There was nothing to be ashamed of in her hour alone with Mr. Marbrook, of course. They'd only talked—mostly. Still, it *looked* bad.

So she tied her wrapper neatly and went to Tessa's room with her head high but her knees knocking ever so slightly. Her old fears only awakened further when she saw that Tessa had awoken her cousins Deirdre and Sophie as well.

Tessa turned her glare on Phoebe. And now she was about to pay for last night's moment out of time. Oh, heavens, when Tessa told the vicar—and Tessa would, for she would like nothing better than to ruin Phoebe's chances of winning the inheritance—when that happened, Phoebe was going to find herself on the first coach headed back to Devonshire.

Oh heavens, the vicar would be so furious!

"Phoebe, you've received a proposal of marriage."

Marriage?

*Could it be him?*

Phoebe's knees gave out and she sat in the upright chair next to Sophie's. Tessa went on, but Phoebe could scarcely hear her over the rushing of wind in her ears. She sat still, her hopes swirling within her while her aunt rattled off some wordy title. There was only one name among it she was listening for and her heart leaped when she heard it.

*Marbrook.*

The thought soothed the sharp corners of the anxiety she had lived with since she was fifteen, cowering in the shadow of her single, monumental mistake.

*Marbrook.* If she could have *him,* live with him, be his wife, his lady—his lover!—she would be saved in so many ways.

"Phoebe?" Tessa's voice was spiky with suppressed fury. "Have you no response?"

"Yes." It was so easy. With a word, her foggy, desperately uneasy future was cleared and set right, the light of this one man's sword of personality and status slicing through the fog and shining into every corner of her life. "Tell him yes."

"But . . . he isn't a duke," Sophie said quietly.

"No," Aunt Tessa replied sourly, "but he will be."

Phoebe blinked. "What?"

Tessa's eyes were narrow with resentment. "It's true. Within weeks, possibly days. His uncle, the ninth Duke of Brookmoor, lies on his deathbed even now."

A duke. How odd. She'd always pictured dukes as

more . . . stuffy and, well, dukelike. Marbrook hadn't been anything like that. In fact, he'd been a bit . . . scandalous.

"He's a respectable man?" Even a duke could be a bounder, after all.

Tessa rolled her eyes. "I don't know why you care, since he'll be a *duke,* but yes, he is a very respectable man indeed." Her tone said she couldn't imagine what a man like that would see in Phoebe, but Phoebe only smiled to herself.

They were like souls. That was what he'd seen last night. He had a restless spirit in him, too, an adventurous, naughty gleam in his eye that had stirred her own dormant blood. A man such as that would not hold her youthful indiscretion against her.

And soon to be a duke. Phoebe could not believe this further perfection. She would win the Pickering fortune as well?

Something that had long been tied in a furious, regretful knot inside her eased and released. She would be an independently wealthy duchess?

A woman like that need fear no one but a queen! She would be a princess in all but name. There was no door in Society that would ever dare slam in her face, no matter what scandal from her past came out.

*Safe.* Safe forever—and with *him.*

She covered her face with her hands and took a deep breath to strengthen herself against the shivers that ran through her entire body.

The bench creaked slightly next to her. It was Sophie, for there was no rustle of expensive silk.

"Phoebe," Sophie said softly. "Are you upset by this? Would you rather not think on your decision for a moment?"

Upset? Phoebe could no longer fight the delirious laughter erupting inside her. It was as if the pressure of the last ten years were released by the turn of a single screw. She threw her head back and howled, falling back onto the settee in giddy relief.

"I suppose not, then." Sophie smiled shyly.

Still giggling, Phoebe threw her arms about Sophie and her cousin returned her embrace tentatively. Imagine, the vicar's wayward daughter, marrying a marquis! He'd awakened something last night, something fey and careless, that made her toss her head and grin fearlessly at the dreaded Tessa.

"Tell him I said 'yes.'" Phoebe cast a damp but brilliant smile at her aunt and Deirdre. "Oh, is it not unbelievable?"

"Entirely." Aunt Tessa lifted an irritated brow. "Very well. Your father is still visiting with friends on the outskirts of London. He can be reached in a matter of hours."

Deirdre only spared Phoebe a cool glance. "You have not won yet, Phoebe. The Duke of Brookmoor has been on his deathbed for a long time. He could live for months yet."

Phoebe only grinned at them. "It would not matter if my fiancé never became duke, for I would have chosen him anyway."

Sophie looked at her. "Is it love, then?"

Aunt Tessa scoffed. "Love? After one night at a ball?"

Phoebe did not contest her aunt's scorn, but only smiled to herself.

# *Chapter Six*

Sophie rushed into the bedchamber, her usually pale face flushed with excitement. "He's here! The Marquis of Brookhaven is here!"

Phoebe grinned at her cousin from where she stood before the vanity, perfectly dressed and ready to take a first drive with her fiancé.

Her own pulse was jumping with excitement at seeing him again. Everything, absolutely everything, was more perfect than she'd ever imagined it could be. The vicar was on his way back to London, but he had sent a note ahead approving the match. It had contained one line that she'd never thought to hear from him again. *"You've done our family name proud, my dear."*

Now, she smoothed the front of her walking gown and neatened the lapels of her sky-blue spencer, chosen just to accent her eyes. She smiled. Somehow she'd managed to please everyone, be respectable, and still find a man who made her blood sing. "I think I have finally settled matters to my satisfaction," she told Sophie serenely.

"Well, I do wish you'd share your secret!"

Phoebe turned to look at her cousin. Even Sophie seemed surprised at her own tart tone. "Sophie, do not resent my good fortune. You will find a husband here in town, I know you will."

Sophie ducked her head and slanted her shoulders. It made her look like a cringing giraffe. "I don't want a husband. I only came to London for the museums and galleries."

Phoebe went up on tiptoe and gave her cousin a quick kiss on the cheek. "Then go to the Royal Academy today. Ignore Tessa and simply go. What can she do—send you back to Dartmoor? She needs your portion to pay for this house."

Sophie blinked and a small smile warmed her lips. "That's true, isn't it?"

Phoebe twirled away from her, letting her gown bell out around her ankles. "I would not have met Marbr—the Marquis if I had not defied Tessa, you know. Perhaps it is an unworthy thought, but sometimes I wonder if perhaps she isn't trying to—" She shrugged, letting the words go unsaid. Although they were in direct competition against Deirdre, surely their own aunt would not act against them . . . would she?

Apparently, Sophie had much the same thought. "Sometimes I wonder that as well." She looked down at herself. "I don't think I'm going to let her choose any more of my gowns."

Phoebe waved gaily at her as she danced down the stairs. "That's the spirit. I shall tell you absolutely everything when I return!"

Well, perhaps *almost* everything!

Phoebe paused in her headlong trot down the stairs. The gentleman standing—nay, looming!—in the entrance hall was tall, handsome, and oddly familiar, though she was sure she'd never laid eyes upon him before. He was also in her way.

"Pardon me," she said as she walked past him on the way to the parlor.

He turned to watch her as she went. She could feel his eyes on her when she rushed to the parlor to see Marbrook.

There was no one in the parlor. Would Tessa's rather sullen manservant have put him in the drawing room?

No Marbrook in the drawing room.

The man in the hall was still watching her as she searched. Nosy prat. Finally, irritated with Marbrook's disappointing invisibility and this odd intruder's persistent interest, Phoebe turned to the fellow with her fists on her hips.

"Is there something on my dress?" she demanded.

He blinked. "I—what?"

She turned, swishing her skirts about for his view. "Are you sure? Not a streak of soot, perhaps, or the unfortunate leavings of the dairyman's cob?"

He straightened and scowled. "Are you a little bit mad, perchance?"

She folded my arms and scowled right back. "Well, I thought there must be something wrong, the way you stared." Tessa would die if she heard her, but what did she care? She was affianced to Marbrook, and likely he would only laugh if he knew.

*I think I love you, Marbrook.*

The man—what was it about him that was so familiar? He had an astringent twist to his lips that made her think of the vicar's face when he was thinking about the incident. So, despite the fact that this fellow was very good-looking, Phoebe didn't like him much at all.

"Miss Millbury," he began.

She swallowed, for he had mastered the vicar's disapproving tone as well.

But what need she care for the disapproval of a stranger? She lifted her chin and thanked the Fates for giving her Marbrook. It was only too bad they had to wait for the reading of the banns, for she would marry him within the hour if she could. "Yes?"

He narrowed his eyes at her tone. "Miss Millbury, perhaps

I ought to inform you that I am not in the habit of suffering such insolence from . . . well, from anyone, actually."

Phoebe nodded. "That explains your sour expression. What explains your rudeness in my aunt's house?"

He blinked, opened his mouth to speak—then closed it.

Phoebe shook off her twitching impatience and began to move past him. If Marbrook wasn't here, she was going to put crickets in Sophie's bed for this prank.

A large hand wrapped itself about her arm. Shock went through her at such outrageous insult. "Sir! Unhand me at once, or I will forced to report this misconduct to my fiancé!"

He gazed down into her face, his brow clearing as if he'd only just realized something. "Ah." He released her, although not without a lingering touch that made her think he rather liked her.

He stepped back and a slight, rather creaky smile crossed his lips. "Miss Millbury, we seem to be laboring under a misunderstanding."

She raised a brow. "I understand that my fiancé is within his rights to slap his glove across your face."

The smile didn't fade. He bowed. "Miss Millbury, Lord Calder Marbrook, Marquis of Brookhaven, at your service."

*Wrong. Very, very wrong.*

"Ah—" She cleared her tightened throat, forcing a normal tone. Something bad was nipping at her belly, sending darts of fear through her. She'd done something wrong and she was very much afraid she knew what it was.

The fellow bowed, then raised his gaze to meet Phoebe's shocked one. "My dear, I *am* your fiancé."

# *Chapter Seven*

The Marquis of Brookhaven stared at her for a long moment, then blinked. "Forgive me. What did you say?"

Phoebe froze. She'd said "bugger" right out loud, like a common street urchin, except even a street urchin would refrain from saying it directly to a lord's face!

"Sugar!" Which was meaningless, but she pasted on a winning smile. "I'm supposed to ask Cook to buy more sugar! If you'll excuse me for a moment?"

With the insane smile still on her face, she turned woodenly and walked away from him. She went through the first door she came to and shut it behind her. With a thump, she let herself go limp against the wood, disregarding the latch pressing into the small of her back.

"Oh, damn, blast, *bugger!*"

What could she do? Explain to the marquis that she'd meant to accept another man? That would likely go down well. Of course, he'd want to know who, and she could hardly turn around and marry his brother without him noticing!

There was no help for it. She couldn't leave him standing in the hall much longer. She must simply tell him, now, before this went any further. Taking a deep breath, she pasted on a polite vicar's-daughter smile and left the room.

He was right where she left him, in the same position

with the same, vaguely impatient expression on his face, like a toy soldier abandoned after play.

Wild giggles threatened to bubble up. Phoebe suppressed them with difficulty, for the situation was heartbreakingly ridiculous and she didn't know whether to laugh or cry.

As she approached her fiancé, she eyed the powerful and wealthy Marquis of Brookhaven, most emphatically *not* the man she knew as "Marbrook," and tried frantically to think of some way to explain her hideous—although completely understandable if a person stopped to think about it—mistake.

Then someone rapped the front knocker in a peculiar, five-point manner—a habit that Phoebe was very familiar with.

Oh, God, no. *The vicar.*

That was all it took. The strength left her knees and her belly went icy with old fears. The new woman was gone. Only the old Phoebe remained to face what the new Phoebe had mistakenly wrought.

She must have breathed the name aloud, for Brookhaven brightened. "Ah, excellent. Your father and I have much to discuss and this shall save time." He granted Phoebe an approving nod. "Most efficient of you to arrange it."

Most efficient of her to arrange her most embarrassing admission to simultaneously humiliate herself in front of both Brookhaven and her father?

"Yes, well, I do have a knack," she said breathlessly, scrambling panic rising within her. She was definitely going to cry—or worse, laugh in a fit of unstoppable hysteria. She could hide, but that wouldn't work for long.

And there was Marbrook. What would he think of her when he learned of this?

Despite her panic, the thought of Marbrook soothed her somewhat. Marbrook would understand, once she explained things to him. He might even be able to think of some way out of this mess!

She cleared her throat, trying to think quickly before the vicar made it past the butler. "My lord, tell me—" Quickly! "Your brother, Lord Marbrook—" Was that correct? She scarcely knew, although Brookhaven only gazed at her attentively, so it must be. "When will you be informing him of our . . . ah, match?"

"Oh, Rafe already knows," Brookhaven said. "As a matter of fact, it was his idea. He thought you and I might suit."

Rafe? Was that his given name? How manly—

*His idea?*

No, that could not be right. "Lord Marbrook? Are you sure? Is he about your height and coloring, with similar—" Similar everything and of course it was the same Lord Marbrook.

Pain lanced through Phoebe's heart, laying it open in such a way that she suspected it would never heal. His idea.

Marbrook had met her, talked to her, taken her into the dark garden and proceeded to make her fall entirely in love with him—had almost-not-quite kissed her!—then had suggested his brother marry her? Like some sort of—of—*agent?*

She'd been an idiot again, when she'd promised the vicar—and herself!—so fervently that she wouldn't be.

Her chest ached as if she hadn't breathed in far too long and a sort of strange clarity came over her vision.

Then the vicar was there, engulfing her in an awkward but enthusiastic hug. That bizarre occurrence alone was enough to snap her from her strange sinking moment, but then he kissed her forehead and said the words she had longed to hear all her life.

"You've done marvelously well, my dear. I'm very proud of you."

Words she'd never hear again if she broke this engagement.

It was so clear. If she spoke up at this moment and announced her mistake, there would be no more awkward hugs, no more pithy approval. She would instantly go back to being the vicar's wayward daughter, who must be watched like a thief lest she backslide into her old ways.

Old pain swirled with new pain and Phoebe buried her face in the vicar's weskit as she'd not been permitted to do in so many years. He seemed somehow less in her embrace—more worn and thin.

*Frail.* What a strange word to describe her tall powerful father.

She squeezed her eyes shut, picturing the man she'd seen for so long, even as he'd begun to disappear into the man now before her. The vicar had always been angular and just a bit looming . . . but now he only seemed somehow breakable.

The shock of white hair, the emphatically bushy brows that added weight to the sharpness of his icy blue gaze . . . still there, yet thinner, less vigorous.

Age had an end. She would never have believed that there might be an end to the vicar . . . until now. The pain and loss of years welled up within her. So much wasted time . . .

*It doesn't have to be that way anymore.*

The weight of responsibility settled upon her with concrete permanence. With so few years left, could she deny them both this chance to make them good years? The sensible thing to do would be . . . to take what she'd been offered and be glad of it.

The tears came then, quiet hot ones that leaked from her eyes despite her best effort at control. "Oh, Papa . . ."

Astoundingly, the vicar merely put his arms about her and patted her rather too firmly on the back. "There, there, my dear. I suppose a bride is entitled to a bit of an exhibition, as long as she keeps it among family, eh, Brookhaven?"

Brookhaven cleared his throat. "Might I assume there won't be many such occasions?"

The vicar chuckled crustily. "Oh, no need to worry about that. My Phoebe is a most sensible young lady."

*My Phoebe. My dear.* Words she'd ached for.

She had inadvertently made her father's dreams come true.

*What of your own?*

Despair and loss mingled with the desire for more of the vicar's rare approval. Phoebe inhaled deeply of the vicar's tobacco-scented weskit, then straightened, dabbing at her eyes with her demure-vicar's-daughter smile upon her face. "Pray, pardon my excess, my lord, Papa. I am quite all right now."

And she was.

*No you're not. This is not how it is supposed to be and you know it.*

Yes, she was. She was engaged to a fine, handsome, wealthy man who just might make her one of the richest women in London—and she was basking in the vicar's unqualified approval for perhaps the first time in her life.

What wasn't fine about that?

Something inside her gave a last despairing wail, and then finally, thankfully, shut up.

# Chapter Eight

The early sun still slanted through the windows of Brook House, but each moment passed like an hour in Rafe's swirling thoughts. He'd tapped the brandy decanter immediately after Calder's departure this morning, but the fragrant amber liquid wasn't up to its usual ability to make him forget.

Now he stood, white-knuckled fists braced on the window frame, staring unseeing at the street visible from the front of Brook House.

Calder was engaged to Miss Phoebe Millbury.

*His* Miss Millbury!

Rafe had tossed and turned all night, trying to compose the perfect "this is romantic, not raving mad" proposal to present to Miss Millbury.

He tried to shut out the memory of himself humming the latest off-color ditty as he'd tied his cravat and pulled one of his signature silver-buttoned blue coats on over his shirt and waistcoat.

Downstairs in the breakfast room, Calder, of course, had been up for hours. Rafe had joined him silently, still pondering the best way to present his potential engagement to his brother. Calder had casually cleared his throat.

"You should be the first to know, Rafe. I took your advice and this morning I received word that Miss Phoebe Millbury has consented to be my wife. Her aunt has guardianship of her for the moment, but Lady Tessa believes there will be no objection from the girl's father. Thank you for saving me much tedious study and consideration."

*No.*

For an eternal moment, Rafe could not draw a breath. Then, through the roaring in his mind, he'd managed to speak. "It has been only hours since the ball." His voice had croaked. He hadn't cared.

Calder had only chuckled, apparently oblivious. "That sort of thing does not take long if one employs the right people to investigate. She is entirely suitable; although her great-grandfather was in trade, there has been adequate rise in the family's station so that the difference is not inappropriate. She brings no wealth, but then, I don't need it."

Still Rafe could not breathe for the fury that consumed him. Once again, the ripest fruit fell easily into Calder's oh-so-deserving hand.

But wait . . . simply because Calder had proposed didn't mean that—

"She accepted my offer with dispatch," Calder had gone on to say. "I find that admirably decisive, don't you? Miss Millbury must be a very practical, nonromantic sort."

*With dispatch.* She hadn't even hesitated, it seemed. And why would she? That moment in the garden, that soft whisper of possibility that had hung in the air between them . . . in truth, he'd been the only one to feel it.

Cain and Abel—murder between brothers. Vengeance on a biblical scale sounded good just then.

Rafe couldn't kill his brother, but he could sure as hell pound his face into the marble floor of the foyer and relish every moment of it.

*Phoebe.*

Rafe's hands had clenched into fists, snapping the fork's

mother-of-pearl handle in two. He hadn't noticed the stabbing pain as the edges dug into his flesh.

As much as he hated to admit it—and it took several snifters of brandy to make him admit it—he had no one to blame but himself. He could see so clearly where he'd gone wrong.

Hindsight was no comfort to the loser, however. The fact that he'd turned Calder's attention to Phoebe like a well-trained pointer indicating a choice fowl to the hunter only made the facts all the more agonizing.

Of course, then he spent a good hour telling himself that one moonlit evening in a garden with a saucy and delightful angel didn't matter at all.

Then he swung back to blaming Calder for yet again taking everything good for himself.

And she had accepted—how could she have accepted?

*How could she not? A girl like that, a vicar's daughter—what was she to do, turn down the richest man in London? "No, thank you, my lord. I don't care to be your marchioness."*

Well, Calder wasn't the richest man in London—quite. He wasn't the most powerful either, although there were only about four or five others above him. He was handsome as well, since he looked a great deal like Rafe—and Rafe had never had any complaints. So how could one expect a young woman fresh from the country to say no to the Marquis of Brookhaven?

*Perhaps none of that is the case. Perhaps she simply likes him better.*

*Everyone else does, after all.*

The better man.

Their father, the previous marquis, had said that many times to Rafe in his wastrel days. "Thank God that Brookhaven will be in the hands of a better man than you!"

Hating Calder and despising Phoebe, while darkly entertaining, was not going to supply an answer for this dilemma.

What was done was done. Calder could hardly break his engagement without disgracing the woman and damaging his own closely protected reputation—something Calder wouldn't do.

Phoebe, on the other hand . . .

He rubbed a hand over his face. She'd seemed the perfect answer. So sweet, yet full of earthy warmth.

And exhilarating. He smiled slightly. Sweet yet tart, dreamy yet spirited.

No. She'd never back out of the engagement. A girl like that didn't change her mind once made. It killed him to think of all that loyalty and sweetness wasted on dour, automaton Calder.

Nor could he in good conscience say a word about last night. It had been innocent, for the most part. He would not compromise the lady.

He straightened, a quiet, despairing certainty settling over him.

Rafe looked down at his hands, which were still fisted and pale of knuckle. He willed them to open and relax.

So now Calder had it all. The estate, the title—

And her.

His fingers curled with old fury once more.

THE GUEST PARLOR in Tessa's rented house was a formal room carefully decorated not to give offense, which only made the mingled bland floral and muted stripes jar Phoebe's eye in their own way.

Or perhaps it was just her. Perhaps this was all some sort of ghastly dream, the sort one had when one overindulged on chocolates. No, it was all horribly real. The vicar was beaming, Tessa was trilling, Deirdre was looking on in sardonic silence, and Sophie was gazing dreamily at the window.

Phoebe sat in perfect stillness on the settee next to the Marquis of Brookhaven and tried dutifully to listen over the buzzing in her ears. The world had an eerie sharpness, yet the color seemed leached from Tessa's salmon-pink gown and the vicar's dark coat.

Seated next to her, Brookhaven was garbed in perfect black and white. Phoebe herself was in proper virginal white muslin with nary a sprig or pattern. Together they seemed a proper indication of her life to come.

Black and white. Wrong and right. No room for error. No easing of expectations. No freedom. No laughter.

No passion.

For Brookhaven, for all that he was every bit as young and handsome as Marbrook, seemed rather more like the vicar at heart. Both men were strict with themselves and others. Both men had precise views of the rules and obligations of their positions. In fact, the resemblance in their personalities was so striking that Phoebe took a certain dismal comfort that she was not to marry a complete stranger after all.

Yet Phoebe couldn't suppress the notion that the vicar had aged in the last week since she'd seen him. Or had she stopped noticing at some point as she had sleepwalked through her life in Thornton?

The vicar seemed inordinately worn by his short journey back from the next county where he'd been visiting friends. Subsequently, the drive through Hyde Park had been canceled in favor of tea in the parlor.

All of which was magically accomplished without any of the ladies managing to put in a word. Brookhaven certainly had a commanding air about him. Even Tessa's sullen staff jumped to carry out his every wish with alacrity.

Now, the vicar turned to her at last. "Well, my dear, you've done nicely for yourself, I must say. He's a capital fellow. I couldn't have chosen better myself."

*Then why don't you wed him?*

Oh, heavens—she hadn't just said that aloud, had she?

No, no one seemed shocked or taken aback. In fact, the insipid smiles just went on and on. It had only been that the irreverent remark had sounded so loudly and defiantly in her head that she could have sworn she had voiced it.

Brookhaven seemed equally pleased with the vicar. "How gratifying to learn that Miss Millbury has been influenced by such sensible thinking all her life. So many young ladies these days seem to have no thought in their heads but balls and gowns," he said approvingly.

Phoebe had the sudden mental image of him patting her on the head. *Good dog*. Just let him try it, she thought in a giddy panic.

Phoebe saw Deirdre bite her lip, hard. At least she wasn't the only one who was bursting to round on the pompous Brookhaven. Then Tessa placed an apparently affectionate hand on Deirdre's shoulder—and squeezed until her knuckles turned white with effort.

Although it had to have been extremely painful, Deirdre never twitched. She only maintained her vapid smile while patting Tessa's hand with daughterly affection.

Phoebe was distracted from her own predicament for a moment by the way Deirdre had taken the painful abuse with such casual familiarity. It seemed all was not as perfect between the two as Phoebe had thought. Perhaps it was better to have a father like the vicar after all.

*And now you can wed a man just like him and never, ever be allowed to grow to womanhood. From vicar's perfect daughter to duke's perfect wife with nary a moment of relief between.*

Except for one thing—she wasn't perfect. How was she going to explain *that* on her wedding night? The vicar would be no help there, for he believed she'd been deserted before she'd been deflowered—and Phoebe had never had the nerve to correct that impression.

The marquis was speaking. Phoebe pulled her wandering attention back with an effort.

"Upon reflection, I have decided that it will not be efficient to continue to visit here."

He was planning to make himself scarce until the wedding? How . . . relieving.

"Instead, I should like to invite your entire party to move to Brook House for the coming fortnight. Lady Tessa, you will be able to assist Miss Millbury with the arrangements with the help of my excellent staff—"

So he'd noticed the lackluster service. Phoebe couldn't blame the poor folk burdened with working for Tessa. One had to be paid a decent wage, and on time, to enjoy one's employment.

Still it was a kind offer—even if it clearly originated in his own desire for convenience. Phoebe opened her mouth to politely decline.

"What a lovely notion!" Tessa's eyes absolutely glittered with social-climbing glee. "We'll pack up at once!"

"No need," Brookhaven said crisply. "I shall have your things moved by this afternoon."

"Oh, that will be grand!" Tessa fluttered and trilled and generally made a rather nauseating show of gratitude. Then her gaze sharpened. "*Until* the wedding, did you say?"

Oh, no. Tessa was playing for hospitality for the entire Season. Since Phoebe would rather stick needles in her eye than live with Tessa one minute more than necessary, she held her breath waiting for Brookhaven's response.

Brookhaven gazed at Tessa. Tessa gazed unrelentingly at Brookhaven. Phoebe watched, fascinated by the clash of wills between two people who were obviously used to getting their own way.

On one hand, it was nice to see Tessa meet her match. On the other hand, Brookhaven had not consulted her, Phoebe, as to her preference in the matter. In fact, he'd not spared her so much as a questioning glance during the entire exchange.

That did not bode well for the future.

Then a belated warning bell sounded inside her. There was more to consider here. On one hand, if she went to Brook House, she'd see Marbrook a great deal. On the other hand, if she went to Brook House . . . she'd see Marbrook a great deal. Either way she was doomed to be in his company more than she'd like—or dangerously less than she wished.

Lord Brookhaven turned to the vicar. "Sir, I can take you to Brook House now. My valet will be happy to tend to your needs." Leaving the vicar to blink in bemusement at the thought of having his pants buttoned by another man, Brookhaven turned back to gaze benevolently at the rest of them. "I thought perhaps you ladies would prefer an outing to visit Lementeur. I hear he's quite the favorite in our set."

By the way that Tessa gasped and even Deirdre's eyes lighted up, this Lementeur was something both desirable and exclusive. Phoebe hadn't seen Tessa this excited since Deirdre had managed a second waltz with the septuagenarian duke.

"After all," Brookhaven went on, "Miss Millbury will be needing a trousseau befitting a marchioness."

Now Phoebe felt like a clay target in a shooting match. Bright envy sparked from the gazes of both Tessa and Deirdre. If sharp glances could kill, Phoebe would be dismembered.

"Who is Lementeur?" Sophie asked.

Phoebe was glad Sophie wasn't afraid to appear unsophisticated, for she was burning to know herself.

Tessa tilted her head and looked at Sophie with unconvincingly fond pity. "Dear child, you really must climb out of your butter churn. Lementeur is only the most exclusive dressmaker in London. It is almost impossible to get an hour of his time, much less to have him agree to make an entire wardrobe!"

Phoebe blinked. "That is very generous, my lord, but I—"

He patted her hand unctuously. "It is no matter, my dear. After all, one cannot have one's wife looking tatty, can one?"

*Tatty.* Phoebe doubted he even knew he'd been insulting.

The vicar cleared his throat. "I do not wish to offend, my lord, but Lady Tessa felt it necessary to speak to me, so I fear I must speak to you. What of your . . . brother?"

Brookhaven went quite still. "What of him?"

Phoebe was every bit as frozen. What of Marbrook? Why did the vicar sound so . . . tentative? It was as if he wished to speak about a subject not fit for ladies' ears, which was ridiculous because Marbrook was a perfectly respectable—

"Your—ahem—brother will be residing at Brook House along with the young ladies, my lord?"

Brookhaven didn't move a muscle. "He will. As will both you and Lady Tessa. I hope you are not implying that there will be any impropriety, sir."

Tessa bent her head to whisper furiously to Deirdre. Phoebe was torn between listening in and paying attention to the mounting tension between the vicar and the marquis. The vicar, who seemed in near ecstasy over the engagement, would never be so offensive—unless there was something very wrong with Marbrook.

*"Rake."* Phoebe heard the word clearly in Tessa's distinctive hiss, the tone she kept for the very tastiest—and most unseemly—shreds of gossip. *"Degenerate."*

*No.* And yet . . .

He'd not denied it when she'd asked him if he was a rake. He'd only smiled.

And hadn't she herself sensed that he was somehow not quite respectable? After all, to whisk her off onto the terrace without introduction—

He had rescued her. She was still grateful for that.

*"Scandal follows Marbrook like a faithful hound,"* was Tessa's final triumphant hiss on the matter.

*Scandal.*

# Chapter Nine

As Phoebe sat next to the man who had made her father so happy, she had the breathless sensation that she'd very nearly been run down by a racing cart—and had only just been snatched from beneath its wheels.

How fortunate she was. She had almost faltered for the wrong man. *Again.*

Old shame engulfed her. Not shame for her ruination, but the crushing feeling that there must be something wrong with her that she could be so gullible.

"—I assure you that there is nothing to worry about," Brookhaven was saying with strange lack of emphasis. "The young ladies will be utterly safe in Brook House."

Safe from Marbrook. As if he were a mad dog, prone to biting the unwary.

Brookhaven stood. "I shall send my staff immediately to take the house in hand." He turned to Phoebe. "I have informed Lementeur that you will need one gown immediately. I wish to set matters in motion at once with a dinner party at Brook House tonight. My brother and I—" His eyes flickered toward the vicar. "We shall gather a select group of friends for you to meet."

"Tonight?" Phoebe spoke without thinking. "Who will come on such short notice?"

Brookhaven looked at her oddly. "They will come if I invite them."

Phoebe withdrew. "Oh, yes. Of course." She must remember to whom it was she spoke. A marquis need not worry if his guests had other plans for their evening.

Or if she'd had other plans for her life.


RAFE WAITED FOR Calder in the Brookhaven carriage parked outside the house where Miss Phoebe Millbury lived with her aunt and cousins. He'd come here to speak to Calder, not to catch a glimpse of Phoebe, of course.

The fact that he couldn't keep his eyes off the front of the house made him feel like a fool.

He'd come to a decision. He had decided to leave for . . . well, somewhere as far from the new Lady Brookhaven as he could manage. The Americas might do, or Africa. He hadn't coin for the passage, but he had a few things of value that were becoming worth less and less to him by the moment.

In any event, he would be gone just after the wedding, before Milady moved in. That was important. He didn't want to think about why.

By the time Calder came out, Rafe had concocted and thrown out a thousand ways to broach the topic of his departure. All made him look capricious in the extreme. Such was his desperation that he was beginning not to care.

Calder entered the carriage without more surprise than a raised brow at Rafe's presence there. "I thought you'd make yourself scarce as usual so I can't ask you to accompany me somewhere."

Rafe gazed at his brother, lifelong fondness and hatred warring in his heart. "You look different."

Calder smiled slightly. "I noticed last night that Miss Millbury had a preference for green, so I sought out this waistcoat from my wardrobe. Do you think she noticed?"

Rafe watched in surprise and a bit of awe as his brother actually tugged self-consciously at his weskit. "You truly care?"

The mere twist of the lips that passed for a smile on Calder did not fade. "She is a pleasing girl. I thought I'd best do a bit of pleasing in return."

The fact that his brother was actually happy about his engagement—rather than simply satisfied at concluding a business matter—sent arrows of fury through Rafe.

*But she's mine.*

Calder adjusted his cravat further. "I've arranged for her to be fitted at Lementeur today. I think that's a good idea, don't you? Indulging her now will increase her attachment, don't you think?"

Rafe choked. "You're—you're asking me?"

Calder turned to look at him strangely. "Did I not just ask you? What is your difficulty? I thought you approved of Miss Millbury?"

Thank heaven he wouldn't have to see her again until the wedding . . . and then it would be too late. He managed to find his voice. "Yes. Yes to the visit to Lementeur. Yes to the approval. Yes to the damned bilious weskit."

Calder frowned and turned back to his cravat. "You're in a mood today. I hope you intend to improve it. Miss Millbury and her family will be joining us later today."

His pulse jumped at the thought of seeing her again. Well, perhaps he could make it through one dinner. He nodded shortly. "Of course. Dinner."

"Yes, dinner . . . and I've asked them all to move their things to Brook House immediately."

It was another blow on top of so many today. "To Brook House." Next Calder was going to tell him that he'd decided to consummate the union in public and that Rafe was required to sit up front.

"I am not a fool," Calder said gruffly. "I know that it was

the fact that I was not attentive enough that drove Melinda into another man's arms." The automatic motions of adjusting cuffs became somewhat less casual, but Calder's tone did not change one iota while speaking of his late wife.

Melinda Chatsworth Bonneville was a suitably pedigreed daughter of the aristocracy, groomed from birth to marry high and well. A demure brunette beauty with exquisite manners and large green eyes, she was the toast of the ton from the moment she first stepped dainty slipper through the door at Almack's.

Calder, having decided it was time to marry soon after rising to his father's title as Marquis of Brookhaven—entirely understandable, everyone said while looking askance at Rafe's steady decline into depravity, since the young marquis had no *real* heir—went about the selection of a wife as carefully as any breeder would compare the bloodlines of new brood mares.

Marry too high and one was likely to find one's fortune drained by the great houses and estates of one's highborn and usually useless new relatives. Marry too low and one would find one's own house filled with social-climbing in-laws hoping to stand on one's shoulders to rise higher.

The Honorable Miss Bonneville had no such undesirable attachments. Her parents were sensible people well-situated with their own small but profitable lands. She had no irritating siblings or cousins to drain one's resources and launch into society and she had a spotless reputation as a biddable but not unintelligent young lady who possessed excellent taste.

Calder set about securing this admirable acquisition to the bloodline with his usual swift and rational efficiency. Within weeks of her debut, Miss Bonneville's ownership had been contracted and paid for and all parties declared themselves satisfied . . .

Except that Miss Bonneville respectfully requested to put

off the wedding until the end of the Season so that she could fully enjoy her first visit to London. Calder, having had his way in all things so far, indulgently agreed. He penciled in the September wedding date on his calendar and promptly went back to his previous absorption in his factories, sure that his well-laid plans could not go astray in his absence.

Melinda, however, had other ideas. It seemed that she was less happy with the match than her parents were. She'd hoped for several Seasons of enjoyable society and a legion of admirers to choose from at her leisure. Now she was eighteen, engaged, and rather less carefully chaperoned than other girls her age . . . and angry at her swift entrapment.

There were mere whispers at first, which Calder likely never heard in his distraction. Then there was rumor, but he ignored that as well. He'd experienced the jealous tongues of Society when he'd inherited so much so young. He knew that idle minds manufactured their own entertainment.

Then rumor became flaming gossip and gossip exploded into scandal—and there was nothing Calder could do about it but marry the girl he'd so unwisely left unattended all season long. Dissolving the engagement himself would have besmirched him and ruined her forever— neither of which were desirable entries into the family history. He was assured by Melinda's humiliated parents that she would settle properly into her wifely role once the wedding took place. There was nothing to do but go through with it and hope for the best.

The best did not happen. Melinda, furious that her actions had made no difference and now madly infatuated with a man she'd met during her adventures, continued to make headlines in the gossip sheets. Matters finally seemed to settle a bit and the couple even seemed to achieve a sort of happiness—Rafe didn't know why precisely, for he and Calder were not on the best of terms at that time—until two years into the marriage when occurred Melinda's next and tragically final act of rebellion.

It was the stuff of grand theatre—the fleeing wife, the mocking cuckold, the shattered husband, and the dramatic cross-country escape which ended in the carriage accident that killed two. It was all so very tawdry and cliché—and ferociously private Calder found himself in the center of it all.

Rafe, who had passed that night in the energetic embrace of a happily married mother of six children—who were shamelessly mismatched in coloring and features all, although thankfully his own black hair and brown eyes never appeared there—learned about Calder's tragic mishap the same way the rest of England did.

The papers were merciless, rooting out every scrap of old gossip and rumor from Melinda's outrageous season and shoring up any weak points with wild speculation as well. Calder found himself in the excruciating position of being openly pitied—and snickered about—by an entire nation. Unbearable for a proud and aloof man.

Rafe packed up the rooms he kept and came home and Calder opened Brook House to him. Neither spoke a word about the tragedy, but Rafe told himself that Calder appreciated the show of support. It was a grim, hushed time.

Calder's determined and dignified silence—and the stature of his enormous wealth, no doubt—eventually outlasted the storm of scandal. Rafe stayed on in Brook House and did his best not to add fuel to the gossip fires. One by one, he gave up his self-indulgent pleasures, although neither Calder nor the rest of Society ever seemed to notice. Perhaps it was simply Rafe's own form of penance. Melinda's wildness was not his fault, but he'd taken a certain bitter amusement in seeing Calder hoist on his own sanctimonious petard.

He would never have wished this seething madness on anyone however, and it bothered him to see Calder retreat even farther into his stern shell.

Calder never gave up his blacks after his year of mourning was over, and his new brooding demeanor did nothing to deter the gossips who still loved to paint him as an object of romanticized pity.

Calder's thoughts must have followed a similar vein, for he scowled slightly into the glass. "I do not intend to make that mistake again. That is why the wedding will take place within weeks. If not for the reading of the banns, I would take care of it tomorrow."

Rafe was quiet for a moment. "Do you truly mean this? You intend to be a true husband to Ph—Miss Millbury?"

Calder slid him a glance. "I was a true husband to Melinda. She was not a true wife to me. But Miss Millbury has not been in town long enough to form any attachments and I intend to see that she does not have the opportunity."

"Cage the bird quickly, you mean." Rafe's chest tightened. "So she has no opportunity to fly."

"Of course. It is much more efficient. She will not miss what she never had."

*I wouldn't wager a farthing on that, brother of mine. One can miss quite a bit that one never had.*

"Her cousins are coming as well. Very demure and proper girls, those two."

Stay away from the young ladies, in other words. Rafe gave a short bark of laughter. "I'm sure they are. I shall see you then."

He slammed his palm down on the door latch and exited the carriage. Better to walk the rest of the way. As he shut the door and turned away, he heard something he would have wagered he'd never hear in all his days.

Calder was humming, rustily and a bit off key, but humming nonetheless. Rafe could quite honestly say that he'd never seen his brother so happy.

How appropriate then that it made him so miserable.

# *Chapter Ten*

Moments after Brookhaven made his goodbyes, another gentleman arrived at the house on Primrose Street—a Mr. Stickley, from the firm of Stickley & Wolfe, the executors of the Pickering trust.

"Yes, well . . ." The thin gentleman peered at them all doubtfully as they sat in a semicircle facing him in the same guest parlor where they had received Brookhaven. Mr. Stickley took up decidedly less room than their previous caller. "Lady Tessa, are you quite sure the vicar himself isn't available?"

Tessa smiled daggers at the man. "The vicar has gone on to Brook House with the marquis. All the affairs of the Pickering heiresses have been left in my hands."

The man blinked. "Still . . ."

Tessa's smile evaporated. Mr. Stickley tapped his fingers on his file case as if he debated waiting until an actual male could be found. Phoebe admired his fortitude, then realized he was probably simply too myopic to see the danger he was in.

"Sir, I fear we must get on with things. You see, Miss Millbury has an appointment with Lementeur, himself, this afternoon. We"—she waved her hand at the others and herself—"are going to have fittings as well, since Miss Millbury insisted on it."

Phoebe gazed at Tessa. The woman was unbelievable. "I did?"

Tessa's eyes sparked danger. "You did."

Phoebe smiled. Tessa suddenly seemed rather tiny and, well, insubstantial. Lady Tessa did not compare to the Duchess of Brookmoor, after all. Not even to the Marchioness of Brookhaven, come to think.

Phoebe's smile became wry. She tipped her head lightly. "It would my honor to ask you all to accompany me to Lementeur's for fittings."

Deirdre's eyes flashed something that might have been resentful respect, but Sophie only shrugged. "Do you think it will take long?"

Mr. Stickley frowned, for he clearly cared little for such nonnecessities. "I suppose we must begin—although I will enter it into record that I wished to delay until the vicar could join us."

"You may enter it anywhere you like, Mr. Stickley," Tessa said with loaded emphasis. "As long as you begin. Now."

"As you ladies have doubtlessly been informed, the Pickering fortune now stands at twenty-seven thousand pounds—"

Someone gasped. Phoebe realized it was her. The others seemed less startled, although Sophie seemed vaguely confused, as if that outrageous amount were difficult for her to grasp.

Mr. Stickley turned her way. "Is this the young lady who is engaged to the marquis?"

Phoebe nodded, her mouth still dry. Twenty-seven thousand pounds? That wasn't just a fortune, it was an obscene one.

Mr. Stickley regarded her with wan approval. "Well, it seems as if you might well win the day. I have it on reliable information that the current Duke of Brookmoor has taken a turn for the worse yet again."

An old man was dying. Phoebe's stomach turned that this was good news . . . and yet it was. His death and her marriage would free her forever. She wanted that safety more than she'd ever wanted anything.

*Except Marbrook.*

She managed a noncommittal noise for Mr. Stickley, who nodded.

"Now, should Miss Millbury inherit there will be small annuities for the other two—I believe the will states that they will receive fifteen pounds per annum . . ." He trailed off, for even he must have realized what a paltry sum that was.

A decent governess made more than that, and had her room and board supplied as well. He cleared his throat. "It is regrettable that Sir Hamish did not account for rising costs . . . but there is no adjusting that amount."

Phoebe didn't want to meet her cousins' eyes, but she forced herself to. She needed to win the Pickering fortune. Her father's dream . . . her mother's dying wish . . . her future was not hers to change.

Deirdre was beautiful and well connected. She would do well enough.

Sophie . . . Sophie was gazing into space, her brow slightly wrinkled. It occurred to Phoebe for the first time that Sophie had never expected to win a cent of Pickering money.

Why was she here in London, then?

Mr. Stickley cleared his throat again. "Now, you must understand, Miss Millbury, that Stickley & Wolfe cannot release the inheritance until you are married and your future husband is officially named the duke. Nor can word of this arrangement leave the family or the entire matter becomes null and void."

Deirdre frowned. "But that is the part I've never understood. We could all catch a duke if we could wave twenty-seven thousand pounds before him."

Oh, no. Deirdre wasn't resentful, not even a little tiny bit.

Mr. Stickley nodded sadly. "Precisely. Your great-grandfather realized that. He wishes you to *earn* the inheritance with your own resourcefulness."

Of course, Phoebe could understand Deirdre's ire. If fair hair and sapphire eyes did not count as the finest of resources . . . well, what was the world coming to?

"What happens to the money, then, if someone tells?" Everyone turned. It was Sophie, speaking for the first time since the proceedings began. All eyes shot back to Mr. Stickley, who reddened in a rather splotchy manner and tugged at his collar with his index finger.

"In the unlikely case that not one of you ladies secures a duke—or if the contents of the will are leaked to non-family members—in that case . . ."

Furniture creaked as all four women leaned forward, the intensity of their regard apparently enough to dismay even a cold fish like Mr. Stickley. He coughed and cleared his throat yet again. "In that case, the entire account . . . well, Sir Hamish had very decided views on the excise tax . . ."

He gazed about him at all their expectant expressions and shrugged helplessly. "He left it all to the smugglers."

"Smugglers." Sophie looked down and smiled. "Whisky smugglers, I take it?"

Mr. Stickley looked as though the very idea of all that lovely money going to a lot of unwashed criminals made him want to vomit. "Yes. The entire fortune will go to pay the fines and penalties of men convicted of distilling and transporting whisky without paying lawful duty."

Phoebe thought of the portrait of Sir Hamish that hung in Thornhold. With sandy hair and piercing blue eyes, yes . . . she could see the rebel in those eyes.

*Oh, look, Great-grandfather. I've won.*

The smugglers wouldn't see a penny. She would marry

Lord Brookhaven and quickly, too, for it meant she would never have to be afraid again.

She didn't give a hair on her head for rich gowns or jewels, but the thought that she might never again have to bite her tongue or lose sleep wondering if she'd said too much or ponder any stray whisper she might hear, trying to ascertain if someone knew something terrible about her—that thought was worth all her integrity and her heart besides.

*The Duchess of Brookmoor. Just remember that you will be the duchess.*

# Chapter Eleven

Mr. Stickley entered the austerely elegant office of Stickley & Wolfe, appointed as it was in a classical style that quite matched the elegant exterior of their Fleet Street building. There were no papers cluttering up the vast gleaming desks, there was no murmur of clerks busily seeing to the more mundane tasks of a busy firm.

Stickley & Wolfe had only one client—one purpose in the world, one might say. For the past twenty years, the sole occupation of Stickley & Wolfe had been the protection and management of the Pickering trust.

There had been other clients when the original Stickley & Wolfe held court in this office. Mr. Stickley senior had been the sharp, detail-oriented partner, while Mr. Wolfe senior had been the charming social representative, bringing in new high clientele with his wit and good looks. Although there had been a prevalence of freshly baked widows in the clutch, it had made for a profitable business.

Mr. Stickley the younger, however, was not interested in the accounts of widows, who had the irritating tendency to actually want to *spend* the money. Mr. Wolfe the younger had inherited his father's good looks and charm, but not the innate class that had made his father welcome among even the highest society—if there were an odd number of ladies that must be matched at dinner.

Mr. Wolfe the younger was more inclined to be found at a gaming hell with a ladybird on his lap—at least while he was still sober enough to want one.

So one by one, the large client list that was inherited from the fathers was lost by the sons until only the Pickering trust remained. Sir Hamish was long deceased, thankfully, or his business might have gone the way of the merry widows.

To be truthful, the state of things suited both Mr. Stickley and Mr. Wolfe to a fine stitch. Mr. Stickley nurtured and petted the trust into its current astonishing growth, while Mr. Wolfe gambled away his retainer with gusto, for there would always be more to come. After all, the odds of one of the Pickering great-granddaughters capturing a duke were well worth playing.

Stickley sat himself in the large tufted leather chair that he loved so dearly and listened to the welcome quiet of the serene office. Thankfully, Wolfe was rarely present but for the occasional visit to pick up his portion for that night's wastrel fling.

Stickley despised Wolfe with all the exquisite delicacy of a man who would never dare to free his inhibitions so, but he would not have parted with him for the world. Aside from the fact that he would have to use his personal monies to buy Wolfe's half of the firm, where else would he find someone who would leave him so delightfully alone?

This was why, when Wolfe breezed in an hour later, Stickley was able to peer at the useless bounder over the lens of his spectacles with a certain degree of friendly disdain.

"Hoy there, Stick. I'm here to fill me purse."

Stickley rose in no particular hurry. "Your father didn't send you to Eton so that you could murder the King's English so."

He went to the safe, casually keeping his back to Wolfe's chair. He'd had the combination changed years ago, fully intending to share it with Wolfe should he ever ask, but he hadn't. Therefore, why put the poor, morally unstable fellow in the terrible position of having to restrain himself from cleaning out the vault?

Stickley filled a small bag with several large pound notes and coins. He was always entirely generous with Wolfe, never scrimping on his "purse" as he called it. When there was a rise in the trust's carefully managed investments, Wolfe's purse was increased accordingly.

Stickley wouldn't dream of cheating the son of his father's beloved partner—although it would be incredibly easy to do so. In fact, over the years, Stickley had thought of any number of ways to leach more from Wolfe's retainer, but one must set one's moral compass high and never allow it to falter, or one would lose oneself in sin.

Stickleys didn't steal.

Without turning, he tossed the purse over his shoulder, knowing that Wolfe would catch it in the air. That done, he closed the safe box and carefully reset the combination, all with his back blocking the process from Wolfe.

Then he turned, fully expecting to see Wolfe already on his way to the door. Instead, his absurdly handsome partner sprawled disrespectfully in the matching tooled leather chair, gazing at him narrowly.

"You're losing your hair a bit young, aren't you, Stick?"

Stickley passed his palm over his scalp before he caught himself. He jerked his hand back to his side and stalked to his side of the great desk. "I haven't the slightest idea what you mean." He seated himself with a precise flip of his coattails, perfectly centered in the fine chair. He looked up to see Wolfe grinning at him fondly.

"Stick, don't let it worry you. Neither one of us is a lad anymore."

Eyeing his partner's dissipated pallor, Stickley nodded sharply. "Indeed."

"I think you need a wife, Stick." Wolfe rolled forward to plant both elbows on the pristine parchment blotter on his side. Stickley's was not so perfectly clean, but then Stickley's was actually used. "Someone to give you a couple of little Stickleys—a son to carry on the firm and a daughter to brighten your old age."

"I am perfectly content as I am," Stickley countered. "You, on the other hand, might benefit from cleaving to only one woman." Less likely to die from nasty pox or be shot by some objecting husband.

He didn't speak aloud, but Wolfe grinned unrepentantly, as if he'd heard every word. "Stick, at least when I die, someone will notice. You'll just be left here, sitting at the desk until you turn into one those African mums."

"Egyptian mummies," Stickley corrected acidly. "Which you would know if you ever used a newssheet for anything but to line your boots."

"Not even that. My valet lines my boots for me." Wolfe leaned back in the chair and plunked both said boots on the blotter, crossed at the ankle. He laced his fingers behind his head and gazed across the desk with a slight frown on his face. "Stick, I think I've been neglecting you."

Stickley went very still. *Pray, do not say you wish to take more responsibility within the firm!*

Wolfe nodded as if he'd come to some sort of decision. "I think it's time I take more responsibility within the firm."

"No!" Stickley nearly leaped to his feet in protest. Then he forced himself to calm as he slowly sat more deeply in his chair. There was no need to panic. This was Wolfe, after all. Give him a page of figures to account and he'd be asleep or gone within the hour.

Stickley took a deep breath and tried a patient smile on for size. It must not have looked well, for Wolfe's gaze became somewhat alarmed. Giving up on smiling, Stickley merely pursed his lips. "Wolfe, please forgive my . . . argument. Of course you are welcome to take over some tasks. I must say, with all the hullabaloo over Miss Millbury's engagement, I could use a bit of help."

Wolfe blinked. "One of the Pickering girls is getting hitched up? When did this come about? They've only been in town for one day."

Stickley pressed his lips more tightly. "They have been here for one week, and apparently that was enough for Miss Phoebe Millbury to secure the affections of one Marquis of Brookhaven—whom you might recall is shortly to inherit—"

Wolfe waved a hand. "Yes, I know who Brookhaven is—likely better than you do." He rubbed his other hand across his lips. "This is a pickle for us, isn't it?"

"Not necessarily." Stickley took a small gold case from his breast pocket and withdrew his spectacles. Although they were spotless, he cleaned them automatically. "We have served the trust well for all these years. The girl certainly won't need the money if she is to marry Brookhaven. I don't see why we cannot convince her to leave it safely in our hands indefinitely."

Wolfe gazed at him pityingly. "Stick, you know nothing about the aristocracy, do you? They're all paupers, in debt up to the roots of their hair, if they have any left."

Stickley twitched slightly at the reminder of the impermanence of hair. "Nonsense. I passed Brookhaven in the street myself today. He was most elegantly turned out, with a very fine equipage."

Wolfe waved a dismissive hand. "Oh, they hide it well. Borrowing on their expectations, they call it—but they borrow again and again and somehow those expectations never seem to bear fruit. Land-rich and pocket-poor, I call it. I'll bet that once Brookhaven finds out about Miss Millbury's pretty packet, he'll gut it to shore up his crumbling estate and pay off just enough of his vowels at White's to borrow more."

Stickley looked down at his hands, which were trembling on the blotter. "He—he has a crumbling estate?"

"They all have crumbling estates, old Stick. Vast miles full of tenants and cottagers who need new roofs and plows. Miss Millbury's twenty thousand pounds will be gone in a puff of smoke."

Stickley didn't bother to correct Wolfe as to the amount. What Wolfe didn't know wouldn't hurt him—or require explanation. Instead, he looked with desperation at the only person in the world he could count on in this, his hour of need.

"Wolfe, what are we going to do?"

Wolfe leaned forward, his eyes narrowed. "We're going to do the only thing we can do. We're going to stop this wedding."

# Chapter Twelve

When Calder had returned to Brook House, he had rather indifferently ordered Fortescue to secure a lady's maid for Miss Millbury. After thus briefly seeing to his fiancée's future comfort without so much as a pause in his stride, he disappeared into his study to immerse himself in his factory concerns once more.

Rafe watched him go with concerned disbelief—although not surprise—then turned to the butler.

"Fort, Miss Millbury—well, she's not the sort to complain, even if she doesn't like who you choose . . . just find someone young and likeable, will you? Someone she can be herself with, someone she can be—"

Fortescue gazed at him with no expression whatsoever, which was how Fortescue always gazed at him. However, this time there was just a trace of speculation in that sea of blandness behind those pale sharp eyes.

"Indeed, my lord. I shall take care to choose someone perfectly suitable . . . as always."

Translation: I knew that, I've already seen to it, and you're not the only one around here with eyes.

Rafe persisted. "I am serious, Fort. I want her to have someone cheerful, not one of those dour, creaking old tarts who lace too tight and make her wear shoes that pinch and—"

Fortescue nearly had a tremor of expression. It stopped Rafe mid-sentence. "What?"

The butler cleared his throat. "If your lordship will permit me, I have already chosen a likely girl from the present staff. Patricia is no older than Miss Millbury, is an intelligent and attractive girl who has a sort of . . . kindness about her—" Fortescue stopped short.

If Rafe wasn't mistaken, the wintry bastard also colored a fraction, turning from pale to not-quite-so-pale.

Struggling for words? Fortescue? Ho ho! Perhaps something other than ice water ran through the usually imperturbable butler's veins! Rafe contemplated teasing the man, but he wouldn't want the poor bloke to have a seizure from too much unaccustomed emotion. Besides, he presently had a great deal of sympathy for those afflicted with unrequited . . . well, anything.

Rafe let the corner of his lips twist upward. "You're a good man, Fort. If you ever want to leave this pit of slavery I'll hire you myself."

Since the only way Fortescue could advance his career from this breathless peak would be to work for the Prince Regent himself, it was a measure of the butler's aplomb that he could greet such a jest with a dignified, "I shall consider it, my lord."

Rafe turned his gaze toward the as-always closed door of Calder's study. "I'll be moving on soon, you see, Fort." He grimaced. "No room for bastard bachelors in the honeymoon house."

"I'm sure his lordship would prefer you to stay, Lord Raphael."

"Oh, that's not a good idea," Rafe breathed, thinking of his brother's bride-to-be living and laughing and dreaming around every corner. "Really, truly it isn't."

◆ ◆ ◆

FORTESCUE CAME UPON Patricia while she dusted the
newel post at the bottom of the grand curving staircase.
She worked meticulously, kneeling on the floor to get the
most minute crevice shining to Brook House's exacting
standards.

Fortescue watched in helpless fascination as her industry made her bottom wave invitingly in the air. Ogling
housemaids went against every rule in the butler's code of
ethics. Unfortunately, from the moment he'd heard
Patricia O'Malley's musical Irish lilt asking for work at
the service entry behind the kitchen, he'd found himself completely unable to control his fascination. Hide
it, yes. Control it, deny it, dispense with it—no.

He'd followed that sweet voice from where he waited to
collect the Marquis's breakfast tray to lurk behind the impatient footman who'd answered the bell.

"Get on w' ye, then," the man had ordered the cloaked
figure who stood wreathed in morning fog and humble dignity. "We want no Irish here."

Her head had lifted sharply at that, giving Fortescue a
view of alabaster beauty and sharply flashing green eyes.
"'Tis no crime to be from Ireland," the girl had told the
sneering footman coolly. "Though *you'll* be wantin' to pray
God'll forgive your conceit."

The footman moved to shut the door in her face. Fortescue had caught it in one hand without realizing he'd moved
closer.

Lovely Patricia—who'd removed her cloak to reveal
hair the color of sunset, God help him!—had accepted the
position of lower housemaid with dignified gratitude,
though the rest of the staff had stared in shock and astonishment. Brook House needed no more help and certainly
not some common Irish right off the boat!

None had the nerve to gainsay Fortescue, of course, though they might comment plenty among themselves.

He ought not to have done it. It was unheard of, at this level of service. She was the sort of uneducated creature who'd think herself lucky to find grueling factory work, not one of the members of the generations-old highest servant class in Britain.

Now, having broken so many unwritten rules already, he shattered more of them as he let his gaze wander over the lithe figure kneeling before the stair. The way she looked, the lilt of her voice—he was unable to deny that he went rather desperately weak-kneed at the merest breath of her.

Her brilliant hair was mostly hidden beneath her proper mobcap and the Brook House uniform wasn't meant to be alluring, yet even that couldn't hide her supple grace, or the way her auburn lashes lay upon her fine pale cheeks, or the way her anatomy responded to her industry as she scrubbed—

She caught sight of him and froze, gazing up at him in surprise. Fortescue clenched his fists together behind his back and hoped his gaze betrayed none of his erotic fascination.

After a moment, she raised her fine brows at him. "Mr. Fortescue . . . sir?" He made her nervous. She was very aware of him as well, but only as the head of the staff, the man who held her future in the balance.

Fortunately, she was doing well, though untrained. It wouldn't last—but not because she couldn't do the work. Even now, he could see the ties of her homeland stretching behind her like threads of a dream. She'd come to find work, to help her family, but she wasn't going to stay.

Not unless he did something to make staying irresistible.

In a moment, he would clear his dry throat. In a moment, he'd be able to speak without a trace of love-starved schoolboy stammer. His body reluctantly obeyed at last. He cleared his throat. "Good morning, Patricia."

Her gaze flicked to the front windows of the hall, then back to him. "Good afternoon, sir."

Afternoon. Of course. He continued to gaze at her stonily, unable to think of what he'd come to say. Her gaze went from curious to worried. She thought she'd overstepped with her gentle correction, he could see.

*God, so very beautiful—*

And so very young and so very in his direct employ. He was her superior. He was above tawdry entanglements with housemaids. His life was his service to the marquis. He was the very nearly the highest of the high, at the apex of his career. He was better than this.

Lady's maid. Right.

He cleared his throat again, aware that it made him sound like a stuffy septuagenarian. "His lordship has officially announced his engagement to Miss Millbury."

She smiled at that, transforming herself from stunning to breathtaking in an instant. His chest tightened. Oh, he had it dire, he did. Twenty years of perfect service, without so much as a pat-your-fanny on his ledger, and all he wanted to do was to drag this girl into the nearest linen closet and—

"'Tis good news, sir. 'Tis not good for a man to be too much alone."

"What?" He choked. She was talking about the marquis. "Oh . . . yes. The wedding is to take place quite soon." Shockingly soon, but he was in no position to pass judgment at the moment. "In fact, Miss Millbury and her family will be moving into Brook House immediately to begin preparations."

Her smile grew. "So many fine ladies will certainly brighten the house, won't they, sir?"

"Indeed." He was already blinded. Doggedly, he clenched

his fingers more tightly over sweating palms. "As it turns out, Miss Millbury does not currently have a lady's maid of her own. I thought you'd do."

Her smile disappeared in surprise—nay, complete shock. "Me, sir?" She blinked at him. "M—*me*?"

The household would be up in arms at the topsy-turvy appointment. Miss Millbury herself might quite possibly object and if the marquis bothered to take note, he certainly would. Fortescue simply didn't care.

"You're to begin immediately. Miss Millbury's things are already on their way. I assume you do know what to do with those things?" he asked sternly.

She closed her mouth with a little snap, challenged out of her shock, just as he'd intended.

"I'll do my best, sir."

He nodded briefly. "Very well then." He turned sharply and strode away, before he lost all control of himself. He did glance back once, to see her leaning limply on the newel post, shaking her head in disbelief.

Even then, she was the most beautiful creature he'd ever seen.

He was entirely doomed.

He'd never felt so alive.

# Chapter Thirteen

The entrance to Lementeur's was unmarked, merely an elegant portal among the more obvious shops on the Strand. However, Tessa strode up to the lovely carved oak door, rapped the bird-shaped knocker smartly, and stood her tallest.

Waiting for someone passing by to see her entering the most exclusive dressmaker's door, no doubt. Phoebe considered offering applause, but thought Tessa might not see the humor of it.

The door opened on a rather gorgeous young footman who seemed not at all impressed by the sundry and various degrees of feminine beauty awaiting outside.

"Good afternoon," Tessa began. "I am—"

The fellow didn't even look Tessa's way, instead fixing his aloof gaze exclusively upon Phoebe. "Lementeur will see you now, Miss Millbury. Your . . . *friends* may accompany you, if you so desire."

Oh, my. This was going to be interesting after all. Then Phoebe caught the seething rage on Tessa's face. The last thing she wanted was to give Tessa any more reason to attack Sophie.

Phoebe gazed at the haughty young man evenly. "I do not believe my aunt was allowed to finish her sentence," she said with mild firmness.

The fellow's eyes flickered slightly. "Of course," he said, bowing deeply to Tessa. "But Lady Tessa needs no introduction to anyone with taste." The irony was deep, but Tessa had never been all that discerning.

Tessa preened, Deirdre rolled her eyes, and Phoebe breathed a sigh of relief. With her distant gaze, Sophie seemed completely removed from it all, as if her body were present but her mind was miles away.

*I know those eyes. Those are my eyes when I'm being Miss Millbury, the vicar's perfect daughter.*

The young man led them into the entrance hall and took their bonnets and wraps. Then they were guided into an elegant room with a curtained dais to one side. The fellow bowed deeply. "Lementeur will join you momentarily."

In spite of matters, Phoebe was beginning to feel some anticipation. She'd never truly had her choice of gowns, for the cook had ordered them when she was younger and the vicar had forced—er, influenced—the choices after that.

The door opened and a rather curious gentleman entered. Unlike the gloriously beautiful footman, he was a small, spry fellow with puckish features and twinkling eyes. Phoebe liked him immediately. Tessa sprang to her feet, her face wreathed in smiles. Good heavens, Phoebe hadn't known Tessa's face could *do* that!

"Mr. Lementeur! Thank you so—"

He held up a hand. "It is only Lementeur. It is more a title than a surname, you see."

"Le Menteur. The Liar," Sophie breathed. By the look on her face when the man turned to her with delight, she'd not meant to translate aloud.

"But of course!" Lementeur tilted his head, smiling at Sophie as if she were his dearest new friend. "And can you guess why an honest man such as myself would take that name?"

Sophie obviously knew the answer. She had "good stu-
dent" written all over her, yet she hesitated. Phoebe leaned
forward, for she dearly wanted to know.

Tessa shifted restlessly. "Sir, we—"

"Come on, sweeting," Lementeur said gently to Sophie.

Sophie pressed her lips together, glancing at Tessa.
Then she looked back up at Lementeur. "Because you are
an illusionist. You make people—women—look finer than
they are."

Lementeur reached for Sophie's hand, bending to kiss
the back of it. "At last, someone understands. Only I prefer
to think that I make them look finer than they knew they
could." Then he straightened briskly and gazed at all of
them in turn.

"Miss Millbury. Miss Cantor. Miss Blake. And of
course, the memorable Lady Tessa." He walked slowly
before them, inspecting them with his head tilted. Phoebe
felt compelled to sit her straightest. Deirdre seemed
bored, although Phoebe knew she was as excited as any
of them. Sophie was gazing curiously about the room, as
if Lementeur's assessment had nothing to do with her.
He stopped before to her "What an elegant form," he ex-
claimed.

Tessa drew up. "Sir, it is an unfortunate fact that my
niece is as pl—"

Lementeur swung on Tessa in full artistic fury. "Your
niece is a dressmaker's dream—an untouched canvas, a
figure of such pure elegance and refinement—"

He threw up his hands and turned back to Sophie. "You
could wipe them all from the minds of Society if you
wished it, my darling. All you need do is say the word and
I will make you my muse, my *pièce de résistance*, my mas-
terpiece!"

Sophie drew back from the little man's outburst of adora-
tion. Doubt and hope raced each other across her expression.

Tessa began to pale with rage. At last, Sophie shook her head. "I shall have to decline," she said shakily. Then she shot a single, hot glance at Tessa.

Lementeur took her hand and patted it gently. "That's all right, little one." It wasn't at all absurd, for some reason, though Sophie towered over him. "You will come see me, if you change your mind?"

Then he turned back to Phoebe. "Miss Millbury, if you will please ascend?" He took her hand and placed her on the round raised dais, standing her there like a reluctant doll. Pushed back from the platform stood a number of tall mirrors, currently shrouded in white cloth.

"I do not wish to be distracted by reflections," Lementeur said when he saw her looking over her shoulder at them. "Now be still."

Phoebe stood as straight and still as possible, suddenly horribly aware of every possible flaw in her appearance.

Lementeur circled her, murmuring. "Yes, yes, the bosom is very good, the waist divine . . . the hips, heaven help us . . . not to worry, not to worry . . . there are ways . . ."

Since he was obviously not speaking to her, Phoebe worried plenty. Her hips? She'd never given them a thought! She suppressed the desire to run her hands over herself, to see if larger hips had mysteriously materialized. Perhaps she ought to skip that second crumpet at tea . . .

He came around to the front of her and peered into her face. "Marvelous skin. You've been most diligent with your bonnet." He pondered her for a long moment, tapping one finger against his lips. "What colors . . . ?"

Tessa spoke up from across the room, where Phoebe became aware that they had all been watching with extreme fascination, even Sophie. "Mr. Lementeur, I believe Brookhaven prefers blue."

Lementeur sent Phoebe a long-suffering look. Phoebe sympathized completely. Without turning his head, he raised his voice to answer Tessa. "Everyone knows that Brookhaven prefers *blue*, my lady. Yet which blue is best? Cerulean? Lapis? The color of Turkish stone? The deepest royal blue?" He shot one scathing look over his shoulder. "Do let me think, if you please?"

He turned back to Phoebe with a small smile on his lips that told her he'd enjoyed that. "Now, my dear, tell me— for we must appeal to more than his lordship's sense of color—what, in your perception, led him to focus his attentions solely on you?"

"I—I haven't the foggiest notion." She looked away. "I never met the man before the engagement . . . but I know it was on his brother's recommendation that he chose me." A rather humiliating admission.

Lementeur raised a brow. "*Really?* Marbrook, eh?" The other brow joined the first. "Actually, that does make . . ." The murmured thought trailed off and he clapped his hands together and smiled. "Yes. Yes, I have it. I have something that will do for this evening. It was meant for Lady Reardon, but she'll understand when I tell her. She believes in true love, you see." His eyes twinkled.

*True love?* The marquis was a respectable man, but that was overstating the case. Then again, what did it matter what people thought?

"I'll have it sent over as soon as I have it hemmed, along with a few other things. Now go. Begone. Come back in two days for your first fitting."

"Two days?" Phoebe hadn't had many gowns made in her life but she knew it generally took longer than that.

"I do not get paid by the hour like some lowly seamstress!" He shooed her off the dais with both hands. "Leave. All of you. I must work."

Phoebe shooed, hopping off the dais and rejoining the others. Tessa gazed at Lementeur in bewilderment. "Leave? But what of our—"

Lementeur crossed his arms and rolled his eyes. "Cabot!"

The beautiful young man appeared from nowhere to escort them all from the room. Once the door was closed, he deigned to offer them a chilly smile.

"The master's eye does not require such props as measuring tapes. Miss Millbury, your trousseau will be ready to fit in two days. There will never be another fitting required, unless your figure changes." He nodded to the others, not quite a bow, but more respectful than before.

Tessa sputtered. "But I must consult as to color and style—"

Cabot's gaze became absolutely glacial. "My lady, if you desire an *ordinary* gown, perhaps you wish to go elsewhere."

Tessa swallowed quickly. "No, no, of course not. Er, please thank Mr. Lementeur for us?"

They left, Phoebe now pondering the possible reasons behind Brookhaven's selection of her, Tessa unusually quelled, Deirdre sporting an amused half-smile, and Sophie looking very thoughtful—and very much present.

"How do you think he can make a gown without measuring?" Sophie ventured when the carved oak door had shut behind them.

Deirdre shrugged. "I haven't a clue. What does it matter? His gowns are always superb, so he must know his business."

They passed another shop, one with gentlemen's accessories displayed in the window. Phoebe's eye was caught by a stock pin, a dark yellow topaz set in gold that winked at her, twinkling like Marbrook's brown eyes. She felt the impulse to buy it and give it to him.

*You are not allowed to give Marbrook gifts. Your giftgiving is now restricted to Brookhaven and Brookhaven alone.*

That fact brought home her situation as nothing had

before it. She would never be able to entertain the possibility of another man again, not for the rest of her or Brookhaven's life.

Some women might not be so bound by their vows, but Phoebe wasn't one of them. If—*when*—she married Brookhaven, she would abide by those vows forever and never look back.

Resolutely, she turned her eyes away from the topaz stock pin and looked for one to suit Brookhaven. After a moment she spotted one that made her smile. It was a golden figure, a bullheaded man, the mythical Minotaur. There was no earthly reason why it should remind her of Brookhaven, but it did.

Before she could allow herself to reconsider, she walked smartly into the shop and purchased it for him. She would give it to him tonight.

If it made him smile as well, then she would know that she had made the right choice.

*And which choice is that—the man or the pin?*

Well, now, that was best not thought about, wasn't it?

# *Chapter Fourteen*

Rafe knew that he ought not to be loitering here on this street full of shops, hoping to get a glimpse of Phoebe as she left Lementeur's. He knew that he was heading down a dangerous road, but he found himself there all the same.

And then she was there as well, across the street. Her aunt and cousins milled about her for a moment, obscuring his view. Then they walked on while she paused before another shop.

She was just another pretty girl, he told himself savagely. A girl in a bonnet, shopping on the street with her family. There was no reason for his pulse to jump, world to narrow down to only her, no reason for his feet to step forward off the walk, into the street—

A shout jerked him back to awareness just in time to leap backward out of the way of a fast-moving cart. By the time he found his footing again, Phoebe was gone.

Damn. Or perhaps it was better this way. Now he'd only see her tonight, at dinner, surrounded by family and servants. That would be a safe way to meet her again.

After all, it had only been one evening—only an hour of that evening, in fact.

So she preferred Calder. What of it?

*How do you know whom she preferred? You didn't ask her.*

He'd hardly had the chance, had he? Calder had moved with uncharacteristic impulsiveness—or was it merely Calder's usual decisiveness? What if Calder really loved her?

God. Rafe ran a hand roughly over his face. Calder had been so alone for so long. Rafe doubted his brother had so much as touched a woman's hand since Melinda died.

Could he in good conscience try to take that from Calder?

And what if Phoebe truly did prefer Calder? His eyes narrowed as he tried to sort it out in his mind. Yes, she had liked him, he was sure of it—but that was only liking. He'd reacted very strongly to her, but what if her reaction had only been champagne and the relief of being saved from humiliation?

The thought that chafed, was that in a scarce fortnight, Miss Phoebe Millbury would spend her wedding night in Calder's arms.

He clenched his teeth.

Only a fortnight left until the wedding. Then she would be Calder's wife and even Rafe's shaky morals did not sink that low.

He hoped.

PHOEBE EMERGED FROM the shop with her gift in her reticule, looking about for the others. Next to the gentleman's shop was a hat shop—a bit of clever salesmanship, really, when one considered that few gentlemen truly had the patience required for a decent bout of hat shopping.

When Phoebe peeked through the front window, she saw that Tessa and Deirdre were already happily engaged in lively debate over . . . feathers? Even Sophie was wistfully fondling a sweet concoction of straw and ribbon. What fun! Phoebe moved to the door and even had her hand on the knob—

Until she smelled the chocolate.

Chocolate was one of her secret sins—really her only sin these days, unless one counted a tendency toward unvoiced sarcasm. She managed to hide the occasional caustic thoughts that crossed her mind, but she had never quite conquered the longing for all things wastefully pleasurable.

There was not a large selection of sweets available in Thornton—aside from rose-petal gelatin—nor was the vicar one to waste money on such decadent luxuries, so her opportunities to submit to this particular vice were few and far between.

With one last longing glance into the hat shop, Phoebe set off to find the source of that delightful scent.

Now before her eyes, there rose a miracle of self-indulgence and pleasure. A confectioner's, a real sweet shop of the sort she'd only heard of. The tiny place wasn't much larger than a market stall, but it was filled from ceiling to floor with the sin of gluttony—sin shimmering with crystallized sugar, sin tinted in every color of the rainbow. The heady scent of sugar and cocoa was intoxicating now, making Phoebe's knees weak with desire.

A woman popped up from behind a rack of red twists. Her pink cheeks and white hair made her seem like just another sweet. Her blue eyes twinkled and her smile dimpled when her gaze fell upon such an avid customer.

"Stopped in for a treat, 'ave ye, pet?"

Phoebe fell instantly in love—with the shop, its proprietor, and with the rows upon rows of gleaming treats before her eyes. From the amber of caramel to the deepest coffee-color of fine chocolate, everything looked entirely and completely heavenly.

There was a spare farthing in her reticule—"spare" meaning that it had no immediately useful purpose. It sang to her, a high sweet note that said, "Spend me!"

A moment later Phoebe was skulking guiltily back the

way she'd come, a tiny paper twist of purchased candy in
her hand and the first taste of chocolate on her tongue. Oh,
it had been *years*. She must consume it quickly, for she
could imagine what Tessa would have to say about it. For
Tessa, the figure was paramount. Nothing, not wine or beef
or cakes, could be allowed to come between a woman and
the tightest laces of her corset.

Phoebe turned the last corner quickly—and nearly
choked on her first taste. Her three companions gazed at
her curiously.

"Where have you been?" Tessa's eyes were narrowed.
"What do you have there?"

With a tiny silent mew of loss, Phoebe dropped the paper twist of candy behind her back and stepped on it. She
spread her hands before her. "I don't know what you mean.
I was only looking for a hack to take us home."

Tessa gazed at her sourly. It only made Phoebe think
longingly of lemon drops.

"Hmm. Well, I suppose we ought to begin our preparations for this evening. Let us go home then."

Phoebe allowed herself to be towed away, casting only
one longing glance over her shoulder at delicious sin left
undone, squashed on the pavement.

Through the milling crowd she thought she saw someone stop and bend to pick up her discarded paper twist.
Then skirts and parasols came between.

Phoebe sighed. When would she learn? Sin didn't pay.

# Chapter Fifteen

The mistress's bedchamber at Brook House was a vast, feminine fantasy of cream silk dressed in shimmering gold velvet. There were three rooms, if one counted the enormous dressing room, with its racks upon racks to hold more gowns than Phoebe could imagine, much less owned.

With the matching sitting room, the bedchamber was larger than the entire ground floor of Thornhold. Two opposing fireplaces blazed against the spring chill in the air, making it a good bit warmer than Thornhold as well. Phoebe wandered through the room, almost afraid to touch the delicate crystal bottles on the gold-leafed vanity or the exquisite mother-of-pearl inlay on the dainty escritoire. She had never seen such grandeur in her life. It seemed meant for someone else, not for her.

She avoided looking at the other doorway discreetly set into the painted paneling with determined exactness. Her ladyship's room came with its very own portal into his lordship's room right next door.

A discreet throat-clearing came from the doorway. "You won't be staying here yet, of course, Miss Millbury." Fortescue, the tall and eminently correct butler of Brook House, said approvingly when he noticed her shy avoidance of that blasted door. "But I thought you might like to see where your ladyship will live after the wedding."

*Your ladyship.* He was talking about her, Phoebe Millbury, vicar's daughter—the future Duchess of Brookmoor.

The beautiful room seemed to close in on her. The roaring fires—lighted just to warm the rooms for this tour?—seemed to burn all the air from the room. Phoebe closed her eyes against a wave of dread and pressed a hand to her constricted throat.

Fortescue might think her actions proof of her maidenish fears of the marriage bed—after all, the thing loomed like a great golden barge in this sea of wheat-colored carpet!—but Phoebe cared nothing for his opinion. It wasn't the wedding night that frightened her.

It was the marriage itself.

The vicar, Tessa, Deirdre, and Sophie—they were all in their rooms by now, settled in to stay until the wedding.

And after the wedding as well, for her.

*Forever.*

She would never leave Brook House, except to go to another one of her husband's houses. She would say goodbye to her cousins and her aunt and her father after the wedding and they would leave and she would stay . . . forever.

That word kept getting stuck in her mind, the way a torn nail snagged on fine fabric. This marriage business was so very . . . permanent. What if she didn't like Brookhaven, in the end. What if she eventually began to hate him?

*Forever.*

She turned her back on the lovely room and opened her eyes. Forcing a bland smile, she took a breath. "It is very fine. Now will you show me to my room?"

Fortescue led her down the hall, past many doors, to one apparently sufficiently far enough from his lordship's to calm her virginal fears.

Phoebe breathed a sigh of relief at the sight of the pretty but understated room before her. It was spacious enough and the furnishings were very fine, but it was clearly a guest chamber, not a room fit for a queen.

The bed was large and lavishly hung in pale green velvet, yet was still more modest than the marchioness's chamber and the walls were papered in white with delicately tinted vines running from floor to ceiling. The patterned carpet was a darker green and the furniture was elegant rosewood, sans decoration for the most part.

If the other room was a golden cage, then this one was a garden pavilion. It even overlooked the sculpted rear gardens of Brook House.

A cheery fire crackled in the petite hearth, welcoming Phoebe to a room she could live in forever. She turned to the butler with a real smile this time. "How lovely! Thank you, Fortescue."

"You'll find your things have already been stored away," Fortescue told her. "I've assigned a girl to you for the time being. I'm sure you'll be selecting your own lady's maid soon, but you'll find Patricia to be intelligent and teachable in the meantime."

Her own maid. From pauper to princess in a matter of hours. Had it only been this morning that she'd accepted Brookhaven's proposal?

*No, you accepted Marbrook's proposal. Brookhaven just happened to be attached to it instead.*

"If it meets with your approval, Miss Millbury, I should like to introduce the entire staff to you—after you've rested, of course."

Oh, dread. She was to be paraded before the servants and expected to remember everyone's name and station.

"Oh, no," Phoebe blurted. Then she recovered her bland smile. "I think I'd prefer to wait until I am officially the lady of the house. Until then, I am merely a guest like any other."

"As you wish, Miss Millbury." Fortescue didn't so much as blink, yet now disapproval radiated from his very bones. He really was the perfect foil for Lord Brookhaven, wasn't he?

Another time, another place, Phoebe might have found herself intimidated by the elegant manservant. Now, Fortescue and his opinions were the least of her worries.

She let out a breath and moved to the vanity to set down her reticule. There was a flat, satin-covered, beribboned box there, approximately the size of a silver salver. "What is this?"

Fortescue blinked. "I'm afraid I do not know, Miss Millbury." This bothered him, she could tell. "Perhaps a gift from his lordship?"

"Oh." That flat vowel caused a flicker of too much concern from Fortescue, so Phoebe reapplied that damned smile and opened the box.

"Oh!"

It was filled from side to side, end to end, in two layers, with more chocolates than Phoebe had ever seen outside of the sweet shop this afternoon. Her jaw dropped at the generous plenty.

"This must have—" *Cost a fortune.* A silly statement in a grand house like this. Unable to hide her surprise and glee, Phoebe turned to Fortescue with breathless delight. "How did he know? I didn't think anyone on earth knew how I love chocolates!"

Fortescue was gazing at the box with glacial consternation. "Er . . . his lordship can be most astute."

Phoebe touched the satin-covered lid with thoughtful fingers. If Brookhaven had already discerned something so personal about her . . .

She'd had the impression all day that Brookhaven had very little real interest in her. Perhaps she was wrong. Perhaps he merely had difficulty showing his emotions.

Well, anyone who would make such a lovely gesture deserved more of a chance than she had so far given him. So he wasn't his brother—what of it? Marbrook was a handsome, flirtatious fellow who likely toyed with the affections of a dozen women every evening. The more different Brookhaven was from Marbrook, the better!

Fortescue cleared his throat. "The dressmaker sent word that your gown will be delivered shortly. Patricia is awaiting it downstairs even now. Should I ring for her to help you freshen up from your afternoon?"

The gown, and the entire trousseau, were more evidence of Brookhaven's openhanded generosity. All she had to give him in return was a piddling gold cravat pin.

*So give him your loyalty and your consideration—and stop acting like you lost your favorite kitten!*

"That's fine, Fortescue," she said absently. "Would you mind showing me where my cousin, Miss Blake, is staying?"

"Miss Blake requested a room at the other end of the hall from Lady Tessa." Fortescue's tone was not altogether disapproving of this decision.

Sophie was indeed at the other end of the grand house. "Goodness, Sophie!" Phoebe smiled at her cousin. "Was it so terrible to share a room with me?"

Sophie looked up from where she was seated tailor fashion on the floor, sorting through piles of papers. "Hello, Phoebe. Did you know that Brook House has the most astounding library? Your father has already lost himself in there. I doubt we'll see him for days."

Phoebe didn't wish to be disloyal, but the very idea appealed. "And will you disappear as well?" Her tone came out a bit more wistful than she'd intended, for it penetrated even Sophie's preoccupation.

Her cousin looked up, blinking behind her spectacles. "Are you all right, Phoebe? I thought you wanted this match."

"Yes. Absolutely. I do." Or at least, she was sure she would, once she became accustomed to the idea. "It is only that everything is moving so quickly . . ."

Sophie nodded. "Brookhaven is a very efficient fellow, isn't he? I don't think I've ever seen anyone accomplish so much before teatime."

"Yes." Phoebe flung herself stomach down over Sophie's bed. "Gowns. Chocolates." She opened the box and offered them. "A beautiful room. I am being most efficiently swept off my feet." She rolled over to stare at the tester above the bed. "I wonder if I should tell him he needn't try so hard? I feel a bit . . . suffocated."

"Stop complaining," said a tart voice from the doorway. Deirdre strolled into the room uninvited. She gazed at the chocolates longingly for an instant but did not indulge. "I heard the butler say you requested a room far from Tessa, Sophie. I wish I'd thought of that."

"I'm rather glad you didn't," Sophie said absently as she paged through the stack of notes on her lap. "Then Tessa would only move closer still."

Obviously stung, Deirdre stiffened. "Tessa would not target you so often if you did not give her such pleasure with your reactions! The way that you shrink up—and that slouch! Honestly, Sophie, sometimes I just want to slap you myself!"

Sophie didn't turn from her task. "Feel free to try it."

Deirdre made a noise of frustration. "Sophie, listen! When Tessa carries on, simply smile and nod and say, 'Oh, do you think so, Tessa?' or, 'I hadn't thought of it that way, Tessa.' "

Sophie drew back. "Why should I let her think I agree with her cruelty?"

Deirdre stared at her. "To survive it, of course."

Sophie frowned slightly. "Is that what you do, Deirdre? Do you merely survive?"

Deirdre went quite still and then smiled her most brittle, Tessa smile. "Whatever gave you that idea?" With a toss of her head, she turned and swept from the room.

Sophie watched her go, then turned back to Phoebe, who was silently tracing the pattern of the coverlet with one fingertip.

"Is Deirdre very unhappy, do you think?" Sophie sounded as if she'd never before had the thought.

At that moment, Phoebe herself felt the urge to shake Sophie, just a little bit. She pushed herself off the bed and stood. "Yes, Sophie, I—and everyone who has spent more than fifteen minutes with Deirdre—think she is very unhappy. And who wouldn't be, living their childhood at Tessa's mercy? The question is, Sophie . . . why is that you've never seen it before today?"

Phoebe left the room before she found herself joining the general mistreatment of Sophie. Once in the hall, she halted and closed her eyes, reaching for patience and tolerance and all the things a good vicar's daughter ought to have a plentiful supply of.

Two weeks in this house with Marbrook, Brookhaven, the vicar, Tessa, and the warring cousins.

Perhaps the dreaded wedding could not come soon enough.

# Chapter Sixteen

The damned wedding could not come soon enough.

Rafe was in his suite, frankly hiding—not to mention cracking open the brandy a bit early—trying not to hear the hubbub from the guest rooms down the hall.

Had she liked the chocolates? Was she nibbling on them even now, as she had in the street, with that look of guilty exultation on her face, her eyes half closed in sensual pleasure as the dark sugary confection melted on her tongue? Was she thinking of him at all?

Stop it.

Now.

He tossed back what remained in his glass, then slouched in the large chair by his fire, his booted feet stretched toward the flames although he was not cold.

How could he be cold when she was in the house? God, she would be everywhere—at the dinner table, down the hall at night, bathing in her room in the firelight, all golden and slippery and flushed from the heat of the water . . .

He groaned and poured himself another glass. He was going to hide in his room for the next two and a half weeks. If he had any luck at all—and if the cellars of Brook House held enough brandy—he would manage to stay drunk until the happy couple boarded the coach for their honeymoon.

He would simply leave now, but Calder would never understand if Rafe missed the ceremony itself and there was no way in hell that Rafe was going to tell him why.

Then Calder was there, standing over him, his expression clearly prepared to wax disapproving over the lack of brandy in the decanter.

"Bugger off, big brother."

Calder grunted. "My fiancée has taken up residence. I'll thank you to make a good impression on her family." He folded his arms. "That means you will not interfere with Miss Millbury's cousins."

Rafe raised his right hand and placed his left over his heart in mock earnestness. "I solemnly vow that I will not interfere with Miss Millbury's cousins." Easy enough, for his record of "interfering" with virgins was rumor, not fact.

More or less.

"And do try not to get drunk before dinner."

"Oh, shut it," muttered Rafe. *You got the girl.* "Let me have the brandy, at the very least."

His brother turned to leave, but—being Calder—couldn't go without one parting shot. "It appears to me like the brandy has you."

Rafe glared at the decanter as his brother left the room.

DEIRDRE STROLLED THROUGH the house, pausing to trail a hand over the lip of a large Chinese vase displayed on a hall table. The smooth cold porcelain left not a trace of dust on her fingertips. Of course not. Brook House gleamed with wealth and comfort and good care.

She sighed in acquisitive envy. Their own house in Woolton had suffered greatly from Tessa's alienation of the staff . . . although Deirdre's own chambers were always spotless and warm. Despite the petty satisfaction of seeing Tessa helpless against the combined spite of the servants,

Deirdre did long for the days when the fires were generous and the dinners exquisite—when Papa was alive.

It would be that way here in Brook House—if not far better yet. The lady of Brook House would live a life of luxury beyond compare—coddled by attentive staff, indulged by a generous husband, freed by status and wealth to do as she wished, whenever she wished.

*Well, that certainly won't be you.*

Phoebe was the lady of Brook House—or would be in mere weeks. Deirdre fought back a dark wave of resentment. Phoebe would win it all—the house, the inheritance . . .

And Brookhaven himself.

The worst of it was, Phoebe didn't even seem pleased! Here Phoebe had every dream that Deirdre had ever had the imagination to compose—and that covered a lot of ground!—yet she seemed as pale and reluctant as a prisoner being walked to the gallows.

It was enough to make Deirdre hate Phoebe . . . if the damned girl wasn't so pitiful. God, that father of hers! Tessa might be a vile and pitiless bitch, but Deirdre needn't take her abuse personally, for Tessa wasn't blood. Tessa's status as her guardian was a temporary one—the more temporary the better.

But "the vicar" as Phoebe called him—never "Papa" or "my father"—was as cold and remote as Tessa was hotly interfering. He seemed to care nothing that Phoebe was obviously unhappy with the match, or that she grew quieter and paler by the hour.

Of course, Brookhaven, the huge lout, was just as oblivious. He took Phoebe by the arm, held her hand, spoke to her and never, ever actually saw her.

*I'd never let a man like that ignore me. I'd make him see me. I'd make him ache for me.*

Deirdre floated down the hall, opening door after door, finding every room more exquisite than the one before. At last, she opened to door to a small, private parlor that took her breath away.

Beautiful landscapes covered the walls from the wainscot to the ceiling. Pale velvet draperies framed the large high window with its view of the garden. Delicate spindled furnishings in fine ebony seemed to float on the luxurious blue carpet like pleasure boats on the sea.

She wanted to go in, to take her place at the delicate escritoire that was obviously meant for her ladyship—the very place to plan menus and arrange the household matters!—and run her fingers over the carved mantel that was a frilly, feminine confection of pink marble, and lie back on the ivory velvet fainting couch and dream her afternoons away—

Where Phoebe would dream her afternoons away.

Deirdre shut the door on those dreams, pulling the latch to with a decided slam. Damn Phoebe anyway.

AT BROOK HOUSE, the guests were gathering for dinner.

Phoebe tried not to twitch with nervousness as she waited to meet the party. She knew she had never looked better in her life.

The gown from Lementeur was a treasure in silk of perfect hazy summer blue, perfectly constructed to look simple while in fact it was anything but. There was no trim other than a darker velvet ribbon just below her bustline, yet the entire effect was one of exquisite opulence. Her waist had never seemed so tiny, nor had her bosom ever sat so high. She preferred not to look down, although Sophie had assured her that the neckline was no lower than they had seen other respectable ladies wear.

"It is only your figure that is out of the ordinary," Sophie had said admiringly, without the slightest trace of envy. "Brookhaven will be speechless."

Brookhaven had indeed been speechless, but not with admiration. His brow had creased slightly when he'd seen her, as if she were not at all what he'd had in mind. He'd been equally underwhelmed by her gift, although he'd dutifully thanked her and pinned it to his cravat.

Then it was time.

Marbrook was there, just across the room, when Phoebe entered on Brookhaven's arm. Her gaze went directly to him as if it were magnetized. He glanced up once, then glanced away again immediately. Phoebe ordered her spine to straighten and her chin to lift. The man owed her nothing, not even explanation. She'd spent an evening with him once, which had meant nothing.

Matters were awkward enough without dwelling on one misspent evening.

*I wish I'd kissed him properly. I wish I'd seen him without his shirt. I wish I'd—*

He was still not looking at her, but was instead gazing across the room at no one at all. Well, two could play as well as one. Phoebe turned her attention to the other guests, determined to do his lordship and the vicar proud as the future Marchioness of Brookhaven. She smiled, she curtseyed with just the right amount of subtle awareness of her new status, she spoke sweetly and without opinion, just as Tessa had instructed her. She was perfect in every way.

She could scarcely stand herself.

*If I met me, I wouldn't want to see me again either.*

Nonsense, perhaps, but at least she was free to be nonsensical within the confines of her own mind.

If only said mind would stay away from thoughts of Lord Rafe Marbrook, who had never looked at her again so far this evening.

Instead, he stood, arms folded with one shoulder braced against the mantel, scowling at nothing in particular. The

other guests avoided him, even Brookhaven, who occasionally glanced at his brother in dry puzzlement.

Calder himself, on the other hand, seemed positively
expansive this evening. He didn't actually smile, but he did
relax the grim steeliness of his jaw on occasion and even
spoke unnecessarily once or twice.

Phoebe watched them both, these two brothers, one
whom she'd pledged to marry, the other she'd lost to only
dream of. They were both handsome, astonishingly so, both
highborn, both extraordinary in every way—which made her
wonder what in the world either one of them had ever seen
in her.

*Instead of wondering why Marbrook didn't propose, you
ought to wonder why he ever spoke to you in the first place.*

Right. She was lucky to have this opportunity, she was
lucky to have caught Brookhaven's eye, she was lucky,
lucky, the luckiest girl in London.

So why did her heart feel as though it were being ripped
in two?

# *Chapter Seventeen*

Rafe almost hadn't recognized her when she came in on Calder's arm. She looked beautiful in a sky-blue gown that coincidentally happened—or perhaps not—to be Calder's favorite color. Her hair was up without a strand out of place and her smile was just the right degree of beautifully turned lip . . .

She looked like Phoebe's much more restrained sister, although the gown was a celebration of sin in the making. Yet, where was the flash of defiance in her blue eyes? Where was the tumbling, riotous hair that begged to be splayed across his pillow? Where was the girl who had tried her first champagne and ended up in his arms?

She spoke, she smiled, she even laughed—but it was never in her eyes. That sweet effervescence had been lidded, trapped, and suffocated.

She looked his way and he quickly glanced aside—only to turn his gaze upon her reflection in the large mirror across the room. It was perfect. He could see her, gaze at her, fill his eyes with her—er, rather, gaze casually in her general direction—and she might never even know she was being watched.

Something that looked like disappointment crossed her features when he looked away, but it was so swiftly gone that he knew he had only imagined his own feelings on her face.

His gaze followed her in the mirror as she made her away around the room on Calder's arm. She did everything perfectly, smiling and nodding and curtsying, yet she looked so . . . distant. It was as if she were asleep and all that surrounded her was naught but a dream.

*I could wake her, if I chose. I could pull her onto that darkened terrace beyond the doors and bring her back to life—*

Rafe killed those betraying thoughts, or at least stabbed them thoroughly and left them to bleed on the carpet. He would not allow those thoughts. She was now Calder's. She was as off-limits to him as if she were on the moon.

Then she appeared in front of him. Her hand was still on Calder's arm so Rafe could not actually run from her, much as he might want to.

"You're being a wallflower this evening," Calder said cordially. "Are you still fretting over that farmer?"

"That farmer" was a man with seven children and an ailing wife who had been a prosperous and productive tenant until recent rains had wiped out his crops. To Calder, he was merely a machine that had stopped working properly and must be replaced. To Rafe, he was a member of the Brookhaven family and Calder was failing his duty—by every ancient custom of honor and stewardship—to help the man recover instead.

But Calder hadn't listened and there was nothing that Rafe could do about it. Helpless rage swept through him, fueled by the sight of Phoebe's hand tightening on Calder's sleeve.

*Already depending on him to save you, are you? Already thinking he's your knight in shining armor, going to slay the dragon to save fair maiden?* Fair maiden had best remain price-worthy and efficient if she wanted to register on Calder's scale of importance!

"All done making the rounds, Calder? Did you count the steps required and figure out a more efficient way to do it next time?"

Calder's brow rose. "Not necessary. I had the servants guide the guests to spots ranked in order of importance, so that I would not waste time crisscrossing the room."

Rafe saw Phoebe's startled gaze go to Calder's face. Her expression was priceless. *Is he quite serious?*

Rafe laughed sharply. "He is entirely serious, Miss Millbury."

Phoebe's eyes locked with his. Something jolted through him, something sweet and fiery. *At last.*

He hardened himself against that rare allure and bowed stiffly. "You are looking every inch the future marchioness this evening, Miss Millbury. Did my brother choose your gown?"

She might have flinched, he could not tell. Then her eyes became entirely without expression and she returned his bow with a very proper curtsy. "I am flattered that you think so, my lord. It was chosen on my dressmaker's recommendation, in fact. Why do you ask?"

Nothing. She was again as lifeless as a stone—perfectly carved and faceted and glittering, but without any light of its own. He must have been drunker than he thought last night at the ball.

Then she rose from her perfect curtsy and raised her gaze to his once more.

Rafe had felt electricity once, at a scientific demonstration. He'd been the only one brave enough to touch the tip of the wire when the fellow had urged them all to feel this astonishing new force. That nip of startling energy was nothing next to the fierce jolt of thrilling possessiveness that tore through him at the miserable longing in her eyes.

*She is mine.*

His woman—on his brother's arm. His woman—soon to be in his brother's house, in his brother's bed.

Then she glanced away and the spell was broken.

The glint of gold caught Rafe's eye. He clutched at

anything to take his mind off her. He bent forward to peer at his brother's cravat pin. "The Minotaur?" He straightened, one eyebrow raised.

Calder patted his cravat. "A gift from my intended," he said smugly.

A harsh bark of laughter escaped Rafe. He covered it with a cough as he glanced at Phoebe. Her gaze was averted, but her cheeks were pink and her lips were pursed. She was trying not to laugh as well.

Calder, of course, missed the joke entirely. "What?"

"Your brother finds it most fitting, I believe," Phoebe said demurely. "Although I could be mistaken." She did not so much as cast Rafe a glance as they walked away, every inch the grand new couple of the ton.

Rafe felt confusion tangle with his earlier desire. He had the distinct feeling that there were two entirely different Miss Phoebe Millburys living side by side behind that now-distant blue gaze.

Which was mad, of course. He was imagining the flashes of desire in her eyes. She was no more than a pretty girl, like a hundred others. If Calder wanted her, he could have her.

So why did that thought not have the finality it should? Perhaps because he'd already thought it a hundred times today and it still didn't ring true.

HE WAS STILL tall. He was still achingly handsome. He was still just a tiny bit lost beneath his dashing demeanor.

He was the wrong man. Phoebe turned her back on Marbrook, determined to give Brookhaven the chance she'd secretly promised him. "You set great store by efficiency, don't you, my lord?"

"Indeed. When I was but thirteen, my father made sure I understood that I would someday have guardianship of not one, but two major estates. He said, 'You'll have to be in two places at once, lad.' "

"An intimidating prospect!" And a heavy load to place on a thirteen-year-old boy's narrow shoulders.

"To be sure. In order to prepare for that day, I began to investigate efficiency. I became fascinated by the new practices being used in some of the more modern factories. I bought my first factory when I was twenty-one. Since then I have accumulated a great many—and all are more productive now than when I purchased them."

Phoebe feared her eyes were beginning to glaze over. "I'm sure it's a most diverting pastime," she said, trying not to give away the fact that she'd only heard every fourth word.

A brief silence made her realize she'd said something wrong. She glanced up to see the beginning of a faint scowl on his handsome face. What could it have been? She'd called his passion a pastime—yet he was a marquis! What more could it ever be? As she understood the nature of all things aristocratic, his ancestral lands ought to be his priority, not his widget makers.

Still, best to cover as well as possible. "And so . . . productive!"

He grunted slightly, but she thought he seemed appeased. It was so blasted difficult to read his various and sundry nonexpressions!

She racked her mind for something to fill the wounded silence. "Can not your brother take some of the burden from your shoulders? Two estates, two sons—it seems most . . . *efficient* to me."

The sudden and utter silence from Brookhaven—and everyone within a ten-foot circle!—made her realize she'd done it again, but worse. She looked about, but everyone carefully did not meet her gaze.

What had she said? Brookhaven had a brother, she—if anyone!—knew that was a fact.

A deep voice spoke at her ear. "Half brother, Miss Millbury."

She turned her head to see Marbrook next to her, his eyes dark and furious and a slight, wry smile on his lips.

"My lord?"

He leaned closer, until she could feel the warmth of his breath on her ear. "From the wrong half of the bed, you see."

Oh, God. Marbrook was a bastard—which was obviously such common knowledge that no one had seen the need to mention it. The family name and the "lord" were some sort of courtesy, then. He must be one of those rare accepted bastards.

No inheritance, no grand title, no estate. So little, when his half brother had so much!

"Ah." She gazed helplessly at Marbrook. What could she say? "I'm . . . sorry?"

His lips twitched. "Don't be. You had nothing to do with it. It was all the old marquis's doing." He raised his gaze to meet Brookhaven's, his smile turning into something altogether darker and fraught with meaning she couldn't interpret—except to guess that Marbrook wasn't entirely happy with his lot. "Isn't that right, Calder?"

"Indeed." Brookhaven's tone was dry. He gazed at Marbrook with stolid dislike. "What a fine Michaelmas gift it was, too. A brand-new brother, just my size, to take half the toys."

Marbrook chuckled without humor. "And all the girls."

"Not all." Brookhaven's hand tightened over Phoebe's, pressing it firmly into his arm. He turned to her. "Come, my dear. You haven't met our neighbors from the north."

Phoebe went, for Brookhaven's grip was rather implacable, but as she left she cast a glance over her shoulder at Marbrook. He stood in the center of the drawing room, tall and rigid and alone, his dark eyes locked on hers.

*Don't walk away from me*, his gaze commanded.

She had no choice but to turn away.

# Chapter Eighteen

Moments after Brookhaven walked Phoebe away from Marbrook he found an excuse to slip from the room. Apparently he'd not been as crafty as he'd thought, for he was followed almost at once.

Phoebe caught up with him in the hall. "Marbrook, wait!"

Rafe stopped reluctantly. She came even with him and dropped the skirts she had picked up to run. Her cheeks were pink and that flicker of vulnerability shone again in her blue eyes.

"Yes?"

She took a deep breath. "I'm so sorry about—no one told me about your . . . birth. I didn't know."

Now he knew he hadn't lost her due to his lack of birthright. That must mean that she was after the title.

He raised his brows with polite inquiry. *Yes. Be merely polite.* "I see. Is there anything else?"

She flushed anew and looked down at her hands. Pressing her palms over the wrinkles she'd just made in the blue silk, she kept her gaze low. "No. I simply wished . . . to thank you for not mentioning last evening to your brother."

"There was nothing to tell. We danced and we talked. This morning you accepted my brother's proposal of marriage."

"My lord, did you . . . were you merely interested in me for Lord Brookhaven's sake?" That part came out in a rush. Her cheeks grew pink but she gazed steadily at him, determined to have the answer.

"Does it matter?" *Yes, it matters!* No, it could not. Not ever. "Yes, I pointed you out to my brother. Evidently, he liked what he saw. You accepted him, so you must have as well."

Phoebe felt something new and precious start to die inside her. Yet she knew from personal experience that one magical night didn't necessarily mean dreams came true. "I see. So you checked the teeth of a horse he wanted to buy, is that it?"

"If that is how you choose to perceive it." Something dark flickered behind his eyes.

Abruptly Phoebe wanted nothing to do with either of them. Calder was cold and stern, Rafe was obviously capricious in the extreme.

Yet to walk away from such an advantageous match? It was a hard world. She must take care of herself. A wealthy titled lady had a better chance of doing that than a tarnished vicar's daughter.

So she gave a polite smile, the one she could do in her sleep—the one, it turned out, that she could smile while her heart was tearing itself in two. She curtsied and then straightened and held out her hand. "Well, since you are not bothered by it, neither shall I be. Shall we go in to dinner?"

Abruptly Rafe regretted his own distance. Where had she gone? He missed her already. He stepped closer, then a bit too close, until he could feel her soft breath and detect the subtle floral scent of her skin.

He came closer, until she could feel the fire emanating from him. It was more exciting than a touch, for she was doing no wrong. She was simply standing, her hands at her sides, her eyes downcast. No wanton recklessness, no deviation from her path.

It was only that he was *there,* so close she could feel that heat, smell the fine, clean male scent of him, let it fill her lungs without regret. She was only breathing, after all.

She studied his boots and the way the finished leather clung to his ankles and muscled calves. Her gaze shifted slightly higher almost without thought—although she was still being most well-behaved—and she let her eyes drink in the sight of his long, rippling thighs. He was so close she could see every shift of his body in those thighs. The muscles swelled and relaxed, swelled and—oh, heavens, *that* wasn't a muscle!

She must shut her eyes and turn away. She must feel shocked and demeaned by his earthly . . . er, display!

Then again, her lids were still lowered, her lashes still hiding the direction of her gaze. Who was to know if she peeked a bit?

She peeked. A great deal.

His male organ lay to one side, along his thigh, pointing at a downward slant. As it stiffened—why would it do that, when she was only standing before him in a most demure state?—as it grew and filled before her eyes, something like heat began to gather in the pit of her stomach.

No one could see it, of course, so there was no danger. It was only that her thighs began to tense in response, for it felt so good to squeeze slightly against the rising pressure inside her. Her breasts felt odd as well, the tips tingling and tightening—something she hoped he was ignorant of. She was safe, silent and unrevealing in her growing desire. No one knew.

When Phoebe raised her gaze to Rafe's, he could see nothing in their blue depths. She made no reaction at all. No spark, no fire, not even predictable virginal jitters at his presumption.

*She smells like Eden.*

Any woman could wear perfume. Most women who bathed smelled fairly nice.

*She would be warm and soft in your arms, in your bed. She would bear fat, laughing babies and smile at you over breakfast for all of the years of your life.*

Again, nothing unique there. Most women could fill that bill.

*She could make you forget any other woman.*

*Or perhaps she already has.*

The chilling danger of that thought made him step back swiftly. "I'll be along in a moment," he said hoarsely. God, don't let her detect the naked need he heard in his own voice. "Go—go in to Calder. I'm sure he's waiting for you. You're better off with him, anyway." He smiled, a bitter slice of white in the shadowy hall. "You've probably heard all about me by now."

She gazed at him soberly. "You are generally considered to be a rake, a rotter, and a bounder. You neglected to mention that when I asked."

He shrugged, his smile growing sharper. "I lied. That is what rakes, rotters, and bounders do, you know."

She nodded. "So I've noticed." She lifted her chin. "Well, we will be seeing a great deal of each other in the future. You should know that I—I don't hold last evening against you. What is past, is past."

He bowed briskly. "That's big of you, Miss Millbury. I'll endeavor to do the same."

"Oh." She blinked. He could see her confusion—*what did I do to him?* What indeed? After all, no woman in her right mind would choose the black sheep when they could have the golden boy, would she?

She raised her chin and smiled that perfect, remote smile that revealed absolutely nothing. "I shall see you at dinner, then."

Rafe despised that smile.

She turned and walked away, a portrait in serene uncon-cern. Rafe watched her go, letting something die inside him.


TESSA STEPPED AWAY from the door, with its fascinating view of the hallway, and moved smoothly back into the guests gathered in the drawing room.

That wretched vicar's daughter had a secret . . . and now so did Tessa.

For Tessa knew that Phoebe was a volatile creature—like gunpowder, she was perfectly safe until someone put a match to her.

The handsome, notorious Lord Raphael Marbrook might just be the man to do it.

It seemed the game might not yet be won, after all.

When Phoebe reentered the room, Tessa was speaking to Deirdre in the far corner. When Lord Marbrook rejoined them, Tessa was smiling at Lord Brookhaven, laughing though he'd made no joke at all.

What an intriguing evening this was turning out to be.

# Chapter Nineteen

Later that night, after the guests had all given her their goodbyes and congratulations, Phoebe paced her room in her nightdress, feeling caged and twitchy like a captive animal.

Never before had she felt like such an impostor. She was no marchioness! She certainly wasn't what any of them saw in her—not even Sophie, who thought her so fortunate—and she certainly wasn't the proper virtuous vicar's daughter that Brookhaven saw!

Marbrook had seen her. He was the only one who had ever seen past the pose—and she had mucked it up.

*Would you have truly tied yourself to a scandalous bastard?*

The very thought filled her with dread. *Scandal follows Marbrook like a faithful hound.*

Doubt plagued her. She thought she saw more in him than the rest of the world, but what if she was wrong? What if she was only being duped again. She had believed in Terrence absolutely and look what had happened.

How could she be sure? Even Marbrook himself didn't deny his history. No. She was where she ought to be, and if she was not the woman they thought her, then she must try very hard to become her . . . she must become the marchioness—and someday the duchess.

And soon.

One of the guests, Lady Oh-would-she-never-remember-all-these-names?, was asking Brookhaven about the wedding plans. Brookhaven looked up, his expression one of faint surprise. "I've posted the banns and the church has been secured for that date. I need no more plan than that."

Every lady at the table had gasped in simultaneous horror. Phoebe didn't wish a prominent display, of course. Girlish daydreams of a romantic and opulent celebration didn't seem to matter when the transaction was as businesslike as theirs.

*No flowers? No wedding breakfast with rose-petal gelatin and cream? No smiling, happy crowd to wish the new couple well?*

No, she told the voice firmly. It was silly and wasteful and . . .

*And a mockery of what might have been?*

There could be no repeat of this evening's silent moments of communion with Marbrooks. For the next fortnight in Brook House she would be in close proximity with him—God, perhaps sleeping mere yards from his room! Seeing him at breakfast and at tea and—she closed her eyes at the horror of it—more eternal, heart-aching dinners like tonight!

Even at this very moment, Marbrook was in his room . . . perhaps in his nightshirt . . . or perhaps bathing, wearing nothing but warm soapsuds and the glow of the fire on his muscled body—

Two more weeks of it, and then more, if he stayed in the house—her house!—after the wedding. A horrible thought struck her, making her wrap her arms about her stomach and nearly double over.

He would be in the same house on her wedding night—only a few steps away while she was giving herself to Brookhaven—there'd be no way to hide it, everyone knew, so he would be aware of every moment that she betrayed him—

No. Wait. She would be Brookhaven's wife.

In love with Brookhaven's brother. Who was she betraying there?

She clutched at her head, willing the conflicting thoughts to subside. Please stop. Please let it be simple. Why wasn't it simple?

A tentative knock on her door. Sophie. Thank God!

She threw open the door, grabbed Sophie's hand and dragged her into the room. "Sophie, you must help me. I've made the most tremendous error! I cannot marry him!"

Sophie blinked. "You don't like his lordship after all?"

Phoebe sat on the bed, not caring if she wrinkled the counterpane, and buried her face in her hands. "I like his lordship's brother better," she murmured, a frantic, panicked laugh escaping her, cracking her voice.

"What? Please sit up and talk to me, Phoebe. I can't understand a word you're saying."

No, she couldn't tell anyone, not even Sophie. Oh, heavens, the vicar's face if he found out!

Lifting her face from her hands, Phoebe forced an awkward smile. "It is nothing. It is only that I am just now realizing that all of this is real."

Sophie sat down next to her. "You are very lucky, Phoebe. You know that, don't you? A fine, handsome man wants you to be his wife. Do you realize what that is worth?"

Phoebe nodded, knowing what Sophie was saying—that Sophie herself would never have such an opportunity. She took her cousin's hand in hers. "You'll get one too, Sophie, see if you don't!"

Sophie shrugged, her gaze going dreamy once more. "I've already gained more than I ever thought I would. New adventures . . ." A small smile crossed her lips. "New friends."

Phoebe took a breath. "Yes. Friends." Marbrook would make a marvelous friend. He'd been the only one to understand the stock pin. If she could ever forget the way he'd made her feel before—and the way he made her feel tonight, simply by standing near her in the hall!—then she might yet manage to be his friend.

She turned to gaze out over the dark night garden.

Someday.

A WAXING MOON brightened the garden, but not enough to dim the red tip of Rafe's lit cheroot as he lurked in the shadows.

*I'm not lurking. It's my garden, after all.*

Or not really. It was Calder's garden. Brook House was Calder's house. Bloody Calder.

Rafe reluctantly allowed his gaze upward once more to the large square of light on the wall above. Phoebe's room—the pretty green one with the view of the garden—the one Rafe had suggested to Fortescue that morning.

She'd liked it. She'd liked the chocolates as well, Fortescue had told him. Rafe felt ridiculous, depending on secondhand information like a schoolboy with a crush, yet he hung on every word.

A shadow moved before the window. He went still. Then the gleam of auburn and the lithe silhouette told him it was the maid, Patricia. He blew out a stream of smoke, discouraged and mightily disgusted with himself.

Not so disgusted that he left, however.

A while later, another shadow—this one altogether more buxom and soft. He straightened. *Phoebe.* Honeyed light struck her hair as she leaned against the embrasure and gazed out at the garden. He couldn't see the color of her eyes from here but he could imagine them softened, like a twilight sky.

Yearning tore at him. Why? What was this hideous ache, over a girl he barely knew?

He ought to fling himself out into the city and take up with the first likely widow who happened by! Tossing down his cheroot, he stamped it out with emphasis. He would, by God! Right now!

She turned her head in his direction. He froze. She lifted a hand to swipe surreptitiously at her eyes, so the maid wouldn't see.

There could be a thousand reasons for her tears. She could be weeping for someone passed, like her mother. She could be weeping for any one of the lost souls lurking in the dire London streets at this god-forsaken hour. She could be weeping for joy.

Fiery hope detonated within him.

Those tears belonged to him. He couldn't say how he knew, but he *knew*.

She wept for him, even as he stood out in the cold like a cast-off hound, shivering for her warmth.

She wept for *him*.

# *Chapter Twenty*

By the next morning the invitations had already begun pouring in. Phoebe sat at the table with Deirdre and Sophie in the comfortable breakfast room at Brook House, sifting through the vast pile. "I don't even know most of these people."

"Well, the Marchioness of Brookhaven will." Deirdre didn't bother to hide her peevishness. "Did you think things would remain the same?"

"Not that I'd mind," Sophie interjected slowly, "but I think Tessa would dislike it if you accepted invitations that did not include all of us."

Deirdre snorted into her teacup. "I think Tessa would have kittens, but don't let that stop you." She put down her cup and leaned forward. "Or accept none of them. Brookhaven won't care. He despises social events."

Phoebe blinked. "He does? How do you know?"

Deirdre stared at her. "How do you not? It is obvious the man would rather tot accounts than dance a step."

What a relief, if that were true. Then again, why not behave as if it were until proven otherwise? Phoebe smiled and nodded at her cousins. "Thank you. I will take your advice. After all, Tessa can hardly feel slighted if I decline them all."

Deirdre leaned back in her chair and shook her head, a

dry smile on her lips. "Never underestimate Tessa's ability to take offense. She's quite expert."

Sophie glanced at Deirdre nervously, then back at Phoebe. "There's something else."

Phoebe smiled. "What did I miss?"

Deirdre heaved a sigh. "You won't like it. I would, but you're not the sort to appreciate it."

Phoebe looked from Deirdre to Sophie. "What is this? Tell me."

Sophie drew a folded newssheet from behind her back. She hesitantly handed it across the table to Phoebe.

Laughing, Phoebe picked it up. "Look at your faces! What could possibly be so—"

There she was, on the front page of the newssheet. The drawing was spare and hurriedly done, as if someone had only a moment to catch her likeness as she paused, but it was most definitely her. Next to her image was one of Brookhaven, although his was more finished, making her seem wispy and insubstantial next to him.

She and Brookhaven, on the front page of the most popular newssheet in London—her face sent out all over the city and beyond—her face handed out by newsboys on every street corner. She closed her eyes in horror, then opened them again, unable to look away.

*"Brookhaven Chooses a Bride! Vicar's daughter snatches up London's premier bachelor before the Season is fully under way! Mary Mouse and the Marquis!"*

If the headlines were bad, the text was worse. *"Your Voice of Society has discovered that Miss Phoebe Millbury has only been in town for a week, yet she has managed to do what three Seasons of London's loveliest young ladies have failed to accomplish—she has caught the eye and the betrothal of one of England's most desirable men, the dashing Brookhaven! Moreover, she did it in last year's sprigged muslin with puffed sleeves, if you can believe it!"*

Phoebe felt her belly tremble. She carefully put the gossip sheet on the table and cleared her throat. "Mary Mouse?"

Deirdre popped a bite of sausage into her mouth. "The country mouse. From the story."

Phoebe inhaled and exhaled, but it didn't ease the tightness in her chest. Her face began to go numb. Sophie jumped up in alarm.

"Dee, she's going to faint!"

Sophie and Deirdre made it to her just in time. They eased her back into her chair and made her lean forward until her head hung in front of her knees.

"Just breathe," Deirdre urged, her voice not unkind. "You'll get used to all this soon enough, I imagine. After all, as the Duchess of Brookmoor, you'll be in the papers every time you sneeze."

Phoebe whimpered.

"Dee, you aren't helping," Sophie hissed.

"No." Phoebe straightened, one hand pressed to her breast bone to make sure her lungs were still in working order. "No, she's quite right. I just never thought about it like that—" *And I thought I'd be facing it with Marbrook instead.*

Every eye upon her, every move she might make watched by all of Society and beyond . . .

*So, let them stare. You'll be a duchess.*

A rich duchess, wealthy in her own right. Immune.

Yes, she must not forget that word.

*Immune.*

Her breathing steadied and she could feel her color rise once more. She smiled up at her cousins. "Thank you. I'm all right now."

Deirdre snorted as she returned to her chair. "I should hope so. You're the luckiest woman in London and yet you faint over a little gossip. Milksop."

Phoebe smile wryly. Apparently Deirdre had a very

shallow well of concern in her soul. Probably best not to tap it too deeply. "You're right. Besides, who really reads these things, anyway?"

Both cousins stared at her blankly. "Everyone," Sophie said. Deirdre nodded, chewing.

"Oh." Well, no matter. It was all such a lot of nonsense. She would not be ruled either way by it.

Soon, she would be immune.

SOPHIE FOUND THE family parlor empty and sighed with relief. The library was not nearly as pleasant as this sunny room, especially now in early afternoon—not that the murmuring presence of the vicar would stop her if it were the only place she could be alone.

Of course, Brook House was far superior to the previous small house in that respect. Wherever she had turned there had been a cousin or an aunt or a dratted servant wishing her to *do* something. She was accustomed to rattling about in an old, large manor house where servants were rarely spotted and easily avoided. Only the bell pulled from her mother's bedside drew her away from her studies and the quiet days stretched on and on.

Here in London, however, life moved at a much faster pace—one which Sophie enjoyed as long as she was left alone to observe it, not participate in it.

And why should she? The competition for the Pickering fortune mattered nothing to her, for she had no chance of winning against elegant, stylish Deirdre or pretty, buxom Phoebe. The only reason she'd come was to escape Acton and her eternal servitude there.

Seating herself at the card table, Sophie spread out her notes on the folklore collection she was translating from the original German. Such entrancing stories . . .

# Chapter Twenty~one

Phoebe was hiding from Tessa, who was on a riotous tear about something—last night's sweeping defeat at the hands of Marbrook, probably, although Tessa would never admit to it—so the wise choice seemed to be tactful retreat.

The attractively shabby—although still very fine—family parlor was empty but for Sophie's stories spread out on the game table. Phoebe wandered over to peer at them without disturbing them.

Deirdre appeared in the doorway. "Oh." She looked reluctant to enter, but then, after casting a glance over her shoulder, she joined Phoebe in the parlor and shut the doors.

Phoebe had been hiding from people in general, but Deirdre was high on the list of "in particular." She bit back a sigh. "So who are *you* hiding from, Dee?"

Deirdre tossed her head and smiled confidently. "Why, no one! What a silly question." Still, she flung herself down onto the settee and lounged rather more horizontally than was proper. Flinging one arm over her eyes, she let out the sigh that Phoebe hadn't allowed herself.

Phoebe eyed the door, although to be honest, she didn't want to brave the tigress. Tessa didn't actually want to see her and Phoebe didn't actually want to cross the path of her vision, so it was for their mutual benefit that Phoebe stay put.

She sat in one of the chairs at the card table and smoothed

her skirts. She would have loved to lounge the way Deirdre was doing, but she felt the weight of "your ladyship" on her shoulders. Instead, she leaned her head back and closed her eyes.

The door burst open and Sophie darted into the room. She shut it behind her as if pursued by a pack of wolves, then turned to see Phoebe and Deirdre, who had uncovered her eyes, staring at her.

"Oh." Sophie looked as though she were contemplating returning to the wolves. "I only left for a moment . . . I was out of ink."

Phoebe couldn't help but laugh. "Why don't we all just sit and pretend the others aren't here?"

Deirdre smiled slightly and crooked her arm over her face again. Sophie looked from one to the other, then took the other chair next to Phoebe.

Phoebe closed her eyes again, still smiling. She'd wondered if she would find anything in common with her cousins. Now she knew there was one thing the three shared. They all feared Tessa's wrath.

Someone cleared their throat near her. She opened her eyes to see Sophie hovering, a crinkle of worry appearing between her eyes. Phoebe shook her head. "Don't worry, I didn't touch a thing. I didn't even read it. Should I get out of your way?"

Sophie's mute desperation told her enough to spur her to her weary feet. "Perhaps I'll retreat to my room," she said unenthusiastically.

"Don't." Deirdre spoke without uncovering her eyes. "You'll never make it through alive." Then she rolled over, propping herself up on her elbows. "Believe me when I say that. I *know*."

Phoebe sagged. "I'm sure you do."

Sophie pulled the other chair back to the card table. "We can share, if you like," she said shyly. "Would—would you like to read my translations? On my journey to London I came across a true find in a bookshop." Her eyes glowed. "It is a collection of folk tales from Germany."

Frankly, Phoebe would rather bang her head against the floor than read some dry text, but when the alternative was an early demise at Tessa's spiteful hands . . .

She sat and leaned forward to look at the paper nearest her. "Will it take long?"

"Oh!" Sophie was all eagerness and enthusiasm. "You'll simply love it, I promise!" She took up the paper Phoebe had been eyeing warily. "This is one of my favorites so far. It's really rather romantic—" She faltered, as if waiting for Deirdre to poke fun, but Dee was listening willingly enough. Apparently any form of diversion won out over facing Tessa.

Sophie cleared her throat and took a breath. *"In times of old there lived a king and queen, and every day they said, 'Oh, if only we had a child!' Yet, they never had one. Then, one day, as the queen went out bathing, a frog happened to crawl ashore and say to her, 'Your wish shall be fulfilled. Before the year is out, you shall give birth to a daughter.'"*[1]

Deirdre snorted. "A frog? A talking, wish-granting frog?"

Phoebe turned sharply. "Shh! Or I'll tell Tessa you're lying on the sofa, wrinkling your gown."

Deirdre quailed. "Oh, very well."

Sophie sent Phoebe a grateful glance and took another breath. Her voice came out stronger this time, more sure. *"The frog's prediction came true, and the queen gave birth to a girl who was so beautiful that the king was overjoyed and decided to hold a great feast. Not only did he invite his relatives, friends, and acquaintances, but also the wise women, in the hope that they would be generous and kind to his daughter."*

[1]Jack Zipes, *The Complete Fairy Tales of the Brothers Grimm*, New York (Bantam Books), 1987, p. 186.

Soon Phoebe found herself entranced by the tale, read in Sophie's breathy, light voice—which was very pretty, now that she listened carefully to it. There was a curse, which was exciting, and an evil wise woman, which was distressing, and an innocent young girl of fifteen—

*Weren't we all?*

Phoebe swallowed back a surge of bad memory and focused on Sophie's narrative. A girl, who—through no fault of her own—was sentenced to a magical sleep . . .

Sophie stopped reading and put down the paper.

"What?" Deirdre sat up from her sprawl on the sofa. "That's it? That can't be it! She spends forever shut up in her castle behind a wall of thorns?"

Phoebe was gathering a bit of upset herself. "I can't believe that—"

Sophie shook her head. "Oh, no—there's more. I simply haven't finished translating it yet."

Phoebe shot up from her chair and pushed Sophie down into it. "Go. Begin. Translate."

"Yes," Deirdre added. "Translate like the wind."

Sophie blushed, pleased. "Do you really like it? I thought I might bind them when I'm done—"

Deirdre raised her hand. "Less talking. More working."

An endless hour later, the next paragraph was done. The hapless princess was still trapped and now countless fine young would-be suitors had died, impaled upon the thorns.

Deirdre refolded her handkerchief to find a drier spot. "All those handsome princes . . . such a terrible waste."

Phoebe sniffed. "The poor princess . . . locked away, punished forever . . ."

Sophie dabbed frantically at her notes, trying to dry her own tears from the paper before the work was ruined. "All those people, their lives frozen still . . ."

A good bawl was had by all, in fact. Phoebe felt the better for it, and even waspish Deirdre seemed softer around the edges afterward. Sophie leaned back in her chair, one hand limp on her midriff. "I can't do any more. I'm exhausted and my eyes burn." She took off her spectacles and glared down at them. "I hate you."

"As well you should," Deirdre agreed. "Spectacles are guaranteed man-repellent. Which is odd, when one considers it. I mean, most men aren't really interested in one's eyes, are they?"

Sophie turned to her, squinting. "What do you mean?"

"Teats and arse," Dee said flippantly.

Sophie gasped, but Phoebe only burst into horrified giggles. "She's right."

Sophie fixed her spectacles back over her ears and gazed from one to the other. "Really?"

They nodded as one. Sophie shook her head. "Then it's a good thing I'm not on a husband hunt, for I'm sorely short on bait."

"You've enough to catch a very short, very poor sort of banker person," Deirdre consoled her. "Perhaps someone bookish."

Sophie blinked. "Bookish would be all right, I suppose . . ." Then she shook her head, covering her face with her hands. "But I'm such a clumsy ninny whenever I—" She raised her face and gazed at them hopelessly. "I can't even *talk* to a man without—you simply don't know!"

Phoebe tilted her head. "You talk to men all the time. There are several male servants in the house."

Sophie drew back and shook her head. "I don't speak to them."

Deirdre leaned forward, rather as if she were repelled and fascinated at once. "Never?"

"That's ridiculous," Phoebe said. "You must speak to the menservants at Acton—"

Sophie shook her head again. "We haven't any. Mama says that deep voices hurt her head."

"But your vicar—?"

"We've only a sexton, but no. He visits Mama, but he likely thinks I can't speak."

Phoebe threw up her hands. "But the—the butcher? The blacksmith? Little boys playing in your way on the village street?"

Sophie shrugged. "The cook negotiates with the butcher and we've no horses and little boys usually run when they see me coming."

"A world without men," Deirdre breathed. "I don't know whether to be horrified or envious."

Phoebe made a face. "I'm a little of both, I think." What would her life be like without the vicar's harsh disapproval shadowing her all day—

But those days were over, weren't they? She was her father's "dear" once again. Bolstered by that thought, she dusted her hands in a businesslike way. "Deirdre, stand up. Sophie, fetch that book on the table."

Soon she had Deirdre pacing sedately about the room, demonstrating the classic feat of ladylike grace, although why in the world one needed to know how to carry a book on their head was apparently beyond Sophie.

"That looks ridiculous."

Phoebe put her hands on her hips. "Well, it was the only thing I learned from my brief and bitter bout with a governess. If you can do it, you'll never have to worry about being clumsy in front of a man again. Just try it."

Deirdre paced back and forth, the picture of elegance. She sat, stood, curtsied, and even danced while the book remained as if nailed to her crown. Phoebe was moved to applause. Deirdre ducked out from under the book, caught it with one hand, and bowed theatrically, the book acting as a sweeping feathered cap. "Tessa, if nothing else, is a persistent teacher," she said with a grimace.

Sophie's evident doubt only grew. "I'll never be able to

do that. Just thinking about having to speak . . . converse . . . heavens, you don't mean to make me dance—" She swept her arms wide in her distress.

A cut-crystal vase crashed to the floor as Sophie stood like a simpleton, watching it fall.

Phoebe looked at her strangely. Deirdre tossed the book onto a side table and plunked her fists on her hips. "Honestly, Sophie, how do you ever expect to marry a man if you can't even think about one without spontaneously shattering valuables?"

Sophie paled, then flushed. The shards of vase lay winking derisively on the carpet. The door burst open and Tessa came striding in, her skirts hiked in one hand.

"Oh, for pity's sake! What happened to the crystal?" Her tone so matched Deirdre's that for a moment Phoebe thought it was her cousin speaking again.

Then Deirdre stepped forward. "So sorry, Lady Tessa. I was showing Sophie how you taught me to walk balancing something on my head."

Tessa smoothed her skirts and rolled her eyes. "Well, next time use something unimportant, like a book! Not that it will do Sophie any good. If you don't learn that sort of thing by the time you leave the schoolroom, Sophie, it will never look natural."

She waved vaguely at the mess. "Do have someone sweep that up, Deirdre."

Sophie tilted her head to whisper to Deirdre with some surprise. "Why did you lie?"

Deirdre smiled slightly. "What a thing to say! I never lie."

Sophie looked at Phoebe, who only laughed helplessly and spread her hands. "She didn't actually lie, you realize," she whispered. "She *was* showing you the walk."

Instead of her former pout, Tessa now had a sly look of satisfaction on her lovely face.

"Thanks to Brookhaven's status in Society," she announced, "the guest list for the wedding ceremony contains the very finest of Society. The splendor of this event will reflect directly upon me, so I will have everything just so. I have left the tedious details to the staff, of course. Phoebe, you will assist me. Deirdre, you will see to your wardrobe, for you will never have another chance like this one to meet the most eligible men in London. Sophie . . ." Tessa grimaced. "Just . . . do something with your hair and try not to fall on your face during the ceremony."

Sophie's attention was on her table full of notes. "Mm. Yes, Aunt."

"Phoebe, come along now. We have much to do."

# Chapter Twenty~two

Wedding plans would have to wait for a while, unfortunately. That afternoon, the parlor of Brook House was filled to the brim with callers. Phoebe's engagement had rocketed her into an entirely different social stratum and apparently no one wanted to miss out on their chance to ride along.

For hours there was a constantly shifting parade of anyone who had ever been introduced—or wanted to believe they had been introduced—to the cousins in the brief week they'd been in town.

Sophie wasn't taking it well, it being her own personal version of hell. Phoebe was coping fairly well, until she began to notice an annoying trend of clumpy, off-center buns on the young ladies who came by.

Deirdre only rolled her eyes when Phoebe mentioned it to her. "You should be flattered. They're all trying to figure out how you did it, so they can do it, too."

"It" translating as "bagging a marquis in seven days or less."

Phoebe frowned. "My hair doesn't look that bad from the back, does it?"

Deirdre smiled. "Keep telling yourself that," she said, then turned back to her gaggle of ganders, led by a particularly ardent young poet by the name of Baskin, who was inclined to spiel long-winded verses about Deirdre's eyes and hair—all very "moon" and "June." The afternoon seemed to stretch on forever, while Phoebe began thinking longingly of the wedding planning still to do. Apparently, Deirdre could hold court for hours, although her disappointment in the rank of those involved found itself revealed in small, smiling barbs that were greeted as wit by all who were not targeted.

Sophie did her duty, remaining seated in the farthest corner, evidently engrossed in a book. Phoebe did her best to seem interested and polite, but her thoughts revolved around only one man.

"Lord Raphael Marbrook!"

*Rafe.* Phoebe's eyes flew open, her spirits instantly rising, filling like a sail in the wind.

He stood in the doorway, tall, dark, broad-shouldered . . . and beautiful. The room became smaller and emptier at once, as if the other gentlemen were nothing but shimmers on water beside the solid masculinity he exuded.

He was clad in dark colors—almost mourning-black—and his face was absolutely expressionless, as if he'd rather be anywhere else in the world but in his own parlor.

His brother's parlor, actually. Phoebe knew that bothered him, though he'd told her no such thing. How could she know that? How could she know that he'd had to force himself to come in here, that he intended to leave as soon as humanly possible, and that, in spite of all that, he'd been unable to stay away?

Because that was precisely how she felt. The only reason she was truly here and not hiding in her solitary guest room was that somewhere deep within her, she'd been hoping to catch a glimpse of him today.

He looked away and the connection broke, leaving Phoebe feeling odd and a bit foolish. What a world of fantasy she was building concerning Lord Marbrook!

By the mooning expressions of the other young ladies in the room—with the exception of Sophie, who was staring out the window, and Deirdre, who was far too pragmatic to moon—Lord Marbrook affected all women that way, including several of the nongeriatric chaperones . . . although a few of those were giving him the eye as well.

He took up residence with one elbow on the mantel and began to exchange laconic comments with a few of the more highborn gentlemen in the room. He bestowed pretty words on the nearest ladies, greeted Deirdre, Sophie, and Phoebe *en masse,* and apparently timed his departure to fourteen and a half minutes after entering.

As he turned away, Phoebe was treated to her second favorite view of him—second only to full eye contact—the flexing of his tightly muscled arse as he walked away.

*Extraordinary.*

"Well, Miss Millbury, then I suppose it's a good thing the brothers look so much alike. I believe your betrothed has one of those, as well," one young woman said loudly with a trilling laugh.

Phoebe froze. Oh, no. Oh, *drat.* She'd said it out loud—while gazing longingly at Marbrook's bottom—in a roomful of self-proclaimed wits who were more than a little bit envious of the social accomplishment of Mary Mouse.

"Don't let her get away with that, Ph—Miss Millbury." It was Marbrook's warm voice in her ear. "Go on."

He'd returned to the group, settling next to her on the sofa even as she'd found herself skewered by the Society woman's challenge. Phoebe didn't—couldn't!—look at him, but she felt the solid heat of him like an outpouring of strength soaking into her.

"Give her what for," he whispered.

"I suppose," she heard herself say loudly, "it is true that—unlike some—I am engaged." She knew what to do now. She gave all present a mischievous smile. "However, last I checked, I am not yet dead."

Laughter echoed through the room. Mary Mouse or Marchioness—either way she'd scored a point and all knew it. The girl took it well, considering. Her eyelids drooped slightly, acknowledging a worthy adversary, then she turned back to idly charming the few men who were not in Deirdre's thrall.

Phoebe took a deep breath, then turned to thank Marbrook for his support. The place beside her was empty. She looked toward the door, only to see a broad back disappearing from the room.

# Chapter Twenty-three

The callers were gone and the servants were setting the formal front parlor to rights, cleaning up escaped tea cake crumbs and blotting drops of tea from the fine furniture. Rafe passed the room by, smiling reluctantly to himself as he thought of Phoebe's touché earlier.

As one ventured more deeply into the house, one found other, more comfortable rooms that callers rarely saw. To Rafe, the contentedly overstuffed family parlor of Brook House had never seemed so inviting.

From where he stood in the doorway, he could see the top of a fair head, the tip of a pert nose, and an entirely delicious view down a lace-edged bodice. Phoebe had apparently given up on keeping her lists sorted out on the card table and had moved the entire planning of the wedding to the carpet where there was more room to spread them out.

She sat very properly on the sofa, but had leaned so far over to read her lists that she might as well have sat on the floor. While Rafe watched, she chewed intently on the end of her pencil and jiggled her heels against the floor. Other parts jiggled companionably along.

She was adorable. She drew him like a bee to her bright bloom. Rafe took four heedless steps into the room before he could stop himself. She noticed his boots come into her range of vision.

"Oh!" She looked up and her eyes brightened at seeing him. He smiled warmly down at her, helpless to remain cool against such welcome.

"What are you trying to decide?" He dropped to one knee just beyond her regimental rows of paper and tried to peer at them upside down. "Is this the guest list?"

She nodded and blew out a long breath. A few loose wisps of hair floated away from her face, then settled back down along her pink cheeks. "I've been at them for hours but I simply cannot figure it out."

"Your aunt requested that I help you."

She grimaced slightly. "I'm afraid I lost patience with her. She took exception to a remark I made, snarled that my petard needed hoisting, and then left in a huff."

Rafe chuckled. "What did you say to her?"

She glanced away sheepishly. "I said that if we were one lady too many at the wedding breakfast then perhaps she ought to volunteer to stay in her room."

"Ouch. Whom did she wish to cut?"

"Sophie, of course. Tessa dislikes me, but she despises Sophie for some reason."

"I vote you keep Sophie," Rafe said stoutly. "She's quiet, which makes her infinitely preferable to Tessa."

Phoebe's eyes widened, but then she spoiled the effect of her genteel shock by snickering. "I ought to scold you for that."

Rafe grinned. "You can't scold me if it's true." Then he craned his head to read the lists right side up, and pointed to one. "You can't seat the Earl of Eastwick near the Mayor of London. They're in the midst of a feud—something about Eastwick's young and lovely mistress who used to be the Mayor's young and lovely mistress."

Phoebe gasped. "Oh, no! That won't do." She scratched out the mayor's name and scrawled it on another list, then handed it to Rafe. "How about there?"

Reading the seating list, Rafe rubbed a hand over his lips to hide his smile. "I don't think so. *That* gentleman happens to be the father of the aforementioned young and lovely mistress."

It was amusing to Rafe, but Phoebe seemed to melt before his eyes.

"I don't think I can do this," she whispered, her face starting to crumple. "I don't know these people—I don't know anything about being a—a—"

Oh, God. Not tears. Anything but tears! "I do," he said quickly. "I know them all and I know most of their secrets."

She brightened for a moment but then shook her head. "I don't think that would be a good idea. We shouldn't . . ." She trailed off, but the look she gave him spoke volumes.

Rafe smiled slightly. "We cannot avoid each other forever, Miss Millbury. You're marrying my brother."

She looked down at the lists and bit her lip. "I suppose you're right. After all, it's not as if we—" She stopped, then lifted her chin to gaze at him with the light of determination in her pretty eyes. "Very well. My lord, I would much appreciate your help with the seating arrangements.

He smiled and stepped over the lists to join her on the sofa.

The instant he settled next to her, however, he regretted his impulse to offer help. She still smelled astoundingly good, she still fit next to him like a puzzle piece, and he still—*forever*—wanted her in his arms.

He'd been a bad fellow in his life and apparently now he was meant to pay for it, for surely there was no worse hell than being constantly confronted with what he could not have. Swallowing hard, he forced an easy smile. "So, who first?"

She leaned forward to choose a list and he felt the aromatic warmth of her leave his side, turning him instantly cold. She was inches away but he missed her already.

Then she sat up, list in hand, and turned to him with a smile. Her lips were a breath away from his, he could see right down her bodice, and she was again jiggling her feet nervously.

There was no help for it. He was a dead man.

IN THE FINE offices of Stickley & Wolfe, Solicitors, an argument was brewing.

"Go tell her about him. She's just a poor country girl. She has no idea what she's getting into with a man like that."

"A man like what?"

Wolfe stared. "You really ought to get out more, Stick. Brookhaven! He looks all right from the outside—in fact, I wish I could afford his tailor—but by all accounts the man's a brute."

Coming from Wolfe, this epithet was either amusing or alarming. Since Mr. Stickley had no sense of humor whatsoever, he gasped. "Is he? How do you know?"

Wolfe spread his hands. "There are some who believe he killed his first wife. Of course, it was all hushed up at the time, but I could see it in his eyes."

Stickley gave an affronted sniff. "He ought to be locked up." Then his eyes widened. "Poor Miss Millbury!"

Wolfe shook his head sadly. "Poor Miss Millbury, indeed. So you see, Stick, it isn't just for our own gain that we must stop this wedding."

Stickley stiffened. "It never was—I only wish to preserve Pickering's trust!"

Wolfe nodded. "Absolutely. God bless Sir Hamish."

Then he leaned forward. "So you see what you must do. Miss Millbury must be told what a dangerous position she's put herself in."

Stickley stood, dusting his impeccable suit briskly. "I will see to it immediately."

"Good on, you!" Wolfe watched him go, then reached into his desk to pull out a bottle of excellent whisky. "I'll drink to that, Stick," he murmured. "You annoying little prig."

The office quietly his at last, Wolfe leaned back in his fine leather chair and set his heels upon the desk, the bottle cradled in one arm. "God, how I hate that bloke."

THE SEATING CHART was done at last. Everyone was arranged according to rank, wealth, secrets, and peccadilloes. Phoebe closed her eyes and sank back onto the cushions of the settee. "Oh, thank God."

A warm chuckle sounded close to her ear. "You're welcome."

Phoebe turned her head and smiled, eyes still closed. "All right then, thank God and Marbrook."

He did not reply. The silence stretched a bit too long. Phoebe opened her eyes to see his face inches from hers, his head braced on one fist, his elbow propped on the back of the settee.

She was abruptly, viscerally reminded of that first evening at the ball. From his tormented expression she could see he was remembering as well.

His eyes . . . she could spend her life looking into those eyes, healing the pain she'd caused in them. The darkness that hid there behind the light that everyone else saw—how could the world be so blind to the thoughtful and honorable man she saw behind the rogue?

He lifted a hand to touch a strand of her hair that had

fallen during their chore. With one finger, he brushed it back, letting his touch linger on her temple, then cheek. Such a simple, innocent touch—such an impossible ache it caused within her.

She'd not been wrong then. He did feel what she felt.

She didn't move, didn't speak, for if she did the truth, the reality, would come crashing in on them and she wanted it gone just a moment longer. Just a moment to be with Rafe, to be his lady, to be the woman she might have been were she not an idiot and a coward.

His hand slid around the back of her neck and his forehead dropped to touch to hers. She waited, unresisting. How could she fear that he might do something improper when everything felt so right when they were together?

He didn't kiss her lips, but only turned his face to lie next to hers, cheek to cheek, his breath in her ear. She shivered, then melted. Then waited.

Her pulse trembled in her throat. He found it with his warm mouth, touching the sensitive skin lightly with his tongue. Her thighs relaxed to ease the pressure building between them.

She closed her eyes. And waited.

His mouth moved around and down, leaving a trail of feather-light kisses on her collarbone. She felt the stubble of his cheek on the top of her breast.

He buried his face in her bosom. "Phoebe . . . God, how am I to bear seeing you wed to my brother?"

And so, the spell was broken. The magic fled the room and cold truth came chasing it. Phoebe gasped, then pushed him away to stand. She turned away and tried to cool the heat in her face, in her blood, in her softest flesh.

Rafe pushed himself upright, his breath coming hard as if he'd been running.

*Running home. Running someplace true and right.*

She turned around, her color high, her eyes defiant as

she met his gaze. She was mussed and her hair was coming down—long honey-gold tendrils that threatened to get caught in her generous cleavage—and she was superb, his spirited country darling . . . except she wasn't his.

Yet there was one thing he had to know. "Why did you accept my brother's proposal?"

Her face crumpled slightly. She looked away. "You never told me your entire name. I thought when I received the proposal—"

It was all a terrible mistake. Oh, God. She'd said yes—*to him*!

Joy and triumph sang through him for an instant—until he remembered that she'd not corrected the mistake.

"Yet you said nothing later," he said flatly. "Because you discovered that you'd accidentally landed a much bigger fish."

She looked down at her hands. Her knuckles were white from the intensity of their grip on each other. "It isn't like that . . . quite. The vicar—"

Rafe's indignation deflated instantly. "Of course. You are being forced to continue the engagement against your will."

Phoebe felt sick. She covered her face with her hands before he could read the lie in her eyes. "I wish—" *I wish I'd never met you. I wish you weren't a rake. I wish I weren't a coward.*

He came around the chair and took her into his arms. "It isn't your fault. You are powerless to prevent it."

She shook her head violently. If he did not stop being so kind, she was going to vomit out the truth—and then he would hate her as much as she hated herself.

*Remember . . . immune.*

She took a breath and pulled away slowly, pasting on a wan smile. It would hurt him less if he never knew, if he thought her a victim of fate. It was best this way. Sooner or later another lady would catch his eye and he would forget all about his passion for her. She would become as familiar as that sofa, just another fixture in Brook House.

And just as respectable.

"I am sorry that I was not honest with you from the beginning. I thought—" She swallowed. "You said that you pointed Calder in my direction after the ball."

He looked away, rubbing at the back of his neck with one hand. "I'm afraid I did. I'd meant only to get his approval."

"Ah." Too much gone unsaid by them both. Too late to change it.

"All is not lost, not yet." He took her by the shoulders and touched his forehead to hers once more. "I could speak to Calder, to your father," Rafe whispered, his plea alive in his voice. "My rank is a bit dubious, but I do not come entirely empty-handed."

Phoebe closed her eyes and swallowed. The vicar would go icy at the very thought of Phoebe passing over the inheritance. She could not bear to lose him again. She reached for Rafe's hands and gently removed them from her. "No. It is done, my lord. There is no turning back."

His hand fisted inside her loose grip. "You do not even wish to try." His voice hardened. "Perhaps I am mistaken in your feelings. Perhaps it is not your father who is the matter here."

Phoebe shook her head and kept her face turned away, her eyes still shut tightly. Her silence was the best she could do for the vicar at that moment, for if she even attempted to speak she would beg Rafe to do whatever necessary to end the engagement.

She longed to explain, for if he knew he would not be so hurt—or at least he might begin to understand—but if she broke the silence she would jeopardize Deirdre's and Sophie's portions as well as her own.

"You cannot even look at me, Phoebe." His voice was strained and hollow. "How are we to live out our lives this way?"

Her heart wailed and her spirit ached, but she had been too long desperate to gain the vicar's regard once more. She was unable to go against that habit, too weak or perhaps too well trained to please herself rather than him.

So she waited, frozen in her last shred of self-control, until she felt Rafe leave the settee then heard the parlor door slam. She remained there, eyes closed against the tears that threatened.

She felt weak and used up, like a torch that had burned itself to ash. There was only one thing immovable and certain in her world.

In a fortnight, she must marry the marquis.

# Chapter Twenty-four

Moments after Marbrook left her, when her color was still high thinking about what she ought not to be thinking about, Fortescue introduced yet another caller for Miss Millbury.

Phoebe hurriedly tended to her hair.

"Mr. Stickley, what a surprise!" Phoebe smiled and stood as Fortescue showed the solicitor into the parlor.

It wasn't too hard to pretend pleasure. She liked Stickley. He was quiet and mild-mannered—rather refreshing after spending time with Calder and Rafe. Their scraping edges left her exhausted, and dealing with Deirdre and Sophie wasn't much better.

Mr. Stickley didn't seem nearly so happy to see her. "Miss Millbury, I do hope you'll forgive the intrusion, but a matter arose that I—well, I thought about it a great deal on the way here—" He stopped himself and inhaled deeply. "Miss Millbury, you cannot wed Lord Brookhaven."

Phoebe couldn't help but brighten. "Truly?" Then she caught herself and frowned worriedly. "Oh, dear. Mr. Stickley, perhaps you ought to explain yourself."

She waved him to a seat, but he only began to pace anxiously before her. "I don't know how to tell you this. Oh, my heavens. It truly is most disturbing—"

Phoebe kept her voice pleasant, but introduced just a smidgen of Tessa's steel. "Mr. Stickley, sit."

He sat instantly, but continued to wring his hands. "Oh, my heavens!"

At this point, Phoebe would have found an actual curse quite diverting. As it was, Stickley was wearing at her nerves. If there was some real impediment to her engagement, then she would be free—but would she be fearless enough?

Conflicting hopes assailed her and Stickley's dithering proved fair to driving her mad! "Mr. Stickley, out with it!"

He stilled himself immediately. Really, perhaps Tessa was on to something with that waspish manner of hers.

"Miss Millbury, you cannot marry Lord Brookhaven because . . . because he is a murderer!"

She made a doubtful face. "Brookhaven? Whom did he kill—a rabbit?"

Mr. Stickley went prim. Lord preserve her from prim! But Phoebe recognized the signal that she'd offended. Time to make it up to him or she'd never get anything from the man. She leaned forward eagerly, parting her lips in mock anticipation. "Oh, Mr. Stickley—pray, tell me more!"

He sniffed, but then relented. "Oh, very well. This morning I was told about Brookhaven's suspicious involvement in his late wife's death—"

Phoebe blinked. "Brookhaven had a wife?"

Stickley made a peevish noise. Phoebe shook off her disbelief. "Oh, so sorry. Do continue. You have me on pins and needles . . ." *Blah, blah, blah, anything, only tell it!*

She'd never been any good at all about waiting for the end of a story.

Mr. Stickley pulled a sheaf of newsprint from his pocket. "I never put faith in rumors, myself, so I took the liberty of stopping at the London *Sun* to look into it. I have here the original articles from that time five years ago."

He spread out the sheets. Each headline was worse than

the one before. *"Lady Brookhaven lost in carriage accident—two dead." "Brookhaven carriage stolen?" "Rumors fly—who was the other man?"*

Rich meat indeed for the gossips. Why had she never heard of this scandal? Even Thornton received the newssheets, albeit a day or two late.

Ah, yes. Five years ago she'd been working day and night helping the vicar stave off a cholera epidemic in Thornton village. It had been months before she'd had a moment to read a newssheet. Tessa might have mentioned it, but Phoebe always did her best not to listen to Tessa.

"No one dared accuse him, of course." Stickley sniffed. "There was no real evidence—although what would there be? No one saw the accident. There was only Lord Brookhaven's account to go by. He explained away the other fellow by saying that he was a houseguest of theirs, although one might wonder why a marquis would have a stage actor as a houseguest."

Phoebe had been scanning the articles, looking for anything more substantial than Stickley's gossip. She pushed them away, frowning. "There is no such implication in this," she said flatly. Was she disappointed or relieved? "Brookhaven may not be perfect, but I cannot believe this of him."

Mr. Stickley blinked rapidly. "But—but Miss Millbury! If Brookhaven murdered his first wife, he'll have no compunction about murdering you as well!"

Phoebe narrowed her eyes. "Mr. Stickley, I have just explained to you that I do not put stock in gossip. One small error—one misunderstood mistake!—and it pursues one forever!"

She didn't know if she was still talking about Brookhaven, but she felt fury and helplessness bubble up from somewhere old and deep. "Why can't people see all the good things that someone does? Why can't they talk about the years of hard work, or the charitable efforts, or the many kindnesses—why is it always those little lapses in judgment that follow one to the grave?"

Stickley stood, affronted and alarmed. "I cannot believe you would dismiss such powerful evidence—"

"Evidence!" Phoebe jumped up as well. "The only evidence I would believe of Brookhaven is his signed, sealed confession delivered to my hand by the Prince Regent himself!" She folded her arms and sneered. "And even then I'd first ask Brookhaven to check the handwriting."

Stickley's manner became more schoolmistress than solicitor. "Well, I never! If you've not the sense to save yourself, then I suppose there is nothing more I can do for you!"

Phoebe didn't trust herself not to tear the little prig to pieces then and there. She gritted her teeth and kept her arms tightly folded for his protection. "I'm sure you know the way out, Mr. Stickley?"

He left in a prim and prickly huff. When he was gone, Phoebe closed her eyes and fought to pull herself together. What was the matter with her? She'd just thrown out possibly her last chance to get out of this mess—for even the vicar might take pause at selling her to a man with a murderous past—but she couldn't do it. She couldn't hold a rumor against someone when she bewailed her own fate so often.

*Not even for Marbrook?*

No. She might barter her body and her life for status and protection, but not her soul.

Not even for Marbrook.


RAFE GAVE HIS horse a powerful kick in the sides and the stallion burst from the stable yard in a clatter of iron shoes on cobblestone.

He must let her go.

The streets were yet crowded, so Rafe cut through the alleys, taking a familiar path to Hyde Park. There was only one place to ride away one's fury and anguish in London, and that was Rotten Row, an earthen track that ran the length of the park.

Not nearly far enough away, but it would have to do.

# Chapter Twenty-five

After Mr. Stickley's departure, Phoebe remained in the parlor, pacing in a large circle around her wedding guest list.

Eventually, the bloody thing sent her fleeing the room, into the hall where the darkening evening had outpaced the servants and their fresh candles.

A shadowy figure loomed just outside the door. Rafe?

"Hello." The deep voice rumbled through her belly. No, it was the marquis. Her fiancé.

Remembering Mr. Stickley's tawdry gossip, she slowly moved toward him and took his large hand in hers. "I'm glad I have the chance to speak to you again," she whispered. The dark closed around them. She would be a good wife to him, the poor man.

He let his fingers slowly wrap themselves around hers. "Are you?" he murmured. "Then so am I."

Phoebe leaned into him, letting her forehead rest on his waistcoat. She let the fingers of her other hand slip up over his shoulder to stroke his hair. She heard his heartbeat thud faster in response.

Phoebe froze. What to do now?

Then she realized that there was nothing to do. She had every right to approach and caress her fiancé.

She simply couldn't explain why she felt much more

guilty standing here in the hallway with Brookhaven than she'd felt pressed to Marbrook on the sofa!

So she stepped back slowly, trying not to give away her sudden discomfort. A servant hurried into the passage to light the sconces and Phoebe could see the bemused but very interested expression upon Brookhaven's face.

"Don't you think you ought be dressing for this evening's concert, Miss Millbury?"

Concert? Had he invited her out this evening? Irritation sparked. If he had, he'd forgotten to mention it to her. Then again, it would get her away from the house.

And away from Rafe. She smiled briefly. "Of course. The concert. I suppose it is high time I changed." She moved back and dipped a curtsy. "I shall be ready shortly, my lord."

He nodded formally. "Until then, Miss Millbury."

Just before she rose onto the first step, she turned back. "My lord?"

"Yes, Miss Millbury?"

She swallowed. "I . . . today I learned from . . . from a concerned party . . . I did not know you were married before."

His silhouette went oddly rigid. "You did not? Your aunt assured me that she told you everything."

"Oh, I'm sure she did." She waved a hand. "But, to be truthful, my lord, I never listen to Tessa's gossip."

"I see." He said nothing for a long moment. "And what did you think of what this concerned party told you."

Phoebe took a step toward him. "I think you have suffered great loss," she said softly. "First your parents when you were not much more than a boy, then your wife. So much pain . . ." She took a breath. "I simply wanted to say that I'm sorry. I know how great a hole someone's death can leave in your heart. I cannot imagine what it must have been like for you."

"Thank you, Miss Millbury." His rigid silhouette did not

change, but his voice held something new entirely, something softer and several degrees warmer . . . and just a tiny
bit impressed? "That is very kind of you."

"You're welcome, my lord. Until tonight."

"Until tonight . . . Phoebe."

She fled. There was nothing else to call her headlong
progress away from Brookhaven. She ran up the stairs and
to her room—thank heaven, her very own room!—to hide
far away from her tangled feelings.

Unfortunately, they tagged along.


TESSA SWEPT INTO the dining room, her third best gown
perfectly pressed despite its travel, done by a harried and
exhausted Nan. Tessa's hair was divine, her powder perfect, her most conciliatory smile in place. Brookhaven was
going to be charmed out of his boots and beg her to stay on
after the wedding . . . possibly even beg to come to her
bed. She wouldn't mind a lover again and Brookhaven was
a handsome brute with a dark reputation. It could be he
would enjoy her little amusements . . .

"So sorry I'm late," she cooed. "I—"

There was no one there. Only one place was laid, with a
Brookhaven servant standing attentively over it with a decided smirk upon his face. "Their lordships regret that they
have been called away, my lady. If my lady will be seated,
we may begin to serve."

Oh, he might think he was expressionless, but Tessa always knew when she was being mocked.

"Where are my charges?" Their lordships might be beyond her reach for this rudeness, but the girls would pay
dearly.

The man bowed again, the scraping rodent. "Miss Blake
is in her room with the headache, Miss Cantor is in her

room with the headache, and soon-to-be-my-lady Miss Millbury is at a concert with his lordship, my lady."

Soon-to-be-my-lady. A reminder that if she wanted welcome in this house, she'd better treat that dratted Phoebe with respect. Frustrated that her rage had no easy outlet, Tessa flounced to her chair and let herself be served the soup.

The long formal table stretched out to either side. Even with no one else here, she'd been placed in the socially lowest position, in the center with her back to the door. It was as if the Brookhaven staff knew something . . . something they couldn't possibly know.

*Damn* Phoebe.

# Chapter Twenty-six

The Royal Concert Hall was a gleaming example of Georgian opulence and wealthy splendor. Creamy plaster relief crowned the arched ceilings and gold leaf touched every surface with grandeur. Above them all hung stunning chandeliers, icy concoctions of crystal and glittering light.

This place was meant to display the finer things for the finer folk—to impress upon all visitors that they were indeed the most civilized country in the world.

Such was the splendor of modern London, from the astonishing gas lights in Pall Mall to this sumptuous display. How unbelievable that she, Phoebe Millbury, was at the center of it all. She attended balls and concerts and the opera—dressed in a fine silk gown, seated next to a handsome lord—living just the dazzling life that every girl dreamed of.

All she needed to do to gain it had already been done. This would be her world now. She was already being swept up in it. She need only allow it—if she could only be sure it was a world she truly wanted. Or was it simply what she ought to want?

The soprano's voice soared toward the frescoed ceiling. Lord Brookhaven leaned close and murmured something approving. Phoebe nodded automatically. Her entire existence was like a beautiful dream.

Why then, did she so desperately long to wake up?

"MARBROOK, WHERE IN the world have you been?"

A tall willowy woman, wrapped in the finest of furs, waited for him eagerly. She let the cloak drop to reveal a deeply cut wisp of clinging silvery silk that had the nerve to call itself a gown. Hair the shimmering blue-black of a raven's wing tumbled freely down her back in defiance of the latest style. A gaze the disturbing silver of a wolf's eyes swept him from boots to brow as the woman raised her chin haughtily.

Lilah. As he entered the grand reception room at the Royal Concert Hall, Rafe considered a swift turnabout and escape, but it was too late. Lilah had spied him. A predatory smile turned her lovely face into something wicked and sexual. Of course, that had once been a major part of the initial attraction, but now it only left him cold. He was already regretting the impulse that had caused him to invite her out this evening.

Lady Lilah Christie was a fascinating beauty and true carnal delight. She had the added bonus of a husband who looked the other way, apparently grateful merely to have her on his unworthy arm. Most men in Society would give half their fortunes to get a mere evening of her attention. Rafe himself had only won her through a relentless and tireless pursuit.

"Hello, darling." Her husky voice held an intimate purr. She came a bit too close and let her gaze roam over his body possessively. Only a few months ago that would have been all the invitation necessary.

Now, standing within inches of Lilah, Rafe's skin

crawled just a tiny bit. He wanted to move away—and possibly bathe.

This—aside from being prickly and odd—was a horrifying development. "Fashionably late, as always, my lady," he said to her uneasily.

Enthusiastically sinful and outrageously imaginative, Lilah had kept Rafe's interest longer than any other lover ever had. Indeed, she had tired of him first, or so she had claimed. Now, she seemed to have reconsidered that rejection.

*You're a lucky man. Keep telling yourself that.*

He offered Lilah his arm with a bow and they entered the concert hall itself in a wave of whispers and sidelong glances. Lilah's affairs always supplied the very best gossip. Rafe resigned himself to being a household name once more.

As he guided Lilah to a seat, he cast a last longing glance toward the exit. Abruptly, his attention was captured by the gleam of light on a certain head of fair hair, on the familiar lift of a particular chin.

*She's here.*

His entire being focused onto Phoebe like a hunting hawk on a dove. The concert went on but he heard not a note. His awareness was narrowed to the pinpoint sight of her sitting next to Calder. Her tilt-nosed profile, the curve of her cheek, the delicate wisps of hair at the back of her neck—all enough to dry his mouth and constrict his throat.

When Calder leaned close to whisper something into her ear, Rafe saw her tense. She did not lean away— quite—but neither did she lean intimately toward the man she meant to marry.

Telling, that.

Or not. She seemed naturally demure in public, after all.

So he tortured himself onward. *She doesn't want him. She does. She loathes him. She likes him.*

Calder himself began as a lump on the periphery of Rafe's focus, but as the evening wore on Rafe could not help but notice that Calder seemed . . . relaxed. The brother Rafe knew could never have borne to waste an entire evening thus—not while there were machines that needed machining and whatsits that needed manufacturing.

Yet here he sat, serenely enjoying the music, Miss Phoebe Millbury quite willingly at his side.

Phoebe turned to Calder and smiled slightly at something he said. *She likes him.*

*She likes the better man.*

The dowager in front of Rafe shifted, mercifully cutting off his view of them, although it did nothing to stem the flood of angry self-contempt.

What was the use of this torture? He hardly needed to prove to himself that Calder had won.

The soprano finished her aria and politely enthusiastic clapping ensued. Rafe took advantage of the moment to make his escape. As he blindly exited the concert hall, he felt a hand on his arm.

"Marbrook?"

Oh, God. *Lilah.*

AS THE CONCERT went on, Phoebe became aware that the evening was becoming slightly more bearable. His lordship had eased considerably in the last two days and Phoebe had almost detected a flash of dry humor. Almost.

Then Phoebe caught the flash of blue from the corner of her eye. *Marbrook.* She turned more fully to see his broad back disappearing through one of the doors.

She didn't even hesitate. "Please, excuse me for a moment, my lord. I—I feel the need for the retiring room."

Why hadn't she hesitated? *No, don't think on that. Don't think at all.*

Calder stood instantly. "Are you ill?"

She smiled quickly. "No, I'm quite well. It's simply the crowd—I'm not used to this . . ."

It was a ridiculous excuse for an excuse, but he seemed to accept it. "Please, let me know if I can—"

But she left him behind, slipping past a sturdy dowager who was complaining of the number of people, moving through the crush like water seeking level, entirely intent on *him.*

*This is not good. This is not the* him *you ought to be thinking of.*

Of course it wasn't.

She didn't care.


IN THE HALLWAY, Rafe found himself pressed to the wall by an advancing Lilah. Unfortunately, he wanted only to have her step back and stop looking at him as if she wanted to have him on her plate at dinner.

Did this mean that he was ruined for other women forever? Could that happen from one evening's sweet—God, so sweet—encounter in a garden and a mere moment in a parlor? Could a man like him catch such a serious case of devotion in such a short amount of time?

Not if he could bloody help it.

He smiled false invitation. Lilah glowed. She hadn't had more than a nodding acquaintance with sincerity for years, so it was no surprise that she did not detect the lie.

She moved closer still. "For a moment there I thought you'd forgotten me," she whispered.

Rafe let habit take over. "I could never do that." He ran his fingertips delicately up her bare arm. She let out a husky sigh that tickled his ear. Her touch felt soiled, although to be truthful, she was no more soiled than he himself. His past covered him in grimy regret . . . and only the understanding in Phoebe's clear blue eyes could have washed him clean. She would have been his redemption and his reward. His new beginning. A chance to be the man he ought to have been.

A chance he'd lost forever. So what was the point of trying anymore?

He quelled his distaste and opened his hand around the back of Lilah's neck. She was beautiful and willing. He was a man, damn it! That was all a man needed, right?

Perhaps sometime between now and getting her naked, he would recapture his free will.

*God, I hope so.* If not, he was in for a bit of embarrassment. Lilah was more woman than most men had in a lifetime. If she couldn't liberate him, no one could.

"Lilah wants," she whispered throatily.

*And whatever Lilah wants, Lilah gets.*

He opened his mouth to give the customary response, a playful bit of sexual banter they had created between them . . . but the words would not come. She was pressed practically knee to chest with him, ready to play out his darkest secret fantasies—if there were any left they hadn't already done—and he couldn't do it.

*Are you mad, man? Grab her hand and drag her to the nearest broom closet to play "Master and the Virgin Chambermaid!"*

*I don't want the chambermaid. I want the vicar's daughter. She can likely play that, too! Just go!*

He closed his eyes and concentrated. Lilah naked. Lilah on her knees. Lilah on top—

Would Phoebe like it on top? He could allow her to set her own pace, to find her own way to orgasm while he supported her, hands about her waist—

She would toss her rebellious honey-gold hair and cry out in surprise, and then her blue gaze would lock on his as the pleasure flooded through her . . .

"That's the lad," Lilah cooed in his ear. Her hip nudged his growing erection. "For a moment I thought you'd forgotten me again."

For a moment, he had. "You always did talk too much," he said gruffly. He reached one hand to grasp her rounded bottom and pull her tighter against his groin, holding on to the image of Phoebe in his head. Phoebe in his arms, Phoebe in his bed, Phoebe—

A startled gasp brought him back with a jolt. He opened his eyes.

Phoebe in the hall, staring at him groping the most diligent whore in Mayfair. He dropped his hands as if Lilah had turned into a slimy insect.

Phoebe's gaze locked with his, just as in his fantasy, but the only thing flooding through her seemed to be revulsion.

And hurt.

Which was ridiculous. What had she to be hurt about? She was engaged to marry another man! It would be best for them both if she never looked at him that way again.

Rafe wrapped a purposeful arm about Lilah's waist and forced an irritated glare at the interruption. "Do you mind?"

Phoebe's slack jaw snapped shut. Her eyes narrowed suspiciously. Damn it, she saw through him, even now!

"I have been assured of the validity of your reputation, my lord," she said primly. "You did not need to prove it to me." Then she turned away as if she'd seen something no lady ought to sully her vision with.

Lilah looked over her shoulder and giggled. "Who's the Puritan?"

Phoebe heard her, for her shoulders jerked slightly. She didn't turn back, but only raised that bloody stubborn chin higher and increased her pace.

"No one," Rafe said, unable to take his eyes from every injured and furious inch of her as she disappeared around the corner. "Just my sanctimonious brother's sanctimonious fiancée."

Lilah laughed, a tinkling scornful sound. "Then they deserve each other, I think." She turned back to nuzzle his neck. "Now, where were we?"

It was no use. "We were done." Rafe stepped back. "Sorry. I guess this time Lilah doesn't get what Lilah wants."

Her silver eyes flashed a warning that would have brought another man to his knees. "Take care, my lord. I *never* offer twice."

Rafe bowed slightly. "Then I hope you never run out of men, my lady." With that he turned and walked away from the most beautiful woman in London—and never looked back.

# Chapter Twenty~seven

"I'm in love with Lord Raphael Marbrook!"

Oh, bother. The secret had barely made it home from the concert and up the stairs to Sophie's room. Phoebe clapped one hand over her mouth and waited for Sophie's reaction. Her cousin merely raised her eyebrows slightly.

"Well, that does pose a pickle, doesn't it?" Sophie turned to look at her properly. "Does he love you in return?"

Phoebe felt her cheeks color. *Does he love you in return?*

She sat abruptly on the bed, wrapping her arms about her middle. The quivers in her stomach were only half caused by unfulfilled desire. Some of the largest were coming from a darker place of fear. Was it only desire on his part? Was he the rake he claimed to be? Was she being a fool?

Again?

"I think he wants me," she said tightly. "But he has not spoken of love." She could not put her faith in what might merely be hot blood. The vicar had warned her many times that such impulses were not real. Hot blood was a lie and sensible girls would want nothing to do with it.

Sophie sat across from her. "I see." She regarded Phoebe for a long moment. "Cousin, are you sure . . . you have made a very advantageous match with his brother. You would be giving up a great deal if you broke the engagement to choose Marbrook. The scandal alone would—"

Phoebe ducked her head. "Oh, heavens. I cannot think on it." The vicar would never speak to her again. The look he would have in his eyes . . . she felt the ashes of old pain curl and blacken with new heat. The quivers in her gut became tremors. She looked up at Sophie helplessly.

Fortunately, Sophie seemed to have experience with helplessness. She stood and strode to a chest and removed a brandy decanter. "I found it in the library. Actually, I took it away from the vicar. He isn't spending all his time reading, you know." She poured a hefty portion into a glass. Returning to Phoebe, she pressed it into her shaking hands.

Phoebe took a gulp, shutting her eyes against the medicinal fumes of the liquor. It burned all the way down, but after only a few moments she felt the tension in her shoulders ease. "That was repulsive," she said, with a small breathless laugh.

"Good." Sophie took the glass away. "Then you're not likely to take it up as a habit."

The brandy eased a bit of the panic, but it did nothing to remove the reasons—either of them. Both tall, broad-shouldered reasons continued to loom over Phoebe, stealing the air from any room she was in.

"Lady Lilah Christie."

"Who?"

"That's her name. I asked . . . afterward. She is—or perhaps was—Marbrook's lover." She sniffed. "*Lilah*. It suits her . . . all sleek elegance and catlike mystique. The memory of Marbrook's hands on that silver silk gown . . ."

"Oh, my," Sophie breathed. "You have had a night."

Phoebe shook her head defiantly. "I'm not jealous—not precisely. I knew immediately that Marbrook was only trying to prove a point."

The brandy was making her head swim. "But . . . that moment in the hall, when I saw another woman in Marbrook's arms, I realized that it would never be me."

"Because you're marrying Lord Brookhaven," Sophie reminded her gently.

Phoebe waved that off. "Yes . . . but that it would some-day be *someone*. I'm going to marry Brookhaven and ful-fill the vicar's dream and Marbrook is going to go on without me, having lover after lover and possibly even someday a wife . . ."

Her face began to crumple. "And it will never be *me!*" She grabbed the bed's dust ruffle and blew her nose mightily.

"Milksop." Sophie gave her a wry smile. "No more brandy for you."

Phoebe flopped back onto the bed and gazed at the de-sign worked in plaster around the ceiling.

"Be careful, Phoebe. You have given your word to Lord Brookhaven. The scandal—"

Phoebe covered her eyes. "I know. I cannot—I will not—fall again. I will not go through that again—the pain, the recrimination, the constant constraint for fear of expo-sure! Always wondering, do they know? Are they whisper-ing about me? Has the end come at last? Am I ruined?"

She rolled over on the bed. "The worst is the secret, shameful hope that it *will* come out," she whispered. "That it will be public knowledge, that I would be ruined in truth and would never have to live masked again."

Sophie put a hand on her shoulder. Phoebe started, for she'd nearly forgotten Sophie's presence.

"Phoebe, I don't really know what you're speaking of . . . and perhaps you ought not to say. If you truly, hon-estly want to avoid scandal, perhaps it might be wise to avoid Lord Marbrook until the wedding is done . . . and perhaps a bit after."

Phoebe sat up and brushed at her cheeks. "Avoid him. Yes. That is precisely what I will do. It will be easy."

She desperately hoped.

# Chapter Twenty-eight

When Rafe returned to Brook House, too late to encounter anyone but the yawning groom who took the reins of his happily exhausted horse, he welcomed the dark and silent emptiness of the halls and rooms. His own valet had long since gone to bed, knowing that after a certain hour, Rafe would likely not come home at all.

In his room he threw off his jacket and waistcoat, yanked his cravat knot free and tossed the linen on the pile. He sat in the large chair before his fire and pulled off his boots, tossing the fine leather aside with all the care he'd give tattered rags. What did it matter? Fine things were only things after all. They would not make his life without Phoebe any easier to bear.

He'd stayed out late to avoid her—for how could he face her after that hideous scene outside the concert!—but there was no escaping her presence. She was so damned *everywhere* in this house. Her scent lingered in the halls, her name was on everyone's lips, her damned cousins underfoot with their lighter and darker versions of the same blue eyes . . .

And although Rafe's body ached, his stomach growled a protest. Off to the kitchens to slake at least one appetite.

His feet bare on the chill floors, he padded silently through the house in search of something more substantial than lovelorn frustration to put in his stomach.

He'd grown up in this house, at least for half of every year, so there was no need for a candle. The dark was an old friend to Rafe. Most of his finest moments—or worst ones, depending on one's moral perspective—had been spent in the dark.

The kitchens were in the cellar, as in most large houses in town. There was the large pantry, the carving room with its vaguely alarming rack of cutting implements, the main kitchen where the stoves were, the scullery with its deep stone sinks and Rafe's personal favorite, the larder.

It was a long narrow chamber, lined with marble shelves for the things that needed chilling, and cool stone floors that stung his bare feet. Since he was in the mood for savory, he easily avoided the sturdy worktable in the middle of the room and bent to feel along the lowest shelves for something of a ham or roast nature.

He found meat pasties, probably made for the lower servants, since the fastidious master would curl his lip at such common fare—although Rafe had never met a meat pasty he didn't like. In spite of the call of the rich potato and meat filling he moved on, feeling his way carefully. He was really more in the mood for big, juicy slices of—

Thigh. Smooth . . . rounded . . . warm . . . lush . . .

"*Eek.*" It was a small protest, hardly more than a whisper.

"Ah!" He snatched his hand back and straightened—and smacked the back of his head into the stone shelf above with great force. "Ow!" He staggered backward with one hand to his skull.

"Oh!"

Something moved on the shelf, there was a rustle of fabric and a metallic clank—and then light seared his expanded pupils.

"Bloody hell!" He slapped his other palm over his eyes. "Sweet Charlotte's Ass! Are you trying to kill me?"

"I didn't—I—who is Charlotte?"

"Phoebe?" He partially unshielded his eyes and blinked. Blurred afterimages still floated in the way, but he could see her before him, clad in nightdress and half-open wrapper, fishing her lighted candlestick out of a flour tin.

She scowled at him in the glow, trying to undo the knot in the belt of her wrapper in order to pull it tighter. "Goodness, my lord! You frightened the life out of me!"

"I? I think I just lost ten years! I was planning to put those to good use, you know."

Her mood turning in a flash, she dimpled at him. "How? Doing good works?"

He grunted. "Absolutely. There are any number of charities working for the betterment of beguiling mistresses. I'm a regular contributor."

Reminded, her humor vanished. She raised a brow. "I'll wager you are. Men like you simply don't know when to stop giving."

She wasn't going to let him off the hook so easily. "What do you know of men like me?"

"I know enough." She attempted to look arch, but with her tousled hair and rebellious wrapper, she merely managed to look adorable. "Rakes and scoundrels aren't exclusive to London, I'll have you know."

He grinned, absurdly happy simply to be with her. "Oh, you breed your own up there in Bump-arse-shire?"

She gave up on the knot and folded her arms over her exposed bodice. "I believe they are primarily imported, my lord," she said sourly.

His smile faded. "You aren't teasing, are you? What happened to you in Thornton? When did you encounter rakes and scoundrels?"

Something flashed across her expression for an instant and he thought she was going to speak. Then it was gone and she merely gazed at him evenly. "Did you come searching for something to eat?"

"Ham. Or roast. Or—" *Thigh*. But just as they were not talking about Lilah, they were carefully not talking about how he'd found her curled up on the shelf, hiding from the intruder with her nightdress rucked up over her knees, were they?

He could respect a good evasion, but he thought he ought to do his part somehow. "You shouldn't wander the house alone. You don't know it well."

She lifted her chin. "It is my house—or it will be in a fortnight. I think I am entitled to raid the larder if I please."

Her house . . . his brother's wife-to-be. "Yes, thanks so much for reminding me. Soon there'll be lots of merry little Calder-shaped brats to keep us all up at night."

She lifted a tray of roast slices to the table which stood in the center of the room. "Cheese?"

He absently reached down a round from a higher shelf for her. "Did you hear what I said?"

She was humming slightly as she pulled half a loaf of bread from the shelf where she'd been hiding. Baked items weren't kept here, so she'd brought it with her. She really was making herself at home at Brook House.

"I heard you," she said. "You're protesting my breeding capabilities." She slanted a disgruntled look at him. "Some of the brats might be Phoebe-shaped, you know."

Little Phoebes, cherub-cheeked and tousle-haired, pattering about the house, perpetually in trouble, charming their way out with dimples and long-lashed blue eyes . . .

For a moment, he was utterly captivated by the image in his mind. Then he remembered that it would not be he who fathered those blue-eyed darlings.

Uncle Rafe. Welcomed for holiday dinners and not much else.

She went on calmly preparing the food with competent

movements. If she'd been affected by this evening's moment at the concert, she didn't seem to be upset by it.

*I want you to be upset. No, I want you to be devastated. I want you to fight for me, to throw everything away to please me, to cost yourself your family's esteem and the life of a duchess so I won't feel like my brother wins . . .*

*So what kind of man does that make me?*

*It makes you Uncle Rafe, because she's smart enough to send you packing, even though she fancies you.*

Which was precisely what he deserved.

If he had known what all his rebellious amusements would someday cost him, would he have done it differently? Would he have fallen in with Calder's plans, would he have studied harder, been more prudent, avoided cards and women and drink?

*Why can't you be more like your brother?*

Had a day of his youth gone by without hearing that hated phrase from his father, or tutor, or even a local cleric? Every utterance had been like a brick in the wall between the brothers, shutting Rafe out—

Shutting Calder in?

No. Rafe shook off that preposterous idea. Calder had everything.

He gazed at Phoebe, who was carefully not looking his way at all. Yes, she fancied him, but she would never choose him over Calder. She was too intelligent to do that.

"I don't want to hurt you, Rafe." Her voice was low, but he could detect the pain in it.

"And I don't want to be hurt," he said, forcing a smile. "And see? We can spend time together without difficulty. We're the only ones awake in the entire house, just the two of us, alone and isolated where no one knows we—"

He stopped, for the vastness of their solitude only made the night feel safer and more secret. Dangerous.

Across the table from him, she visibly shivered. "This floor is icy."

"Then get off it." He rounded the table in a swift movement.

"What—"

Wrapping both hands about her little waist, he lifted her to sit on the table before she could form a protest. Her gasp feathered against his cheek, mingling with her scent. He wanted to tighten his grip, pull her closer and make her forget everything but him—

He backed a step away and bowed deeply to hide his expression. "My queen's royal barge is ready to depart. If Your Majesty will lounge appropriately?"

She laughed. "You're mad."

He straightened. "Lounge," he ordered. "The floor is too bloody cold."

She snickered again, but pulled her chilled feet up to tuck them beside her, then leaned on one hand. "There. I'm lounging. Can you hand me the tray? I cannot reach it from here."

He snatched up the tray and held it out of her reach. "Your Majesty's royal hands must not handle trays!"

"A girl could become accustomed to such a thing," she murmured thoughtfully.

A poor vicar's daughter had likely toted many trays in her life. "Then do so, my queen," he intoned, in his best impression of Fortescue.

She laughed again and then assumed a bored and queenly air. "Very well, then. Serve me the bread."

He pulled a shred of it off and popped it into her mouth, neatly avoiding her reaching hand. Her eyes twinkled as she chewed and swallowed. "So no royal handling of food either, eh?"

"Of course not." He plucked a bite of cold roast from the selection and fed it to her.

She closed her eyes. "Why does stolen food taste so much better?"

"Keep your eyes closed," he said. He fed her bites of bread, roast, and cheese for a moment more. She murmured appreciation as she chewed, reminding him of the way she'd enjoyed her chocolate on the street. He put down the tray and grabbed the candle. "I'll be right back."

The pantry was just down the way and he was back before she could make more than a token protest at being left in the dark. "Sorry about that. I didn't want to put my elbow in the pie."

She brightened. "Pie?"

"Better. Now close your eyes again."

The trusting way she closed her eyes, tilted her head back, and opened her lips . . .

A decent man really ought not to have those thoughts about his brother's bride. Of course, he'd never laid claim to decency, had he?

The treat he'd brought her was a rich chocolate sauce that was probably meant for dessert tomorrow evening. He spooned out the dark delicacy, letting it drip onto her tongue. She rolled it in her mouth and shuddered. "Heaven," she murmured throatily.

Her husky appreciation made his groin pulse. The way her tongue flicked over her lips to catch the tiniest smear made the blood leave his brain and head for those nondecent parts of him.

He eased another spoonful into that rosebud mouth, the throb of his lust the only thing he could hear. His hand shook, losing a tiny drip of chocolate to land on her chin.

Before he could stop himself, he ducked his head and licked it off.

She gasped and went rigid, but her eyes remained closed and she did not move to push him away. Their play, meant to distract them from the tingling heat between them, had lost the match.

Phoebe waited, unable to breathe, unable to think for the longing in her heart and in her rushing blood. Her belly trembled with need. *Kiss me.*

*Don't. It isn't right.*

*It cannot be wrong, not this.*

*Kiss me.*

"You gave me the sweets, didn't you?" she whispered. "How did you know?"

He swallowed. "I followed you," he whispered back, his lips so close to hers. "I . . . watched you."

She did not open her eyes. "I felt you there." She sighed.

"Open your eyes, Phoebe. Open your eyes and see me."

She lifted her lids and her eyes were like twin fires, blazing lust at him, drying his mouth, sending all virtuous thoughts straight to hell with smoke trails fading. "Phoebe?"

She was on him even as he moved toward her. He drove his fingers into her thick fall of hair and dragged her mouth up to his. She wrapped her arms about his neck, going up on her knees to press urgently against him.

He needed her closer. The belt of her wrapper caused a brief problem, which Rafe solved by reaching for the knife she'd cut the bread with. He sliced through the tiresome knot with one swift motion, then the wrapper fluttered to the floor behind them.

Her nightdress would be but the work of a moment. It would flutter away as well and she would be naked in his hands, bared to his every wicked wish. Oh, the things he wanted to do to this sweet, hot-blooded country girl . . .

The candlestick tipped over, rolled off the table, and fell to the stone floor with a harsh clang that resounded through the narrow larder.

They jerked away from each other instantly in the sudden darkness. Rafe scrambled backward until his back met the shelves. He heard a crying gasp, a rustle of fabric, and a harsh thud as the door slammed shut behind the sound of racing feet.

"Phoebe?"

She was gone.

He brought his hands up to cover his face. He could smell her on him. "Oh, God." The silence and darkness pressed down on him, driving him to his knees.

Curse or prayer, God wasn't answering.

# Chapter Twenty~nine

She undulated beneath him, her movements hungry and innocently erotic. His sweet, hot Phoebe, finally to be his in truth, forever his.

"Forever, my lord. I shall love you forever," she gasped as her body shuddered beneath his. "My lord, wake up, my lord."

Oh, damn.

Rafe opened his eyes to see his valet Sparrow standing next to the bed, gazing at him apologetically.

"You asked me to wake you early this morning, my lord."

"Go away." Rafe shut his eyes hard but Phoebe was gone.

"My lord, you had plans this morning. Don't you remember?"

His plans had been to get out of the house as early as possible and avoid seeing Phoebe or Calder or any of the damned wedding party. After last night, that plan was more important than ever.

Not much longer.

Only twelve long, unbearable days.

Yet somehow after breakfast, he found himself among the company once again.

Phoebe was wearing blue again, this time a pale, nearly gray blue that saddened Rafe. She ought to wear the brightest colors of sky and jewels, for only those could merit and inspire the color in her cheeks and eyes.

Fortescue looked harried as he carried a tea tray into the room, then absently left without pouring any. Rafe slid a glance toward Calder. "Is something wrong?"

Calder didn't look up from his absorption with his newssheet. "The cook is sulking. Someone invaded the larder last night, made a perfect mess of everything."

Tessa made sympathetic noises, but Rafe could only very carefully not look at Phoebe. He averted his gaze to see Tessa gazing thoughtfully at him, then at Phoebe.

Tessa smiled slightly, then pressed a hand to her brow. "Lord Marbrook, will you do me a great service and accompany Phoebe and Sophie to Lementeur today for their fittings? I feel a headache coming on."

Lady Tessa didn't look ill. In fact, her eyes sparkled and her color was high, but it wasn't as though he could accuse her of falsifying a headache in order to get out of a shopping trip.

This time it was Phoebe who demurred. "Do not fret, Tessa. We will be perfectly all right with Nan and a footman, if Lord Brookhaven might spare us one?"

Calder looked up. "What? Oh, yes. Of course. I'd accompany you myself, but I've a mountain of reports to look over today. So sorry. Deepest regrets."

Calder didn't look terribly regretful. Rafe knew that his brother liked nothing better than burying himself in paperwork all day. It seemed to hold endless fascination for him.

Tessa smiled, but her eyes snapped in Phoebe's direction. "But I shall need Nan all day, for I'll not be able to rise from my bed at all. And to send two young ladies out with naught but a footman?" She switched her gaze to him and raised a brow.

Ah, his cue. Rafe bit back a sigh of resignation and bowed

his head. "I shall be delighted to accompany Miss Millbury and Miss Blake. I shall call for the carriage immediately."

He stood and left, although he could have made the order from where he sat. Spending another afternoon with Phoebe was the last thing he wanted to do.

*Yes, that explains why you put up such a struggle. You can't stand the sight of her.*

Phoebe watched Rafe leave. *Do not look at his bottom!* Oh, dear. Too late. Then he was gone and uncomfortable silence reigned once more.

Brookhaven sat with his gaze on the window, fingers twitching with impatience. Tessa began to dramatize her growing headache. Sophie had her nose in a book and Deirdre was watching Brookhaven's fingers twitch, looking as if she were about to take a mallet to them. The ticking of the ormolu clock on the mantel filled the room for a few eternal minutes.

Phoebe stood abruptly, unable to bear it. "Well, I suppose I shall make ready for that fitting. Sophie, shall we go?"

Sophie looked up from her book, blinking behind her spectacles. "Fitting?"

Phoebe sighed. "At Lementeur, remember? Lord Marbrook went to get the carriage ready."

Sophie gazed at her for a moment, her gaze sharp. Then the keen glint was gone and there was nothing but hazy disinterest there. "I'm sorry, Phoebe, but I really must decline. I've the headache, you see."

Phoebe narrowed her eyes at her cousin. *Traitor.*

She turned to Deirdre, who held up her hands. "I've callers coming any moment now. I promised to be at home today. You wouldn't ask a lady to break her word, would you?"

*Conspiracy.*

Phoebe waited for Brookhaven to make an offer to accompany her himself, instead of sending her with his brother, which wasn't precisely scandalous, but hardly ordinary, either.

Brookhaven glanced at the clock and stood. "Have a nice time, my dear. I shall look forward to hearing all about it at dinner." He turned and left with an absentminded bow to Tessa and the cousins.

*Trapped.* She had to make the appearance at Lementeur if she expected her wedding dress to be done in time. There was no help for it. How very annoying.

*Annoying? Is that why your heart is beating faster and your cheeks are turning pink?*

She put a hand to her face as she turned to leave the room. Damn her betraying blush anyway. She ran up the stairs to fetch her wrap instead of sending a servant, just to legitimize her high color. She wouldn't want him to think she was excited to go out alone with him!

The carriage was ready when she came down and Marbrook waited in the hall. If she didn't acknowledge the danger of such thought, she might imagine they were a married couple, preparing for a delightful drive on a lovely spring day.

And then home for an intimate dinner in the sitting room of their bedchamber, where they, half-dressed—her in a clinging wrapper and him in an open shirt with his muscular chest gleaming in the golden candle-glow— would feed each other tidbits with their fingers and lick them clean—

"You ought not to run so," Rafe said, his gaze averted as he helped her with her spencer. "Your cheeks are quite pink."

"Ah . . . hmm." Don't think. Don't imagine. Don't breathe him in—

His fingers tangled with hers when she reached to pull the spencer closed. He jerked his hands back—and accidentally brushed his palms against her fantasy-aroused

nipples. Her gasp was part shock and part exquisite pleasure at the sweep of hard, heated palms on tingling, aching
flesh.

"My a—apologies—I— Oh, hell!" Rafe turned away,
pressing his palms together to eradicate the memory of
those rigid, upturned points—or else to preserve it. Her
sighing gasp echoed in his mind. Pleasure? Horror?

Or like him, a bit of both?

She stepped back and did up her spencer with every appearance of great concentration. Then she cleared her
throat and raised her chin. "Yes, well . . . shall we go?"

Rafe took one look at her bosom, where even the wool
of the spencer couldn't hide the evidence of her . . . er,
stimulation. Then he jerked his gaze to the top of the stairs.
"Miss Blake?" *Please hurry, Miss Blake. Hasten down and
rescue me!*

"Sophie will not be accompanying us, my lord." She
seemed quite fascinated with the top button of her glove as
she pulled them on and took her bonnet from the side table.
"She has taken the headache as well."

*Lovely. Perfect.*

*Damn.*

Perhaps he could plead the headache himself. He was
certainly in legitimate pain—although his ache resided
somewhere a bit lower.

It was only worse in the carriage. Once the bustle of
seating themselves was over and the carriage was in motion, Rafe became intensely aware of their solitude. True,
London teemed around them as they made their way to
Bond Street yet that noisy populace seemed only like the
burble of a stream in a silent wood. The tension that
stretched between them hushed all the world, leaving only
they two alone.

Rafe tried breaking it. "Are you pleased with your ac-
commodations at Brook House, Miss Millbury?"

She glanced up, gratitude in her expression. "Oh, yes. My room is entirely comfortable. So big, and even the bed is large enough for two—" She went very still, her flush deepening yet more.

Yes, though not as fine as in the marchioness room, the bed in that room was very large and sumptuously hung. It had always reminded Rafe of a harem boudoir—or at least what he imagined one to be.

*Phoebe, clad only in the brief clinging gauze of a sultan's bride. Phoebe, bright eyes snapping over a seductively concealing veil. Phoebe, spread wantonly on that great, luxurious bed, naked and pink and wet for him—*

Rafe crossed his legs casually, setting his hat on his lap, and gazed unseeing at the city outside the window. He was going to go to hell and soon. Death by eternal erection.

Phoebe bit her lip. How could she have spoken of the bed, for pity's sake!

Luckily Marbrook hadn't seemed to notice anything. He seemed quite cool as he stared out the window—until she noticed the pulsing muscle in his jaw and how he kept shifting his position in his seat, as if something made him uncomfortable.

She herself was beginning to feel the effects of the jostling carriage. The rhythmic vibration of the wheels on the cobbles were doing great harm to her composure, coming as they were on top of her own stimulating thoughts.

Shocking thoughts. Wrong thoughts. She was very ashamed of herself.

She wondered how many times today she could manage to have Marbrook help her with her spencer . . .

*I am betrothed. I am a respectable, moral, virtuous woman. I am betrothed . . .*

It wasn't helping. Not with Marbrook so close she could smell the soap he shaved with. Not with him seated across from her, where she had such an excellent view of his handsome face and his broad chest and his large, well-shaped hands—

*He'd kissed her last night. He'd gone breathless with desire for her.*

The carriage rolled to a stop. Marbrook brightened. "Ah, yes. Here we are!"

He was out of the carriage in record time, obviously eager to be away from her.

Yet he handed her out with gentle courtesy and extended his arm to take her into Lementeur's, where Cabot stood ready at the door.

Once inside, Cabot showed Marbrook to a comfortable manly chair and displayed a selection of cigars and decanters. "Whisky," muttered Marbrook, and one glass of amber liquor was immediately bestowed upon him. Cabot made not the slightest indication that he thought it might be a bit early in the day for whisky . . . and to be truthful, Phoebe wouldn't have been averse to a nice nerve-steadying sip herself, but she wasn't offered one.

Instead, she was urged "backstage" of the dais. Two pretty maids waited there with a vast selection of gowns that could not all be for her.

They were. "The master said to make all new," one of the girls said. "Once you wear Lementeur, you won't want to put your old gowns on ever again."

Phoebe looked on in amazement as Brookhaven's true wealth became apparent. She'd thought the blue gown she'd already been given was very fine, and it was, but now it appeared that it had been a simple gown for an intimate dinner party, not the grand garment she had supposed.

The first thing she was put into—that is, literally dressed like a doll—was a beautiful blue-green silk with a structured bodice that made her bosom rise and float like buoys on the sea. The waist was fitted rather tightly, however.

One of the maids raised her voice. "Corset!" she cried,

for all the world like an army officer calling an order. A corset in matching silk appeared and Phoebe found herself laced into it before she could remark on the idea of a corset matched to every gown.

It was quite comfortable for a corset, but by some miracle of engineering, it also gave her a slender grace she'd never possessed, not even as a child. Her waist was tiny and her hips—so very worrisome to Lementeur two days before—were rounded without being wide. Now the gown slipped over her and closed without protest.

"Mirror!"

Phoebe found herself thrust through the curtains to stand on the dais once more, surrounded on three sides by mirrors.

She caught sight of herself in one and went still, her lips parted. She looked . . . she looked like Deirdre, or Tessa, only she was entirely herself as well. She looked stylish and elegant and every inch the wealthy, refined lady.

Then she saw, reflected in the mirror she faced, Marbrook's unguarded expression—his stunned, awed, hungry blue gaze that roved her body up and down.

Phoebe couldn't resist. She bent to fiddle with her hem, dropping her neckline into the mirror. She watched his face become suffused and his jaw tighten.

Again, the crossed legs and the hat. Aha. Phoebe managed not to smile in catlike satisfaction as she straightened from her very naughty test.

"You are a goddess," he breathed.

She looked up, startled. "What?"

He averted his gaze. "Nothing."

She narrowed her eyes. "You called me a goddess. I heard you quite clearly. The goddess of what?"

He turned to play as a last recourse. He grinned rakishly. "You are the goddess of green gowns. All green gowns must bow down to yours, because it is the finest in all the land, sewn by pixies by the light of the moon."

She raised a brow. "I would think a moonlight gown would be blue . . . or white."

He laughed, relieved that she was willing to play. "Then your gown was sewn by mermaids, princesses of the deepest depths."

She turned toward the mirrors, examining her reflection carefully. "A mermaid goddess." She cast an arch glance over her bared shoulder. The mischievous twinkle in her eyes sent an aching tremor through his gut. She was delicious.

"I should think a mermaid goddess would have her very own minion," she said haughtily. "Goddesses set great store by loyal minions, you should know."

He bowed deeply to hide the hunger he knew was flaring in his eyes. Composure, man! "Then your minion is here, your divine seaweediness."

She snickered, then forced a stern glare. "Behave, minion, or I shall be forced to have my legions of swordfish run you through."

"Then tell me, O thy limpet-speckled greatness, how shall I avoid such a perforated death?"

She turned in a swish of silk and began to count off on her fingers. "Firstly, all minions must know how to kneel. Secondly, a good minion should never say his goddess nay. The only permissible answers are 'yes,' 'as you wish,' and 'if my goddess permits me.' "

To Phoebe, the game was merely a welcome attempt to diffuse the tension she'd created with her shameless display.

Then Marbrook sank to one knee before her, a most peculiar look upon his handsome face. "Yes," he said huskily. "As you wish." His eyes were dark with something that made her ache inside. His lids lowered sensuously. "If my goddess permits me . . ."

She exhaled in a long, helpless sigh as he reached one

hand toward her hem. To have this man—this broad-shouldered, powerful man!—at her feet, calling her his goddess with that black hunger in his gaze . . .

Well, it just about melted a girl's knees, that's what!

She curtsied deeply to hide the shaking in her knees. "You are too kind, minion." When she rose, she stepped forward just as he extended his hand.

Her hem swept over it and his fingers slid over the inside of her ankle. They both froze.

She looked down at him, prepared to laugh it away, but his gaze was locked on the hand he couldn't see. She felt the softest caress in that sensitive place beneath her ankle-bone.

So she kept still when she ought to have stepped away, wobbly knees or no. She waited, frozen in place, as his hand slipped farther beneath the peacock green silk.

His fingers were warm and feather-light. She could barely feel them through the silk of her stocking.

She could barely feel anything else. There was no sound, no light, no world. Only the touch of his warm hand sliding slowly—so slowly it made her ache!—up from her ankle . . . and over her calf . . . and the soft crease behind her knee . . .

There was nothing but the rustle of silk as his hand rose upward between her knees, then past. She could feel the heat of it between her thighs now—no touch now, just heat—and it made her belly quiver.

She ought to move, ought to step away, ought to whirl out of his reach with a shocked and revolted gasp.

The odd thing was, she couldn't even remember what those words meant at that moment. All she could think was that, at the next moment, the heat of him would be on her—perhaps even in her . . .

His gaze flew upward to lock with hers. The heat inside her was nothing compared to the molten lust in his eyes.

"If my goddess permits me . . ." His voice was dark and husky with need.

She swayed forward, her eyes closing against the tide of hot lust that rushed over her. *Touch me . . .*

Her eyes flew open when the curtain behind her whisked to one side with a rattle of brass rings on the rod. She jolted in surprise and turned so abruptly that she staggered. Lementeur stepped forward and reached one hand out to aid her balance.

"My dear, you look entirely delicious." Lementeur considered her with approval. "Don't you think so, my lord?"

A choked sound from Marbrook made Phoebe whip her head around—but he was safely back in his chair three yards away, as if he'd never left.

His hat was in his lap once more.

Lementeur whisked Phoebe away again, leaving Rafe alone with his burning thoughts and throbbing groin.

*Days.* Not years, not months. It would be mere days until the wedding and he could leave this madness behind. Perhaps he would find himself a pretty wife in the Americas and make some fat babies with her. All he had to do was survive the next two weeks and keep his hands off the girl.

Lost in thought, he didn't look up when the curtain was whisked back again.

"Ahem," a soft voice said.

Rafe glanced up—and could not look away.

She was no longer just a girl. She was a bride.

Rich off-white satin was folded and tucked on the bodice of the beautiful gown, the lines arrowing out from the overlapped center to a knotted scrap of sleeve perched on each shoulder like a tiny ivory dove. The skirt fell in long, graceful folds, reminding him of a Greek column. Her skin glowed against the perfect pale color, while her hair outshone the faint golden tint.

*'Tis bad luck for the groom to see the bride before the wedding.*

Where had that thought come from? Rafe swallowed. Could it be that he still entertained some fantasy that Phoebe would change her mind? How mad and deluded could one man be? She stood before him in her wedding gown, for pity's sake!

He met her gaze. She was waiting to hear what he thought. It clearly mattered to her a great deal what he thought.

Which was wrong. She ought to be all atwitter over Calder's opinion, not his.

Damn. He'd done this with his lack of self-control. He'd muddled her mind, weakened her determination to take this advantageous step.

And the only one to pay for it would be her. In the end, he would walk away a free man—albeit with a hole in his heart. But no one needed to know about that.

He stood. "You look astonishingly beautiful."

She blinked. "I do?"

"There is no lovelier woman in all of England," he said gravely. Let her hear it once, for God knew Calder would never say it. "You should never forget that." He bent to pick up his hat. "If you'll excuse me, I find that I must go now. The carriage will take you back to Brook House when you're finished here."

With that, he turned his back on the bride of his heart—though it tore him nearly in two to do so—and walked away.

# Chapter Thirty

The next day, Phoebe managed to go the entire day without seeing Rafe. At this point, the sensible thing would be to avoid him entirely. She took breakfast in her room, kept to the loneliest portions of the house during the morning, pled the headache during calls and made it last all through dinner.

Brookhaven sent an officious message requesting that she inform him if she required a physician. She replied that, no, she was only overtired from the past few days of activity and she was going to bed early.

Activity that had been a great deal more strenuous and breathless than Brookhaven could ever be allowed to know!

He sent another message, reminding her that they had seats at the opera the next night. Phoebe knew there'd be no more hiding tomorrow. Brookhaven expected her to plan the wedding and be on his arm, ready to play marchioness.

It hadn't worked, anyway. It did no good, trying to avoid Rafe. He was everywhere . . . in the servants' conversation, in the portraits on the wall, in his hat and gloves on the front hall table, his voice rumbling through the halls . . .

She heard him coming once, the distinctive stride of his

down the hall. She spun about, thinking to flee to the front of the house.

Brookhaven's deep voice resounded in the front hall, just coming in the door.

Rafe was behind her and Brookhaven on the approach. She turned to duck into the library. No, blast it. The vicar was ensconced within. He would know she weakened. His sharp eyes still followed her every move.

There were simply too many men in this house!

Across the hall another door beckoned. It was a servants door, flush to the wall, disguised as part of the paneling. Phoebe was through it in a flash. She carefully closed the door behind her, then pressed her ear to it. Had she been spotted?

Footfalls on the hall runner, then more from the other direction.

Both sets of footsteps paused before the linen closet.

Phoebe shook her head in the darkness. Of course.

"Ah, Rafe—I'm glad I caught you. I've been meaning to speak to you about my fiancée."

Oh, dear. Phoebe didn't know whether to shrink back and cover her ears or press herself more tightly to the door and listen.

"What about Ph—Miss Millbury, Calder?" Rafe's tone was wary.

Calder cleared his throat. "Well, I have noticed you have a tendency to gaze at her. And you do seem to be always *about*. Even the staff has commented."

Oh drat. Someone had seen them in the larder—or the parlor—or the hall—

*My my, we have been busy* . . .

She wrapped her arms tightly about her chilled midsection and tried to listen through the roaring in her ears.

Scandal. Disgrace. Notoriety.

Oh please, no.

"What of it?" Rafe was bristling, she could tell.

Calder harrumphed. "There's no need to take offense. After all, you built your own reputation. You can hardly expect me to ignore something you've worked so diligently on."

"Why not? You ignore everything else I care about."

"Meaning Brookhaven?"

Brookhaven? Phoebe sat back slightly. This wasn't about her, but the estate?

"Of course I mean Brookhaven!" Rafe's voice began to rise. "You've ignored every suggestion I've made!"

Calder snorted. "Well, but really, Rafe. You're hardly in a position to know what's best for an estate the size and complexity of Brookhaven."

There was a moment of silence. Phoebe waited, scarcely allowing herself to breathe. Did Calder even realize what he'd just said?

When Rafe did speak, his tone was so quiet she almost couldn't hear.

"Because I had the wrong sort of mother, you mean?" His tone was like the furious snap of a whip. "Did that accident of birth cause a deficiency in my brain, do you think?"

Calder let out an impatient sound. "Don't be ridiculous. There's nothing wrong with your brain—when you choose to use it."

"Ah. You're saying I don't think matters through—say perhaps like the matter of proposing to a woman you've never met?"

Ah, now it was back to her. Except . . . was it her imagination or were she and Brookhaven somehow tied together in this brotherly clashing of antlers?

Calder grunted. "Why I so promptly proposed to Miss Millbury is of little moment."

Really? Because Phoebe was perishing to know.

Rafe continued in his too quiet tones. "I think it is of vast moment. I believe that if you were to answer that question truthfully, that you and I might just have to take this outside . . . or choose weapons."

Phoebe swallowed, her chilled gut turning to pure ice. Oh, no. What had she wrought here in this grand house?

Or was the battle simply far too ancient for her to influence either way? Was she simply a new pennant in an old war?

"You've been drinking again." Calder's tone was of condescension covering alarm.

Rafe let out a long breath. Phoebe breathed with him, willing him to back down from that perilous stance.

"Actually, no," Rafe said in lighter tones. "Not a drop since the ladies encamped, in fact."

Phoebe heard his steps begin, moving away down the hall.

"Although your brotherly *concern* for my well-being does make me want to swallow great amounts of brandy," he called back to Calder. "Great, amber *oceans* of brandy."

His striding steps faded then and silence reigned outside Phoebe's hiding place. Was Calder still there? Should she open the door a bit to peek?

Then she heard the rumble of Calder's muttering. "Bloody, damn buggering *hell.*"

Phoebe's eyes widened at the profanity. Not that she was shocked to hear it—she'd assisted at more than a few village childbirths, after all!—but she was most certainly shocked to hear it from the stiff, cool, upright Marquis of Brookhaven.

Apparently she wasn't the only one subject to fits of strong emotion when it came to Lord Raphael Marbrook!

She heard Calder's usually measured tread march off in the opposite direction in relatively unseemly haste.

Although it was dark as pitch in the chamber where she was, suddenly things were becoming all too clear. Her heart sank and she slid down the wall with it until she crouched with her hands clasped about her drawn-up knees.

Two dogs, circling warily, and she was the bone—or the symbol of the Brookhaven bone—or something such. Her head ached.

A discreet tap came at the door. "Miss?"

Phoebe sighed. "Yes, Fortescue?" She answered without lifting her forehead from her knees.

"Miss Millbury, might I be of some assistance?"

"No thank you, Fortescue. I'm perfectly fine."

"A candle perhaps?"

"No, thank you." She paused a moment. "Fortescue, what room is this?"

"'Tis the closet where we keep the table linens, miss."

"Will anyone be needing linens for the next few hours?"

She could almost hear the elegant Fortescue purse his lips in barest amusement.

"I believe we can make do without, miss. What should I tell his lordship if he asks after your whereabouts?"

She leaned her head back against the door. "Fortescue, have you ever seen two dogs fight over a bone?"

"Yes, miss."

"Well, this particular bone needs a bit of a holiday."

"Indeed, miss. I shall tell his lordship that you are indisposed."

"You're a treasure, Fortescue. Now go away."

"Yes, miss. Have a nice holiday, miss."

So here she was in the dark and silence and privacy she'd craved so desperately. She ought to take this time to plan her honeymoon or learn the staff's names or consider which charities Lady Brookhaven ought to endow—but there was one only thought on her wayward mind.

Three days—and she'd not managed to keep her hands to herself for any one of them. She didn't know how she was going to bear another eleven!

♦ ♦ ♦

OUTSIDE THE LINEN closet, Fortescue pondered the door behind which the future Lady Brookhaven cowered.

She was a lovely young lady, so sweet and unassuming.

The poor thing was going to be chewed alive by Society. If their lordships didn't manage it first.

A soft laugh from nearby sent a quivering tingle up his spine. He did not turn. "Good afternoon, Patricia."

Light footsteps approached. "Good afternoon, sir." She came to stand next to him—not too close, of course, but it didn't matter. He could still catch the warm, cinnamon scent of her.

"Will she be comin' out soon, d'you think, sir?" The laughter in Patricia's voice was gentle, not mocking. "I've a sudden need for a tablecloth, like."

Fortescue inhaled carefully and managed not to close his eyes and moan in pleasure. "I believe Miss Millbury is taking a bit of a holiday from the tensions of preparing for the wedding."

"Aye," Patricia sobered. "But has she decided which one?"

Fortescue swallowed. "We do not gossip about our employers."

Patricia shook her head, sending more aphrodisiac scent to enfold him. "I'm worried about her, sir. She's a real lady, for all her simple ways. I hate to see her so sad."

So his Irish flower was kind as well as lovely. The flames threatened to burn him alive.

"'Tis nice that she has your understandin', sir," Patricia went on, approval making her voice softer yet. "Most men would think her daft for hidin' amongst the napkins."

He felt a touch on his sleeve. "You're a good sort, Mr. Fortescue."

No one touched him. Ever.

His arm felt cold once she'd moved away.

# Chapter Thirty~one

Rafe could bear it no longer. He'd spent most of yesterday pacing, except when he couldn't resist venturing out into the house to catch a glimpse of Phoebe, who was apparently avoiding him. It was for the best.

He hated it.

An entire day without her caused an ache so deep that it alarmed him. And convinced him. The emptiness he felt when she was not close by—as if his life would always stay the same shallow lonely existence it was now.

There was no help for it. He was going to have to leave. Now. Calder was going to want to know the reason. Hopefully, Rafe would think of a convincing way to explain his sudden compulsion to be very far away.

Rafe found Calder standing by his desk, gathering papers into a leather file. Calder was dressed to travel.

"Going somewhere?"

Calder didn't so much as glance up. "Yes. There's a problem at the china factory. One of the kilns caused a fire. I'm off to assess the damage."

Rafe folded his arms. He didn't understand Calder's fascination with manufacturing, especially with Brookhaven crying out for more of his brother's attention. "Don't you have people who have people that look into that sort of thing for you?"

Calder snorted and tied the file folder shut. "And wait days for unsatisfactory information to travel back and forth? It's much more efficient to simply go there and put my decisions into action firsthand."

"What about Ph—Miss Millbury?"

"What about her? My business matters are no concern of hers."

*You'd do that, wouldn't you, brother? You'd shut her out of everything that matters to you, just as you did to Melinda, and then wonder why she is unhappy! You have this woman, this lovely, loving, precious woman—you have* everything—*but you'll never appreciate a shred of it.*

That didn't bear saying, unfortunately. Calder didn't speak of Melinda. Ever. Rafe worked his jaw against the words that wanted to spew out. "Don't you and Miss Millbury have an engagement tonight?" His tone was short, but not as heated as his brother deserved.

Calder halted in his swift exit. "Oh, hell. The opera seats." He tucked the file under his arm and bent over a sheet of paper on his desk. With a jab of the quill into the ink, he scrawled a quick message and folded the note once. Straightening, he thrust it at Rafe. "See that it gets to her, will you? I've a horse waiting."

Rafe took the note as Calder hurried by him. "God forbid you inconvenience the horse," he muttered. "To hell with the rest of us."

Of course, Calder heard none of it, for he was already gone.

Rafe gazed down at the note in his hand.

*My dear Miss Millbury, I regret that I am unable to fulfill my promise to you this evening.*
    *Brookhaven.*

A good brother would see that the message was delivered. A good brother would fling himself on the first ship bound for other seas.

He crumpled the note and shoved it in his pocket. "Apparently I am not a good brother."

He couldn't do it. He could not leave now and desert Phoebe to a life of luxurious neglect, to know that her discontent would grow until the day that, like Melinda, she was flung from a disintegrating carriage like a broken doll in her attempt to flee the pain and emptiness of her life.

Phoebe's unhappy future rose before him. He must try once more to convince her not to go through with this marriage.

Apparently, Melinda had known something about Calder that Rafe had never wanted to believe.

In his own perfectly correct, wintry, and heartless way, Calder really was the Bastard of Brookhaven.

TESSA WAS LISTENING again. Oh, if anyone had passed, she would have seemed to be purposefully headed down the hall.

She was rarely caught in the act, however. She'd had a brutal, violent father who'd not always been susceptible to her carefully doled-out charm. It had been a fine line between cajoling him from his black moods . . . and attracting him too much. She'd learned to manipulate, to scheme—and to win.

Not to mention how to move quietly in a man's house, ever alert to things like the smell of cigars, the clink of a whisky decanter against a glass, the heavier step. Such a skill never seemed to become less useful, she thought, smiling to herself.

Brookhaven was away . . . and it seemed the mice were going to play.

Well, far be it from her to stand in the way of young

love. Especially when helping it along just might make her—or rather, Deirdre, of course—a very rich woman.

IN THE OFFICE of Stickley & Wolfe, Solicitors, a new plan of battle had been hatched.

"His lordship has seats to the opera tonight. I've confirmed with a delivery lad to Brook House that himself is taking his bride-to-be. They've their own box, of course, which means that his lordship will be ducking out occasionally to stretch his legs, have a smoke, et cetera."

"Et cetera?"

Wolfe endeavored not to roll his eyes. "Take a piss, then. At any rate, we can dress up to fit in and wait outside his box. The upper levels of the opera house are a maze of little halls. We'll snatch him, overwhelm him between the two of us, and . . ." Stickley's twitching became no longer ignorable. "What?"

"I don't have anything to wear."

Wolfe shrugged. "Any evening suit will do—"

Stickley's twitching intensified. Wolfe's eyes widened. "You don't have an evening suit."

"I've never had a use for one," Stickley said primly. "I do not condone expenditures on unnecessary clothing."

Wolfe snarled. "*Fine. I'll* wait for him, *I'll* overwhelm him, and you'll wait at the back door of the theater with the cart at the ready."

Stickley nodded nervously. "All right. If you truly think it is necessary to go to such extremes."

Wolfe grinned toothily. "Stick, old son, she can't marry him if he isn't there!"

UPSTAIRS IN HER bedchamber, Phoebe had three of the new gowns from Lementeur laid on the bed and was regarding them with a frown. What to wear to the opera with the Marquis of Brookhaven?

First of all, she'd never been to the opera, and while it was assumed that one dressed very well, she had some doubt as to the degree.

Second of all, what would be appropriate for an affianced bride of a marquis?

Deirdre would likely know and might help, but she was off driving in Hyde Park with one of her admirers. Sophie— well, never mind.

*This is one of those times when having a mother would truly be a blessing.*

"Having trouble, dear?" a kind voice inquired.

Phoebe started, whirling toward the doorway of her chamber.

But it was only Tessa, stepping gracefully into the room, a gentle smile on her face—which was out-and-out bizarre, actually. Phoebe stepped back warily. "Lady Tessa."

Tessa's smile deepened. "Surely you can call me 'Aunt' by now, dear?" She came even with Phoebe and perused her choices. "Oh, how pretty! You've done well. However . . . oh, dear. Ordinarily, these would do perfectly well but . . ."

Phoebe eyed her gowns, her doubts rising anew. "But what?" She might not trust Tessa but there was no denying Tessa's exquisite taste—in her own fashions, at least.

"Well, this is your first evening at the opera as the marquis's betrothed bride. One wants to make a lasting first impression, doesn't one?"

Phoebe's stomach turned over. All eyes upon her— tongues wagging—

*Don't do it.*

"Help me, please, aunt!"

*Now you've done it.*

Tessa beamed. "Of course, dear!" She turned toward the the bounty of gowns Phoebe had received from Lementeur.

Phoebe followed Tessa like a worried puppy. "I'd thought blue, for his lordship, but I did not know if a deep color would be appropriate or if I should select something light—"

Tessa waved a negating hand. "Theatrical is always the order of the day at the opera. All the ladies wear their very most dramatic and exciting gowns—ah, this will do perfectly!"

Tessa reached for the one gown that Phoebe had especially avoided—the blue-green extravaganza that made her look as though she were made entirely of bosom.

And made her think of the look in Rafe's eyes when she'd tried it on for him . . .

"Oh, no! I couldn't."

Tessa turned with the gown in her hands and blinked at her in puzzlement. "Whyever not? What is the use of a gown you will not wear?"

"But it makes me very—" Phoebe indicated with both hands before her, blushing.

Tessa gave a tinkling laugh. "Well, then it will stifle those wits who can't see why Brookhaven chose you from all the others!" She seemed completely unconcerned that she was lumping herself and Deirdre in that group.

"I—I thought you were upset about the match," Phoebe said hesitantly. "With the chance that I'll win."

Tessa shrugged. "Well, I won't deny that I was a bit miffed at first. Yet why should I care, really? No matter what the outcome, I personally would never receive anything but the satisfaction of seeing Deirdre nicely set—and I've no doubt she's entirely capable of securing a fine future for herself. Brookhaven's connections will make that all the easier now. So there is little point in holding your good fortune against you, is there?"

Tessa in general made Phoebe uneasy, but her words did make sense. Deirdre was one of the beauties of the Season.

She might very well make a match worth far more than twenty-seven thousand pounds.

She found herself smiling shyly. "Very well. I shall wear the gown." It was a beautiful creation.

"Lovely!" Tessa turned her toward the mirror and held the gown to her front, reaching from behind and gazing encouragingly over Phoebe's shoulder. "See? Brookhaven won't be able to resist you!"

*Brookhaven.* Phoebe felt that same twisted guilt at the thought of getting close to his lordship.

Yet that was how it should be. She should be dressing to please Brookhaven and no one else. And perhaps . . .

Perhaps if she made herself as tempting as possible— perhaps Brookhaven would be driven to long for her as Rafe did.

And perhaps that would inspire her to long for him right back. Perhaps that was all that was lacking. Perhaps then things would be as they should be.

Perhaps.

# Chapter Thirty-two

Two hours later she was dressed and she knew she'd never looked more tempting in her life. Tessa had magnanimously sent Nan to help Patricia and had even supervised the various choices of hairstyle.

In the end, both the maids and Tessa had agreed that the hair should be as simple and elegant as possible, so as not to draw attention away from the gown—"And your pretty face, dear."

Of course, to Phoebe's eye, that meant that the primary draw of the world's—and Brookhaven's!—attention would be her bosom. It was disconcerting to think about going out in public so . . . so exposed.

Yet Phoebe had seen Tessa herself in worse, and other ladies of the ton as well. Apparently what was not acceptable for the daughter of Thornton's vicar was entirely expected of the new Marchioness of Brookhaven.

*I—and my breasts—are simply going to have to get used to this.*

So was the vicar, apparently. He was waiting for her outside her bedchamber door when she emerged, wrap in hand, peacock feathers waving high above her head.

His eyes went wide and there was a severe bout of throat clearing. Finally he pulled himself together—but only by staring somewhere over Phoebe's left shoulder. She herself was blushing mightily at the thought of her tightly bound father seeing quite so much of her—ah, assets.

He cleared his throat one last time.

"My dear—" he began. "I wish to speak to you for a moment."

Tessa and Nan had moved discreetly away already. "Yes, Papa?"

"I—er—I thought it was high time I commended you for the way that you've overcome your—" He cast one helpless glance downward, then squeezed his eyes shut. "Your previously wicked nature."

The hypocrisy was almost more than she could bear. All those years of perfect behavior had garnered nothing but criticism, yet throwing herself on her betrothed while half clothed met with praise.

She'd been a silly child. She'd made a terrible mistake.

In shocked response, the vicar had essentially put her in gaol, hiring servants whose sole purpose was to watch her. From ignored to imprisoned in one swift move.

*What is the primary difference between a rich marquis and a poor dancing master? Coin. And the brood mare goes to the highest bidder.*

And what was the rich marquis going to think when he discovered that he'd purchased soiled goods?

"Papa . . ." She had no one else to talk to. "Papa, what am I going to do on my wedding night when Brookhaven discovers that I'm not—"

"Not prepared?" The vicar interrupted too quickly—and his ruddy flush was not due to squeamishness.

Phoebe blinked. "You know?"

He looked away, clearing his throat. "Nothing to know. *Nothing at all.*"

Phoebe was stunned. The vicar, self-righteous man of God, was a liar. Moreover, he fully intended for her to lie in order to bag and bed a marquis. Was he even particular about that order of events?

*How dare you judge me so harshly for my poor misdirected heart? At least I sinned out of love!*

Out loud, all she said was, "Yes, Papa."

He huffed, obviously pleased by her decorous meekness. "Well, never let it be said that I don't give credit where credit is due! You have come a long way from the wild and wayward girl you used to be, my dear."

"Have I?" And yet, who was she now—wild, untamed, sensual Phoebe of the past or prim, demure, faultless Phoebe of the present? One man wanted one woman, the other man wanted the opposite.

*I miss that girl.*

*I miss myself.*

But that girl would never be the Duchess of Brookmoor. That girl would never be immune.

RAFE WAS COMMITTING the unforgivable and he knew it. As he prepared for his departure, he saw to every detail of his affairs, leaving nothing behind that he might ever need to come back for.

The gamble for Phoebe's heart was a sure thing—a sure thing that he would somehow lose by it. He was simply in too much pain to care. The devil on his shoulder had spoken and he'd listened—he intended to take this last chance with her.

If she accepted him, he would lose his brother forever.

If she rejected him, he'd lose Calder anyway, for he would never be able to face the future here in England— living out his days in his brother's house, watching his brother live happily evermore with his lovely new wife.

There was one last thing to take care of. He stood before

his dressing table, gazing down at the Marbrook signet ring that was as much a part of him as the finger it had spent the last twenty years circling.

There was no possibility of coming back from this betrayal of his brother, no way to come back home . . . ever.

The signet hit the crystal dish, ringing like a bell.

The voice in his mind took on an edge of horror.

*What are you doing? Are you mad? You are a Marbrook! That is the only thing you have left!*

It didn't matter. His heart was torn from him, kept prisoner in another's hands, and he couldn't even regret it. If ever a woman was worth a man forfeiting his soul, it was Phoebe. The agony of living without her, of breathing and eating and sleeping for the rest of his life with this hole in his chest was more than he could bear. She loved him as well. He must believe it. He could be the man she wanted—he must believe it or he would surely die.

He rubbed the heel of his hand against the place where his heart used to reside. The ache did not subside, the need did not abate.

There was no help for it.

At least, one outcome or the other, this torture would at last be done.

# Chapter Thirty-three

The footman was dressed in the usual blue and black, the carriage standing in the street before Brook House was one they'd used before. There was nothing to make Phoebe suspect that there was anything odd in the gloved hand that reached from the darkness within.

Yet the instant she placed her own gloved hand within it, she knew.

She made to pull back, but Rafe's hand tightened on hers and implacably pulled her inside.

Or perhaps she went willingly. It wasn't as though she could think clearly when he touched her!

At any rate, she found herself in the dark carriage alone with a man she should not be alone with. He had released her instantly when the carriage door had shut, but she could still feel the heat of his fingers on hers. Her belly tightened and she shifted uneasily. Just being near him had the most disturbing effect between her thighs. Every bump and rattle of the carriage threatened to worsen her condition, and the longer he let the silence stretch, the higher her tension ran.

Finally, she could not bear it. "Where is he?"

She heard him draw a deep breath.

"In Hertfordshire. Something blew up."

She waited for him to elaborate, but the silence fell

again. She ought to have filled it with more questions, or even something inane about the evening fog, but she'd hesitated too long for normal conversation and could not bring herself to speak again.

He was watching her. She could feel his gaze on the skin of her face, neck, and upwelling breasts. The light from the forward carriage lantern cast a yellow glow on her while keeping him in total shadow, but she knew he was staring. She'd worn the blue-green gown for Calder's titillation—a heavy-handed attempt for the attention of a rather dense man. Now she wished she'd borrowed a nun's habit instead. Rafe obviously needed no such stimulation.

"You look like a lamb for slaughter."

"The only one I want slaughtered is you," Phoebe shot back instantly. "What are you thinking, sneaking up on me this way? You know I cannot resist you!" Then she blinked. Where had that come from? Damn the man! He always brought out the "other" Phoebe in her!

As the wheels rolled through the London streets, Phoebe considered her options. She might scream. She might fling herself from the carriage, or beg assistance from the footman even now clinging to the rear of the vehicle.

She did none of those things. This was Rafe, who hadn't done a thing to her that she'd not been a willing, if later shamed, party to.

They did need to talk, that was a fact. She needed to make sure that he understood that she was serious in her decision to move forward with her commitment to Calder.

There would an opportunity to speak in the box at the opera, and they would be most public there. No danger of undone buttons or flung cravats. It was odd that she was accompanied by Rafe and not her betrothed, but perhaps not too scandalous.

So she decided to bide her time and wait for them to reach the opera house in Covent Garden. She gazed out the window, although the fog-smeared view was little more than a series of dark outlines and blurs of light.

Then she noticed that the blurs of light had become fewer and the darkness more dense and closer to them. She peered outside, alarms sounding within her—along with the distinct sensation that she'd missed her opportunity for escape.

"Where are we?" She stood to press her hand to the latch of the carriage door.

"Phoebe, don't—"

She opened the door, which swung outward—

Into the sweeping branch of a tree. It knocked the door shut, hard. The impact flung Phoebe backward.

*"Oof."* She landed on large, warm man. She was sprawled across his lap!

She tried to scramble to her feet. Hard arms came about her, keeping her where she was. "Shh." His breath was hot in her ear, sending shivers through her body to mingle with the trembling of alarm.

She used her hands to pull her upper body off his, although his arms about her waist kept her bottom firmly planted on his lap . . . where matters were developing at an alarming rate. She struggled. "Where are you taking me, my lord?"

"Phoebe," he gasped. "Stop wriggling or we won't be talking at all soon."

She went completely still, although she did not relax against him. Now she could feel him, every inch of him, hardening against her. She was leaning forward, gripping the opposite seat handle in her attempt to get away. Unfortunately, that tilt of her hips only planted her most sensitive area right on top of his rigid, pulsating erection.

The tissue-thin gown and sheer petticoats were no barrier at all. His trousers were fine as well, leaving nothing but a few frail fabrics between seeking and finding . . .

He groaned, shifting spasmodically beneath her. She gasped, jolted by the rush of pleasure. He moved again, slowly this time, as if he could not help himself.

The pressure of him there, the heat of his body, the way his hands slipped down to grasp her hips.

The jolting of the moving carriage added delightful bumps and shudders to the process, as did the feeling of his heated panting on her bared back and the hard, nearly painful grip of his hands on her.

The ride grew frantic—chaotic—breathless—

At last, Phoebe tossed her head back, letting out a cry as the jolting motion brought pleasure that took her higher, pushed her farther, snatched her up, and threw her over the edge of heaven to let her fall, headlong.

She fell forward, panting, her hair tumbling down over her shoulders and face, bracing her hands on the opposite seat to keep from falling apart completely.

Then she noticed that the carriage had slowed and now jolted to a stop.

"My lord?" The driver's voice preceded the sound of the small latch that held shut the square speaking hole in the roof of the carriage.

Swiftly, Rafe flung Phoebe into the darkest corner of the opposite seat, just before the square of lantern light fell upon his upturned face. He put up a hand to shield his eyes.

"My lord, is everything all right? Was the ride too rough?"

Phoebe clapped a hand over her mouth to stop her horrified laugh.

Rafe cleared his throat. "Everything is fine."

"Yes, my lord. Ah, my lord, how much farther are ye wantin' to do down this road? We passed the last inn for miles near five minutes ago."

Phoebe saw the hand-caught-in-the-biscuit-tin amusement fade from Rafe's face as he shot her a disconcerted glance. "We'll halt here a moment," Rafe told the driver. Phoebe felt her own pleasurable lassitude seep away to be replaced by dismay.

He'd meant to bring her out of town, to an inn far from interruption—or aid.

She'd just been kidnapped.

SLIDING FROM HIS seat, Rafe went to his knees before her in a sudden rush that made her gasp.

"Phoebe, please! I'm sorry. I had to do it. I cannot stop thinking about you . . . about the way you look at me—as if I am more than a man. As if I am a hero. When I am with you, I am the way I once was—before bitterness and resentment came between me and the world like a hard shell."

He reached for her hands, grabbing them like lifelines. "I was a boy who worshiped his father and dreamed of being like him someday." He smiled crookedly. "Perhaps without the production of bastards with the widow down the lane . . . but a man who took pride in his lands and his people, who wore the mantle of master with humility and care. It wasn't until I realized that every stick and stone and rivulet was actually Calder's that I—"

He halted the torrent of confession, for she was gazing at him in horror and consternation.

"I'm going about this all wrong, aren't I?"

"You aren't seriously suggesting that I jilt Calder and run away with you? How? Tonight? In a gown your brother bought for me, in his carriage, driven by his servants?" She drew back. "How can you suggest such a thing!"

"Because he cannot make you happy! He never will, don't you see? He is stone, icy impervious stone! Your heart will shrivel and die with him! He will never understand you as I do—he will never listen to your dreams—he will never play Goddess and Minion, or Lady and Knight! Can you truthfully tell me that you will be satisfied to live out your days without another moment of daydream or delight? That you can go on, joyless year after joyless year, without laughter or love, and not turn into either a dead, frozen imitation of the woman you are now or go wild with desperation and bring harm to yourself somehow? It has happened before!"

She looked down at her hands clasped in his. "Melinda," she said flatly.

"She was not so different from you, you know," he said urgently. "She thought she could be satisfied with the trappings of wealth and status. She thought that if her life looked beautiful, it would be so, but in the end she wanted more than empty, icy distinction—she ached for more!—until she decided she simply couldn't live another day without it."

His gaze searched her face for her response, but she felt frozen.

"Phoebe, don't you see? You can stop this now, right this very minute. Change the course of everything! Choose me!" He dropped his forehead to rest on their clasped hands. "You can be happy," he said huskily. "I can give you a happy life, I swear it."

*A happy life.* Rafe, hers for always. The nights—oh heaven, the nights!—and then the mornings, with the sun streaming in the windows of some small but wonderful cottage. And when they went out together—

When they went out together, it would begin. Whispers. Sideways glances. Derision.

*"The rake's bride—"*

*"—wed in scandal—"*

A lifetime of notoriety. She had been in Society long

enough now to realize that her father had been accurate all along. Gossip never went away. It lived forever and grew and grew, until no one knew the real truth or even cared.

Panic swept her, until her ears roared and her throat began to close. She pulled away from him, gasping. "I cannot breathe—I cannot think—" She shook her head wildly. "No! I never want to feel that way again! I am too afraid!"

"Afraid?"

Her hands began to shake. *Yes, afraid. So afraid of that bleak, desperate place of being everlastingly in the wrong.* She pushed at him wildly. "Oh, no. I could not bear it!"

"Bear what? Phoebe, speak to me!"

She tried to catch her breath enough to answer. "I am already watched, emulated, talked about—simply for becoming engaged! What do you think the world will think of me for throwing away a marquis for a bastard rake!"

She saw the pain flare in his eyes and shook her head. "I'm sorry. You know that I don't hold your birth or your past against you . . . but they will hold it against me! Wherever I go, for the rest of my life, they will whisper, they will point. I will be known as the Bastard's Bride, or the Runaway Duchess, or something else more horrible."

"They are whispers," he said softly. "Only whispers. What do they matter?"

She choked on damp and bitter laughter. "If wedding you gives me this much pause—when I feel the way I do about you," she gasped, unable to catch her breath. She suffocated under the burden of that future even now! "How do you think my father will react? My cousins? The family in the house next door, who won't let their children play with ours—the people who will leave the ballroom when we walk in!"

"Let them walk! We will dance alone if we must!"

"Alone? Do you understand what alone is? You have always had Calder. I have only the vicar. You do not know what it is like, having someone's love by a thread. The worry that one wrong move will cut that thread and you will lose them forever . . ." The thought stole the air from her lungs once again.

His brows drew together. "Have you not met my brother?"

She shook her head. "No. Calder loves you. You've tested him for years and he's still there."

"No he isn't." Rafe pulled away to sit wearily in the opposite seat. "Not after tonight, at any rate." Rafe smiled crookedly. He reached upward to knock on the small trapdoor above.

There was a pause. "Yes, my lord."

Oh, God. Phoebe closed her eyes tightly.

"Do you and Stevens think the lady and myself might have a moment to ourselves now?"

"Yes, my lord. Stevens and I will just walk down the road a bit, eh?"

Phoebe waited as the two jumped down and their steps faded to silence.

# Chapter Thirty-four

Deirdre wandered into the music room where Sophie was working on the next phase of her translation. Sophie gave a brief finger wave but did not break her concentration. Deirdre flung herself across the settee with a small world-weary "oomph."

"Tessa's up to something," Deirdre stated firmly.

Sophie sighed inwardly at the determined interruption, then marked her place with care. Putting down her pencil, she turned her attention fully to Deirdre. "What makes you say that?"

Deirdre snorted. "Years of practice." She sat up and frowned at Sophie. "She helped Phoebe dress for the opera tonight. Tessa never helps anyone unless there's something in it for her. What could she possibly gain from Phoebe looking so beautiful at the opera tonight?"

Sophie shrugged. "I have no idea, since Phoebe isn't going to the opera tonight."

Deirdre blinked. "What?"

Sophie tried not to let her gaze wander back to the page she'd been working on. "I heard Fortescue tell one of the footmen. Lord Brookhaven's been called out of town on business."

Deirdre snapped her fingers. "Sophie, concentrate! Are you sure about this?"

Sophie blinked, realizing that Deirdre was truly worried about something. "Of course I'm sure. I saw him ride away hours back. I'm sure Phoebe knows by now."

Deirdre shook her head slowly. "Phoebe left an hour ago—with a man who apparently isn't Lord Brookhaven."

It was Sophie's turn to snort in disbelief. "Who in the world would she have left with, if not his lordship?"

Deirdre raised a brow. "Who indeed?"

Alarm and a bit of envy began to shimmer in Sophie. "Did you say she looked beautiful?"

Deirdre nodded gravely. "I've never seen her look so . . . delectable."

"Oh dear." Sophie bit her lip. She didn't know whether to be happy for Phoebe or heartbroken. "And you think Tessa knew about this?"

Deirdre narrowed her eyes. "Tessa can be very perceptive if it's for her own gain."

Sophie considered Deirdre for a moment, forgetting all about her translation. "You know about Phoebe and Marbrook?"

Deirdre leaned back upon the settee and folded her arms. "Not as much as you, apparently. Why don't you fill me in?"

Perhaps not surprisingly, Tessa was not amused by their suspicions when they confronted her a few moments later where she loitered in the front parlor, flipping through the latest gossip sheets.

"I'm sure I don't know what you mean. I was only trying to help poor Phoebe. She's so useless when it comes to fashion." She laughed, a musical sneer of a laugh. "Rather like dressing up a cow for a parade."

Deirdre gazed at her stepmother coldly. "Did you dress the cow for a parade or for milking? You knew Brookhaven called off the evening at the opera."

Tessa blinked in overdone surprise. "Did he? I'm stunned. I had no idea. Phoebe must have kept it from me in order to maneuver a tête-à-tête with . . ." She snickered. "Another man!"

Sophie gasped. "That's a lie!"

Deirdre could have told her cousin to save her shock. Tessa hadn't been within a mile of the truth for as long as Deirdre had known her.

Tessa actually seemed to take offense at Sophie's righteous stance. "Why do you care, either way? Whether Phoebe or Deirdre wins the Pickering inheritance, it can't possibly make a difference to you, you dough-faced stick insect! It's a good thing you're getting that fifteen pounds a year, for you're too repellent even to be a governess!"

Deirdre wouldn't have thought Sophie could become any paler than she already was, but Tessa managed to make her nearly white as paper. Even Tessa seemed dismayed by her own unsubtle cruelty. The three of them stood frozen in a moment of awkward silence.

Then Tessa huffed and strode to the door. With Tessa gone, the mood eased somewhat, but Deirdre didn't know what to say to Sophie who remained frozen and pale. She wished she knew how to remove that look from her face!

"Sophie," she said brightly, "let's have a game of cards." It was the only thing she could think of.

Sophie took a deep breath, then another. Deirdre watched her walk shakily to the card table and pull the deck from its drawer. She paused a moment to squeeze her eyes shut, hard. Deirdre knew from experience that this sometimes worked to hold back tears.

It seemed to do the trick for Sophie, for she was able to turn back to Deidre and say with something close to a smile, "Yes, let's."

Deirdre sat at the table as Sophie walked over with the cards. If she could make her forget all about Tessa's horrible insult then it would be worth the effort.

Well, not forget, perhaps, but ease the sting.

Besides, what could they do to help Phoebe until she returned to Brook House?

# Chapter Thirty five

The servants walked away carrying one of the carriage lanterns, the glow growing indistinct in the shreds of fog yet remaining. Phoebe kept her gaze out the window, unable to look at Rafe.

"You don't know what it's like," she whispered. "I have been there before. I have lived in that place for years. There didn't a day pass where I didn't wonder at someone cutting their eyes at me when I walked by, or bending their heads together to talk, or why someone crossed the street when I approached. The fear that it had happened was so great that I would find myself unable to breathe."

"You cannot live that way. You cannot be forever worrying that the ax will fall."

"You're right. I cannot. That is why I must marry Calder instead of you." She looked stonily ahead, not meeting his eyes. "To be a duchess—a rich duchess yet—that is the only way I can ensure that I need never fear again."

He drew back. "Do you so wish for fine gowns and jewels?"

She closed her eyes, her jaw unrelenting. "I care nothing for such things."

"What then?"

"You pretend not to understand, when I know that you already do. If I marry you, I will be a living scandal—the woman who threw aside a duke for a rake. It will persist, like a rot in my life, for as long as I live. And our children— do you not think of them? A story like that is good for generations of gossip!"

"I have been the source of gossip all my life," he said. "It does not kill."

"Oh, yes it does," she whispered. "It strangles slowly, it bleeds your friends from you one by one. It takes a pound of flesh every day until you are nothing but bones and nerves. I fear it would leach my love until I had nothing but regrets. If that fear makes me weak, then so be it. I am every bit the coward you think me."

He flinched at that and drew a sharp breath. "Is that true? Would Society truly have so much power over your feelings for me?"

"It isn't that simple!"

"Yes, it is. It is as simple as breathing, as the beat of your heart. I am yours. You are mine. All else falls away and the truth of us shines like the brightest of suns. You are mine. *Forever.*"

She averted her face, her fingers twisted tightly together. "Don't." She took a long shuddering breath. "Just . . . *don't.*"

Rafe drew slowly back, his chest tightening with realization. "It isn't that you don't love me, is it? No, I can see now. It is that you *won't* love me."

She said nothing, letting her silence answer for her. He swallowed, the pain in his chest twisting the action into agony.

There was no storming this keep. There was no charming this objection away. Phoebe, so soft and warm, so sweet and smiling, was stronger than she seemed. Her iron will *not* to love him, for whatever reason—and he was the first to admit that she had many—was not susceptible to his pleas or blandishments.

The moment stretched on, the silence growing like an impenetrable wall between them. Rafe felt the chill radiating from the cold stones of her resolve. The force of her rejection drove him back against the tufted cushions in a slow surrender. "I see."

He tried to inhale against the weight pressing into him. His chest ached. "I will importune you no more then. My apologies for the pain I have caused in my ignorance." Was that his voice? He sounded like a man pinned beneath a great boulder.

He reached out to the door handle, preparing to exit and fetch the servants, when her shaking hand lit lightly on his arm. He gazed at that small hand, at the trembling fingers just barely touching the cloth of his sleeve. "Miss Millbury—"

"Rafe—" There was agony in her whisper, agony that matched his own. "I'm sorry."

"No," he said softly, never lifting his gaze from her gloved hand, white lambskin against black wool. "It is I who am sorry. I'm sorry that I spent my life avoiding respectability instead of earning it. I'm sorry that I didn't strive sooner to be a man worthy of a woman like you. I'm sorry I didn't beg for your hand that first night at the ball. I'm sorry that I came to you too late, with too little to offer."

Her hand stroked down his arm to twine her fingers with his. "No. Too late, perhaps, but never too little. If I could only tell you . . ."

He groaned. "What is this, Phoebe? Why do you reject me, then tease me with your touch? Why do you push, then pull?"

She laughed, a damp and broken sound. "It is not I who—someday soon you will learn something about me. I will marry Calder and then he will become duke and you will learn something. When that day comes, please—please realize that I had no choice. You will remember that I obeyed my father and that I was a coward—but you must also remember that I loved you dearly and well. The man you are isn't the reason I refuse you. The man you are is the reason it is so difficult to do so."

"You are not a coward." He lifted her hand to his lips. "You are a woman of honor, who won't break a promise to a good man. I couldn't love you so if you weren't. And Calder is a good man. He will never intentionally hurt you." *Unlike me, who has already caused you so much pain with my persistence.*

She couldn't have heard his thought, but as always, she seemed to know. "And you're a good man as well, Lord Raphael Marbrook. You may not think it, but I would not love you so if you weren't." Her voice shook and he felt the trembling of imminent tears in her fingers.

He reached for her, pulling her into his arms, tucking her head beneath his chin. "It will be all right, sweet Phoebe. You'll have a brilliant life and I will visit someday and be a good black-sheep uncle to your children and give them sweets that make them ill and toys that make too much noise."

She laughed into his waistcoat, but the chuckle transformed into a sob between one breath and the next. He held her tightly as she cried, feeling the heat of her tears through his waistcoat and shirt, like brands on his chest. There would be scars left there, though he'd be the only one who ever saw them.

It was going to kill him to let her go.


THE CARRIAGE SAT unmoving, parked on the side of the road, when Stickley and Wolfe caught up with it. They stayed across the road, hiding in the shadows. The brush on the side of the road was wet and clinging from the recent rain.

"What are they doing?" Stickley hissed. "I thought they were going to the opera?"

Wolfe brushed at his smudged and torn finery. "They had better not go now. I'll never pass in the opera hall in this state."

Stickley worried the buttons on his weskit. "We'd better call this off. It's all wrong now. I don't like this dark and quiet. There might be bandits or some such about."

Wolfe grinned, his teeth flashing white in the darkness. "Ah, Stick, you're a genius. Give me that pistol of yours."

"I will not! I need it for when I make deposits at the bank. I am very careful with other people's money, you know."

Wolfe nodded. "Absolutely. I know that. And right now, I'm going to save Miss Millbury and her money from a murdering lord with a crumbling estate—if that's all right with you, of course."

Stickley drew back in horror. "You're going to kill him?"

Wolfe closed his eyes and sighed.

Stickley frowned. "You're the third person to make that noise at me this week."

Wolfe raised a brow. "Can't imagine why. Now, Stick, I'm not going to kill Brookhaven. I'm going to capture him, just as we'd planned. This is better than trying to grab him at the opera, for there was no one to deal with but a coachman and a footman."

"And Miss Millbury. You won't frighten her too badly, will you?"

Wolfe raised both hands. "I am here to save Miss Millbury, remember? We are the heroes in this piece, right?"

Stickley smiled tightly. "Right. Of course." He handed the pistol over to Wolfe. "Be forceful, but not too violent. And don't give away your identity!"

Wolfe pulled a blue silk handkerchief from his pocket.

"Does this look black in this light? Good enough, I suppose." He used a sharp stick to poke eyeholes, then tied the silk about the upper half of his face like a mask. "There. Neither Brookhaven nor Miss Millbury has ever met me, so I'll be safe enough. You stay back here."

"But it's my pistol. I want to be a hero as well."

"Stickley, stay." Wolfe turned toward him, his eyes suddenly sinister in the mask. "I mean that."

Stickley subsided. "Very well."

But Wolfe was gone, a shadow among shadows drifting toward the parked carriage.

# Chapter Thirty~six

Phoebe lifted her head from Rafe's chest and brushed the tears from her cheeks. "Did you hear that?"

Rafe turned his distant gaze outside. "Hear what? Are the servants back?"

Phoebe frowned. "I could swear I heard someone calling out for 'sand and liver.' "

Rafe made a noise. "Sand and—" He jerked upright and pressed her back into her seat. "Stay here!"

In one smooth motion, he opened the door on the wooded side of the carriage and slid out and down, out of her sight. Phoebe stayed where she was told, fear beginning to boil beneath her heart. When Rafe was gone, she got down onto all fours to peer out the windows on the road side.

"Stand and deliver, damn you!" The voice was hoarse and deep. A dark figure appeared in the moonlight, a man all in black with a mask over his eyes. One hand carried a pistol, aimed directly at her!

She ducked down, although she wasn't at all sure that the walls of the sleek, lightweight carriage would stop a bullet. Should she follow Rafe out the other door? Should she stay put, to do as she was told?

If she were a highwayman, she'd check the carriage first.

So be it. She scuttled backward, cursing the full skirts of her opera gown. If she could rip them up the side for better motion she would, but the sound would ring through the night like an alarm bell. For the moment, she was just going to have to hike them high and hope no one could see her pantalets—oh, criminy, she'd not worn pantalets. All in the cause of seducing Calder.

All right, then, perhaps she wouldn't hike the skirts quite so high.

The door had never truly closed, so it was a simple matter to push open the well-oiled hinges and slither, silk and all, into the mud beneath the carriage. Sheltered and dark, yet she could see danger coming. Hopefully, no one would think to look for a lady between the wheels.

The mud made her progress more difficult but blessedly silent as she slithered on her stomach to the other side. Her elbows planted deep in the mud, she pushed her hair out of her eyes with filthy hands and looked for the highwayman.

He still stood, alone in the center of the road, brandishing his pistol. "I know you're in there, Br—guv'nor! Come out peacefully and I won't harm the lady."

Phoebe didn't put much stock in the word of a bandit. He looked the proper brigand, tall and powerful, his gold buttons gleaming in the moon's glow—gold buttons?

Thievery must pay better than she'd thought.

A hand, cold and slimy, closed over her ankle. Phoebe started violently but made no sound.

"I thought I told you to stay in the carriage." Rafe's whisper was nearly soundless, coming from just behind her.

Phoebe closed her eyes. He was going to pay for that—perhaps not now, but soon. "I didn't like being a bird in a cage," she whispered back.

Rafe slithered up beside her. "Then don't get caught." He peered out at the highwayman, who looked as though he were losing his patience. "I don't think this fellow has much experience."

Phoebe nodded. "Yes, he does have the air of a beginner. Is that a good thing?"

"It might not be. An accomplished thief is in control of the situation and of himself. I don't think this fellow is either."

The man moved, approaching the carriage. "Shh!" Rafe pushed her down, hiding her face in his shoulder—his wet, muddy shoulder. Phoebe pulled away to breathe and spit out a taste of mud.

Rafe pressed his mouth to her ear. "When I give the signal, slip out the back and hide in the woods. I'll come find you."

Phoebe nodded, the fear turning hard and spiky within her. This was real, the bandit was real, and his pistol was very, very real. "Be careful," she breathed.

Rafe dropped his head to press a quick kiss to her lips then stopped a half-inch away. The kiss ended up on her cheekbone. "Don't worry," he whispered. "I'll be there to dance at your wedding. Now . . . *go*."

Phoebe pushed herself back as Rafe sprang from the concealing darkness, a silent and lethal leap at the armed man. Slithering backward until she was free of the carriage, hiking up her leaden, muddy skirts with both hands, turning to run, she listened every second. She heard a shout of surprise, grunts, and the sound of scuffling. She took a few steps into the wooded copse, stepping over a fallen branch, one hand before her as she left the revealing glow of the moon.

A cry of pain sounded from the scuffle—Rafe!

To hell with obedience.

Phoebe turned and reached for the branch on the ground. Heavy, but not too much so for a country girl. She wrapped both hands about it and raised it high, then took a deep breath and rounded the carriage screaming like a banshee.

There were two highwaymen now, pulling at Rafe's still form on the road. Phoebe's screech became a howl of rage as the two men looked up just in time to catch the branch across their faces.

They scrambled backward, out of range, cursing—one voice high, one deep. She could see them clearly, but the masks had held—except the slighter man seemed to have made his mask from a sleeve of a shirt. The cuff flapped behind his head with every motion.

Bloody beginners.

She planted a foot on either side of Rafe's still form and brandished her weapon with a snarl. "Get out of here, you goat-rutting bastards!"

The slight man gasped. "Language!"

The larger man pushed his companion back with one big hand to his chest. "Shut it, St—Stone."

"What?" The smaller man slipped in the mud, then recovered. "Oh. Right . . . *Fox*."

The big man snarled at his companion, then turned back on Phoebe. "Now, miss . . . there's no need for you to get so upset. We have a bit of business with this gentleman, but we've no intention of harming you."

Phoebe bared her teeth. "That's too bad, for I've every intention of harming you."

She took a mighty swing, making the branch whistle in the night air. Both men jumped back, staggering in the quagmire they'd created in their struggles with Rafe. She cocked the branch back again, braced like a cricket player.

The big man held up both hands. His smile beneath the mask was white. "There's no call for that, miss." His deep voice was smooth and cajoling. "You're much too pretty to be so violent."

Phoebe faltered, letting the branch sag slightly. "I—I am?"

Encouraged, the fellow took another step. "You certainly are. A fine figure of a woman, if I may be so bold. Why, this fellow isn't man enough for the likes of you!"

Phoebe looked down at Rafe, facedown in the mud. "He isn't?" She let the branch rest on her shoulder as she thought about it. Then she looked back up at the man in black. "Are you?"

He chuckled and took one more step toward her.

One more step had been all she needed. She swung with all her might, snapping the branch up and across his jaw. She heard teeth shut hard and a deep grunt of pain as the impact sent shocks reverberating up the branch to her hands. The big man seemed to float backward for a long moment before hitting the road hard, his big body sliding in the mud.

"Wo—Fox!" The slighter man ran forward and dropped to his knees beside his companion. "Fox! Can you hear me?"

The big man groaned. "Bloody Paris can hear you, St—Stone!" He pushed the other man aside and rose, one hand feeling gingerly at his jaw.

In his other hand, he held the pistol, pointed directly at her heart.

Oh, damn. She'd forgotten about the pistol.

The smaller man gasped. "What are you doing? You can't shoot a lady!"

The big man growled. "Oh, yes I can. She hit me!"

Stone backed away a step. "You'll do nothing of the sort." His voice seemed different, authoritative and sharp. "Kindly remember who you are, sir."

Fox seemed to have trouble remembering that, whoever that was. Phoebe waited, her breath coming short, her hands shaking, her rage fading under the onslaught of her terror. Then the big man let the pistol drop.

"Another day, then," he said wryly. He tipped the pistol at her like a hat. "Miss."

Then the highwayman raised his pistol and fired over the heads of the Brookhaven carriage horses. The animals started and lunged and fled off into the night, their bunched haunches carrying away themselves and the carriage and any hope Phoebe had of an easy course to rescue.

"Oh, dear," Stone said softly.

Fox smiled meanly. "Have a nice walk, my dear. I do hope his lordship isn't too heavy."

Then the two melted into the shadows—well, sort of. She heard a great deal of crashing and cursing before their voices faded away completely.

Only then did she dare toss her weapon aside and kneel beside Rafe. She rolled him over and wiped the mud from his face, peering at him closely in the moonlight. "Rafe? Rafe, my darling, can you hear me?" Heavens, did everyone say that when someone was unconscious? "Rafe, please wake up! We must get away from here!"

# Chapter Thirty-seven

After a quarter of an hour of slipping and skidding beneath the weight of Rafe's stumbling body, Phoebe spotted the bodies of the two servants sprawled on the side of the road. After carefully letting Rafe slip to his knees, she ran to them. Both men were unconscious, but had normal breathing and heartbeats and she couldn't find any wounds other than lumps on their heads.

For a moment, she contemplated leaving Rafe with them, but he was too disoriented. He might stumble off into the wood and never be found.

Hiking Rafe's arm higher over her shoulders, she turned resolutely toward the inn. "Two miles. Two tiny, little miles. Piece of cake."

Rafe revived enough to maintain a stumbling walk, although it was as if he were sleepwalking. She was getting desperately worried about his dazed state. Surely he ought to have roused by now?

Once he turned to her and said very clearly, "Phoebe, my head hurts." Then he returned to his confused state, muttering about Brookhaven and Calder and "his damned factories."

Phoebe answered him when he seemed to require it, and if he went too long silent, she threw down fodder for argument. "Calder's plan for his factory is brilliant" or "It's

Calder's estate, he can do what he wants with it." Such contributions were guaranteed to stir a response.

Then his thoughts apparently returned to her. "She's the one," he said, over and over, breaking her heart every time. "I found her."

"She doesn't love me," he said once, quite clearly. "I can't make her love me."

"Oh, I think you're doing a damned fine job of it," she whispered back to him, but he was off again on Calder.

"Bloody know-it-all. Bloody perfect heir."

It wasn't hatred, really. More of a strange sort of rivalry, like two hounds living too closely together. And apparently, the fate of Brookhaven was the bone.

It was fascinating stuff, and did a great deal to explain the events of the last week, but Phoebe was fast losing strength. Even country girls didn't last forever.

At last she saw the glow of lanterns ahead. The relief was such that her knees weakened and she nearly went down with Rafe on top of her.

"Not what I had in mind, my love," she laughed damply as she strained to resituate him. "Perhaps after we've bathed."

She threw Rafe's unresisting arm over her shoulders and hefted his weight as best she could. Heavens, he was big! She made it through the inn yard and was coaxing Rafe's stumbling feet up the steps when someone came out and spotted them.

"Great Scott! Here, let me help you!"

Phoebe turned Rafe's greater weight over to the stranger with relief, for spots were beginning to form before her eyes from the effort. As it was, her knees were trembling greatly, although that might have been from the sudden realization that it was over—they had survived.

She placed one shaking hand against the doorframe for balance as the stranger helped Rafe into the inn. She wasn't done yet—not quite. "Sir, our driver and footman are injured. Please send help back down the road for them!"

The lights and sounds of the inn struck her like a welcome fire glow when she stumbled through the door at last. She heard cries of alarm at their appearance and the shuffle of hurried feet as people sprang up to help them inside. Someone took her elbow gently and guided her to a seat by the fire. She was seated much too close, for the heat scorched her face, but it felt wonderful.

Safe, and apparently unrecognized. Now, it was time to come up with some story that would save—

"Lord Marbrook! What has happened to you?"

Oh God. Phoebe jerked her head up to see a handsome young man leaning over Rafe, prodding him in the arm. Rafe's head rolled and his eyes blinked rapidly—he was trying to regain his awareness, but what might he say before he had his thoughts in order?

Phoebe jumped up and put herself between Rafe and the newcomer. "Sir, I beg you not to question him now. We have been through much tonight."

The fellow frowned. "Rafe is my friend. You, I do not know."

"I? I am—" This was where a planned story would have come in handily. "I am his sister, of course."

The fellow blinked suspiciously. "I've known Rafe since we were in school. He never mentioned a sister."

Oh, God. Not just a friend, a good friend. "Well . . . I . . . I keep close to Brookhaven."

His eyes narrowed. "What is your name?"

Lady. Rafe's sister would be Lady Something, or would she? "I am Lady Nan—" No, too common. "Dei—" Oh, God no. Deirdre would kill her! "Tess—" Criminy, even worse!

"Lady Nanditess?"

Phoebe raised her chin. "It's a family name."

The man raised a brow, as if he could suddenly see why the family had kept her under wraps all those years. "I see." At last, he shrugged, unable to confirm or deny her. "How may I aid you, Lady Nanditess? Should I obtain two rooms for the night?"

Phoebe refrained from mopping her brow in relief. "Yes, thank you . . . ah . . ."

The man bowed. "Forgive me. I am Somers Boothe-Jamison."

Since she was teetering on the edge of exhaustion and panic that Rafe had not yet truly regained consciousness, Phoebe merely nodded regally and waved the fellow on. "If you don't mind . . . those rooms?"

When he'd gone, she sat next to Rafe and examined his wound by the light of a small candelabra from the center of a table. There was a nasty bump and a cut which had bled heavily but was not terribly large or deep after all. His pulse seemed strong and his pallor was improving by the moment. She framed his face in her hands.

"Rafe darling . . . wake up. Wake up, please."

He twitched and his eyelids fluttered, but he did not wake completely. Beside herself with worry, Phoebe scarcely noticed when Mr. Boothe-Jamison returned with help to carry Rafe to his room.

It turned out to be "their" room, actually. Mr. Boothe-Jamison shrugged apologetically. "It was the only guest room left. I took one in the attic for your injured servants, as well, but I thought you'd want to be close by—"

"Yes, thank you." Phoebe knew she was being abrupt, and after he'd been so kind, but if she didn't get all these people out of the room, someone was sure to decipher Rafe's murmurings and realize that he was saying, "Phoebe, where are you?" over and over again.

Shooing the crowd from the room, promising Mr. Boothe-Jamison a visit with Rafe when he recovered sufficiently, and exacting a vow in return that he would do his best to get a physician for Rafe and the servants immediately suctioned the last bit of strength Phoebe had left.

When the door was shut at last, she leaned her back to it and took a long breath. Then she rushed to Rafe's side to smooth his hair and feel his brow and generally reassure herself that he was alive and safe at last.

Then she gasped one raw and terrified sob and pressed her shaking hands to her burning eyes. The tears of reaction and exhaustion came at last and she slid down next to the bed to sit on the floor, her arms wrapped about her knees, sobbing until she had nothing left to cry.

At last her breathing steadied and her tears ran out. She swiped at her eyes with her torn and dirty skirt, then gazed at it with revulsion. The gown of a temptress, meant to tease Rafe's brother into a mad passion.

She stood quickly and stripped it from her, popping buttons in her hurry. She contemplated burning it, but when might she find another? In compromise, she hurled it into a corner and stumbled to the bowl and pitcher on the stand across the room clad in only her shift.

She washed away the burning in her eyes and did her best to remove the stains of her ordeal from her skin, but without soap, Rafe's blood did not want to come off. She took the softest of the towels to clean his poor bump and wash his handsome face clean of the road dirt. They'd beaten him badly, poor brave dear.

She knew he likely would have fought so powerfully for any lady's protection, but the fact that he'd fought so for her—and had been so beaten for it—did something irreparable to her heart.

Love. It welled up full and warm and permanent within her. There was no denying it, no passing it over, no believing that it would ever diminish or fade.

She loved him.

And he loved her.

That was when she realized that it had never been Society's reproof that she had feared. It had never been scandal that had turned her into a coward.

It was this . . . this longing ache, this vulnerability . . .

This love.

She had almost loved Terrence, and that had been bad enough. The pain had lasted years and the humiliation even longer. Even then, somewhere inside her, she had known that if she were ever to experience the true depth of real love, there was a possibility of pain so deep that forever could not heal it.

How foolish she'd been. Love was not a drink one tasted and then rejected. Love was not something that could be avoided or arranged. Love was a highwayman, standing by the road of life, just waiting to strike at the reckless and fortunate few.

As she had been struck.

How simple it had all turned out to be. In a world where she'd been blinded by shades of gray for the last ten years, there was sudden black and white clarity. She'd heard that dire circumstances could strengthen and refine some people. She was glad to find out that she was one of those people.

There was nothing in her but love for Rafe. There were no decisions to make, no strategies to form. She was his woman. He was her man.

There came a knock at the door. The physician had arrived. After wrapping her cloak about herself, Phoebe brushed Rafe's dampened hair back from his forehead and pressed her lips to his. "I love you," she whispered.

*Forever.*

# Chapter Thirty~eight

In the now-quiet inn room, the physician had come and gone, pronouncing that Lord Marbrook needed rest and care. He emphasized "rest" while looking sourly at Phoebe. He was a gentleman who had seen a great deal in his long life—apparently the "sister" façade was a tad overused.

Now Phoebe sat on the edge of the bed next to Rafe. She reached out to brush a lock of dark hair away from his temple. He turned his face toward her touch, even while barely conscious, seeking her out.

Love.

How strange and vulnerable this thing within her. It was love in infancy, first blazing hot in passion, then warm in acceptance. The way she'd felt for Terrence was nothing compared to the way she loved Rafe. A single blossom compared to a valley full of roses. She loved this rakish, impossible, beautiful rogue. His charm delighted her and his handsomeness pleased her, but the wounded aching lonely man inside him was what snared her heart and seemed fated to never release it.

He was imperfect. His life before her had been a maze of short, callous affairs and hard, careless living. Could he love forever? Could he see only her and never set his eye roving again? Should she gamble her future on his shy and wild heart?

Such a simple word, "yes." Why not say it? Why not say yes to love and happiness? She'd already said yes to him once, though he remembered it not—one night filled with moonlight and imaginary roses . . .

"Excuse me, my darling," she said to Rafe as she rose from his bedside. "It is time I officially jilt your brother."

Calder would be disappointed and likely angry, but she did not think he would be truly hurt. Someday Calder would hand his heart over to a woman, but that lucky woman wouldn't be her. Funny, now that she was thinking about leaving him, she could see Calder clearly for the first time as a man, not an obstacle.

As a respectable, honorable man, Calder deserved better from her than simple desertion. He deserved an explanation.

Her heart calm at last, her future clear, she rang for someone from the inn and waited by the door, listening for footsteps. Before they could tap and disturb Rafe, she opened the door and requested paper and ink. When they arrived she set herself down at the small table to explain herself to the man she could never marry.

*Dear Lord Brookhaven,*
   *I ought to have told you at once, before we set about this betrothal in earnest, but I made a terrible mistake . . .*

When the letter was done—and it came much more easily than she would have thought—she sealed it with a bit of candle wax. She pulled her still-damp cloak over her borrowed nightdress and stepped quickly up to the next level, where the driver and footman had been given a room.

The footman opened the door, his eyes widening. "Yes, my la—miss?"

"How is the driver?"

" 'E's all right, miss. Just a crack to the 'ead. 'E'll be right as rain come mornin'."

Phoebe considered him for a long moment. She had little choice, after all. "Are you Brookhaven's man, or Marbrook's?"

The fellow scratched his ear. "Well . . . I suppose I'm both, miss."

Phoebe frowned. "Oh, dear. That is not an enviable position."

Something like respect flickered in the man's eyes. "No, miss. I suppose ye would understand that if anyone would—if ye don't mind me sayin'."

At his sympathetic tone, Phoebe smiled. "I don't suppose you would consider working for me, just this once? I must be sure that this letter reaches Lord Brookhaven immediately. Do you know where his lordship is?"

The man blinked. "As a matter of fact, I do, miss. I've been to 'is pottery factory with him before."

Phoebe handed him some coins from Rafe's purse. "Get a good horse from the hosteler and ride fast. I want Brookhaven to see this as soon as possible." She smiled again. "It seems I'm going to wed Lord Marbrook instead."

At that, the man quailed. "Er, do ye wish me to wait for an answer?"

Phoebe wrinkled her nose. "Heavens, no. Throw the letter at him and run for your life."

The footman took the letter, nodding. "Yes, miss. I'll be sure to get a *very* good 'orse!"

Phoebe waited by her inn room window until she saw the man ride off at great speed, his Brookhaven livery nearly invisible in the darkness. One man disappointed. Her father, she must tell in person. For all his faults, she owed him that.

Then she turned to look at Rafe, his bruises still alarming but his sleep easy and natural now.

Her man . . . forever.

Feeling the conflict of these last days fall from her shoulders like a great weight, Phoebe smiled softly as she undid her nightdress and let it slip from her shoulders. Naked, she walked to the other side of the wide bed and slipped beneath the covers.

RAFE GROGGILY BECAME aware of two things. One, his head hurt. Two, his head really, really hurt.

He sat up, spasmodically trying to escape the pain. It intensified cruelly, driving him helplessly back down. He landed on something soft.

"Mm-mm."

The sweet female sigh jolted him into full waking. Warm skin, soft flesh—he knew what that was. There was an entirely naked girl in bed with him.

"Uh . . . hello?" It had better be Phoebe—except that if it was Phoebe—oh, God, he was in such trouble either way!

"Rafe?"

Joy and pain sliced through him in equal measure—all right, perhaps not equal. To hell with his soul, to hell with Calder—he had Phoebe in his bed! He reached for her, pulling her into his arms. She came willingly, softly melting herself into him, laying her head on his bare chest.

"How is your head, my love?" she whispered.

"It hurts, but—" *My love?* Rafe closed his eyes tightly, willing himself to remember. Women tended to take it ill when a man couldn't remember. They'd been alone in the carriage. He'd released her, given her up, sacrificed his heart for her happiness—

And then what? There was something else, something important . . .

"Sand and liver?"

She laughed, propping herself up on his chest, as naturally as if she'd lain naked in his arms for years. "You're making fun of me now."

"There was a highwayman!"

"Two actually. I believe the second one sneaked up on you, otherwise I'm sure you would have thrashed them most properly," she said staunchly.

He tried to sit up again. "I didn't? Then how did we get away with our lives?"

She pressed him down again. "Shh. Your poor head." A cool hand soothed his brow. "I thrashed them for you," she said. "Well, one of them, at any rate." She snuggled closer. "I'm quite good at cricket, you know."

His head throbbed and he felt as if he were floating or falling—either way, as if he were not in control. "Phoebe, please start at the beginning."

"Must I? The middle is much more interesting."

"Phoebe."

She sighed. "Oh, very well. You and I were talking in the carriage, after you'd sent the servants away. Do you recall that much?"

"Yes, I remember everything up until I told you to run. Which you apparently ignored."

She shrugged. Delightful things happened against his ribs . . . things he meant to thoroughly investigate when the throbbing subsided in his head.

"I could hardly leave you in their hands. They were trying to drag you off!"

He frowned. "Why would they do that? Highwaymen steal and sometimes kill, but I've never heard of them kidnapping. They tend to strike and flee."

"Well, that's what it looked like to me . . . although I might have been mistaken. There was still a bit of fog.

Perhaps they were only searching your pockets for some-thing to steal." She made a grumbling noise. "Well, that makes my rescue a bit less exciting, I suppose. I faced down a pistol to save your pocket watch?"

His arms tightened about her. "Never do that again!"

She twined her arms about his neck. "I promise," she said soothingly. "Next time I'll hand it over myself."

"Next time you'll flee when you're told!"

"Yes, my lord . . . my love." She kissed his chest softly. "Next time I'll flee."

*My love.* There it was again. "And . . . after you drove them off with a cricket bat—how did you get a cricket bat again?"

"Tree branch. I only hit one of them. The hard man. The other one was . . . different. He didn't seem to want to hurt anyone. He made the hard man leave us be, but they fright-ened the horses away and left us there in the road. I man-aged to get you on your feet and we lasted long enough to walk back to the inn we'd passed."

He doubted he'd done much walking. More likely she'd done a great deal of dragging. "What of the driver, Afton, and the footman?"

"They're here, being tended to. Don't worry. I don't know if anyone has found the carriage but I'm sure they will soon. I had you put to bed and then I—"

He gave her a squeeze. "Then you what?"

She laid her head down on his chest again. "I wrote to Calder," she whispered. "I told him that I could not marry him because I love another."

Him. She'd chosen him. This was not another illicit en-counter, a brief flash of heat between him and his brother's intended. She was with him because she was *with* him.

*I love another.*

She loved him.

She was waiting for his response. He knew that

because she poked him and said, "I'm waiting for your response."

He hesitated still. How could he express—what was there to say? How to tell her the way that his world had just expanded, that his heart had burst its bounds, that he was a man remade?

"Thank you," he said formally.

She pushed herself up on her hands to stare down at him. "What?"

"I said th—"

"Wait. Stop. One moment." She scrambled over him—and he enjoyed every moment of it—to climb from the bed and pad across the room. He heard the rustle of fabric, then a clink and a snap. She was lighting a small lamp. The glow steadied as she adjusted the wick.

She carried it back to the bed—regrettably now clad in his shirt, which covered her to her knees. She had very pretty calves, however. Nicely turned ankles as well.

She put the lamp on the table. "Sit up," she ordered, then rearranged the pillows behind him when he did so. "Now lie back."

He was propped now, facing her as she perched on the edge of the bed. She moved the lamp slightly closer, then peered into his eyes. "All right. You can say it now."

He smiled slightly. "Thank you," he repeated. *Thank you for not giving up on me.*

She gazed at him for a long, silent moment. Then a beautiful smile bloomed. "Well, all right then." She leaned forward and softly kissed his chest, just about where his heart began to beat hard. "You're welcome," she whispered against his skin.

*I love you,* his heart whispered back to her.

She lifted her head and smiled at him, the corners of her lips curving mischievously. "Are you feeling well enough yet?"

He reached to cup her cheek in his hand. "Well enough for what?" His thumb stroked down over her full lips. She kissed it.

Then she gently bit the pad. "Are you feeling well enough to make love to me properly?"

He toyed with a strand of her beautiful hair. "I suppose I might be able to muster the strength soon—"

She sat up and whipped his shirt off over her head, revealing herself to him for the first time. He coughed in surprise. "Or perhaps now."

She flung herself onto him, kissing his chest, her hands roving rather more adeptly than one might suppose from an innocent maid—not that he cared, really. He was no angel himself, to worry over a tiny flaw in this gift from the gods.

She wrapped her hand about his erection and squeezed it slightly before moving in a rhythmic manner. She rained kisses on his chest, moving lower over his flat stomach, following the trail of dark hair there. Surprising—but not disappointing.

Her touch, somewhere between skilled and innocent, her kiss, urgent and yet sweet—all this only made her more herself—more Phoebe.

Still, she was in a tearing hurry—when they had all night this time. He caught at her hands and pulled them away. "Sweet—please—"

She went still. "Oh, no. Already?"

"What? Oh." He grinned. "No. Not that you aren't tempting, darling, but I've a bit more control than that."

She blinked. "Control? Men can control . . . that? All of you?"

He looked at her. "Of course we can. Most of us, at any rate. There are always exceptions . . ."

She suddenly looked very consternated. Why?

Then he knew. His mind might be muddled, but it did work eventually. She'd apparently known just such an exception. How to handle this without making her feel as though he blamed her? "Did—did you know someone who . . . ahem . . . couldn't?"

Phoebe hesitated for a very long time. She'd never told—the vicar had been so adamant. Now that she probably ought to tell—after all, she did not want there to be secrets, not with Rafe—she couldn't seem to form the words.

"Oh, *bugger.*" No, those weren't the words, although the vulgarity did make her feel a bit better. "Rafe . . . I . . . I'm not—" She gazed mutely at him, unable to continue.

Rafe smiled gently at her, his eyes crinkling in that way that made her turn to mush inside. "Phoebe, I'm not upset with you. You'd be surprised how many of the prim young ladies of the ton . . . well, aren't. The myth is preserved for the sake of some gentlemen, but I assure that I am far too blackened myself to be one of those."

She continued to look at him, loving him more by the minute, but unable to say what needed saying.

He reached to the floor, holding his pounding head on with the other hand, and handed her back the shirt. "Why don't you put this back on for a moment? You'll be easier if you aren't nude."

She slipped it over her head, grateful for the understanding in his eyes. Then he took her hand in both of his and rested it on his hard stomach.

"You aren't a virgin," he said for her. "There was a man."

"Terrence," she blurted.

"And Terrence was . . . ?"

His grip was easy and comforting. She took a breath. "Terrence was my dancing master."

His grip tightened, just for an instant. "He was your teacher." His voice was just a tad flat, with something dark flashing in his eyes . . . then it was gone and only comfort remained.

Phoebe nodded, finding it easier to swallow now. "You don't know very much about me, Rafe."

He stroked a lock of hair away from her face. "Then now is a good time to learn more."

# Chapter Thirty-nine

Phoebe took a deep breath, then let it out slowly. "Most of it isn't very exciting. I lived in the vicarage of Thornhold all of my days until coming to London. I don't remember my mother very well, but I do recall that she always seemed to be coming and going. She had all the duties of a vicar's wife, visiting the ill and infirm, mediating disputes between the village wives, looking after me and my father, plus she took on the duties of several servants in order to save money. She died when I was but five years of age—probably of exhaustion.

"I was too young to be left on my own, but the vicar said there was no money for a nurse or governess and I might as well do that job myself." She smiled in memory. "In many ways I did not mind such glorious neglect. For the most part I ran wild with the less supervised children of Thornton. I climbed trees with the butcher's son and beheaded my dolls with the poacher's daughter. In my ignorance I believed myself to be well loved and tended, for I knew nothing other than the vicar's rather vague affection, rarely bestowed."

Rafe nodded, pulling her close to him. "Lost little girl."

She sighed, snuggling deeper into him. "This might have done me well enough, but it went on too long. No one seemed to notice that I was a child no longer, but was becoming a young lady who ought not to be lying in the meadow after dark, staring at the stars, holding hands with the milliner's son. I did not mean to be bad, but I knew little of what was right and wrong. The vicar said I ought to have listened more closely to his sermons, but after hearing the same ones all my life—he only has a dozen or so—I found other matters to occupy my mind while at church."

Rafe chuckled. Phoebe closed her eyes to let the sound she loved rumble through her. "Then one day, when I was nearly fifteen, Lady Tessa arrived with Deirdre. She pointed out to my father that I was blossoming right out of my childish dresses and doing it rather nicely indeed. In his surprise I suppose he overreacted. He all but locked me in my room while he searched high and low for people who knew how to teach a young lady the things she needed to know. All I knew was that after a lifetime of freedom I was imprisoned for no reason I could see."

Those days so long ago . . . she'd been so confused, so unable to understand what she'd done wrong. Rafe's arms tightened about her. "Go on," he murmured.

"Well, eventually, the vicar engaged a governess, a lady's maid—who knew less about hair than I did, thank you very much—and a dancing master, an impoverished young gentleman by the name of Terrence LaPomme. The governess stayed for less than a week before throwing up her hands and declaring me hopeless. Thank heaven that Thornhold had a decent if rather mouse-eaten library, for I was able to learn many things on my own.

"My new lady's maid immediately discovered the butcher's son—my former playmate, if you recall, who had grown into a strapping fellow, indeed—and thereafter spent her nights sneaking down the trellis from my bedchamber window and leaving me to my own resources.

"The only person who seemed to care that I learned about being a lady was Terrence. I was willing to learn anything he would teach me, for I was much impressed. He seemed so fine to me, so elegant and handsome, in an 'if only the world had not been so cruel to me' sort of way. As I look back, it is obvious to me now that he was merely dissipated, but at the time I only saw the romantic tragedy of his self-proclaimed 'wasted brilliance.' "

Rafe had gone very quiet beneath her, but she could hear his heartbeat quicken. He was angry at Terrence, of course, as she had been for so long. She smoothed her hand over his chest, wordlessly thanking him for listening instead of leaping up to find Terrence and beat the stuffing from him.

"Terrence did teach me to dance, I'll grant him that much. In addition, he convinced me that he loved me and that we had been brought together against all odds because we were fated for one another. It quite did the trick at the time, of course. My head was most remarkably turned. I agreed to run away with him.

"So, foolish child that I was, I followed my maid down that trellis one night with my possessions wrapped in my shawl and slipped away into the darkness with Terrence LaPomme, useless rake and despoiler of virgins."

She sighed deeply. She'd kept that secret for so long . . . and yet the world had not ended when she'd uttered it at last.

"What happened?" Rafe kissed the top of her head. "What happened to Terrence?"

"After the one night with me, he disappeared the next morning. The vicar found me a few hours later, of course. There was only one road from Thornton toward Scotland and I had left that note about fleeing to Gretna Green, despite Terrence's warning not to. But it was too late. I spent the night in the same bed with Terrence and I am quite thoroughly ruined."

He laid his cheek along her crown. "Not to me."

She breathed him, feeling so light she thought she might

fly. His heat surrounded her, protected her—she was safe in his arms, as she'd never been safe in her life.

"Well, Terrence apparently thought so, for I woke that morning alone. I looked out the window to see the back of him, riding away as if his life depended on it. I never saw him again. Then the vicar came and took me home."

"Was he very angry with you?"

"Cold." Phoebe shivered. "From that day onward he was so cold to me. He covered my absence with a lie and then he locked me in my room to think on what I'd done, for three solid months—"

*"What?"*

She pressed him back down, easing his fury. "Another man might have beaten me within an inch of my life, but he didn't . . . although there were times when I would have rather been struck than be treated with that icy distance.

"By the time I was released, I was so horribly lonely and trembling for the slightest freedom that I found myself quite able to conform to the vicar's new rules of decorum."

"Rules?"

"Oh, yes. I was to wear only the most demure of gowns. I was to keep my hair tamed at all times. I was never to run, or laugh out loud, or speak to strangers, or to men at all, even if I had known them all my life. I was never to venture anywhere without the company of my new middle-aged and shrewish lady's maid—who refused to come to London, thank heaven.

"Let me see, there were more . . . I was not to chew too quickly or to ask for seconds. I was only to leave the house to manage domestic affairs, for I became in effect the housekeeper, or to go to church, accompanied by the vicar, of course. I was not to voice opinions or to beg for treats or make complaints or—well, you get the general idea."

"I cannot imagine that went well at all. You are not so pliant."

She shook her head. "You don't understand. I did it all. I committed myself completely to becoming the new Miss Phoebe Millbury, perfect daughter and lady. It wasn't that difficult. All I had to do was to kill the old Phoebe."

She trailed her fingers over his chest. "At least, I thought she was dead, but I think perhaps she was only sleeping . . . until that night in the moonlight when you awakened her."

He caught her hand and laced his fingers into hers. "You are not the only one who awakened that night."

She sighed happily. "Oh, good. I was hoping you'd talk, too. I shall settle back and listen to your story now."

He laid his head back and gazed up at the cracked plaster ceiling. "My story . . . well, my mother died when I was quite young, as well. I was eight when Brookhaven came to get me. I knew I had a father who was someone important, but I had never seen him before that day. I like to think that he truly cared for my mother—that I was not born out of a mere moment of lust—but I suppose I'll never know. Lady Brookhaven, Calder's mother, lived somewhere else entirely. We rarely saw her. She didn't seem to care about my presence one way or the other. She died a few years later, but I'm not sure Calder even noticed. He was entirely his father's son."

Phoebe nodded against his chest. "The heir."

"Of course. For our entire lives, Calder came first. First to the table at dinner, first to receive his own high-blood horse, first at our father's hand in learning about the estate and the legacy of the Marbrooks.

"What about your father? Did you believe he preferred Calder?"

Rafe shrugged. "All I knew was that Rafe was the enemy. Our father was the ground we battled over. Since Calder was first at Brookhaven, I took the other firsts." He let out a breath. "This is the part that is hard to tell you."

She raised her head to look at him. "Are you trying to tell me that you're not a virgin?"

He laughed and gave her a little shake. "Don't jest. I didn't jest when you were doing the telling."

She kissed his chest in apology.

He went on. "I was first to swive one of the willing, giggling chambermaids, first to go brawling with the burly smith's sons, first to drink myself insensible with wines stolen from the family cellars. First to be thrown out of the better schools, first to have a married woman as a mistress, first to be a scandal in the newssheets."

"And your father? Did he notice how much effort you put into this?"

He smiled. "Indeed. I was an embarrassment. I was a smear on the family name. I was on the road to ruining Brookhaven with my gambling debts.

"You're not who they thought you were."

"Yes, I am. And they didn't know half of what I've done."

"What you've done . . . but not what you are."

He kissed her for that. "Yet you see, I was also the last—the last to realize that what I really loved was Brookhaven and its people. Brookhaven, which will always and forever belong to Calder and his heirs." He let out a long breath. "Belong to the Marquis of Brookhaven, who has no heart for it at all."

She reached up to stroke her fingertips over his cheek. "But you changed for Brookhaven."

He smiled sadly. "Too late. Calder does not see that I have paid my debts or that I have made good investments since. I have nothing to show for it at the moment, but I believe in what I have done. I believe that it will pay off in the end. But Calder will never allow me to help him run Brookhaven. And now—"

"And now he will never trust you. Because of me."

"Phoebe, I lost nothing there. There was no possibility that Calder would ever look beyond my past. I could spend the next ten years wringing myself into knots for him—to no avail. He gave up on me years ago."

She frowned. "I suppose I do not understand this brother thing. He is not your father. He is but a few months older. How does he become the one whom you must please?"

"He *is* Brookhaven. He is my home . . . my only family." Until now. For the first time Rafe was beginning to get a glimmer of what he'd destroyed in his need for Phoebe.

She raised herself up on her elbows and gazed at him soberly. "The vicar might never forgive me. Calder might never forgive you. Are you sorry?"

She was so beautiful, her eyes dark with worry, her mussed hair falling over them both, her sweet face saddened by what they had both given up . . . for this very moment, in each other's arms at last.

Uncomfortable with the conflicting joy and loss within him, Rafe grinned instead of answering. "Phoebe, I think I feel well enough now."

Her eyes searched his for a moment longer, then her slow smile began. "Why, my lord, whatever do you mean by that?"

# *Chapter Forty*

The first kiss was what their first kiss in the larder should have been, had it not been the explosion of so much repressed lust.

He rolled her over until she lay beneath him, then he slid one knee up between hers. Taking his weight on his elbows, he brushed the hair back from her face with both hands. "I love your eyes," he murmured, now that he had the right to. "I wish I could swim in them."

She drew her brows together. "Is that a nice thought or an odd one?"

He laughed. "I'm not sure. Is it a good thought to want to dive into you and never come up for air?"

She reached up to sweep back the hair that had fallen over his forehead. "Come on in . . . the water's lovely."

He dropped his head until their noses touched. "You are an astounding creature, Miss Millbury."

She slid her fingers into his hair. "Only with you."

Their lips touched then, softly, carefully, with that tentative promise that there was more to come and plenty of time for it. She wrapped her arms about his shoulders, keeping her hands in his hair, pulling him to her until their bodies melded.

Perhaps this truly was their first kiss. Before they had been forbidden lovers, fighting their natures and their commitments. Everything before now had been tainted with guilt or compulsion.

They were free now—which, in Phoebe's mind, made this their very first kiss.

His lips were warm and firm on hers. He gently pulled her lower lip into his, then released it. She melted into him and let herself be kissed in luxurious capitulation. The tip of his tongue, hot and wet, slid between her lips, just for a second—a mere knock on her door. She parted her lips and let him in.

There, covered by his body, her head cradled in his hands, Phoebe was kissed with pure love for the first time in her life. Behind it were the coals of passion, banked and patient, but this kiss was a gift and a vow and a beseechment all at the same time.

She tightened her fingers in his hair and gave and promised and answered him with her own lips and tongue.

He ended the kiss in order to look into her eyes. His were black and urgent in the candlelight. "I love you, Miss Millbury."

She kissed his chin. "I know."

"Do you? How can you? I have not been good to you."

She shook her head. "You rescued me."

He smiled. "And then you rescued me."

"Rafe?"

"Yes, Phoebe?"

"I don't want to talk anymore."

He laughed, low and wicked. Then he took her nipple into his mouth.

Hot magic lanced through her, making her arch her back with a cry, pressing more of her soft flesh into his eager mouth.

Her passionate noise unleashed him. He grabbed her with hot, hungry hands and dragged her to him, then under him. She lay on her back with her hands willingly trapped between their bodies, her breast bared and wet and in his hungry possession.

He suckled hard, making her keen and squirm at the mingled pleasure and pain. Then he wrapped his hot, hard hand around it and moved his attention to her other one. Then he slid down her body, kissing her skin softly all the way.

"Where are you going?"

"I am going to make you forget all about Terrence LaPomme." He drove his tongue between the sweet folds of her.

She gasped in surprise and stiffened. "What—"

He lifted his head. "Phoebe, who is in charge here?"

She thought about it a moment too long. He bared his teeth to bite gently at her soft white thigh.

"Ow! I thought I was the Queen . . . or was I the Goddess?"

"Then it is long past my turn, don't you think?" He pressed her thighs gently apart, but did not relent. "Say 'yes, my lord.' Then stop talking."

She went pliant in his hands. "Yes, my lord," she said throatily.

"That's better." He dipped his head to taste her again.

Phoebe, forced to do nothing to protest, allowed herself to descend into the wicked pleasure of his mouth on her. Was it wicked, truly?

He rolled his tongue over the stiff little button that was the center of her pleasure. "Oh, yesss." It was most certainly deeply, darkly wicked. Bad, even. Hopefully it would continue to be bad for a long, long time.

It did so, until he changed his motion to drive his tongue deeply into her. She cried out and dug her fingers into his hair, rotating her hips, moving against his mouth, abandoning herself completely to the pleasure purring through her body.

When her breathing had calmed and her trembling had eased somewhat, she tossed back the damp hair that had fallen over her face and lifted her head. "My lord?"

He kissed her mound softly. "Yes?"

"Nothing." She dropped her head back on the pillow. "I simply wondered if it would work to say it again."

He chuckled, his breath hot on her sensitive flesh. She lay open to him in her sensual abandon, her inhibitions gone the same place as the rules her father had imposed on her. "So this is what free feels like."

He moved up the bed to lie beside her. "No. This is better. I've been free—and it is lonely and cold. I'd much rather be your Minion."

She rolled over to lie nose to nose. "And my Master."

He smiled. "It is always best to take proper turns."

With one hand on his shoulder, she pushed him back to lie flat. "So what does my Master want?"

He stroked a thumb over her bottom lip, then kissed it. "To give you pleasure, of course."

She bit him. "That is not a good answer. Tell me what to do, or I'll simply be forced to muddle through on my own."

His eyes widened. "I'm fairly certain that 'muddle through' has never before been used in reference to love-making."

She shrugged. He liked to watch the side effect of that. "Very well. On your head be it." She repeated his movement, sliding down his body, kissing all the way. Unlike the first time, she did not stop to grasp his erection with her hand. Instead, she greeted the tip with wet open lips.

A deep groan ripped through him. His big hand came to rest upon her head, not pushing but simply guiding. "I would not ask you—"

She lifted her head. "Minion, who is in charge here?"

He dropped his head back on the pillow. "I have created a monster," he gasped.

She opened her mouth and took his enlarged head into her mouth. It was firm and round and salty. She licked around it, exploring with her tongue. He made deep vulnerable noises which emboldened her. She dropped her jaw to take more of him in her mouth. She found that she could not manage more than half, so she wrapped her hand about the rest so it would not feel chilled.

Somewhere in that maneuver, she accidentally caused suction. The aching, heartfelt moan that erupted from him was enough to encourage more study. She began to slide him deeply in and out of her mouth, sucking on the way out and rolling her tongue over the staff on the way in.

His hand tightened painfully in her hair but she ignored it, intent on her task. She was on to something, she just knew it. She increased the speed of her method. He grew in her mouth and in her hand until she needed to wrap her other fingers about him to cover him completely. Goodness, he seemed to never end!

The blunt head of him began to further swell in her mouth. Much more and she wouldn't be able to—

"Damn it!" He reached for her roughly and pulled her away, dragging her up to roll onto her and between her thighs. He was panting as he pushed her hair back to gaze pleadingly into her eyes, his dark and needing. "Now—I must have you—"

She opened her thighs and wrapped her arms about his ribs. "Now."

He wrapped his hands over her shoulders and drove himself hard into her—

The pain was harsh and ripping. A keening cry escaped her. He froze. "What—"

She pushed at him, gasping. He held her close. "No. Shh. If I leave now it will only hurt more." He smoothed her hair and kissed her face. "Relax into it, sweeting. Breathe."

He was warm and strong and, despite her sudden panic, she knew he had not meant to hurt her. She was safe in his arms. She buried her face in his neck and forced her lungs to slow. If she bore down just a little, would it ease? It would. After another moment, the sharp pain was gone, ebbing to a dull, stretching ache.

He ran his thumb over her cheek, taking away a tear. "Better?"

She sniffed and nodded. "What was that?"

He shook his head. "That was your virtue, my sweet. Apparently your Terrence was a bit of a failure."

She blinked. "But I spent the entire night with him. We did . . . things."

"Did you do this?"

She bit her lip. "Don't talk down to me. Of course we did this—well, something like this. Terrence would press into me a bit and then—"

He shook his head. "And then Terrence the Early would be finished, wouldn't he?" He dropped his forehead down to her shoulder. "I would have known if I had thought to check your readiness. Even with an experienced woman, it is the courteous thing to do." He rolled his head back and forth. "If not for your damned talented mouth . . ."

She laughed damply. "Don't put this on me, Lord 'I swived everything in sight' Marbrook! I'm only a proper little virgin from the country."

He lifted his head to smile ruefully. "Not anymore."

She put her finger over his lips. "Shh. I've believed I was ruined since I was fifteen. I'm owed a few moments of prudery."

He blinked. "Oh, hell, I hope not!" He began to withdraw from her.

The hot pleasure made her gasp. He went still once more. "Did I hurt you?"

She shook her head, rolling it on the pillow. "Do it again," she moaned.

He held her closer, then slowly, carefully, drove into her once more. The hot stretchy ache gave in to a rush of thick pleasure that took her breath away. She felt her fingers dig into the rigid muscles of his arms. "Oh, yes, please!" she gasped. "Again!"

He kissed her softly. "Yes, my queen." He stroked his thick, rigid erection more deeply into her, pulling out so slowly she keened with pleasure, driving in with just enough speed to make her gasp again.

She wrapped her arms about him, needing to hold on to something solid as she was swept away by a warm, exquisite sea. Deep strokes, the drive and retreat, the ebb and flow of him inside her, expanding her, giving to her, owning her—

She rose sharply and hard, then flew spinning out into pure light. He went with her, whispering his love as his powerful arms held her tightly through the shimmering tremors of her ecstasy.

# Chapter Forty-one

Phoebe became aware of her own sobbing cries as the light ebbed from her body. She swallowed and buried her face in his chest, her breath still coming too fast. "I—was I—loud?"

His deep laughter rumbled through her. "Don't worry, my sweet. It began to rain again a while ago. I don't think anyone could hear you."

"You had better not do that again, just the same," she said seriously. "I told everyone at the inn that I was your sister."

He gave her a scandalized look. "They'll all think me depraved! You howled like the north wind!"

She laughed and slapped at his shoulder. "I did not." Then she frowned. "Did I?"

He chuckled again. "I don't recall precisely." He pressed more deeply within her. "I suppose we could try it again and see."

She shuddered at the renewed pleasure. She was more sensitive now. It was as if she could feel every rigid vein in his organ as it drove into her. He shuddered now too, as he stroked deeply into her, letting his careful control loosen a bit.

"Is that all right?" he gasped. "Not too fast?"

He needed it. She lifted her legs and wrapped them around his back to ease the fit, then linked her hands behind his neck. "I'm fine," she said breathlessly.

It was harder this time, faster and more untamed, and she resisted the pleasure for a bit in order to watch the darkness of his passion on his face. Then his wild need excited her too much and she gave in to the throbbing rush of his heat within her.

He took her on and on, his hard powerful body sweating and rippling under her touch. He swelled further within her until she was nearly sobbing with the pain/pleasure of his invasion.

Then, with a deep animal roar, he stiffened in her arms, thrusting deeply, pulsating into her. She cried out at the final increase in his size, exploding into her own sharp, instant pleasure at the feel of his eruption.

He remained there, gasping hoarsely, his face tucked into her damp neck, as the shudders continued to rack him for a long moment.

"Oh Sweet Charlotte's Ass," swore Phoebe breathlessly. "What happened?"

He laughed weakly into her skin. "I'm not sure. I think I finally experienced 'making love.' It seems you weren't the only virgin in the room."

She wrapped her arms about him and pulled him down to relax over her. "See? We were meant for each other, like . . . like bread and butter."

He slid the greatest part of his weight off her, then stroked her hair away from her perspiring face. "Like toast and jam?"

"Like kippers and eggs."

"Bangers and mash."

"Precisely," she said with satisfaction.

"Horse and cart."

She turned her head to look into his eyes. "Who is the cart?"

"What?"

"Am I the cart? I'd prefer to be the horse, I think . . . although the horse isn't precisely driving, is he? Then again, the cart makes no decisions whatsoever . . ."

He drew his brows together in a helpless expression. "You're having one of those conversations that doesn't include me again, aren't you?"

She looked up at the ceiling. "I think I'd prefer 'prince and princess,' like in Sophie's story."

She told him about the princess cursed to a hundred years of sleep.

He toyed with her hair and listened, but then he frowned. "What does it mean? It doesn't make sense."

"She's alive, but it is as though she is dead . . . or sleeping. To me it seems as if she were attacked and she . . . she retreated. She stifled her deepest self—sent it to sleep. She remains that way for a very long time."

He kissed her temple softly. " 'Tis a sad tale. What happens next?"

"I don't know—but I hope that she awakens soon." She yawned. "I am so weary. I don't think I can—"

"Shh." He drew the covers high and tucked her into the curve of his warm body. "Sleep. You've had a trying day, what with cracking highwaymen's skulls and finding your lost virginity and all."

She curled up small into him, as if she had never slept any other way. "Only one highwayman," she murmured with another yawn. "I'm sure you would have thrashed them both . . ."

# Chapter Forty-two

Morning rose over the shabby little inn yard. Rafe watched it from the window of their room, not really seeing the cloud-shrouded sun as it peeked over the stable roof or the way the mist-edged yard began to fill with activity.

He leaned with one hand braced high on the window frame, wearing nothing but his trousers and a piece of toweling around his neck. Phoebe slept in the bed behind him, exhausted and spent from the passion of the night and perhaps from the strain of the last week as well.

He'd risen sleepless from that bed hours ago, for there was no halting the thoughts that swirled through his mind. Blame, for one. Regret. Joy. One hole in his heart had healed, but another had opened. The future . . . that he could scarcely bear to let his mind light upon.

Yet, with the fever of his passion now abated—somewhat, he thought with a rueful half-smile—it was past time to face the cold truth of what his actions had wrought.

He pushed away from the window, the cheerful scenery below suddenly unbearable. He crossed to the rustic washstand and tossed the towel down by the pitcher and bowl there.

He'd thought it would be over when he won her, but he'd been wrong.

It had only just begun.

He closed his eyes against the self-loathing that rose within him. He had stepped over a line that even at his lowest he'd somehow never really believed he could cross. Somewhere deep inside him he'd clung to the hope that he was, or at least someday could be, an honorable man.

He looked into the small, age-spotted mirror, blind to the haggard eyes and the purpling bruises that distorted his features. He saw nothing there but a man who would betray his only brother.

He began to dress absently, pulling on the shirt that smelled just a bit of her soap, finding his boots flung into a far corner. He took care not to look at the woman—his woman—in the bed, for he feared that if she knew his true feelings of loss and despair that she would blame herself . . .

The only hope for him to reclaim a bit of that honor was to make a clean breast of it all to his brother, face-to-face. He didn't want to. He'd rather have stolen Phoebe away into the night, hidden far away, and lived out his days without owning up to what he'd done to the only person who had ever given a damn whether he lived or died.

He certainly hoped that Calder would dish out a beating because he really ought to be required to pay for what he'd done.

The second-oldest sin in the recorded world. Brother against brother—the wickedest battle, the one that no one wins. It was likely that Calder would never forgive him.

"No," he said aloud, "but we all knew that, didn't we?"

"Who are you talking to?" Phoebe's sleepy voice came from the bed. He turned.

She was watching him mangle his cravat. Her eyes were wide and dark, with circles beneath them betraying the few hours she'd slept, and the flush on her cheeks betraying the reason why.

She'd never looked more beautiful than at that moment,

sleepy and mussed and tangled in the sheets with her softly rounded limbs splayed in innocently awkward sensuality, like a newborn colt's. His heart thudded dangerously at the sight of her.

He smiled at her in the mirror as he beat his cravat into some sort of submission. "I'm going to have to learn how to do this myself," he told her, a teasing note in his voice. "I don't think Calder will be continuing my allowance after I see him today."

Worry flashed across her expression. "Do you think he is very hurt?"

"At losing you?" *It would kill me.* Rafe looked down to hide the flare of guilt in his own eyes. "I shouldn't think it too much worse than damaged pride." He turned to her, his hands spread wide. "There. How did I do?"

She smiled wanly. "I think I had better fix that." She rose to her knees, keeping the sheet demurely in place. Luckily, she needed both hands to fix his neckwear, so he managed to have her naked and panting by the time she was done. At last she put both hands to his weskit and pushed him away.

The chill of missing her warmth sent a feeling of foreboding through him. He grabbed her hand and pulled her back.

"Let's never leave this room," he begged. "To hell with the world. We'll take trays of food at the door and never leave the bed!"

She tilted her head to gaze at him sympathetically. "We cannot hide from what we've done, my love. I would go with you, but I think that might make matters worse." She gave him a last kiss and gently pulled her hand free.

"If you're going to go, you'd better leave before that cravat ends up wrapped around the chandelier again."

She was laughing again, the way he'd meant to leave her. He'd almost made it out the door when she stopped him one last time.

"Rafe . . ."

He turned. She'd covered herself once more, but her gaze was naked and vulnerable. "You'll come straight back?"

He strode back to the bed where she sat very properly erect on her knees, oddly dignified in her mussed and many-times-violated state. He took her face in both his hands and kissed her long and hard. She melted into him, the way she always did, so damned wholeheartedly.

*I love you. I'm going to marry you and live in blissful exile forever.*

No. When he came back, his honor washed as clean as it might be, then he would bring his ring and bestow it upon her properly, as she deserved.

He forced himself to pull away.

"If I'm going to go, I must go now."

She managed a near-smile. "Of course. Poor Calder. I will survive until you return this afternoon."

Phoebe remained where she was as she watched Rafe depart the room. Then she tried to recapture the warmth of him by climbing back into bed. The room looked remarkably shabby in daylight—reminding her of the last time she spent the night in an inn.

*He's left you.*

She smiled slightly as she scoffed at herself. What a ridiculous thought.

Awake permanently now, she slid out of bed. She wrapped the coverlet around her to ward off the chill. The day was gray and misty out, but it would warm soon.

Rafe was riding away.

She pressed her nose to the wavering glass. Was it Rafe? It could be any man—any man who was tall and dark haired and well dressed in a blue surcoat and rode a rented black horse with four white stockings . . .

*He's left you, just like Terrence did.*

She straightened and turned away from the window and the view of the road which had been empty for several minutes now. Rafe would be back. A man like Rafe would never abandon a lady in an inn!

*You're not a lady. A lady would never sleep with her fiancé's brother.*

Calder was no longer her fiancé. She'd broken the engagement before she'd permitted Rafe to—

*Permitted? More like ravaged the fellow against his will! Are you* sure *you're a lady?*

Inside her mind, Phoebe took a riding crop to the voice, humiliated it, and drove it out of town. Rafe would be back. He loved her. He had fought for her. He was hers and she was his.

She waited, but blessed silence reigned.

Letting the coverlet slide from her shoulders, she went to where someone had kindly left her somewhat less muddy clothing in a neatly folded pile—Rafe!—and dressed. She fixed her hair as best she could, pinning up the front with the few pins she could find on the carpet, letting the back fall nearly to her waist. Her gown was creased and dirty, the sleeve still torn but Phoebe only sat herself regally in the single chair to wait for Rafe to return.

For he *would* return. Of that she had no doubt.

AS CALDER STRODE through his second favorite china factory, having just laid the first brick in the replacement kiln he'd ordered built, he was stopped by a familiar looking young man in Brookhaven livery.

"My lord!"

"Hello . . . er . . ."

"Stevens, my lord."

"Yes, Stevens, what is it? Is everything well at Brook House?"

The young fellow looked nervous. He dug into his coat to pull out a folded paper. "She said I was to bring it straight to you, and I did, my lord. I rode all night."

"She?"

Stevens swallowed. "Miss Millbury, my lord."

Calder grunted. He had more important matters to tend to. "Is she here?"

"No, my lord. She's . . ."

Something in the footman's voice made Calder look at him sharply. "Where is she?" he said, his voice low and hard.

Stevens paled. "Blue Goose Inn, on the road toward Bath, my lord."

He took a step back as Calder flipped the page open and began to read.

*Dear Lord Brookhaven,*

   *I ought to have told you at once, before we set about this betrothal in earnest, but I made a terrible mistake . . .*

Calder read the letter carefully. Then he crumpled it in his fist until his knuckles whitened.

It was happening again.

"Stevens!" He looked around him, but the footman was gone.

Apparently, fleeing him was becoming contagious.

# Chapter Forty~three

After she washed and dressed, Phoebe visited the driver, Afton.

He lay in his bed, looking like a prunish child in the vast borrowed nightshirt. His head was bandaged and his face bruised, but he'd fared no worse than a serious concussion.

"To be sure, miss," he assured her worriedly. "We didn't go far, but we was set upon as soon as we'd turned the bend and lost the light of the carriage lanterns. I'm shamed to say I went down like a felled tree—didn't make account of meself at all."

Phoebe patted Afton's hand. "You couldn't have known. And his lordship and I came away well enough. You bore the worst of it, I fear."

"Oh, don't you worry none, miss. I'll be set to drive you and himself back right soon." He tried to stir but his eyes lost their focus and he fell back against the cushions. "Or might be I'll let Stevens drive," he gasped.

Phoebe pressed cool water on him and sat at his bedside until the headache had eased and he'd fallen asleep.

By the clock in the main inn room, that had absorbed only a few hours of her morning. She spent another hour brushing the worst of the mud from her gown and petticoats. Then she thought to order a full hot bath, for surely it would do her good to relax away the tension of waiting.

She was out of the bath within a quarter of an hour, unable to sit still. She dried her hair by the fire and braided it. Then she brushed it out and twisted it into a knot at the back of her neck. Then she took that out and experimented with a crown of braids. This consumed a mere half hour.

There was nothing to worry about. It would take Rafe hours to ride there and back, although not as long as the carriage ride had been.

And anyway, it wasn't as if Calder would actually harm Rafe—or at least not permanently. They might argue for a while. She could definitely imagine someone throwing a blow. There might even be a bit of a brawl . . .

An hour later she was positively twitchy with impatience, unable to do anything but pace from the bed to the window and back again. Rafe had said he'd hurry back—

Terrence hadn't even said goodbye. She'd looked out her window to see him racing away on his rented nag, sans saddle or even his coat!

Which had no relevance to the present situation, of course. What a silly notion to cross her mind right now! She laughed away the sick lurch that the memory of Terrence's desertion always caused. He'd done her a great service by fleeing the scene of her seduction. If he hadn't, she would be Mrs. LaPomme at this very moment, trying to sweep under her layabout husband's dirty boots!

She laughed again, thinking of Rafe's sedate departure and the longing glance he'd cast over his shoulder before he'd turned the bend in the road. It was quite the reverse of Terrence's desertion!

Unfortunately, the eternal stretch of the day made it very difficult to remember that. Noon came and went. Afternoon lengthened interminably into an endless evening. Her spirits collapsed every time she heard booted feet in the hall, yet he did not come. She tried to rally, she truly did, but eventually the words she repeated to herself ceased to carry meaning and became only sounds.

The inn's chambermaid entered with coal for the fire, but the glow did nothing to dispel the growing chill within Phoebe.

Where was he? Being that she'd never observed a conversation with Calder that took more than three minutes and contained more than fifty words in total, she doubted that he and Rafe had whiled the day away in a heart-to-heart.

Unless there had been drinking.

Her spirits rose slightly at the thought. Spirits did tend to make men forget where they were supposed to be.

Until she recalled that Calder never partook, not a single drop of it, not even beer.

As the evening came to full night, she began to feel the cold presence of real worry. Lateness might be inexcusable, but to not come at all? Something terrible must have happened to him!

Should she rally the inn staff for a search? Rafe could be injured, thrown from his horse in a ditch—a ditch anywhere between here and Brook House! She added hand-wringing to her pacing and began to chew her nails for good measure.

Then she heard it, that familiar brisk stride—that decisive clop of fine boots on worn wood of the hall floor—

It wasn't until she flew to open the door that she remembered why that stride was so familiar.

It wasn't Rafe who stood there, glowering at her from his great height.

It was Calder, who did not look as though he'd spent the day coming to any sort of resolution with his traitorous brother.

"Where is he?" Calder growled. "Where is the conniving bride-stealing bastard?"

# Chapter Forty~four

Phoebe backed up in dismay as Calder pushed his way into the room.

He turned, his gaze flicking into every corner. "I'm going to rip him apart," he growled.

"Now, my lord . . . you cannot blame him alone—" Phoebe stopped and swallowed hard, belatedly remembering the stories Mr. Stickley had shown her. The rumor that claimed that Calder had killed his wife and her lover in a jealous rage.

She probably ought to have remembered that before she'd let Rafe go back to—

"Wait—" Ice struck deep within her. "Rafe didn't find you?"

Calder glared at her, his rage unabated. "*I* was not lost."

She shook her head, waving aside his fury. "Listen to me. Rafe left early this morning to speak to you. He thought it was the right thing to do—"

"I was not hard to find. Your letter found me easily enough. Then again, my brother doesn't worry about the right thing to do—as you may have noticed. All his life he has tried to take what is rightfully mine—"

"Oh, shut it!" Phoebe made a sound of frustration. "Calder, put it behind you and listen to me!"

He stared at her in surprise, then huffed out a breath. "No one tells me to 'shut it.' Ever."

Phoebe waved a hand. "Yes, yes, I know. Everyone quakes in their boots when you stride by, blah, blah, blah."

He scowled and opened his mouth. She clapped her hands together sharply. "Now listen to me! Something terrible has happened to Rafe!"

"Good."

She narrowed her eyes at him. "You don't mean that."

"I—" He ran a hand through his hair in a gesture that reminded her so much of Rafe that her heart hurt. "I don't know what I mean. I never do when it comes to Rafe. My brother is the only one who can turn me inside out like this—"

She let out a breath. "Trust me when I tell you that it is mutual."

He shook his head. "No. Rafe always knows exactly what he's doing—whatever will plague me off the most, usually."

"And would leaving me here alone while he *didn't* go to see you plague you off?"

Calder hesitated. "No. He'd be more likely to stick around to watch the fur fly."

She threw out her hands. "Exactly! I mean—it is not in character to disappear, either way, is it? It's almost as if someone—" She went very still. "Oh, no. The highwaymen!"

Calder gazed at her. "I'm listening but I'm not following."

Phoebe began to pace worriedly. "Last night—on the road—we were attacked! There were two of them—one had a pistol! They disabled the servants and jumped Rafe—I beat them off with a tree branch when they were trying to drag him away!"

He held up a hand to stop the torrent of words. "You beat off two armed highwaymen with a tree branch?" He frowned at her. "You aren't at all who I thought you were, are you?"

She hesitated, then shrugged. "Not even a little tiny bit. So sorry."

He blinked. "And yet, I am not sorry . . . which is odd."

"Lovely. Right. Let's get back to Rafe, shall we?"

He sighed. "It seems we always do."

She went to the window, though there was nothing but the night to see outside. "He left here early, barely past dawn. If we retrace his steps, and question anyone who might have seen him, we might be able to find him—"

"Not we. Most especially not you." He folded his arms. "I shall hire investigators—Bow Street runners—to find him, assuming he wants to be found. You and I will go back to London."

She shook off the suggestion. "No. I want to go looking for him—"

"Phoebe."

Perhaps it was the unexpected gentleness in his voice, but she turned in surprise to see Calder gazing at her with compassion in his eyes.

She beat back the tide of fear and worry. "He didn't leave me, Calder. He would never leave me."

His lips tightened. "Then he will know to look for you at Brook House, won't he? If he comes back to the inn, we'll leave a note for him here." He bent to pick up her abandoned wrap. "You cannot stay here, Phoebe, and you cannot tromp the roads looking for him."

She pressed her fingers over her mouth, thinking hard. She didn't want to leave this shabby room—*their* shabby room—the only place in the world where they were not a rake and a wanton, but simply lovers, meant to be together forever.

However, Calder was right. She'd not hear a thing, waiting in this tiny room while the walls closed in and her nerves wound tighter. At Brook House, she would have Sophie, and clean clothing, and first stab at any news Calder received from his investigators.

She let her hands fall and trailed her fingers over the dingy bedpost. *Sorry, my love.*

Then she took the wrap from Calder's hands and preceded him out the door, her head held high.

RAFE WOKE TO feel pounding in his head.

*Not again.*

This time he didn't expect to find his arms full of naked Phoebe, the finest cure known to mankind. This time he immediately remembered how he came to be where he was.

They'd been waiting for him. Not a mile down the road, where the hedges grew high and the morning traffic toward London had not yet begun.

And he'd ridden right into it, scarcely aware of his surroundings, his thoughts occupied with memories of Phoebe, trembling and perspiring in his hands, her hair tossing on the pillow as he played her like a flute . . .

A man stepped from the bushes, a small, dapper man with a handkerchief tied over the lower half of his face. Not the highwayman of the night before—at least not the one he'd seen.

He'd turned to try to spot the other one, but it had been too late. The first blow glanced off his temple as he tried to duck, but the second must have done the trick.

Here he was, bound and gagged, in the back of a cart that smelled of rotten vegetables, covered by a length of scratchy burlap that let the light spike through his aching eyes in tiny bright squares.

He suppressed the need to struggle against the tight bonds and simply closed his eyes. There was no point in wasting strength and losing his one chance at surprising whoever his abductors were.

It would be nice if he could first figure out why anyone would want to abduct him. Once upon a time he would have assumed he owed someone money, but no longer. His tally sheets were clear. He was broke, but not indebted.

Phoebe wasn't in the cart with him, so he hoped that meant they weren't after her. Of course, if they had been, they would have taken her the other night, tree branch or no.

She'd be safe there at the inn, with the servants around her. She would wait for him while he figured out a way to get himself out of this mess.

He was tied very securely. It was obvious that he was going to stay right where he was, until someone else released him.

Damn it.

# Chapter Forty~five

At Brook House, the next several days went by with excruciating slowness. Sophie tried to help by finishing the translation.

*"Then he leaned over and gave her a kiss, and when his lips touched hers, Briar Rose opened her eyes, woke up, and looked at him fondly. After that they went downstairs together, and the king and queen woke up along with the entire court, and they all looked at each other in amazement."*[2]

Deirdre listened to the end of the tale with irritable scorn. "So that's it? All those men die and this one walks right in—and he's her true love?"

Phoebe looked up from where she'd been staring into the coals. "Sometimes I suppose love is simply a matter of timing." She wished Rafe had had better timing—to propose first, for instance.

During the day, when everyone's doubts about Rafe's character roused her protective instincts, it was easy to be steadfast and faithful.

At night, however, when the household took their doubts to bed, her own secret ones began to rise.

[2]Jack Zipes, *The Complete Fairy Tales of the Brothers Grimm*, New York (Bantam Books), 1987, p. 189.

*Are you sure he's coming back to you?*

She was sure. Absolutely positive. Adamant, even.

*You were sure about Terrence, remember?*

The familiar ache throbbed, deep in her heart. No. She'd been too young then, too lonely and susceptible. This was entirely different.

*Then why does it look so much the same?*

TESSA, WHO WAS most satisfied with recent events, sat down at her cluttered vanity and began to plot to get Phoebe to leave forever. One unfortunate side effect of this delightful mess was the way that Brookhaven's protective instincts had been aroused. He was actually acknowledging that damp whiner Phoebe's existence!

It would not do for Brookhaven to get truly attached now, not when Deirdre's chances had just risen so dramatically.

Tessa smiled into the mirror, distracted by her own beauty once again. "Why of course, Your Highness!" she cooed. "I simply adore my daughter's new home at Brookhaven!" She winked. "Why, Your Highness, I thought you'd never ask!"

PHOEBE WAS WAITING for Calder in his study when he arrived after breakfast. There was something to be said for a man who was always precisely where he was supposed to be.

She stood when he entered. "My lord, I have only this morning realized that you have yet to formally call off our wedding."

Brookhaven glanced at her once, then continued around his desk to rifle through a stack of documents. "I don't see any point in rushing into things."

This from the man who had proposed less then seven

hours after seeing her at a ball. "It must be done, my lord! I will not have the world thinking I'm wedding one brother when I intend to wed the other!"

He still didn't look at her. "I don't see that it is any of the world's business one way or the other."

She drew back. "Well . . . no, of course it isn't." She raised her chin. "And I don't care what anyone thinks! But to leave matters as they are . . ."

Oh, no. He didn't, did he?

"You don't . . . you cannot still want to marry me?" She gazed at him with a frown. "Why would you—after what I've done?"

"I could hardly end the engagement without making your . . . indiscretion public knowledge. I wouldn't reveal it, but that sort of scandal only causes more speculation and curiosity. Trust me on that score. Eventually someone would put it together and you would be disgraced."

She folded her arms and tilted her head. "All very noble of you, I'm sure. Except that a man like you—you do not forgive easily, I think. I spent the night in an inn with your brother—"

"Half-brother."

She shook her head and went on. "With your brother, whom I love completely."

"Who has abandoned you."

She didn't flinch. "He did not. You underestimate him, as you always have done."

"Then where is he? It has been days!"

She closed her eyes and took a breath. "I do not know. I worry—" *Oh God, the worry!* She opened her eyes and fixed him with renewed ferocity. "Wherever he is, he needs our help, not our censure. If I married you, I would be guilty of the same abandonment you accuse him of—and so would you be."

"You are loyal," he said. "I admire that. The fact remains,

however, that he is not here. You are now ruined, you have no commitment from him that the two of you will marry—"

She brushed that off. "I told you, it is understood."

He snorted without humor. "Miss Millbury, if I list for you all the women who thought they had some sort of 'understanding' with my brother . . ." He trailed off, for she was smiling at him. "What is it?"

"You called him your brother."

He sighed. "You will hear nothing against him, will you? How can you be so blind?"

She smiled again, this time a bit sadly. "I am not blind. I know who he has been, just as you do. More than you, perhaps, for he held nothing from me. I know that he aches to belong, that he wishes no more of life than to care for Brookhaven, which he loves. I know that he is in agony over what we have done to you—"

"That I doubt."

"That you should never doubt," she retorted. "It was I who seduced him, you know. He did his best to resist the attraction at every turn. I'll admit, he wasn't very good at it—but he's had so little practice, you see. All those married ladies and merry widows . . ." She shrugged. "I fear he's a bit too good-looking for his own good."

He frowned slightly. "He told you all this? I am surprised. Confession is not his usual form of persuasion."

"That's what I'm trying to tell you, Calder. He does not play a role with me. He is only Rafe, bastard son and scorned brother, gambler and light-footed lover no more— simply a man without a true home in this world."

Calder stiffened. "I never scorned him. He has never been turned from my door."

"No. He knows that. But it will never be *his* door, don't you see? Can you imagine what it was like for him, to be brought up with you, knowing that his home, his heritage, his world would never truly be his? A legitimate brother, even a younger one, might hold out some hope that he will inherit, or at least be part of the legacy. A bastard son, especially one with all the love for the land that any father might hope for, taught and groomed for every responsibility that you have—but he will never know."

"He had possibilities," Calder said stiffly. "He was given his rightful portion when our father died. He wasted it on cards and women."

"He was eighteen! And angry and lost, as well. He loved your father, despite how the marquis favored you over him. He made mistakes, a great many of them. Yet have you not noticed that since your . . . your crisis . . . that he has changed his ways? He came back to support you, so you would not be alone."

Calder stood abruptly, moving to the window with jerky strides. After a long moment, he passed a hand over his face. "I thought he'd simply run out of money. I thought he'd seen my situation as insurance that I wouldn't be likely to throw him out."

She lifted a hand, but did not touch him. He wasn't the sort of man one reached out to comfort. "He has changed. He has paid off his debts. He no longer frequents the tables. He hasn't been blind drunk in years."

"Once."

"What?"

"He drank himself into a stupor on the day I told him you had agreed to wed me."

"Ah." She let out a breath. "That was a mistake, you know. I thought the proposal came from him. I didn't know his full name."

Calder turned back to face her. "I figured that out eventually."

"You did? Then why—?"

He looked away. "I liked you. You are . . . a rather different sort of girl. I thought that if you grew to know me, you might . . ." He shrugged. "Anyway, it wasn't as though I could break the engagement without causing an enormous scandal."

Too true. It had been threat enough to keep her from doing the same for far too long. "It would have been less of a scandal then than it will be now," she said ruefully.

He fixed her with his black gaze once again. "Then don't do it. At least . . . at least let the matter lie for now. If—when Rafe returns, there will be plenty of time to straighten the matter out then."

Put off the madness until Rafe was back by her side? It was tempting. God, she missed him. Worry tugged at her constantly, like a fishing line snagged on something vital. *Oh, Rafe.* She wrapped her arms about her chilled midriff. *Where are you?*

Calder was waiting for an answer. She took a breath. "But the world is watching, my lord. Won't anyone think it odd that the wedding arrangements have come to a halt? We must tell the bishop—"

"We will . . . in time. Right now, I think it best if we go on as if nothing has happened. Give Rafe time to do whatever he has gone to do. Give the world time to talk of something else. Who knows, perhaps someone will do something more scandalous in the meantime and we will be nothing but a sentence at the bottom of the scandal sheet."

Phoebe managed a choked laugh. "That would be lovely. I long to be nothing but a sentence."

The corner of his lips twitched. "As do I."

The agreement made her uneasy, but she nodded. "We will wait, then. For now."

*Coward.*

It would only be until Rafe returned. Only until she could tuck her hand in his when she had to face the world's censure. He would never want her to go through it alone.

Her reasoning was sound and Calder was right, she knew. So why did she feel as if she'd committed something a little bit like a betrayal?

# Chapter Forty~six

In the quaint little village of Burnhill, deep in the Cotswolds, Wolfe left the village tavern whistling. He'd thought to bring along enough coin on this venture to tempt a tryst from the pretty innkeeper's daughter.

After an hour in his company, Wolfe had left the girl pink-faced and bemused, with her eyes wide and damp but her fingers wrapped tightly around the gold in her palm. She wasn't likely to squeak—or if she did, what did it matter? Her father wouldn't like it much, but this wasn't Wolfe's village, was it? He and Stick were only here long enough to stop the wedding—

Then what? He stopped right there in the street at the thought. What would happen when Brookhaven missed his wedding date?

Why, once he was released, he'd go right back to being engaged to Miss Millbury. After all, it wasn't as if she wouldn't forgive a man for being kidnapped!

Wolfe stood there in the spring sunshine, blind to the way the evening light made the stones glow golden, ignoring that he forced carts and villagers to go around as they stared at him oddly, and contemplated—without the merest glimmer of distaste, he was rather surprised to notice—committing cold-blooded murder.

At the very least, the brutal murder of Miss Millbury's dreams.

The actual murder would have to take place when Stickley was out of the way.

AT BREAKFAST ON the fourth day of Rafe's absence, Tessa began to talk of sending Phoebe back to Thornton.

"I realize that the wedding has not been officially canceled—but there are rumors," she warned Phoebe blackly.

Rumors started by Tessa? Phoebe gazed evenly at her aunt. "I will remain here, thank you very much."

"But I am your—"

Phoebe frowned. "You're not really my aunt, you realize."

Tessa blinked. "What do you mean?"

"You are not my mother's sister. You are merely the woman who married my uncle." She turned to Deirdre. "Dee, have you considered tossing this woman from your house in Woolton? I'm quite sure your father left it all to you. I should talk to a solicitor—"

Tessa laughed lightly. "Why, Phoebe, what a ridiculous notion! I only mentioned it because—what with all the rumors and the fact that the plans for the ceremony have been left uncompleted—I thought you wouldn't want your . . . situation . . . to reflect badly on Deirdre or . . . ah, Sophie. Decorum must be preserved." Her expression was prim.

Phoebe lifted her head swiftly. "Why?"

Tessa drew back at Phoebe's glare. "What?"

Phoebe stood, her body like a coiled spring. "Why must we preserve decorum? Who are we preserving it for? I don't give a bloody damn what Society thinks anymore. I don't care what you think of me—you or my father. Rafe is gone, Tessa. Gone!"

She pressed her hands to the ache in her chest. "He is

missing and there is nothing but a hole where he was." She spun away, too raw to bear the vast lack of understanding in her aunt's eyes.

Tessa cleared her throat uneasily. "You are too emotional, Phoebe. You always have been. There is no need to be so—so very passionate about—"

Phoebe whirled. "About passion? About a love that makes every sunrise a pleasure for the sole fact that I might see him that day? About a man who can see right through the pretty poses and the fluttering fan—who can see *me,* just as I am, as I truly am—see me and care for me anyway . . ." Her throat gave out on a gasp and her knees went weak.

She sat abruptly. "I think . . ." She swallowed. "I think that I need to be very passionate about a man such as that."

She turned back to the fire. "Leave me alone, Tessa. Just . . . leave me alone."

RAFE LOOKED UP from his work and listened. Voices again. This time they were arguing loudly enough for him to hear them clearly. He walk-crawled to the door to press one ear to the thick, slimy wood. On either side of his head, his hands pressed to the door as well, but he paid no attention to the pain of torn nails or the reek of his filthy fingers. Closing his eyes, he concentrated on the men in the house above him.

Behind him, a new shadow graced the grimy root cellar. High on the wall, there was a new hole—soon to be a window—where two stones had been clawed from the wall with nothing but bare fingers and desperation. It was a small hole, but slowly growing larger. Had the wall not been laid two stones deep he would have seen daylight already.

Now, listening with all his might, he could hear one

bellowing voice clearly and one lighter tenor less so. They were arguing about . . . a letter?

WOLFE SLAPPED THE letter they'd found in Brookhaven's pocket down onto the rickety tabletop and fisted his large hand on top of it. "You know I cannot copy the handwriting! You, on the other hand, have been signing my name for years!"

Stickley blinked rapidly. "I—what a thing to say!"

Wolfe rolled his eyes. "See here, Stick, I don't care. You keep the practice going and you don't cheat me more than I'd say was fair, so it doesn't matter."

"Ch—cheat? I—"

Wolfe's fist slammed the table with a thud, making it jump, making Stickley jump, and causing a twitch to pass through the aching exhausted shoulders of the man listening downstairs. "Stick, I told you—I care nothing about it. We have a partnership that works. You take care of business. I make sure nothing interferes with that business."

Stickley forgot to quiver long enough to sniff indignantly. "And precisely what does that consist of?"

Wolfe tilted his head and narrowed his eyes. "It consists of making sure that we don't lose the trust to Brookhaven's pockets. It consists of making sure Miss Millbury gets a letter from Brookhaven telling her how he just couldn't face marrying her and how he simply had to take a holiday from the strain of his existence."

Stickley frowned skeptically. "He's about to be made Duke of Brookmoor. He wouldn't take a holiday now."

"Sure he would. After all, Brookmoor's been dying for years now. That sort of strain can tell on a man."

Stickley reached one hand to slide the letter closer. "Well, I suppose I could duplicate the handwriting—and this one is actually to Miss Millbury herself, so the greeting will be appropriate . . ."

He muttered on while Wolfe took the other wooden chair, flipping his coattails out grandly as if he seated himself on a throne. Pouring himself a glassful from the wine bottle on the table, Wolfe swirled it, sniffed it, then downed it in a long easy draught.

Stickley looked up, glaring over the spectacles perched on his nose. "We've only the one bottle left, you know. We'll have to go back into the village for supplies and I'd really rather not. The less people see us the better."

Wolfe thought rather regretfully about the innkeeper's daughter, who might have been up for another go-round now that she'd already lost her virtue. Still, it was all in good cause. "Agreed." He corked the wine. Sacrifice wasn't something he was accustomed to, but this was a very important undertaking, after all.

Stickley returned to his study, frowning. "I can match the handwriting well enough, but Brookhaven has an extremely complicated signature. Perhaps after several days of practice—"

Wolfe's chair came back down onto four legs. "Days? God, Stick, I can't stay in this moldy cottage for days while you scribble! Think of something else!"

Stickley shrugged. "I could just forgo the signature altogether. After all, how many fiancés does she have to be jilted by?"

Wolfe smiled and clapped Stickley hard on the shoulder. "That's the lad!" Then he leaned back in his chair once more. "I've a plan to add a bit of realism myself. I hate to lose that fine horse of his, but it's a bit too fine for the likes of us. We'd be better off without it."

He stood and went to the pile of things by the fire. "It's a good thing we hadn't gotten around to burning these." He pulled a fine blue surcoat from the pile and shrugged into it. "It's a bit tight, but a fair number of blokes wear them that way."

He went to the window to gaze at his own reflection with a satisfied smile. "Oh, yes. Don't I look the proper marquis?"

BENEATH THEM IN the earthen vault, Rafe let his breath out in disappointment. He'd heard something about a letter and then their voices had quieted, argument apparently resolved.

His eyes ached from trying to see in the dimness and his lungs felt squeezed by the ill air, but he turned back to the hole in the wall and began to dig at the ancient mortar with his torn fingertips once more. Phoebe was outside that wall, somewhere, hopefully safe and sound, and he intended to get to her if he had to tear this cottage down with his bare hands.

One stone at a time.

# Chapter Forty-seven

When Phoebe entered the master's study on the sixth day of Rafe's disappearance, Calder looked up from the papers he was reading. There was a shadow in his eyes that told her he knew something.

"You have heard from him."

Calder shook his head as he stood to show her to a chair. "No, but I have heard *of* him. I followed the trail of the horse—" He smiled grimly. "Actually, it was a money trail, leading me to the village of Burnhill, where a man matching his description sold one of my horses to a hosteller in exchange for a lesser mount and some coin."

"And you are sure it was Rafe." It wasn't a question.

Calder rubbed a hand over his weary face. "The innkeeper described him right down to the silver buttons on his blue surcoat. Rafe never did care to wear gold like the rest of us."

Phoebe paced the room, forcing the niggling voices to silence. She would remember his voice. She would concentrate on the way his every touch was a caressing vow. She would roll herself into the bedcovers at night and pretend that the warmth came from him.

He would return.

And if he didn't, she would find him and strangle him with his own cravat—

She halted, frozen by that thought.

*She would find him.*

Calder's hired men were doing their best, she was sure, but she *knew* Rafe. She knew his habits and his preferences— and she knew where he'd last been seen. She could start there, following her instincts and her knowledge of Rafe until she found him. What if he needed her help?

She became absorbed by the strength of that idea. Yes. Rafe needed her help. He needed her, she could feel it.

Why not? She had nothing better to do at the moment and the waiting was fair driving her mad. Calder wouldn't like it. Nor would the vicar, but she'd already gone a bit past caring what they thought, hadn't she? She was no child to be ordered to her room!

The ache in her chest eased immediately. If not happiness, taking action at least brought her a sense of purpose and control over her future. She would find Rafe, rescue him from whatever mess he'd found himself in, and they would come home together.

Let the bloody world say what it might.

Calder had plenty to say.

"Absolutely not! I forbid it!"

Phoebe shook her head. "With all due respect, my lord, you don't have a word to say about it."

"Well, your father will surely forbid it!"

She laughed shortly. "My father hasn't stepped ten feet from your library in days. He doesn't even know what happened between us, or that Rafe is missing." She shook her head in disbelief. "He's gone completely native in Mayfair. It's going to come as a serious blow to him when he loses your valet and your whisky."

She tilted her head and gazed at him with stubborn regret. "I dislike having to act against your wishes when you've been so kind to me and my father, but—"

"But it has not stopped you before and it will not stop you now," he said rigidly.

"No." She took a breath. "It won't." She turned to go. "I'm packing a small bag and using my own funds for the journey. I shall let you know immediately should I learn anything new."

He did not try to stop her and it was not long before she stood in the front hall in a traveling dress with a satchel in her hands. She'd written a rather evasive note to the vicar—heavens, no need to tackle that mountain just yet!—and a more explicit one to Sophie.

A knock came at the front door. A footman hurried past her to answer it as she drew her gloves on. She glanced up to see that it was the post.

Should she wait? There might be something—

"For you, miss."

Who—? It was posted from Burnhill.

She dropped her other glove to the floor and ripped through the seal on the letter.

*My dear Miss Millbury,*
*I regret that I am unable to fulfill my promise to*
*you . . .*

The letter was short, almost a note, really. As Phoebe stood there in the great marble front hall at Brook House, bag at her feet, a distant part of her wondered at how such great damage could be done with such economy of words.

The pain in her chest swelled, squeezing the air from her lungs. *I have decided against wedding you . . .* as if he'd chosen not to purchase a new suit or a bottle of ink. The image of his back, broad and straight, clad in blue superfine, fading away in the morning mists, leaving her alone in their bed after . . .

A single sound escaped her then—a hoarse sob cut brutally short.

Then . . . nothing. No emotion but the welcome chill of

her control. It froze the pain in mid-thought, leaving it a spiky, weighted ball of ice in her breast. Better that than the roiling, exploding fireball of agony it had been.

She carefully refolded the letter, keeping the creases sharp. She would investigate the one thread of hope left to her—not that she dared keep faith in it, but she would not take anything for granted, not this time.

Calder was still in his study. He scowled at her when she entered. "I thought you were preparing for your journey."

"I—" She swallowed.

He must have realized her shock, for he stood quickly and rounded his desk to take her arm.

"Sit down, Phoebe. What has happened? You look like death."

She handed Calder the letter. Her hands were not shaking. "This is not signed. Is this his handwriting?"

Calder read it slowly. Then he looked up, the truth in his eyes. "Rafe and I had the same tutor. I used to do his work when he scorned his lessons. Our handwriting is nearly identical. This—" He folded the letter and set it away from him as if he could not bear to look at it. "This could have been written by me."

Time stopped. The light turned to gray. Even the air in her lungs felt like winter.

She realized dully that she had crossed the room to stare blindly out the window. She was there, braced against the window with her ungloved hand—yet she felt oddly as though she floated above them both, looking down at two forlorn people in the silence of lost hope.

Calder took a deep breath and let it out slowly. "Phoebe," he said with gruff gentleness in his voice. "What is the good of loving someone if it goes to waste?"

Phoebe leaned her forehead against the cool glass of the window and watched the spring rain trickle down the pain. "Is that possible?" The gray day did not threaten, but only confirmed her mood. "Can love ever be wasted? Isn't the act of loving worth something, all on its own?"

"Now you're traveling to a place unfamiliar to me." Calder leaned against the giant desk, his long legs stretched out before him. "I am not a philosopher. I do not ponder the meaning of my existence. I already know my place in the world."

Phoebe closed her eyes. "Then you are a fortunate man indeed, Lord Brookhaven. I certainly hope that someone comes along to shake you right out of that smug little tree."

He laughed, a rusty bark. "It would take an army to take me down, I fear."

"An army . . . or an arrow. Love strikes everyone sooner or later, I think—or at least it ought to, if there is any justice at all in the world."

"Are you bitter now?"

Phoebe opened her eyes and gazed unseeing into the misty distance. "I am not. I am . . . I am only sad—and perhaps a little angry—but not bitter." Not yet. Would she become so one day? She could forgive Rafe for pursuing her and she could forgive him for leaving her, but could she ever forgive him if his actions hardened her heart forever?

Probably not. "You are not surprised. I can sense it. What are you not telling me?"

Calder leaned back on the edge of his desk. "I'd rather not say."

Phoebe turned to gaze at him evenly. "You and I have been honest with each other ever since you came to find me at the Blue Goose. Do not fail that now."

Calder studied the carpet. "When he left with you, he took several possessions . . . but he left his signet ring on his dressing table. Since he rarely removed it, I must take it as a sign that he has no intention of ever returning to his family or his home."

So.

She drew in another icy breath that stung her chest. "I will go pack now. I believe it is time I accompanied my father back to Thornhold."

Back to her watchful prison. Back to endless scrutiny, now doubly dangerous. She'd not been nearly as discreet this time. Her ridiculous lie at the inn would be easily penetrated if anyone took the effort. Perhaps if she disappeared now, she would be forgotten by the time word got out that Lord Marbrook had fled London for parts unknown.

Calder stood as well. "Miss Millbury—Phoebe—I cannot but help feel partially responsible for all this."

Phoebe blinked at him in dull surprise. "My lord, you have been nothing but the honorable victim."

Calder reddened slightly. "Not so honorable. I knew—" He cleared his throat, then joined her at the window. He took her hand a bit awkwardly. "I knew when I sent your aunt my proposal that Rafe wanted you for himself. I think I even knew that you preferred him."

She stared at him. "But why? I am not plain, but I am no true beauty. I understand . . . at least, I thought I understood why Rafe chose me . . . but why did you?"

He shrugged. It was odd to see a man so normally sure of himself be so hesitant. "I suppose knowing that he wanted you was enough to make me want you as well . . . at first. Now—"

"I see. So the one of you who ended up with me . . . he gets to be dubbed the pick of the litter, is that it?"

He looked very uncomfortable. "I . . . I believe that is how it began, yes. For me at least."

She held up a hand. "Spare me further wallowing. It is self-indulgent of you. We have both behaved badly."

He met her gaze. "Yes." He took a breath. "I fear Rafe has always brought out the devil in me."

Phoebe began to withdraw her hand. "Our devils are our

own, my lord. We cage them or liberate them of our own free will."

Calder did not release her. "Phoebe, you need not return to Thornhold."

She let her hand stay in his. What did it matter? "Yes, I do. The gossip sheets will go mad soon. I do not wish to face that here in London."

"There is a solution." He loosened his grip, slipping his fingers more intimately between hers. Phoebe watched their hands intertwine without much interest.

Calder smiled, or as close to a smile as she had ever seen on him. "Phoebe, I have come to see in these last days that you are an admirable woman, with strength and dignity to spare. I am asking you to be my marchioness—and my duchess, when that day comes."

He'd managed to surprise her after all. She blinked at him. "My lord, I'd be a terrible duchess. Did you notice that I'm rather indiscreet?"

His fingers curled sensuously through hers. She felt him, felt the heat and strength of his large hand. "Phoebe." His voice was soft and husky as he pulled gently on that hand, tugging her a step closer. "Would you really rather face a future of scandal? Would it truly be so bad to be my wife?"

Phoebe took that step, for she was wondering that very same thing. The thought of belonging to another man now—or ever—to be strung on that reeling line between despair and dizzying joy, to fly on that heartrending passion and fall into that black place between—no, that she would never willingly do again.

When Calder's lips met hers, Phoebe closed her eyes and waited. His mouth was warm, his lips firm and teasing. He slid one hand up her arm to cup the back of her head in his big palm and carefully deepened the kiss.

Somewhere inside her, her body recognized his size and

strength and maleness. She became aware of a slight warming of her lower belly and a tingle in her breasts.

Her heart, however, was left entirely unmoved. It was safe from Calder, safe from that wild ride.

Calder ended the kiss and stepped back. He moved his hand around to tip her chin up so he could see her eyes. "Was that so terrible?"

She could do it. She could wed Calder and shelter beneath his power and status. She would inherit the Pickering trust. She would be immune.

It would not be the life she'd imagined with Rafe. It would be a half-life . . . which was perhaps better than no life at all. She wasn't even sure she could go back to Thornhold. Rafe had changed her with his passion and his intensity. She would never be the same.

Yet she must change again. Could she wear the mantle of a duchess?

"Calder . . . did you ever have a dream about someone that was so real . . . so *glorious* . . . that you thought they must be dreaming it, too?"

He shook his head. "I don't understand."

"I am sure you could do better, Calder," she said gently, a slight thaw in the ice around her soul. "I am not what you need."

His thumb traced her bottom lip. "I like you. I am comfortable with you. I respect you and I cannot deny that I desire you. What more do I need than that?"

Comfort, respect, and desire. Indeed, what did any of them need more than that? The other way lay the swinging blade of agony and bliss. Her choices were clear. Be alone and ruined. Be his duchess and be spared.

Perhaps . . . perhaps it was for the best. Perhaps it was time to be practical. Sensible.

Maybe love wasn't enough, after all.

She turned her face away from his touch. Her gaze fell

upon the "Dear Miss Millbury" letter. It was unsigned, as if Rafe couldn't bear to put his name on it . . . just like he couldn't bear to take his signet ring.

After all, what was his name worth without the man to wrap in it?

*His name* . . .

She looked at Calder, thinking of the things he'd told her about Rafe, and then back down at the damned letter.

*A matter of timing.*

And as simply as that, her decision was made.

# Chapter Forty~eight

*Well, well, my pretties—it looks as though the wedding of the season is on once more! Handsome Brookhaven and his pretty Mary Mouse have thrown themselves back into the bridal fray. It is reported that the flowers for the ceremony have been ordered to the tune of thirty guineas! If you haven't been invited to this splendid event, then you simply don't matter, not in Mother England anyway!*

ANOTHER SLIMY BRICK slid from the root cellar wall, leaving a hole that was heartbreakingly just a tiny bit too small. Rafe cleaned out the crumbling mortar around it and then set it back into place. He had to stop for the night. He'd never been so exhausted. His hands were bloody and throbbing. His shoulders were on fire.

Just a few hours sleep, and then he would start again. It was ridiculous to wear himself to the bone. He'd never make it home once he escaped!

He dropped to his knees and sat there, cold and numb and aching. They had fed him nearly nothing, just bread and weak broth. Were they cruelly trying to keep him weak, so that he wouldn't try to escape? Or were they merely thoughtless and stupid, not realizing that he would die from another week of this?

Ransom had occurred to him, although if those blokes thought they could squeeze a farthing out of Calder after what Rafe had done . . .

*I'm going to pay, it seems, one way or the other. But you were worth it, Phoebe.*

He let his mind wander to her warmth, to her eyes, to the scent of her hair when he held her close to his heart.

With a superhuman push, he stumbled to his feet once more and turned back to the damned hole in the damned wall. Just one more brick and then he would rest . . .

PHOEBE TRIED TO hide from the world in the family parlor, but the world insisted on following her, in the form of Tessa.

Phoebe sighed. "What is it, Tessa?" She had no use for the niceties now.

Tessa narrowed her eyes. "I won't hedge any longer. I want you to break it off with Brookhaven and go back to your moldy little vicarage immediately."

Phoebe didn't blink. "That is hardly news, Tessa. It is quite obvious that you think Brookhaven could be convinced to want Deirdre instead. You might even be right. However, what you think doesn't matter to me in the slightest."

Tessa sneered. "Arrogant twit. I—"

Phoebe interrupted her with a harsh bark of laughter. "I hardly think you are in a position to call anyone a twit, Tessa. Now, I refuse to tolerate you any longer. Go annoy Deirdre."

Tessa paled with fury. "Flee back to Thornhold or face the consequences!"

Phoebe folded her arms and regarded Tessa with boredom. "What consequences, Tessa? Will you dress me in ruffles, like Sophie?"

Tessa moved closer, her chin jutted venomously forward.

"If you do not break it off with Brookhaven immediately, I will make sure that he and everyone else in London knows about Marbrook!"

Phoebe stared at her. "Do you think anyone in London will bring that up once I'm properly and respectably married in a few days?" She shrugged. "And Brookhaven knows already."

Tessa gaped. "He knows? And he still—"

Phoebe rolled her eyes. "God, Tessa, don't be thicker than you have to be! Brookhaven knows and soon no one will care, I promise you. So keep your poisonous, amateurish blackmail to yourself, if you please." Phoebe turned away.

Tessa reached out to grasp her arm with cruel fingers, yanking her back. "I'll wager you didn't tell Brookhaven about that nasty little incident when you were a girl, did you?"

Phoebe went very still. "What are you talking about?"

Tessa bared her teeth in a not-smile. "I'm talking about the foppish little dancing master and the whorish little vicar's daughter." She folded her arms and lifted her chin. "I'm talking about the difference between one mistake and the wanton habits of a lifetime. Do you think he'll still want you when he knows how well-used you are?"

Phoebe stared at Tessa long and hard. "The vicar didn't tell you."

Tessa blinked. "He did!" But her gaze flicked sideways when she said it. "He warned me before he let me bring you to London!"

"No," Phoebe said slowly. "I might hate my father sometimes and I might even wish to flee him forever . . . but he would never betray me to someone like you. He despises you and all you stand for."

She narrowed her eyes and took a considering step toward Tessa. "So how did you learn of this? Only three people in the world knew—myself, the vicar, and the foppish dancing master himself . . ."

Phoebe felt the familiar chains of manipulation and control tightening about her once again. "You sent Terrence to Thornhold. I'd forgotten that. How could you do that to me? I was only *fifteen*!"

Then again, there was no cause for surprise. This was Tessa.

Tessa didn't lose.

Tessa lifted her chin haughtily. "What of it? Your father asked for my help. It was all he could do to contain your wildness. He asked me to select a few qualified people—"

"Qualified? Like the maid Papa hired for me—the one who left me unchaperoned to be with her lover night after night? Like the governess, who drank every drop of brandy in the house and then disappeared after a mere week?"

Phoebe laughed, a short, harsh noise. "And how perfectly I fell into your trap. A lonely, unsure girl and a predatory young man looking for a way to ride free through life—"

Phoebe halted, another outrageous idea taking form. "You told Terrence about the trust, didn't you—although you must have left out a few key bits, or he would have known I'd never get it if I wed him—"

Tessa backed up several steps, nearly at a run. "I did no such thing and you cannot prove I did!"

Tessa looked honestly alarmed now. As well she should, for if she'd leaked the information to Terrence, the lot of them would be instantly disqualified, even Deirdre.

"No," Phoebe said slowly. "You wouldn't have done that . . . although I'm sure you hinted at something of that nature, or he wouldn't have exerted himself so to win me. Terrence ever did have a reluctance to exert himself."

"It's all rubbish," Tessa snapped. "I did my best to help your father through a difficult time and this is the thanks I

get! You always were an ungrateful girl! I knew you'd turn
out badly when that idiot told me you'd given over after
only a month of courtship—" The bolt of shock that
crossed Tessa's expression was very brief, and very telling.

Phoebe felt the chill, sure place of control within her
harden to ice. Her hatred was not hot and flaring, it was
glacial and inexorable.

It was time to end this puppet show.

"What if I had no more secrets, Tessa? What if the
world knew it all? What strings would you pull then?" Her
lips formed a smile, but she felt nothing but the ice. "Would
you like to find out?"

Tessa blinked, confusion finally wrinkling her pristine
brow. "What—?"

Phoebe turned away and stepped slowly toward the window. The world outside was a large one. So many people, so
many secrets. Surely hers were not all that interesting . . .
and if they were, why should she care? "What if I told
all, Tessa? What if I gave the gossips what they want—
Terrence . . . and Marbrook . . . and the Pickering Trust."

Tessa inhaled harshly. "You—you cannot do that! Think
of the family—think of your father!"

"Oh, I imagine he'd survive. He's never much liked being the vicar, you know. With Brookhaven's fortune, I could
buy him a lovely cottage where he can read all day if he
likes."

"But—what of Deirdre? Of Sophie? Of m—" *Of me.*

Phoebe turned from the window, the ice within her hardened to stone. "Deirdre is a well-connected beauty with
many beaus. I'm sure she'll do nicely enough."

"Pray, do not distress yourself on my behalf, cousin."

Phoebe and Tessa turned toward the door to see Deirdre
and Sophie standing there, watching.

Deirdre went on. "I'm sure my *loving* stepmother will
stand by me." The hatred in her voice matched Phoebe's—or

perhaps surpassed it. Who knew what Deirdre had truly suffered at Tessa's hands all these years?

"As for Sophie—" That was a problem, for of all of them; Sophie had the least protection.

"As for Sophie," Sophie interjected, "I have no plans to marry—ever—so I lose nothing by way of possibilities."

Phoebe nodded. Sophie might just prove the most sensible of them all. "So you see, Tessa, no one will suffer all that long—except for you. No one will call. No invitations will come."

Tessa's pallor belied her fear of that very outcome, but she snarled anyway. "I have friends—powerful friends. They will not desert me."

"Truly? What will all your dear friends think of your own virtue as a guardian and chaperone? Isn't that the most sacred duty a lady can perform for merry old England—protecting her daughters from disgrace so we can all wed to advantage and bring many more marketable girls into the world? After all, if I reveal the story of Terrence, I will most assuredly reveal your part in it. Won't they wonder how much of all this was your influence? Will they want you around their own precious daughters?"

Tessa was pale and shaking with fury. "You stupid trollop. You take it all so lightly, don't you? You think none of this affects you—you think you'll wed Brookhaven and no one will care what you've done? Don't be an idiot, girl! You'll ruin your entire future!"

Phoebe thought about that for a moment, her expression serene. "Yes. *I* might. I'll ruin my own life, with no help from you or Papa or even Marbrook. My future—my decision." Then she smiled slightly. "The fact that I could take you down with me would merely be the icing on the cake of my ruin."

Then a deep voice came from the doorway. "Lady Tessa, are you under the impression that I would cancel the wedding just because a jealous, spiteful woman exposed my fiancée's tragic victimization?"

Tessa whirled. Phoebe turned to see Calder now standing in the doorway with a politely inquiring expression on his face, but black murder in his eyes.

Even Tessa was not so self-involved as to miss that. She shrank back. At this moment, Phoebe could well believe that Calder was capable of violence.

But never against a woman, not even one so malevolent as Tessa.

Calder nodded to her. "Miss Millbury."

Phoebe inclined her head. "Lord Brookhaven."

Calder turned on his heel and left, taking any power that Tessa might have yielded over her with him.

He really was a remarkable man. It was such a pity she didn't love him.

# Chapter Forty~nine

The bustle of wedding preparations moved forward with a life of its own. The servants seemed to know precisely what to do to throw such a celebration, though the last Brookhaven wedding had been four decades hence. Phoebe left them generally to their own devices. They were far more qualified than she, anyway.

The vicar spent his days nattering about the library's "stunning collection" and studiously avoiding noticing that anything was awry with his only daughter. Phoebe allowed it, for what could he possibly do to make matters better?

Lementeur delivered the wedding dress personally. The stunning ivory creation was even more beautiful than she remembered.

Remembering meant thinking of Rafe. When she tried the dress on for the dressmaker, she wasn't able to hide the tears that welled forth.

"Oh, sweeting, don't drip on the silk!" He handed her a scented handkerchief and patted her gently on the shoulder while she cried on his.

When she straightened, feeling better in a numb sort of way, he smoothed her damp face and turned her to face the mirror once more.

"You are far too lovely to be so sad," he stated firmly.

"Nor will I tolerate a gloomy bride in one of my gowns. Now, tell me what is wrong."

She told him all—every little hidden aspect of her life, for she'd grown mightily sick of her own secrets. When she reached the part about Rafe's disappearance, Lementeur's eyes widened in surprise for the first time since she'd begun her recitation.

Why surprise just then? Goodness, had he already known *everything* else?

The little dressmaker threw up his hands. "How could you keep such important information from me?" He put his fists on his hips. "Honestly, what people make me go through!"

She blinked at him. "But . . . I'm still getting married tomorrow, sir."

He was in a whirl, clapping his hands for Cabot to gather his items and calling for his driver. "So much to do—" He blew her a kiss as he flew from the room. "Ta-ta, my dear! Happy wedding day!"

Phoebe was left standing alone in her room, all dressed up and wondering what part of her sad tale she'd missed.

STICKLEY GAZED AT the days-old gossip sheet that Wolfe had just thrust into his hands in confusion. Wolfe paced furiously in the tiny shack as Stickley read it.

"Wedding back on?" Stickley looked up. "How can they say this? We wrote the letter—we stole his lordship!"

"We stole someone," Wolfe growled. "*Not* Brookhaven, apparently."

Stickley blinked. "But who, then? He looks like him— he was in the Brookhaven carriage—"

Wolfe tossed back the last drop of whiskey, then flung his empty bottle across the room to shatter against the stones of the fireplace. Glass rained down upon the fine boots roughly tossed there days before. "We stole the damned bastard rake, that's what! We left the marquis warm and toasty in London and risked everything to steal the bloody half brother!"

Stickley drew his brows together, unable to deny the obvious. Then he straightened. "The wedding!"

"What?"

Stickley stood and gathered his hat. "We can still make it if we hurry."

Wolfe sneered. "Why would we want to?"

Stickley tugged his weskit into place and smoothed his coat. "We've already lost, Wolfe—and I think it very good that our plan failed. This matter was far too distasteful for the likes of me. As for the wedding itself, we are invited. At this point, the best we can hope for is to absolve ourselves of any suspicion. Don't you think it would be questionable if we missed the wedding of our only client—the biggest wedding of the year?"

Wolfe blew out a long breath, admitting defeat. "I hate weddings." Then he tilted his chin toward the cellar door. "What about himself?"

Stickley sniffed. He disapproved of rakes on principle. Bastards as well. Bastard rakes who tried to seduce nice young ladies fell far down the list. "He'll keep. We'll send an anonymous note to the nearest village as soon as we're back. Someone will come to let him out."

Once Miss Millbury was properly wed to a nice, decent gentleman!

DINNER THE EVENING before the wedding was extremely subdued. Phoebe remained in her "guest" seat still. There was plenty of time to move to a more appropriate family chair someday. Calder sat at the head of the table, as he had every night since he'd brought her back. Funny, she'd seen more of him since she'd betrayed him.

She used her fork to create lines in the meat juices on her plate. Calder had not kissed her again, thankfully. It hadn't been unpleasant, but it would be a very long time before the fire of that one blissful night would fade from her memory.

Of course, she had all the time in the world, didn't she?

She'd been going through the motions of wedding preparations, although she could not bear to so much as glance at the seating chart with Rafe's notes all over it in a strong, looping hand. "Just do it," she'd told Fortescue, who had nodded gravely and walked away.

When would the mere sight of his handwriting not inflame her memories? She must douse that torch. She must send that Phoebe back to sleep . . . possibly forever.

THE HOUSE ABOVE had been silent now for many hours. At first Rafe had scarcely noticed, intent as he was on his seemingly granule-by-granule removal of the ancient mortar in the cellar wall. It was only when another brick fell through his throbbing hands to crash onto the floor that he froze in alarm, listening.

There wasn't a sound—nor, he realized, had there been for some time. Not a scrape, not a footfall. He listened carefully. They could be asleep.

Or they could both be gone at the same time. That had never happened before. To test it, he took the brick and flung it full force at the heavy iron-bound door of the cellar.

It boomed deeply, sending dust and grit shivering down from the ancient boards above his head.

It also broke a hand-sized hole in the mossy wood. Rafe stared, a hoarse laugh of surprise rasping from his throat. All this time, he ought to have been digging at the moldy door!

He shoved his hand through the hole, but couldn't reach the latch. Bending, he grabbed up the fallen stone and pounded freely at the door. The hole widened instantly enough for him to thrust his entire arm through.

Moments later he was through the door and up into what turned out to be not much more than a poor shanty. There was no one there, but his boots lay discarded by the fire.

He stepped swiftly to them.

"Ouch!" He jumped back and lifted his right foot. Blood welled from where a calling-card sized shard of glass was imbedded deeply into his flesh.

The bastards just wouldn't quit, would they? He yanked the shard out and dabbed at the cut with his filthy shirttail, cursing tightly. The blood stopped at last and he was able to put his boots on gingerly.

There was nothing else of value there—nothing at all but a discarded newssheet on the table. Time to leave. He limped toward the door.

Something caught his eye as he passed the table. *Handsome Brookhaven*—

He paused, reached for the sheet and read.

Oh no. Oh God, no.

Phoebe!

How could she do this? Did she know how he loved her? Didn't she know this would destroy him—

Rafe clenched the newssheet in his hand. She had made her choice after all.

The hell of it was, he couldn't even begrudge Calder his bride. He'd never seen his brother so lighthearted as when he courted Phoebe—nor had he ever felt more like a betraying devil than when he'd woken up beside Phoebe that morning. Calder was a good man—who would certainly never do such a thing to him.

But just because Rafe couldn't hate them for marrying didn't mean he wanted to see them together, year after year, growing closer, having children, until he himself was just a fading face at their table—poor Uncle Rafe who never married.

No. He would go to Johannesburg, try his hand at plantation life . . .

*My dear Miss Millbury—*

How odd. That almost looked like his handwriting on a scrap of paper sticking out from under the table leg. Or was that Calder's note that he'd stolen? He bent to work it free.

*My dear Miss Millbury, I regret that I am unable to fulfill my promise to you—*

What the hell? Rafe stepped quickly toward the grimy window for better light. This wasn't Calder's note—although the similarity of the handwriting was uncanny—nor was this anything he himself had written!

*I have decided against wedding you—*

There was part of another line visible, the upper part of the looping script clear.

*I could not bear to tell your—no, you—in person. This note is ill—no, all—you will rec—*

All you will receive?

Rafe closed his eyes, trying to remember everything he'd heard in the brief argument about a letter.

"Cannot copy—"

"Signing my name—"

"Can match the—"

*Forgery.*

Rafe looked from the scrap of letter to the newssheet with Phoebe's wan face drawn there. "My God."

His kidnappers, for some utterly bizarre reason, had tried to make Phoebe believe that he had wanted no part of her after—

His gut clenched at the thought of the pain she must have felt—and after what she'd already been through in her youth! No wonder she'd turned to Calder—

The wedding!

Rafe scrambled back to the table and madly smoothed the wrinkles from the newssheet, his gaze scanning it, searching for a date. Bloody hell, where was the *damned date*?

There. The twelfth of May— Oh, God, what date was it now? The tenth? The eleventh?

Rafe stuffed both scraps of paper into his pocket as he ran from the cottage, his heart racing ahead to London.

*Wait for me. Oh, God, Phoebe—please, please wait!*

# Chapter Fifty

Her wedding day dawned depressingly clear and fine. She knew that because she watched the sun rise after a long and fruitless night of questions.

Was she doing the right thing? Was she dooming herself to unhappiness? What if she never loved again? Would her life contain enough other things to make it worthwhile to breathe and eat and carry on?

As for living without Rafe—well, she had memories, good memories that she could not bring herself to regret. There were worse things than falling in love with the wrong person . . . of course, she couldn't think of any right offhand.

Except perhaps being powerless. She raised her chin as she gazed out over the green Brook House garden. She would never be bought or sold again, never stolen or traded, never claimed and then discarded.

She would decide her own fate from this day forward.

RAFE TRUDGED HIS way along the road to London. Surely he wasn't the only one traveling this way, even at this early hour with the sun barely peeking above the horizon. However, he was the only one in sight.

Even if carts had passed, he was not sure that any would

have come to the aid of the ragged, filthy fellow limping along in dusty boots. Rafe realized he was unrecognizable—although with his reputation, being recognized might not fare him any better!

Such thoughts did nothing to ease the roiling powerlessness that threatened to choke him. He couldn't move any faster than he was, for he could not force his legs to run any more. He hadn't eaten properly in days. He would have happily asked for help but he hadn't seen a village or even a farm since the sky had lightened.

Only pure will and his desire to see Phoebe kept him upright.

*Don't do it, my love.*

*Wait for me.*

AFTER PATRICIA HAD helped her dress and fixed her hair, Phoebe sent her to tend to Sophie next. The kindly maid was gentle and sensitive, but Phoebe needed to be alone with all the desperation of a cat in a yard full of dogs.

Of course, that meant that the vicar was due for a visit.

He loomed in her doorway, in his usual dark garments and severely tied stock, as if he were on his way to a funeral, not a wedding.

Then again, perhaps she was the one overdressed for such a day. Phoebe's gaze roamed back toward the sunny garden.

"I very nearly killed a man once."

Phoebe turned in surprise.

"He was a rival, one of your mother's suitors. I beat him nearly to death with nothing but my fists and the rage in my heart." The vicar was gazing out of her window, his remote expression and distant tone jarringly at odds with his words.

It was impossible—a lie—yet the vicar never, ever lied. Withhold truth, absolutely, but never lie.

"He lived, but barely. I don't think he ever truly recovered if he even still lives to this day." The vicar reached to flick away a mote of dust from the drapery with one finger. "I would very much like to claim that he deserved it, that he'd committed some terrible crime, or had even indulged in dishonorable behavior—but he had done nothing. He'd merely twitted me about my dogged devotion to Audrey . . . it might have been good-natured, I don't truly recall. I exploded upon him, dragging him to the ground and striking him over and over—"

Phoebe saw a tremor travel through the fingers of the vicar's extended hand. It was the only sign of emotion.

"He was quite correct, of course. I was far too attached to a girl I scarcely knew—yet it had been that way from our first meeting. I touched her hand and all thoughts of others were swept from my mind. I was mad for her—and not in the way you youngsters use the word. I was quite literally out of my mind. I know of no other way to express the feeling. It was as though I could not breathe if she were not in the room—as if she were air itself to me."

*I know. Oh, sweet heaven, I know.*

"She sent me away then. I begged her to allow me to stay, pleaded on my knees . . . I frightened her with my passion, yet she stood her ground and insisted that I take myself off and only return if and when I'd brought my madness under control."

He turned away from the window and the memories it had reflected for him. He inhaled deeply and smoothed the lapels of his coat. His gaze, as cool and gray as ever, rested upon her face. "I joined the church," he went on, as if he'd been discussing nothing more important than a new alter drapery. "I turned to the cold stones of the abbey to draw the heat from my blood and I gave myself up to the service of mankind in penance for my violence. When I graduated I was granted the living at the vicarage at

Thornhold. I sent an announcement to Audrey of my new existence and she answered that brief note with one word. 'Yes.'"

Phoebe swallowed. Who was this man before her? She'd thought him cold, devoid of strong emotion. Yet all this time, he, too, had been masked?

"Papa, I—"

He held up a hand to halt her. "I did not tell you this for any reason but to warn you. Hot blood runs in your veins. I handed my curse down to you. I saw it when you were fifteen and I feared for you. I blamed myself. Now . . ." He let out a breath and almost—but not quite—smiled. "Now I know that I carried the fear and guilt for no reason. You are stronger than I was."

Phoebe felt her eyes burn with poignant gratitude for that crumb of approval—tears he would not want to see. She blinked them back as he went on.

"Of course, it may simply be that as a female, you are incapable of such deep emotion."

Phoebe let out a breath of a laugh, without bitterness. The vicar was . . . the vicar. Life's wheel rolled on, the world unchanged.

She stepped forward and rested her hand lightly upon his arm. "Thank you for telling me," she said, careful to keep her tone even. "I shall take your words to heart."

Which was all he'd truly wanted to hear from her. He nodded, that slight lessening of the tension about his lips the closest thing to the smile she knew she'd never see.

"You see, you can have a life of contentment and peace," he added casually. "I myself have never strayed from mine—but for that once at the inn at Biddleton."

*The inn at Biddleton.*

Phoebe blinked. The vicar had clearly been furious that day, yet he'd not expressed it beyond a terser-than-usual tone and a white-knuckled grip on her arm—

*His hand, wrapped around her elbow, the knuckles scraped and raw . . .*

Terrence's flight, hatless, jacket flapping, never looking back to where she stood at her window, watching him leave her behind . . .

"It took me nearly an hour to bring myself under control that day," he was saying.

An hour of sitting in her room, waiting for Terrence to return to her. "You saw Terrence?"

"Saw him? I beat the living tar out of that cur. I had to threaten his life—and yours!—before he would leave you behind!"

She gazed at him in shock. He looked away from her hurt, guilty self-righteousness on his face. "You were meant for better things! I promised your mother—"

Icy fury began to rise within her. "You drove him off? I loved him!"

He twitched. "Well, he left you, didn't he? And then—why, he sent less than a dozen letters afterward! Hardly true love!"

Letters?

Yet her fury could not be sustained against her present unhappiness. What did it matter now? She'd have been miserable with Terrence, even if he'd meant to wed her. She might not be very happy at the moment, but still her present fate was far superior to a lifetime of washing a layabout musician's dirty stockings.

She turned away from the vicar and rested her burning eyes on the garden once again.

It looked as though the roses would bloom soon.

A FAINT JINGLING of harness roused Rafe from his trudging stupor. He looked up, blinking into the morning light.

As he watched, an apparition appeared. A jaunty little

one-horse cart, pulled by a pony with lavender ribbons in its mane, sporting purple enameled sides and a gold emblem upon the door—an ornate "L."

A small puckish fellow drove it. As he neared Rafe, he smiled gleefully. "There you are, my lord! I thought you might come this way!"

Rafe was too astounded to do more than stand there, his mouth open. The fellow drew the pony up to a halt and hopped out. He wore a purple coat, a shimmering white silk weskit and a dapper little hat, which he doffed as he bowed deeply.

"Lementeur at your service, my lord!"

Rafe blinked. "The dressmaker?"

The fellow shrugged elegantly. "I prefer to be known as a designer of fine gowns, but it will do for now." He waved a hand as though shooing away resentment. "I have come to aid you in your quest, my lord." He sighed happily. "Doesn't the sound of that simply make your knees weak?"

Since Rafe's knees had passed weak miles back, he only stared.

Lementeur popped his hat back upon his head and grinned. "I'll wager you're wondering how I knew where to find you! It was a nice bit of detective work—"

Rafe shook his head dazedly. "Not really. A letter was sent from a village back there." He cocked a thumb over his shoulder. "This is the only road to London."

Lementeur frowned. "Oh. Well, yes." Recovering, his smile returned. "Sorry I took so long but I had the very devil of a time finding a white one."

Since his day—nay, his week!—had already been so strange, this statement elicited only a tiny bit of curiosity from Rafe. "A white what?"

The little man laughed. "A white horse, of course!" With a bow and a wave, he indicated the back of the cart.

Rafe stumbled to the left a bit to see—like an exhaustion-induced vision of water to man lost in the desert!—a fine white long-legged thoroughbred, saddled and ready to ride, tied to the back of the silly cart.

The fire of his need to see Phoebe seared freshly through Rafe, burning away the last of his despair. He turned to the dressmaker. *"What day is this?"*

The fellow tilted his head and gazed back at him with oddly wise eyes. "It is the day, my lord."

An instant later, Lementeur was gazing after a cloud of dust produced by pounding hooves. He smiled and tipped his hat to a more jaunty angle with one finger. "Sir Sprinkle," he said to the fat pony, "we've done very well today." He climbed back into his seat with a happy sigh and clucked to the pony. "Very well indeed. Hurry now, or *we'll* miss the wedding!"

# Chapter Fifty~one

Rafe slid from his fine white horse and stumbled on the cobbles before the cathedral. He would have ridden his wonderful, beautiful horse directly into the apse if he'd thought he could, for his own legs didn't seem to work terribly well at the moment.

As it was, he limped and lurched and staggered through the great doors and into the back of the enormous church—

Directly into a great crowd of onlookers who stood because there was no more room left to sit. The church was absolutely packed and it took Rafe several precious minutes to pardon and excuse and sometimes shove his way through the throng.

He could hear the clergyman giving instructions. The ceremony had already begun! With the last of his desperation, he flung himself through the crowd to find himself stumbling freely down the aisle. His legs gave out and he dropped to his knees.

"Phoebe!" His voice was too weak. He coughed. *"Phoebe!"*

He tried to blink away the exhaustion blurring his vision. Far in front of him he saw two figures standing before the pulpit—one large and dark, one small and white. The white one turned at his rasping cry.

*"Rafe?"*

He heard the murmurs begin around him. Hands came to aid him to his feet. More hands helped him down the aisle. Good Samaritans or spectators who wanted to see the rest of the show—it hardly mattered. At last he stood before them, weaving ever so slightly.

His brother and the woman he loved, standing together before a priest. It hurt—God, it hurt!

Calder stared down at him. "My God, Rafe! Where have you been?"

"I've been imprisoned in a root cellar for the past fortnight!"

Calder regarded him for a long moment. "You look as though you clawed your way out inch by inch."

"I would have dug myself out of the grave to come back for Phoebe . . ." He turned to her. "I know what you must have thought . . ." God, it hurt to look at her, to see the darkness in her eyes. She was so pale, with circles beneath her eyes and hollows beneath her cheeks. She looked awful.

She'd never been so beautiful to him.

"I love you, Phoebe. I love you more than I ever knew it was possible to love anything. I know you think it was only desire—" She started to protest. He held up his hand. "I should have told you I loved you that first night. I should have proposed immediately when I pulled you into my arms to dance you away from the champagne you spilled—"

"I knew it!" Tessa snarled from the audience.

Deirdre and Sophie turned as one to glare at her. "Shut up, Tessa!"

Phoebe never took her gaze off Rafe. "May I speak now?"

"Not yet." He moved to stand before her. "I owe you so much more than I can ever give you." Kneeling nearly made him lose consciousness, but he blinked away the gray fog. Reaching into his shirt, he pulled out a battered rose, a poor wild thing from a roadside bramble patch.

He extended it to her with a bow. "Come away with me, my lady," he rasped. "I have a valley of exquisite beauty beknownst only to me . . ."

"Is this Lord Raphael?" The Archbishop of Canterbury stepped forward. "My lord, are you aware that the ceremony has already taken place?"

"No—" Rafe shook his head. "Yes—I mean . . . what did you say?"

It was over. He turned tortured eyes to Phoebe. She was staring at the crumpled rose in his hand. There were tears upon her cheeks.

She knelt on the floor with him to take the rose. "Your poor hands," she whispered. "What have you done to yourself?"

"This is most unorthodox, my lord." The archbishop reached one hand inside his voluminous robe and withdrew a folded paper. "I was under the impression that you were not supposed to be here today."

"But . . ." Rafe could not bend his mind around this disaster. "But I asked her first."

His voice was weak, even to him, but Phoebe nodded and stroked the blossom across her cheek. "Yes. You did."

"You ought to have thought of that before you signed this proxy, my lord," the archbishop went on stuffily. "I do not approve of these hasty marriages. I told your brother and your wife as much, but his lordship and her ladyship insisted—"

Rafe stumbled to his feet. "What—wait—" He held up his hand. "Proxy?"

*Wife?*

"Yes, Rafe." Calder stepped forward to take the paper from the archbishop's hand. He unfolded it and displayed it to Rafe, all the while sending him a significant glare that

Rafe recognized from a lifetime of semi-allied brotherhood. *Don't muck this up!*

"Of course, you recall the marriage proxy that you signed so that I could take your place at the altar when you became *unavoidably detained*," Calder said. "This is your signature, is it not?"

The agreed-upon response to this signal were the words, "Yes. Absolutely, Father" or "Master" or "Professor."

Rafe looked at the proxy. It *was* his signature, and a hell of a lot better job of forgery than those clods who'd held him prisoner.

Wife.

His Phoebe.

*His wife.*

It was a mad, impossible trick. It was a fantastic, outrageous gift. Joy rose in him, as glorious as the palace fountain. He nodded slowly. "Yes. Absolutely, Your Grace. That is unmistakably my signature."

Calder turned toward the archbishop. "There, you see? My brother was only a bit disoriented from his obvious ordeal. Let us finish this."

"Wait a moment!" Phoebe held up her hand this time. "I don't want to finish this!"

She turned to Rafe with both fists planted on the hips of her exquisite gown. Even dressed as she was, she looked furious and spirited and entirely prepared to take her argument right down to the carpet if necessary.

God, she was superb!

Rafe smiled at her lovingly. "You're going to make me pay for thinking you'd wed Calder, aren't you?"

She glared at him. "You have no idea. As if I could ever marry Calder in truth!"

"I probably ought to take offense to that," Calder said mildly. They ignored him.

"Then shall we start over?" He rose shakily to his feet. "Calder, give me your coat, will you?"

She interrupted, muttering something. He stopped. "What?"

She disposed of her bouquet, tossing it over her shoulder to the avidly watching crowd, and turned to face the archbishop with only the tattered rose in her hand. "Now I'm ready."

The archbishop looked appalled. "But my lord, we've already completed the ceremony. Am I to wed them *again?*"

Calder waved a hand. "I'll pay twice your fee. Call it a wedding gift." He stalked away to sit in one of the pews. Phoebe saw Deirdre turn in her seat to give Calder an assessing look.

Then Phoebe turned away from the crowd of astonished wedding guests and back to Rafe. He stood before her now, hesitant hope shining in his eyes.

"You haven't said 'yes' yet," he said.

Phoebe tilted her head back and gazed up at him. "Don't you need a ring?"

He paled. "Er . . . I've been trapped in a root cellar for days."

"Rafe," Calder drawled. "Catch."

Something glittered through the air, shining double in Rafe's weary vision. He caught it somehow, then grinned at the familiar weight of the gold in his hand. His signet ring.

Apparently, he was a Marbrook still.

"Rafe, will you marry me now?"

He smiled down at his lovely bride.

The one. *Forever.* "What's your hurry?"

She gave him a sultry look from beneath lowered lashes. "Just you wait, Lord Marbrook. In half an hour, you'll be mine forever."

He blinked. "You mean, there's more to you than I've already seen?" It quite boggled the mind.

She laughed out loud. "Oh, Rafe, you're going to need crutches and a tonic when I get through with you—if you survive me at all."

The archbishop was listening, scandal alive on his furrowed face. Rafe grinned a bit giddily. "She's going to marry me," he told the man. "Again."

The archbishop shook his head in wry warning. "I hope you've made your will, my lord."

Rafe raised their clasped hands to kiss the back of hers. "Everything I have is hers," he said, gazing into those bottomless depths of blue. "Everything."

She grinned back, a blissful, wild smile that set his heart free at last. "I'll take it," she says. "I'll take it all."

# Epilogue

"So Sir Pickering declared that we had to prove ourselves by our own merits," Phoebe said into Rafe's naked chest. "I could not tell you, or I would ruin it for all three of us. I could not do that to Sophie and Deirdre, even if I was willing to forgo the fortune. But you are family now, privy to our darkest secrets."

Rafe had gone pale, which was quite an accomplishment considering what she'd just done to him before she'd begun her story. Her jaw still ached.

"Twenty-seven thousand pounds?"

"I think it is closer to twenty-eight thousand. Stickley and Wolfe are quite the miracle workers."

*Stickley and Wolfe.* Why did that suddenly remind her of something unpleasant?

No. Ridiculous.

"But to give all that up for me? I had no idea what I was asking of you."

"It is nothing. I would take you if you were a rat catcher or a chimney sweep."

He smiled. "Not quite that bad. I have something to tell you as well. Calder has agreed to let me take the reins at Brookhaven. He'll be duke soon and he'll have little time to run both Brookmoor and Brookhaven—and it will be many years before any son of his is old enough to take over."

Phoebe rolled blissfully beneath him, wriggling with joy. "That's wonderful! Maybe you'll be lucky and he'll have nothing but daughters!"

His gaze went dark as she writhed against him. "Be quiet, Phoebe-mine. There's something I've been dying to do to you . . ."

Her eyes brightened. "Indeed, my master? What is tha— *Oh!*"

Afterward, limp and perspiring, they lay draped across one another as they fought for breath.

"Goodness," Phoebe panted, "I didn't know I could bend that way!"

"I've always wanted to try that," Rafe wheezed. "I saw it in a book of naughty drawings once."

"Well, thank goodness for the arts!" Phoebe shivered with tiny bursts of continued ecstasy.

Breathless silence reigned for several minutes, until Rafe chuckled deeply. "I thought I would spew my wine when Somers Boothe-Jamison approached us at the wedding breakfast and inquired after Lady Nanditess!" He shook his head. "Poor bloke seemed rather smitten. It was cruel of you to tell him she'd just been married off to an elderly fourth cousin in the Highlands."

"Nonsense. Cousin Harold happens to adore her, and her name, I'll remind you."

He laughed and rolled her onto his chest. "I adore you."

She smiled. "The feeling is mutual, my lord."

"Be my lady of the roses?"

She bit his chest gently. "Always."

STICKLEY RAISED HIS glass to Wolfe. "We did it."

Wolfe smiled. "We did." Between them lay a sheet of paper . . . an agreement signed by Miss Deirdre Cantor that she had no intention of withdrawing the principal of the

trust and that she would be perfectly satisfied with the generous lifetime allowance afforded by the interest. The trust
wouldn't grow as quickly, of course, as under Stickley's
careful nurturing, but it would grow. Wolfe drank deep,
then refilled his glass and topped off the minor sip that
Stickley had taken from his glass. "To weddings!"

Stickley looked down at the agreement. "This isn't really binding, you realize. If she's to marry Brookhaven,
then when he becomes Brookmoor, she'll be within her
rights to take it all."

Wolfe shrugged. "Why would she? Turns out that
Brookhaven has a pot full and as Brookmoor he'll have
plenty more, so what in the world would any lady need with
twenty-seven thousand pounds?"

Stickley smiled smugly. "It's closer to twenty-eight now."

Wolfe punched him in the arm. "Stick, you old dog!
You're a marvel."

Stickley smiled but rubbed at his arm in irritation. Now
that the crisis was over, he couldn't wait for Wolfe to go
back to his ne'er-do-well ways and let him alone to run
things properly. Look at him now, with his heels up scuff-
ing the desk again!

Wolfe was gazing at the ceiling, humming tunelessly.
After a long moment, he stood abruptly and plunked his
glass on the desk, leaving a splash of wine on the blotter.
"Well, Stick, it's been a right pleasure working with you
these past weeks, but I do have business of my own to attend to. If you'll be so kind as to transfer my retainer . . ."

Stickley reached into his desk drawer and sailed the
pouch through the air. Wolfe plucked it from its course and
hefted it with satisfaction. "You've upped it again, haven't
you, Stick?"

Stickley nodded. "Of course. You've worked hard in the
past weeks. It's only right that you receive a larger share. I
do hope you'll enjoy . . . er . . . using it."

Wolfe tapped a forefinger to his temple in an offhand salute. "Righto, General Stickley. Well, then, I'm off."

When he'd gone, Stickley leaned back into his lovely tufted leather chair and breathed a long sigh of pleasure at the silence. Wolfe wasn't all bad. He had most definitely come through in the midst of the madness . . . but it was good to have things back to normal.

And to think, they'd managed to do it all without stealing a dime!

Of course, Stickleys *never* stole.

Turn the page for a sneak peek
at the next Heiress Bride novel

# The Duke Next Door

Coming April 2008 from St. Martin's Paperbacks

In Calder's bedchamber, his valet, Argyle, was all set to prepare the master for his wedding night. Steaming bowls of water for shaving sat next to his best silk dressing gown and the only cologne he cared for, a light woodsy scent mixed just for him at half the strength other men seemed to find necessary.

"May I offer my congratulations again, my lord? What an exciting day for us all." The valet beamed at him. Hadn't the man been present at the disastrous introductions this afternoon?

Calder gazed at the gleaming shaving instruments and wondered if perhaps those were best kept far from his new bride's hands. She was none too pleased with the situation—nor was he himself any too pleased with her—and it simply didn't seem right to embark on . . . er, nuptials at this delicate moment in time.

He cleared his throat. "Her ladyship—is not expecting me this evening." Or was she? Would she coldly go through the motions *now?* After all, by making her vows she had agreed to precisely that. He would be within his right to barge into that scented bastion of femininity and demand, well, pretty much anything he wanted.

*Deirdre naked, golden hair streaming down over her full breasts, kneeling obediently at his feet—*

Which would be abhorrent, of course. No right-thinking man would ever force a woman, not even—or rather—especially not his own lady wife.

*She might like it.*

Calder gazed helplessly at the door to the adjoining chamber. He truly didn't know. He'd married a stranger—again—and so far nothing was going quite as he'd planned.

Again.

But what rose vividly in his mind now was the way that Deirdre, gloriously gowned from their wedding ceremony, had stood in the hall and defied him openly, with anger snapping brightly in her sapphire eyes.

Perhaps . . . perhaps he'd been right about Miss Deirdre Cantor after all. He was a formidable man, he knew. Most people scarcely dared speak to him, yet the lovely Deirdre had raised her chin and called him out, on his turf, in front of his own staff yet.

He didn't let the tug on his lips quite form a smile, but he gazed at the closed door with a bit more hope. She had looked magnificent in that moment, hadn't she? Spirited and furious and arousing, if a man were to be honest with himself . . .

Without quite realizing it, he reached out to press the latch of the door. He was simply remembering her eyes, furious and a bit hurt, now that he thought about it. He could go to her now and—well, he certainly had nothing to apologize for. Still, perhaps it wouldn't hurt to . . . to end the day on a more benevolent note—

The door didn't move. Calder looked down in surprise at the first latch ever to be locked against him in his own house. He pushed harder in disbelief. The door didn't budge.

If he was a cursing man, he'd be cursing now.

He turned sharply and strode from his room, turned a forceful left and took the distance between the doors in a few large, impatient steps. This time the door gave in to his ownership. He flung it open to glare at the woman within—

Who jerked her head up in surprise and covered her wet, naked breasts with soapy hands.

*Oh damn.* His imagination hadn't even come close. There she was, his bride . . . immersed in a great copper tub before the fire—bare, wet, gleaming, dripping in scented suds and succulent flesh—

And more furious at him than ever.

"How dare—!" She halted. It was his house, after all. Every damned stone of it, including those lucky ones in front of the fire that supported the most fortunate copper tub in all of England.

She lifted her chin, though she blushed furiously—her cheeks were nearly the color of the pink nipples he'd spotted for a brief but memorable moment—and narrowed her eyes at him.

"What do you want . . . my lord?"

*You. Now. Hot and dripping all over those sheets there and maybe a bit slippery still, just so that my hands can slide more quickly over your beautiful skin.*

If he'd thought she was lovely when dressed, he'd had no idea what was in store beneath the perfect, stylish wardrobe. He'd angered this outrageously desirable creature on their wedding day? Was he completely out of his mind?

If he'd been a smoother man—like his fast-talking brother, for instance—he would have said something charming, endearing, just a tad bawdy and certain to grant him entrance to more than just the door.

Alas, he was only himself, a man without the inclination to make pretty words. How he wished he'd practiced more. "You locked me out."

*No, that wasn't it.*

He tried again. "This is my house and you are my wife."

*All true, but hardly smooth, old man.*

"I can come and go as I please." Wait, no. That hadn't come out quite right—

*Let's hope she's too innocent to detect* that *double entendre.*

Her eyes widened and she blinked at him, genuinely shocked now.

*No such luck. Too bad. It might have been the best night of your life.*

*Idiot.*

So be it. He ducked the flying sponge neatly and flicked suds from his sleeve. "I shall say no more on the subject. Pray take care not to lock my doors in the future."

He made his escape, shutting the door just in time to let it take the impact of a bottle of bath scent.